ACT OF TERROR

Recent Titles by Richard Woodman

THE ACCIDENT*
ACT OF TERROR*
ARCTIC CONVOYS
ENDANGERED SPECIES
WATERFRONT

* available from Severn House

ACT OF TERROR

Richard Woodman

This first world edition published in Great Britain 1996 by
SEVERN HOUSE PUBLISHERS LTD of
9–15 High Street, Sutton, Surrey SM1 1DF.
This first edition published in the USA 1996 by
SEVERN HOUSE PUBLISHERS INC. of
595 Madison Avenue, New York, NY 10022.

British Library Cataloguing in Publication Data

Woodman, Richard, 1944–
    Act of terror
    1. English fiction – 20th century
    I. Title
    823.9'14 [F]

    ISBN 0-7278-4907-7

Typeset by Palimpsest Book Production Limited,
Polmont, Stirlingshire, Scotland.
Printed and bound in Great Britain by
Hartnolls Ltd, Bodmin, Cornwall.

Contents

PART ONE

HIJACK

'And other spirits there are standing apart
Upon the forehead of the age to come;
These; these will give the world another heart;
And other pulses. Hear ye not the hum
Of mighty workings?
Listen awhile ye nations, and be dumb.'

John Keats 'To Haydon'

Chapter One

"Do you believe there can be new beginnings, I mean *really* new beginnings, in this tired old world?"

"Well the new Prime Minister does. I should have thought as his wife you ought to as well."

"Don't be silly, Johnnie. You're his private secretary, you should know better than anyone."

"That's not quite what you asked, is it? What you mean is, can your husband engineer a new beginning?"

"Don't split hairs. You know very well what I mean, and you also know that a politician's wife is the last person to know what's on his mind."

"Well, then, I think *he* does; but then so do most politicians."

"They need to!"

"They do indeed."

"Oh, I suppose I've just got post-election blues. . . ."

"I'm sure it's something like that."

"You can be so infuriatingly obscure, Johnnie, you really can. . . ."

"Mrs Fraser, we've known each other for a very long time, but I really can't tell you what's on his mind."

"Is there something specific then?"

"I think you know there is."

"Would you like another coffee?"

"Yes."

"So you're not going to tell me?"

"Not if your husband won't. I can't."

"He was looking at his father's photograph yesterday. He

3

stared at it for quite a long time. I thought that it was extraordinary. . . ."

"Why should that be extraordinary in a man who's just moved into Number Ten? I'd have said it would be out of reverence for the paternal spirit . . . worshipping the ancestor who made it all possible, indulging in a little self-congratulation, perhaps, at having lived out all father's expectations. On the other hand it had just been unpacked and caught his eye. . . ."

"Don't be bloody flippant, Johnnie!"

"Sorry."

"You don't look it . . . do you know about his father?"

"Er, he was killed . . . died in the war, didn't he?"

"You haven't done your homework very well. I thought you knew all about it . . . ah, David, there you are at last. Coffee?"

"Yes, please . . . well, Johnnie, what heinous crime of neglect is Jill accusing you of? No, don't get up, this is informal, for Heaven's sake. Just because I'm Prime Minister we don't have to build walls and compartmentalize ourselves."

"Your coffee."

"Thank you. God, I'm shattered! At the very moment I should be taking a rest after the ballyhoo of the election I've got to take up the reins of Government."

"It's what you always wanted, darling. Sugar? Or are you on a health kick?"

"No. Give me sugar tonight."

"What did the American ambassador want?"

"Oh, the usual. He thought the party had been vague on its foreign policy, particularly our stand on the Middle East. Apparently it's rattled the White House."

"I thought we'd made ourselves perfectly clear."

"Oh, we had at the hustings, Johnnie, but now we're actually in power, apparently we're supposed to fall in with Washington. It's what our predecessors did . . . still, it's nice to know we can still rattle the Yanks."

"Dodgy things alliances."

"Don't take any notice of him, David. Johnnie is in a facetious mood this evening. Did you let the ambassador know how you stood on the Middle East?"

4

"No. Not exactly. Johnnie?"

"Yes, Prime Minister?"

"Did you manage that business I asked you to see to?"

"Yes."

"Get the right man?"

"I think so. Highly recommended."

"Good! Well done. What about the others?"

"We've a few days in hand. I'll have people ready."

"What is all this, David? Sounds very mysterious."

"It is. Call it our first covert mission. I can't tell you anything more."

"It's got something to do with the Middle East, hasn't it? And the American ambassador, and the fact that you were looking at your father's photograph yesterday. I don't think you've spared that a second glance in years."

"It's been sitting near my desk for the last twenty."

"I know that. But you were never given to staring at it with such intensity."

"For goodness' sake, dear, why should looking at a family snap be of the slightest significance?"

"Because you are a man of great economy. You never do anything without good reason."

"There, Prime Minister, speaks the loyal wife. . . ."

"Has this got something to do with your lack of homework, Johnnie?"

"Yes it has, David. Do tell Johnnie how your father died."

"What the dickens has that got to do with anything?"

"Tell him!"

"Why?"

"Because I think it's important. I'll bet that you didn't tell the American ambassador. . . ."

"Look, I'm sorry, I don't understand. I'm very tired and if you two want to play word games count me out!"

"Johnnie, *I'll* tell you; you *should* know. David's father was a regular soldier. He was stationed in Palestine after the war. He was shot, wasn't he?"

"He was *assassinated* by the Irgun. . . . D'you think we can get this wallpaper changed?"

5

The cab accelerated on the approach to the bridge and the sparkle of light on salt water appeared suddenly on the left. Tim Palmer rubbed the jet lag from his eyes and stared across the harbour. In the harsh sunlight of South Carolina he could see the ship, tier upon tier of white decks topped off with a fantastically raked funnel painted in her owner's grotesque blue and orange logo.

"Bloody hell!" he muttered to himself. It was worse than he had imagined.

"That your ship?" The cab driver jutted the first of his chins across the water and watched his fare in the rear-view mirror.

"Yes."

"Limey ship ain't she?"

"Yes ... more or less." Palmer shied off an explanation of why the distant cruiseliner wore a flag of convenience over her elegant stern. She *was* British-owned and that qualified her for the cabbie's description. Despite the extraordinary circumstances of his hurried appointment to her as second officer, despite the experience of nearly a year's unemployment, he had not really reconciled himself to what he privately considered to be an act of supreme disloyalty in sailing under such an opportunist device.

"It's a mere formality, I assure you, Mr Palmer," the personnel officer in the company's headquarters had blandly assured him. "High-Seas Adventure Cruises are as British as P & O or Cunard. Flagging out helps us keep our costs competitive and avoid complications with the Argentines ... all the officers are British."

Palmer had suppressed his contempt for the man, swallowed his pride and taken the job. Under the circumstances he could scarcely refuse. Seventy-two hours and several injections later he had hailed the cab at Charleston airport, a hurriedly engaged replacement for a sick man.

"You an officer?" the cab driver asked, straightening the big, soft-sprung Ford as the structure of the suspension bridge rose ahead of them. Palmer tried unsuccessfully to look down on the confluence of the two rivers that formed the harbour.

6

"Yes, the second."

"Lucky bastard!" The cabbie hooked the gum from its wrapper with a practised flick of his pink tongue and began to chew.

"You reckon . . . ?" said Palmer absently. He was wondering what his father would have said about his new job if he had still been alive. A lifetime spent in the now extinct workhorses of the British Merchant Navy had engendered a feeling that cruise liners were not real ships and the men who sailed them were not real men. His grandfather would have had an even more pejorative opinion, having spent his working life in sail, risen to command a Clyde-built four-masted barque and doubled the Horn twice a year. Palmer sighed; neither was alive to recriminate him and both would have preferred him afloat to sitting on his arse ashore drawing the dole. As for their reaction to his peculiar importance . . . that he could not begin to guess at.

"Sure," went on the cabbie, "that fucking ship's full of widows, good American widows all looking for dick." A bubble of pink gum appeared from the corner of the man's mouth and popped obscenely. "Young, Limey dick. Great, eh? Man, you're a helluva lucky bastard!"

Palmer nodded and smiled. The false familiarity nauseated him, but he was an old hand at back-seat small talk with taxi-drivers. It was pretty universal. "Sure," he said.

"A helluva lucky bastard."

Palmer could see brief glimpses of the ship as the Ford began to descend from the bridge and then her huge, wedding-cake superstructure was gone behind the dockside installations as the driver swung the cab off the freeway onto the port road. He fished in his pocket for his papers as the cab hissed to a stop at the security fence.

All he could see of the security man was a tightly buttoned shirt stretched over a pendulous gut which was abruptly replaced by the black visor and helmet, as the hoplite of bureaucracy returned the documents. The security officer jerked his head and the cab moved forward. A few moments later it swung round a shed, passed a mooring bollard from which orange polypropylene ropes led upwards and the sheer, white cliff of the ship's side rose above them.

The cab stopped and the driver peered upwards through the windscreen. "Jeesus . . . call that fucking thing a ship?"

"A dollar a day," said Palmer, getting out and dragging his grip after him. The cabbie reluctantly levered himself out of his seat to open the boot. Puffing heavily he condescended to lug the heavy suitcases out and dropped them into the dust on the quay.

"Jeesus . . ." he repeated, scratching himself in a gesture that indicated his part of the contract was completed.

Palmer peeled off dollar notes and handed them over. "Thanks," he said, his mouth twisted in an ironic smile. The driver counted the notes ostentatiously.

"Would you pick me up in a couple of hours . . . I've some last minute shopping to do before we sail . . . say two o'clock?"

The driver looked up at him, chewing his gum with aggressive vigour and pausing before replying so that that the Limey would realize the enormity of the favour he was doing.

"Can't you buy it on the goddam boat?"

Palmer smiled. "No." He bent and picked up the cases. "Two o'clock?"

"Okay."

The driver waddled back to the open door and the Ford bucked under his weight. "Motherfucker . . ." he said, gunned the engine and departed with a squeal of tyres.

Palmer turned to the great ship. He could hear the hum of auxiliary generators through her shell plating. He glanced along the quay. A bare uncovered gangway led aboard farther forward for the use of the crew. A party of stewards and seamen were unloading stores from two vans. Palmer turned to the nearer gangway. It was covered over and its entrance bore a notice of welcome to the liner *Adventurer*. Two potted palms stood beside the notice.

"Bloody hell," said Palmer as he passed an approaching steward, glaring at the man forbiddingly.

The steward affected to ignore the overloaded newcomer and made ready to receive a second cab which swung round the corner of the shed at that moment.

Palmer toiled up the gangway. He was sweating despite the

cool air that flowed out of the ship's air-conditioning and down the gangway. The rumble of the generators grew and was then replaced by the seductive tone of canned Muzak emanating from the foyer at the entrance of which he suddenly found himself. More plants and flowers reminded Palmer of a Kew hothouse and the rich carpet seemed as incongruous as the palms standing in the filth of the quay below. At a reception desk a bevy of shapely young women were gossiping. The single man among them, wearing the gold and white epaulettes of a purser, indicated Palmer's arrival. One of the women, a young blonde dressed in the ubiquitous uniform of the professional hostess, white blouse, blue pencil skirt and a neck scarf in the company's colours of blue and orange, walked towards him.

Palmer dumped his bags with a thud. He noticed the legs, the slim hips and the mannequin walk.

"Good morning, sir. Welcome aboard the *Adventurer*," she said with professional insincerity, "may I have your boarding documents and your passport, please?"

A gilt badge pinned to the thin blouse announced her to be 'Melanie' and her tan showed through the material. She returned his smile, but he could not decide if it was genuine.

"I'm afraid not," he replied, grinning, "I'm not a passenger."

The girl frowned, the smile slipped. "The crew are supposed to use the other gangway," she said sharply.

"You mean the *forrard* one," he said sharply.

"Yes."

"Well, never mind. I'll know next time. Perhaps you'd be so kind as to show me the way to the second officer's accommodation."

"Oh, you're Mr Palmer, are you?"

"Correct."

Just as Melanie seemed to be treating him like a human being they were distracted by an excited giggling coming up the gangway behind them. Melanie's eyes darted in the direction of the entrance.

"Excuse me, I'll get someone to show you," she turned to the purser's desk. "Lila!"

Palmer winced at the shrill tone of voice as he bent to pick up his bags again.

"Let me take one."

He looked up. The heavily made-up features of the purserette had been replaced by those of a minion. The girl called Lila was dressed in the plain white overall of a labourer, her hair drawn tightly back in a short ponytail, her feet in flat shoes.

"It's okay!" Palmer said, smiling as he straightened up, "Thanks all the same." As he followed the girl out of the foyer it was filled with the ecstatic babblings of a lady passenger who had followed Palmer onto the ship.

"Oh my, this is just wonderful!" He heard her exclaim as his guide led him forward and up a bewildering array of ladders until the floor covering became less expensive and he knew he had reached the officers' accommodation.

He followed the stewardess, noticing that she did not need the benefit of an artificial tan to show her skin through the overall. Her briefs were wickedly scanty and the lines of her brassiere straps neatly trisected her upper back. She held a swing door open for him and he heard the noises of voices and laughter, and the pop and hiss of beer cans being opened further along the alleyway. He muttered his thanks as he drew his heavy bags after him. Their eyes met.

"You the new second officer?" she asked. The accent baffled him, but her swarthy skin and fine brown eyes regarded him with level appraisal from beneath dark brows. A whiff of suspicion crossed his mind, instantly dismissed.

"Yes," he puffed, guessing she was Puerto Rican because of the Yankee twang perceptible in her voice. "And you're Lila, eh?"

"Lila Molina. . . ." She pronounced it *Lee-la* and the knowledge seemed to confirm his suspicions. He smiled at her. She had a wide mouth and a straight nose with fine, flared nostrils and Palmer, struggling in her wake through the narrow alleyway, decided she was infinitely more to his taste than the glamorous Melanie. The purserette seemed out of place at sea, but Lila had that exploited look common to all who are driven to sea for a living. Palmer could identify with that, even if it did spin his grandfather in his grave.

He heaved his gear through the door she held open for him.

10

"Thanks for your help," he said turning, but the girl had already vanished.

Palmer shrugged, peered into the cabin mirror, flicking his fair hair into place, then stepped out into the alleyway. At the door of the cabin from which the noise came he paused and introduced himself.

"Morning. Palmer, Tim Palmer, second mate. Could someone point me in the direction of the Old Man's cabin, please?"

Half a dozen faces looked up at him through a haze of tobacco smoke. They introduced themselves in a bewildering succession of names, declaring themselves deck officers or sparkies, and one of them called Simon something-or-other took him further forward to an open door filled by a curtain.

Palmer nodded his thanks.

"Don't forget to call him Smythe, for Christ's sake!" the young officer hissed before beating a hasty retreat. Palmer knocked on the opened door, wondering how he was going to extract an hour's shore leave from such an apparently forbidding master.

"What is it?" The voice was crusty, imperious in its query.

"Palmer, sir, second officer, reporting aboard." He drew back the curtain and stepped into the cabin.

"Ah, Mr Palmer, come in. It's about bloody time you arrived!"

At the foot of the forward gangway the sweating stewards paused to watch the cabs pull away. They had stopped unloading the cartons of stores from the truck to watch the flamboyant arrival of the American woman.

"She's a bit old for youse, Steph," said a pale young man in the blue-checked trousers of an assistant cook. "Come on let's get this fucking stuff loaded up . . . s'posed to be bleeding spaghetti but feels like iron bars."

The remark in thick Liverpudlian recalled the other two men to their task with a quick exchange of glances.

"Hey, Stephanos, this Englishman is not so strong as he looks, eh? Maybe we show him, eh?"

The speaker was middle-aged but had a powerful physique and hove a box up onto his shoulders with ease. His younger companion, Stephanos, had a similar dark cast of feature.

"Anyways," persisted the Liverpudlian cook, "I thought youse Greeks didn't like women."

The big man paused at the foot of the gangway. "Me, Giorgio, I fuck anything, eh, Stephanos?"

"Yeah ..." both men looked at the cook, "... anything...."

"With a hole in it ..." said the departing Giorgio as he vigorously began the ascent of the gangway.

ADVENTURER, CHARLESTON, SOUTH CAROLINA

"So you are our new secundus?"

Palmer looked up from the opened drawers into which he was decanting his personal effects. The man in the doorway was about 40, greying, but handsome in a dissipated sort of way, with an attractively deep voice caused, Palmer astutely presumed, by quantities of Scotch whisky, a bottle of which he carried in one hand. There was a half-full glass in the other.

Tim rose and held out his hand, then retracted it when he realized the newcomer was fully occupied. "Yes, Palmer, Tim Palmer...."

The stranger stepped into the cabin, avoided the open suitcases and entered the tiny bathroom, reappearing with the regulation tooth-glass.

"Welcome aboard. Have a drink to celebrate your arrival on this fine ship."

It was too late to refuse, though the list of instructions the captain had given him would occupy the four hours he had before the ship sailed.

"It's Scotch, the best Scotch, Glenmorangie ... none of that blended rubbish. We have on board 29 brands of Scotch, eight American – Rye and Bourbon – two Canadian and two Irish, but there is only one Glenmorangie ... cheers!"

"Cheers!" The spirit burned his throat and made Palmer shudder.

"I, by the way, am the doctor, Jonathan Aymes, specialist in venereal and geriatric complaints but not necessarily in that order ... try to ensure that you do not need to consult me on either score during the course of our exciting, adventurous and, hopefully, profitable voyage." Aymes paused eyeing Palmer shrewdly. "You don't have the look of a cruising man, Tim, me lad."

"And what look is that?" asked Palmer putting down his glass and resuming his unpacking.

"Oh, a certain look about the eyes, an incipient turpitude, a reliance upon alcohol, sex and tobacco, a pot belly ... it finished your predecessor. ..."

"What was the matter with him?"

"Excess, my dear Tim, an excess of excess ... he simply couldn't handle it." Aymes emptied his glass and refilled it. "A wee chota-peg," he explained, "before we do battle with the cargo."

"Sorry?" Palmer frowned.

"The passengers ... are you married?"

"God no!"

"Why so vehement ... ?"

"I've been unemployed for a long time."

"Ah! I'm sorry." Aymes was suddenly serious. "It's a common complaint among British seamen these days; endemic one might say."

"It would be epidemic if it was anyone other than the common sailor, but since no one cares a damn. ..."

"No one ever has, Tim," Aymes said soothingly, "the British seaman is as despised now as he ever was. Remember Nancy Astor and the yellow armband?"

"It's all right for you, you're a bloody doctor. The tribe always respects the medecine man. ..."

"Well, I'm only a pox-doctor," Aymes remarked consolingly.

"I'll bet you're like a priest in the bloody confessional once we've dropped the land astern!"

"My, you're a bitter fellow. Here, you need a touch of mellowing." Aymes slopped more malt into Palmer's glass.

"No, I've had enough."

"You can never have enough of the 'Morangie, me lad."

13

Aymes watched the younger man as he completed his un-packing and shut the cases. "The steward'll stow those in the baggage locker. Have you met Father yet?"

"Yes. Captain Symthe gave me enough work to occupy me until sailing."

"Do I detect a note of dismissal?"

Palmer looked up and smiled apologetically. Picking up the tooth-glass he finished the malt whisky. "Sorry. I'm a bit preoccupied, not having been aboard ship for a while."

"Don't air your grievances too obviously, Tim," Aymes said, a note of cordial though cautionary professionalism displacing his flippancy. "Being alienated on a cruise ship can be a disquieting experience. Right! I'll push off ... mind if I steal your paper?"

Aymes held up the crumpled copy of the *Guardian* that bore the previous day's date.

"Not at all, Doc."

"Thanks. See you later."

"Sure." Palmer slammed the last drawer shut and looked at his watch. The cab should be at the gangway.

In the chart room Palmer finished sorting his charts out and felt the ship tremble as the big, turbo-blown Sulzer diesels came to life. They were a dozen decks below him but he felt a sudden thrill of excitement at that stirring heartbeat deep in the hull of the ship. Whatever his private misgivings about the *Adventurer*, he could not resist the sensation of anticipation after so long ashore. Whatever the peculiarity of the circumstances, he *was* afloat again and took consolation from the fact that he could derive a measure of private satisfaction from his duty done well.

He completed his pre-sailing preparations, half listening to the staff captain and chief officer completing their own. Telephones were ringing as department heads reported to the bridge. Bill Andrews, the fourth officer, brought the pilot onto the bridge and the duty quartermaster fished the red and white 'H' flag out of the flag locker and disappeared onto the bridge wing to hoist it on the yard alongside the courtesy ensign of the Stars and Stripes.

14

The pilot waddled across the wheelhouse to shake hands with the staff captain. He seemed impersonal behind his sunglasses and the exaggerated peak of his baseball hat. Andrews put his name in the logbook, giving Palmer a friendly smile as he did so.

"The hands are just going to stations, Pilot," the staff captain said and then turned as Captain Smythe came on the bridge, his gold-peaked cap tucked under his arm. "Good afternoon, gentlemen," he said with sonorous formality, drawing attention to his arrival for the benefit of anyone who had not noticed it.

The staff captain and chief officer reported the ship ready for sea.

"Very well. We will single up then." Smythe shook hands with the pilot.

"Hansen, Cap'n."

"Captain Smythe, Mr Hansen."

"Ain't that," said Hansen pausing to tap a cigarette out of the packet he took from the breast pocket of his shirt, "the same name as the cap'n of the *Titanic*?" He flipped the Zippo lighter with studied nonchalance and Palmer looked up to watch this piece of Limey-baiting.

"That was 'Smith', Pilot. My name's Smythe."

"Smith, Smythe; shit, shite, it's all the same to me, Cap'n. Can I use your VHF?"

Palmer stifled his grin as he caught Andrew's eye. The fourth officer could barely suppress his laughter. Smythe's face flushed above the iron-grey of his beard and his eyes became two hard chips in his florid face, but he held his peace and ignored the rudeness. Helpfully, the chief officer held out the VHF radio handset.

"Hi ... Charleston Control, this is *Adventurer* ... come back. ..."

Palmer checked the chart table and found Captain Smythe beside him.

"All ready, Mr Palmer?"

"Yes sir."

"We may have a Panamanian flag, but I assure you I demand the same high standards as though you were still back in one of Alfred Holt's 'Blue Flues.'"

15

"Aye, aye, sir." Palmer realized that Smythe had been doing his homework on the new second officer foisted on him at short notice

"Your predecessor was a first-class navigator and I understand that your chief qualification was that you were prepared to fly out at a moment's notice. . . ."

Palmer felt a rising anger. Was Smythe relieving his pique at the pilot's rudeness on him? Or was he referring to Palmer's possible lack of expertise, caused by the enforced idleness of unemployment? He could have no other suspicions. Whatever the cause, Palmer was annoyed.

"I am a master mariner, sir." he wanted to add that the qualification was equal to Smythe's own but thought better of it. A lifetime's deference to rank made him hold his tongue.

"Oh, I know that, Mr Palmer, and it's a *British* ticket. But there's no substitute for experience. Just remember I take no shit, or shite," Smythe added lowering his voice, "from anyone."

"Singled up, sir." The chief officer announced, the telephone from fo'c'sle and after-deck in his hand. Smythe turned away and Palmer expelled a long breath.

"Take no notice," whispered Andrews, as he slipped below to supervise the disconnection of *Adventurer*'s umbilical link with the shore. When the last gangway was run onto the quay she would be in isolation, and Captain Smythe the Master under God.

Smythe and the pilot went out onto the starboard bridge wing and the noise of the band wafted up to the bridge. Palmer ventured out for a look over the side. A troup of drum-majorettes were prancing up and down, their short ra-ra skirts fluttering in unison as their knees flashed up and down in the sunshine. The band wore an exaggerated uniform with cross-belts and plumed shakoes and Palmer thought he had never seen anything quite so ridiculous. But the cliff-like side of *Adventurer* was crowded with the heads of her passengers and coloured paper streamers curved gracefully down to the friends and relatives watching the departure from the quay.

"Okay, Cap'n. Leggo fore and aft!"

*   *   *

Mrs Rebanowicz avoided the laboured ritual of departure. She was departing in order to forget and in order to forget she was hungry for new experiences. Besides, she had had enough of ritual; seven months of mourning was enough to cure anyone of blind obedience to social convention. Especially if you were Zelda Rebanowicz to whom widowhood had brought disillusionment. Grief had been swept aside by the knowledge that her late husband had been far from faithful and that the circumstances of his death (on a business trip to Cincinatti) were still not explained to his wife's entire satisfaction. Her presence onboard the *Adventurer* had more to do with the desire for symbolic revenge than any real curiosity about the sights of the remote corners of the world to which *Adventurer* was bound.

Zelda Rebanowicz knew she had made the right decision the instant she followed Palmer into the entrance foyer of the ship: the atmosphere, the vibrations, the whole aura of the ship was so *sympatico* to her distressed condition.

"Oh no! Would you mind putting that over there ... that's so kind of you. You sure you don't mind doing these things for me?"

The steward straightened up from moving the heavy chair and securing the screw into the brass socket set in the thick shag-piled carpet.

"Sure." There was something delightfully lupine about the smile that positively glowed beneath the black mustachios, Mrs Rebanowicz thought.

"Are you Greek?" she asked, a little breathlessly as the man rubbed the palms of his hands on his buttocks. The white trousers emphasized the neat roundness and Mrs Rebanowicz felt a fluttering in her breast.

"Sure," he repeated.

"D'you speak English?"

"Sure. Plenty. Good enough to understand you, Miss. ..."

"What's your name?"

"Giorgio."

"You *are* Greek. That's wonderful!"

"Sure, it's wonderful." He paused, his dark eyes wandering over her. She was the wrong side of 50, he guessed, but with

17

that preserved figure managed by well-to-do American women. It was quite obvious that she was wealthy too. If anything went wrong with the voyage Giorgio was looking for a bolt-hole. His gaze slid over her breasts. Above the rounded stomach they were full and inviting. It was over a month since he had had his last woman.

"Giorgio's wonderful," he said thickly as their eyes met.

He knew he had scored even though she fumbled in her handbag to produce a 10-dollar bill. "Anytime you want anything, you call for Giorgio."

He took the note and stuffed it into his hip pocket. As he left the cabin Mrs Rebanowicz noted how the crumpled greenback made a little wrinkled star on the smooth surface of Giorgio's right buttock.

Somewhere far above her the *Adventurer*'s siren announced their departure.

Margaret Allen heard the noise of the siren from the after end of the long boat deck. She too was avoiding the pomp of departure, but for different reasons. Her first impressions of the ship convinced her that she had made a mistake in embarking. Widowhood had come upon her with its full tide of grief and, but for fear of the crushing weight of loneliness, she would rather have been going north, to an autumn in Vermont, rather than south to a double summer. She stared listlessly down at the empty swimming pools, watching the sunlight on the smooth water and contrasting it with the tiny wavelets running over the grey waters of the harbour. Even the swimming-pool water had an artificiality about it when compared with the reality of the sea. And yet sense told her that a break with the past (and Vermont would be redolent of the past), the stimulation of new horizons and an opportunity to voyage among the lonely archipelago at the very toe of the American continent would undoubtedly repair her shattered soul.

But she felt guilty about making such an effort. Although she suspected such a feeling, and regarded it with a characteristic taste for ruthless honesty, she wanted to retain her sense of grief for as long as possible if only as a tribute to her husband, whom she had truly, faithfully and devotedly loved. Somehow the eclipse of her bereavement by a cruise, a piece of self-indulgence against which her English Protestant upbringing revolted, seemed intrinsically sinful. Yet she must pull herself together and rebuild her shattered life. So she stared uncertainly aft, almost alone on a ship which had developed a slight starboard list as the majority of its 1,000 passengers waved enthusiastically at their friends and families while the propeller wash built up under the ship's stern and the twin bow-thrusters forced her long white hull bodily off the quay.

The paper streamers stretched and began to break, the band thumped and blew its way into a final crescendo of the Sousa march and the drum majorettes' batons twirled in a final pointless climax. Above her head the siren blew another valedictory blast, the swirl from the bow-thrusters eased and the Sulzers thrust the great ship forwards.

Margaret Allen stared at the wake as it formed astern of them and watched the opportunist gulls dip screaming into the swirling water. They passed Drum Island and the thrum of the engines increased. She was no longer alone. People were promenading round the decks; a few teenage children rushed excitedly about and she smiled at their fresh young faces. It seemed that a gulf separated her from them, yet it also seemed a gulf of such a short duration despite the immensity of its experience.

A shadow fell over the deck and such was the extent of her preoccupation that she thought of it for one brief instant as a supernatural visitation. But, looking up, it resolved itself into the mighty curve of the East Bridge flying high overhead, to pass astern and dwindle into the distance, the bright sun-reflected dots of its traffic diminishing in size. As she watched, its dark silhouette gradually lightened against a growing pall of dark cloud which gathered with incredible speed into soaring towers of cumulonimbus. Aware that she had never studied such a build-up of cloud since she was the age of one and of the careless teenagers who continued to rocket round the boat deck, she watched fascinated, as the cloud bank rolled off the land.

Palmer straightened up from the starboard gyro repeater and

cast a cursory glance at the United States flag flying over the low, brown ramparts of Fort Sumter.

"Named after a patriot hero who licked you British,"the pilot was amiably explaining to Captain Smythe, as he lit another cigarette, "That's where the Civil War started. . . ."

"*Your* civil war, Mr Hansen. We'd had ours a couple of centuries earlier," riposted Smythe drily. Palmer caught a glint of good humour in the captain's eye as he disappeared into the chart room to inscribe the bearing onto the chart.

"Pilot ladder port side, Mr Andrews," the chief officer was saying into a telephone.

"Looks like a line-squall building astern of us," remarked the staff captain, peering out of the after windows of the bridge.

They slowed as the pilot cutter surged over *Adventurer's* bow wave and ran into the lee of the hull. Bill Andrews reappeared in the wheelhouse to take the pilot below.

"Well, good voyage, Cap'n. . . ." Hansen pitched his Lucky Strike over the side and held out a pudgy hand to Smythe.

"Thank you, Mr Hansen, and good luck to you." No trace of animosity seemed evident between the two men who, to Palmer, seemed to represent the opposite poles of the same culture. Hansen nodded his farewells and made for the companionway behind Andrews. Captain Smythe moved to the bridge wing and waited for the baseball hat to show itself at the top of the pilot ladder.

"Your first course is one-two-zero degrees true, sir."

"Gyro error?" snapped Smythe without turning.

"Nil, sir."

"Huh . . . give me one hundred and eighty revolutions!"

Palmer stepped forward and eased the engine controllers. The follow-up motors buzzed and the Doppler log clicked as *Adventurer* accelerated slowly.

Suddenly Smythe rolled back off the rail laughing.

Palmer heard the surge of power as the pilot cutter turned away from the ship's side. Next to him the staff captain and the chief officer were exchanging conspiratorial smiles. As it turned back towards the land Palmer caught a glimpse of the pilot cutter. Hansen was making his way aft into the shelter of the cabin, a crewman helping him. He was soaking wet.

Smythe's acceleration before he was clear of the ladder had obviously shot water up between ship and launch.

"Shit and shite are all the same to him," Smythe muttered good-humouredly as he came back into the wheelhouse, smiling at his officers.

The quartermaster came down from the upper bridge rolling up the International code flag that denoted the presence of the pilot.

"And you can take that bloody thing down too," said Smythe, pointing up at the Stars and Stripes, "I've had a bellyful of Yankees."

In his cabin Doctor Aymes was draining the last of the bottle of Glenmorangie and reading Palmer's copy of the *Guardian*. It was his custom to avoid close contact with the passengers until his professional services were demanded, and a study of the passenger list, sent up from the purser's office just before sailing, had convinced him that he had no more than a 24-hour rest period. The usual proportion of first-class passengers were single women, blue-rinse widows from the Mid-West, in search of their last flings and throwing money about with the ease of easy acquisition. The stress-related deaths of their respective husbands had invariably provided them with a maturing Life Assurance policy and their usual behaviour was a sure-fire way to maintain Jonathan Aymes on the unerring path of male chauvinism.

There was, on this particular voyage, a large proportion of tourist-class passengers. They varied in age from retired people to middle-class young marrieds with money enough to allow them to take the necessary eight weeks off work. Apart from the geriatric problems, Aymes could look forward to the odd marital break-up, possibly extending to broken bones: jaws for the women, ribs for the men. Such an objective contemplation of matrimony ensured Aymes adhered to a strict bachelorhood, while the 150 pubescent teenagers running about outside his cabin would confirm him in his long-held belief in birth control. He wondered how many of these adolescents would turn out to be junkies and the thought led him to wonder how many of the crew would turn out to be pushers.

The United States Coast Guard had made a thorough search of the ship before the passengers came aboard, but an object as complex as a cruise liner had an almost infinite number of hiding places if one wanted to exploit them.

Aymes sighed at the folly of mankind, looked sadly at the empty bottle of whisky and dropped it with a resounding clang into his cabin rosy.

"For folly on the international scale," Aymes muttered to himself, "we have the consolation of the media." He turned to the leader page of the *Guardian*:

... it is hoped that the forthcoming United Nations debate on the plight of the Palestinians may take a realistic turn, if only to improve the credibility of the debating chamber of the United Nations. The cynical scuppering of every initiative in recent years has done nothing to elevate the reputation of politicians, diplomats or the national policies of nations, let alone produce even a hope of finding a solution to a single one of the the problems confronting the world community. The growing desperation of the Palestinians has led to an increase in world tension, an escalation of terrorist attacks, acts of merciless reprisal by powerful states and the dismemberment of the Lebanon. If the Palestine question was the only one to confront the statesmen of the world, they might be forgiven their caution; but without grasping the nettle now, all that one can be sure of is an endless vista of violence; of bombings, assassinations and hijacks all leading to God-knows what vengeance from those who consider they should be immune from the ills of the world. ...

Aymes crushed the paper in his lap. It was all too bloody depressing. The cabin suddenly darkened and he saw a young face at the window, its nose pressed impertinently against the glass. Aymes got up and pulled a face. "Sod off," he mouthed. "Christ it's going to be one of those voyages, I bloody well know it...."

Palmer came off the bridge and walked aft along the boat

deck. People drew aside and looked curiously at him in his brassbound uniform. Two children, a girl and a boy, were running towards him and stopped when they saw him. They exchanged glances and giggled, fists going to their mouths. Palmer's brief bubble of pride was pricked and he stared out over the quarter at the masses of cumulonimbus rapidly overhauling the ship.

Reaching the after end of the boat deck he stared down over the array of decks that descended to the stern like enormous sets in a Hollywood extravaganza. Passengers were already lying around in the deck and steamer chairs; catering staff had already begun to circulate among them with the ridiculous drinks that bore pieces of jungle or paper parasols as an indispensible adjunct to the more necessary glass. He looked for Lila but could not see her.

A few brave souls had already ventured into the two pools while a pair of fit-looking men in their thirties were already expending their energy in the netted deck-tennis court. Working up to her cruising speed of 22 knots, *Adventurer* remained bathed in sunshine and none of the passengers seemed to have noticed the approaching black cloud.

Palmer caught the eyes of the duty quartermaster stationed aft to give warning of any passenger who fell overboard. Across the 100 ft or so of crowded decking the two men exchanged glances of professional contempt, or so it seemed to Palmer. He smiled to himself, partly because the quartermaster seemed to share some of his own feelings, and partly out of anticipation of the corporate reaction to the coming squall. He lingered deliberately to watch.

"You're an officer, aren't you? Can you tell me what it is? I've been watching it and it's awesome."

Palmer turned. The voice was cool, well modulated and English in accent, though a certain flatness in its vowels suggested a long residence in the United States. The woman's face was fine-boned with that guarantee of beauty long after age began to desiccate the skin. He guessed her to be 60 or so. He was xenophobically pleased that the only passenger aware of the approaching meteorological phenomenon was British.

"It's a line-squall, ma'am."

"It looks sinister enough to be an omen."

Palmer laughed. "It's merely a local effect. A band of cold air is rolling over the warm, tropical air off the sea. It'll get cold in a minute or two . . . you watch our guests below." Palmer nodded at the sybarites round the pool, one or two of whom had begun to look up as the advancing cloud obscured the sun.

"It's extraordinarily impressive, Mr . . ."

"Palmer, ma'am, second officer."

"You do the navigating; is that right?"

"Well, all the deck officers are navigators, but it's my especial responsibility, yes."

"I'm Margaret Allen . . . professional qualification: widowed housewife."

"Oh," said Palmer awkwardly, "I'm sorry."

"You've no need to be . . . you are right, it is getting chilly."

"You should go inside. The ship is fully air-con . . ."

"Air-conditioned, yes I know, but I actually came on this cruise to taste the salt air, not hide from it. My steward has been trumpeting the thousand and one ways I can be pampered, stuffing my head full of inconsequential things like the fact that there are three swimming pools, a sauna, a shopping arcade, a cinema, a jogging track, God knows how many bars, restaurants, hairdressers and even a room full of dog kennels!"

"But you only came to see the sea?"

"Exactly . . . oh, look! What's that?"

The upper part of the cumulonimbus was overhead now and many of the passengers were leaving the decks; some squealing marked this retreat. Low down on the horizon a hard line was forming, obscuring the disappearing coast of Carolina. They could see the sea whipped white by the approaching wind and on the leading edge of the cloud strange pendulous excrescences hung down and then vanished.

"Golly, they're horrible!"

Palmer laughed. "If you're very lucky you'll see one reach the sea . . . wait, there! Look!"

Margaret Allen followed his pointing arm. The grey append-age was much closer now and she could see it spiralling downwards, waving in a sinuous curve. Below it the sea was whipped white, a whirling of water which, miraculously, began to rise and meet the funnel-shaped cloud. A curious shiver of excitement ran down her spine.

"My God, it's magical," she said, her eyes shining with excitement. In the curious curve of *Adventurer*'s superstructure there was little wind effect but the sight was spectacular.

"It's a waterspout," laughed Palmer, enjoying a real moment of happiness, in his true element.

"Excuse me . . . I couldn't help overhearing . . . did you say it was a waterspout?"

They both turned. An elderly man with bright eyes and a slight stoop had stopped behind them. "I think we have cabins in the same area," he said to Mrs Allen, "my name's Galvin. I apologize for intruding but I was fascinated by your explanation of the change in the weather. I'm afraid I was eavesdropping," he smiled at Palmer, an earnest little man who added, "and I was charmed to hear English again."

"That's quite all right," said Palmer, "I presume you are English?"

"Well yes . . . I never actually renounced my nationality, but I've lived in the States for a long time."

"Then we've more in common than cabins in the same area," said Margaret Allen. She shivered. The line-squall had passed ahead of the great ship and darkened the sea and sky. Alongside them, white horses reared in the wake although the ship's wind neutralized the breeze that followed.

"I suppose that's what they call a sea change," she joked.

"I believe the phrase is meant to mean a more profound change," said Galvin and then, turning to Palmer asked, "Can you tell us roughly where we are heading?"

"Yes. We shall skirt to the east of the Bahamas to head out of the Gulf Stream and turn south-eastwards outside the curve of the West Indian archipelago. . . ."

"It all sounds so . . . I don't know, so grand; a route on the global scale, so to speak."

"That's roughly what it is," explained Palmer.

"Does that mean we go anywhere near the Bermuda Triangle?" put in Mrs Allen.

Palmer laughed again. "Yes, right through the middle of it . . .

but hardly anyone disappears these days. Now, if you'll excuse me, I must return to the bridge. . . ."

"What a handsome young man," said Mrs Allen, "I fear he has a rather poor opinion of us passengers, though."

"Oh, I am not surprised, Mrs . . . ?"

"Margaret, Margaret Allen."

"I'm John, John Galvin." They smiled awkwardly at each other and then she looked away, over the sea astern where the wake marbled green and white through the darkening water.

"I wasn't really sure whether to come on this voyage," she said, "but that young man's obvious enthusiasm for . . . well, what shall I call them? The wonders of the sea, seems rather reassuring."

"I agree, and the case is not dissimilar with me. . . ."

"What made you venture onto the ocean?"

"Retirement, overwork, failing health. . . ."

"Oh, I'm sorry."

"It's all right. It's a case of 'physician heal thyself'."

"You're a doctor?"

Galvin nodded. "Yes. But don't let everyone know. I'd like just two months without a consultation."

"Of course."

"That young fellow, did I hear him say he was the second officer?"

"Yes, that's right."

"Ah, well according to the purser's office he's giving a talk in the theatre tomorrow morning, they call it the forenoon on board ship, about our voyage and what we are likely to see."

"I shall look forward to that."

"Indeed, yes, so will I."

The following morning Palmer found himself in most un-seamanlike surroundings. Caught in a pincer movement by Staff Captain Meredith and Melanie Corbett of the purser's department he found himself instructed to report to the theatre at 11 o'clock, ship's time, to lecture on the proposed track of the *Adventurer*. He was, he discovered, part of the educational package that had featured heavily as an advertising ploy in the cruise's inception. To his astonishment the theatre-cum-cinema could seat nearly 500 people and the first half-dozen rows of plush pink chairs were occupied by restless teenagers. Further back came the adult passengers and, while Staff Captain Meredith made his welcoming introduction, Palmer nervously scanned his intimidating audience for a friendly face. He found Mrs Allen sitting next to Dr Galvin and a row back from Mrs Rebanowicz.

He had recognized Mrs Rebanowicz as the passenger who had followed him on board since he had met her formally for the first time at dinner the previous evening. Relieved to find he had the maternal figure of Mrs Allen at his own table, Mrs Rebanowicz's late and studied arrival had brought a hot and embarrassed flush to his conspicuous cheeks as he stood amid the seated first-class saloon while she settled herself.

While Margaret Allen possessed that fine bred-in-the-bone beauty that defies age, Zelda Rebanowicz exemplified a different standard of looks. Ten years Mrs Allen's junior Mrs Rebanowicz was running to fat and her heavily made-up features were no longer as handsome as when they had first attracted male eyes. But her ample flesh was still voluptuous in form and her disregard of the informal nature of the first night's dinner had ensured that she attracted attention in a gaudy sheath dress that reminded older diners of transatlantic travel in the days before the aeroplane.

For Tim Palmer, Jonathan Aymes's winks from the adjacent table indicated that he was the victim of a conspiracy between the officers responsible for allocating passengers to their tables. This fact was confirmed after dinner when Melanie Corbett waylaid him with a charmingly viperous smile and the instruction to prepare notes on the ship's track by 11.00 the following day for the benefit of an audience. For much of the middle watch, between midnight and four in the morning, when he might reasonably be expected to conduct the navigation of the ship, Tim had been frantically mugging up and jotting down notes on the subject. When he had turned in shortly after four, he had resigned himself to the task. Now, looking at the sea of faces before him, nervous anticipation fluttered through his over-tired body.

"And so before we go any further," Meredith was saying

27

with an urbane assurance that was the hallmark of every good, socializing staff captain, "I will now ask Mr Palmer, the ship's second officer and the chap responsible to Captain Smythe for the safe navigational details of our voyage, to say a few words on the subject. Mr Palmer. . . ."

In the sycophantic applause that Meredith appeared to have earned by his smooth preamble, Palmer was aware of the lights going out and someone, presumably Meredith, poking his stomach with a pointer. On the screen above his head appeared a large map of the two Americas and, just as he panicked at the realisation that he would be unable to read his notes, a spotlight illuminated him so that all he could see were a few young faces immediately in front of him. He took the offered pointer, coughed awkwardly, drew in his breath and began by quoting from the company's brochure.

"Good morning ladies and gentlemen. You are now on board one of the world's newest and largest purpose-built cruise liners. We are, as you already know, able to cater for your every comfort and to minimize any inconveniences that a life on the ocean wave may be thought to entail. . . ."

Palmer ignored the low groan that came from the now seated Meredith. He swallowed hard and continued, aware that what looked adequate at three in the morning lost its assurance in the glare of a spotlight.

"However, this is a luxury cruise only in the sense of your personal comfort. In all other respects you will be sailing in the wake of some of history's most famous navigators, Magellan, Drake, Anson, Cook, Lemaire, Schouten and even the infamous Captain Bligh. Charles Darwin evolved his Theory of Evolution while on board Captain Robert Fitzroy's *Beagle* on a similar voyage and our route is most famous as being the track of the hard-run Yankee Down-Easters that took the prospectors out to the Californian goldfields in the gold rushes of the last century."

Palmer paused for breath and in the silence heard someone mutter, "Here endeth the lesson. . . ."

Undaunted, he pressed on. "The purpose of the ship's voyage is to enable you to enjoy some of the most remote and beautiful scenery in the world and also to sample some of the wonders of the deep as we make our way southwards . . ." He aimed the pointer at a spot south-west of Charleston, "outside the Bahamas, to avoid the north-eastwards push of the Gulf Stream, towards the strait between Puerto Rico and the Dominican Republic known as the Mona Passage and then south-east across the Caribbean and out through the gap between Grenada and Tobago. At our cruising speed of 22 knots, or nautical miles an hour, you will see sunset over Tobago on Friday evening.

"We then move down the coast of South America, crossing the delta of the Orinoco and then, at about midnight on Monday morning, the Amazon. By breakfast time we will have crossed the equator and those of you who have not already done so will be initiated at the Court of King Neptune in the Crossing the Line ceremony. . . ."

An appreciative buzz of anticipation came from the front rows at this news.

"We continue south, during which time you will be able to see dolphins, flying fish and possibly some whales, and at daybreak on Friday week we will enter the harbour of Rio de Janeiro. We will stay a day at Rio.

"From Rio we continue south, and the expectation of whales increases the farther south we go, until, if the weather proves fair, we will enter the Straits of Magellan between Patagonia and Tierra del Fuego two weeks after leaving Charleston."

Without prompting, the map above Palmer was replaced by an enlargement showing the great archipelago that hooked round at the toe of the Americas to that other, isolated Staten Island.

"Our exact itinerary within the straits depends on the weather, but I understand that, if possible, we will pass into the South Pacific Ocean through the Cockburn Channel and then run eastwards through the Beagle Channel, then turn south, past the Woolaston Islands . . ." Palmer stabbed the chart as it appeared between windswept and almost monochromatic slides showing the precipitous slopes of the Cordillera Darwin and the narrow passage of the Beagle Channel.

" . . . To actually double back off Cape Horn, named by Schouten for his native town in the Netherlands. Here we hope you will see the wandering albatross and, if the weather is

29

exceptionally good, Captain Smythe has undertaken to cross the Drake Passage in the hope of sighting icebergs. If, however, this does not prove possible, we will compensate you by spending a longer period coasting up through the Chilean Archipelago towards Valparaiso. . . ."

Palmer went on for another 20 minutes, lingering over the possibilities of seeing varieties of wildlife, of landing at the Isla Robinson Crusoe in the Juan Fernandez group, and of seeing the flightless cormorants of the Galapagos before they arrived at San Francisco.

He found that towards the end he had conquered his nervousness and forgotten to refer to his notes, earning a tight smile of approval from Meredith as he sat down to applause. He caught Mrs Allen's smiling face and her companion, Dr Galvin, seemed to be clapping enthusiastically. Meredith was on his feet again.

"Mr Palmer's very eloquent description omitted one small detail that I had better explain. . . ."

Palmer bit his lip while Meredith superciliously elucidated the problems of the shift in longitude which would make occasional alternations of the ship's clocks necessary. With a voyage whose axis was nearly north-south Palmer had not thought it important at this point to bring the passengers' attention to such a detail and suspected Meredith of putting him in his place. The suspicion, unprovable in the face of the staff captain's suavity, may have been a symptom of his own lack of confidence; but it rankled nevertheless, and continued to make him feel something of an outsider.

As the lecture period broke up Mrs Allen and her companion caught him by the door.

"We thought you did that very well, Mr Palmer," Margaret Allen said, referring obliquely to his confession at dinner the previous evening that this was his first appointment to a cruise ship.

"Very good, young man," added Dr Galvin, "I should console yourself with a line or two of Alexander Pope. . . ."

"Pope?" frowned Palmer, feeling a warm gratitude to these two people, "I'm afraid I don't know any Pope. Wordsworth's 'Daffodils' were my limit at school."

30

"Shame on you, Mr Palmer ... let me quote:

"Sir, I have lived a courtier all my days,
And studied men, their manners and their ways;
And have observed this useful maxim still
To let my betters always have their will."

Palmer could not help laughing. "You are quite right, sir, and thank you. Now you must excuse me, I am expected on the bridge shortly."

Zelda Rebanowicz was not particularly interested in the itinerary of the ship. She had read the brochure and been seduced by the glossy pictures, not of the Cordillera Darwin, but the dancing, the gambling and the sheer thought of being part of such a glamorous scene. Since their eyes had met yesterday afternoon, she had been debating the joys of seducing Giorgio. Not that he needed seducing, Zelda told herself, but the sheer contemplation of the sexual act with such a handsome animal as the Greek steward was, almost, its own reward.

She was old enough not to want to rush the matter, and wise enough to console herself that a slight delay might increase his ardour and, in the unlikely event of his finding another lover, there were plenty more men to choose from. Finally, but looming large in Mrs Rebanowicz's calculations, contemplation of revenge on her late husband would be sweeter in the period of anticipation. However, her stern resolve waned on waking the following morning in surroundings of such extravagant luxury that she melted with lasciviousness, ringing her service bell with enthusiasm after she had made up her face, smoothed the bed and adjusted her nightdress to show her heavy breasts to their best advantage.

But she was to be disappointed. The summons was answered by a girl, a dark and rather beautiful girl whose hair was drawn back in a short ponytail and who brought in the breakfast tray in a no-nonsense manner that irritated Mrs Rebanowicz.

"Good morning," the girl said in a flat mid-Atlantic manner, devoid of any enthusiasm for her task:

"Oh, good morning!" Mrs Rebanowicz studied the girl as

31

she put the tray down. Bent over, the view of her breasts beneath the white overall stirred a feeling of jealousy in Mrs Rebanowicz, a feeling that only increased with the double realisation that this girl maintained her looks without the aid of make-up and, presumably, was a colleague of Giorgio.

"I was expecting Giorgio," she said sharply as the girl straightened up.

"Giorgio is busy with other passengers ... is there something?"

"I thought, never mind, what's your name?"

"You can call me Lila."

"Lee-la, gee, that's an old name. . . ."

"I'll open your curtains, it's a beautiful morning."

The girl threw back the curtains and stood for a moment, arm outstretched. Mrs Rebanowicz noticed that as she stood looking out of the cabin's huge picture window her face seemed to relax. Then she turned back to the woman in the bed. Mrs Rebanowicz had half-expected her to smile, but Lila's face settled into an impassive expression.

"D'you want Giorgio?" she asked matter-of-factly.

"Oh, it doesn't matter, dear," replied Mrs Rebanowicz, unwilling to appear too eager, or to have carnal desire rather than friendly enquiry taken as her motive for asking, especially by this hard-bitten stewardess.

As the girl left the cabin Mrs Rebanowicz fell on her breakfast and rescheduled the seduction of Giorgio.

Lila said: "She asked for you."

"Who?"

"The fat whore in number 8102."

"Mrs Rebanowicz?"

"She's not a Jew is she?" Lila asked sharply.

"She's the widow of a very wealthy Polish businessman, worth several million dollars."

"You be careful, Giorgio."

"Giorgio's always careful," he slid a hand over Lila's buttock.

"Take your hands off me!" she hissed and Giorgio complied instantly, though he muttered to himself as he re-stacked the coffee pots in the deck-pantry.

Lila stared at him for a moment and then said: "Go on then, go and do it if you want to, but remember why."

"I'll remember, Lila ... and try not to enjoy myself too much."

Mrs Rebanowicz was munching toast when Giorgio knocked on the door.

"Who is it?" she called.

"Giorgio, Miss."

"Oh!" her hand flew to her lips to whisk crumbs away, and fluttered over her cleavage. She felt taken at a disadvantage, yet her heart had begun to thump painfully.

"Come in."

Giorgio entered and closed the door behind him. "Lila said you were so kind to ask for me." He smiled, crossed the cabin and lifted the breakfast tray from her lap and set it on the side table. Sitting on the side of the bed he turned familiarly to her. "Now what can I do for you, Mrs Rebanowicz?"

Had she not been reclining, Mrs Rebanowicz would have fainted from the ecstasy of the moment. He was immensely handsome and his torso, half-turned towards her, was taut-muscled beneath the tee-shirt. The thin white fabric of his slacks showed a powerful thigh.

Recovering a little from the delicious sensation of lassitude into which his sudden advance had thrown her, she mastered herself. She placed a hand on his thigh, moving her thumb in a minute stroking motion.

"I expected to see you at breakfast, Giorgio." She pouted. "I did not like the girl ... Zelda wanted you ..." she breathed the last syllable and moved her hand up into his lap and gently squeezed.

His moustache tickled her lips and then their mouths ground together. She felt his hands hot upon her breasts and lay back, letting the first rush of his passion spend itself and securing her own power over him.

The duvet and its satin coverlet still protected her own virtue but she slid one hand from his hard back, over his small buttocks and round to his crotch.

Giorgio pulled back, his own hands flying down to liberate

33

his member. As he lifted his hips she looked down and made admiring noises.

"He's so big ... take those ridiculous things off ... !"

He rolled aside and drew off his slacks and pants. He was all hair and hard muscle as he stood over her to pull away the duvet. The scent of her wafted up as she drew up her knees. Giorgio leapt on to the bed and pulled them apart. Pushing her up against the padded bedhead he bent forward and buried his head in her bosom. She clasped his black curls tightly, muttering endearments, on fire from the ferocity of his lust.

He shook free, his head coming up as she felt the hardness of his bent knees under her buttocks. His hands were suddenly round her legs and she felt herself dragged down the bed and penetrated at the same instant.

"Oh God ... !" she moaned and choked on the syllable of her husband's name, then she was thrusting with the same eagerness as her lovely Greek, and spending as he swore and cursed himself into the little death of orgasm.

Chapter Two

"It's an enormous risk, Prime Minister."

"I know, Johnnie, but no battle's won without risks."

"Or casualties?"

"We must expect those too."

"How heavy?"

"Possibly very."

"I suppose that could be good cover, for you I mean."

"Thank you."

"I'm sorry, but I only meant . . ."

"You meant that I could blow my professional reputation to hell but if we're victimized it'll obscure things."

"It'll be a most effective smokescreen, yes Prime Minister. You've only a hung Parliament, I doubt the popularity you presently enjoy would last. . . ."

"I'd rather obfuscate the Americans, the opposition haven't a thing to go on. Not if I can rely on you that is."

"It's a bit late to doubt my loyalty."

"Yes. I'm sorry. You certainly played your part well as far as Jill is concerned."

"Thanks. She's one of the few who might guess though."

"Yes. What d'you think of this wall-paper?"

"Not radical enough."

"Good man. Another Scotch?"

By the middle watch on Friday morning they had cleared the Mona Passage and Tim Palmer paced the starboard bridge wing of the *Adventurer* in an open-necked shirt. The night air was deliciously warm and the great arch of the tropical sky twinkled with an inexpressible multitude of stars. After so long ashore he was almost choked by the emotion such beauty caused him. The sense of having returned to a much-loved place was irrational for he had only once before been in the West Indies, years earlier as a mere apprentice in one of Alfred Holt's Blue Funnel cargo liners. But he had spent countless watches under the tropic stars and they were familiar to him now as he walked his period of duty away. In the chart room, Simon DeAth, the fifth officer, went through the time-honoured routine, specified in Captain Smythe's orders, of calculating the errors of the standard magnetic compass.

It was a ritual as old as Noah's Ark, a fail-safe device should anything go wrong with their Arma-Browne gyro compass or the Magnavox Satellite Navigator, the Omega or any of the other sophisticated gadgetry that the *Adventurer* carried on her navigating bridge. It was a prudent insurance should her officers be driven back to the old methods of sextant, chronometer and magnetic compass, a comforting link with a familiar past and Palmer had still not got over his regret at its passing. The British Merchant Navy had vanished; been reduced to a handful of ferries, a few tankers and container vessels, a flock of rusting parish-rigged coasters and little else. No one seemed to care, for no one seemed to know it; its officers were compelled to sell double-glazing, its seamen to hire themselves out for starvation wages or sign on the dole.

A few joined ships like the *Adventurer*, painted drabs, trailing their dubious attractions along the fringes of Western decadence.

Looking up at Canopus, coruscating brilliantly as it burned low on the southern horizon, an irridescent sparkle of blue, red and silver, Palmer considered the futile immorality of this scrabbling at the products of excess. He had long ago sensed the extreme danger of its fragile imbalance, the inequality of those who have and those who have not.

He recalled the impact of real poverty as he had first encountered it in the Far East. The abject want had shocked him and given him an innate sympathy with those who struggled against subjection. Now, in his long months of short commons, he had tasted, if not poverty, at least a degree of indigence that would have seemed unthinkable ten years earlier. After all, it was a tenet of his own social order that things generally improved.

He smiled to himself in the darkness and wondered how much of his opinions had been known to the man he had met in London, but the smile faded as he considered the risks and dangers he now ran.

He tried to drive the depressing train of thought out of his mind. It was not for nothing that the middle watch was also known as 'the graveyard watch'. He had been assured the matter was only precautionary, not at all certain. . . .

It occurred to him to wonder what Rosie would have thought of things if she knew. She had always said he was a miserable sod who only had to live for the moment to be happy. She had put her philosophy into practice and the resulting adultery had ended their marriage; but she had been right, he was too much given to morbid introspection.

Perhaps he had learned something, although it had been unemployment, not Rosie, that had taught him. For the moment he was happy enough, despite his strait-laced reservations, and had to admit for all its hedonistic purpose there were compensations on board this great wedding cake of a ship with its deck upon deck of luxury cabins, of pools, saunas, shops and salons; its bars and restaurants, its casino, theatre and upper deck penthouses, such as the one occupied by Mrs Rebanowicz.

He had begun to enjoy the social life, for there was little evidence of the kind of activity he had been warned about. He took pleasure in the company of Margaret Allen and Dr Galvin, had been sworn to secrecy over the private information of the doctor's profession, and had found it of far greater interest that Galvin was a Quaker. They had established a post-prandial ritual of sitting out on deck with their brandies, indulging in that simple philosophizing that sea air and tropic skies induces. It was very pleasant and seemed not to offend their fellow diner, Mrs Rebanowicz who 'just loved dancing' and seemed content to make her own amusement. This delighted Palmer as it backfired on the ship's own doctor.

"Got you a red-hot number there, me lad," Aymes had said, admitting to have arranged for the voluptuous widow to be put at Palmer's table in the first-class saloon.

"Couldn't you have had her put at the Old Man's?" he had asked.

"It's not like the movies," Aymes had said in mock shock, "there's an elder statesman to be accommodated there."

Palmer had recognized the wizened old face of the Zionist. He had wondered if his presence on board had had anything to do with his own meeting in London. He was a precautionary measure, he concluded, besides Aymes had better reasons for sitting Zelda Rebanowicz at the second officer's table.

"Look, you'll have to be seen screwing *someone*, or Meredith'll think you're a queer. He doesn't like the deck officers to be queers. It's all right for stewards, makes them a nice cosy, manageable bunch who keep their in-fighting to the glory-hole, but you, me lad, you've got to prove you're a real man," and here Aymes had beat his chest, "and lay a lassie or two, or three if you like, otherwise you ain't doin' your dooty!"

"Bollocks!" Palmer had said, "An Oedipus complex isn't one of my problems. If Meredith's so keen to test my manhood why doesn't he steer one of his harem in my direction?"

The words wiped the mockery from Aymes's face. "Not Melanie Corbett, Tim me lad, that'd be poaching." and Aymes had swigged the rest of his whisky at a gulp.

It was not that Palmer was impervious to the opposite sex; quite the contrary. But the failure of his marriage to Rosie had cured him of the fever, if not the disease. To complicate his life during unemployment he had become involved with another woman. Oddly and ironically she had been a police inspector, fully employed and bruised in violent clashes with rioting strikers. Kate Meldrum had been the best thing that had happened to him and despite his desperate need for a job, he retained a strong sense of loyalty to her. In any case it was less than a week since he had left her bed.

Nevertheless he was no mysogynist and his easy manner and fair-haired good looks ensured he attracted attention in the ship's public rooms and on deck. Such mild flirtations so publicly performed only served to increase Meredith's dislike. But Palmer, unaware of this, found himself the flattered centre of attraction to a group of the teenage schoolchildren.

They were far from ordinary schoolchildren and had taken passage on the *Adventurer* as part of the curriculum of their highly privileged alma-mater. They came from an exclusive 'International' public school where an 'enlightened' regimen ruled over a thousand adolescents of both sexes in the restored keep of a Scottish castle. Founded by an armaments manufacturer to whom late parenthood had brought a measure of unease, it catered for the children of the wealthy, preparing the upper echelons of the coming generation with a brilliantly wide-ranging education and a suitably narrow international clique of friends who would later become colleagues. Palmer had yet to discover the degree of privilege to which these youngsters were both exemplars and heirs. In these first days he found them merely charming.

He took little interest in the organized social life on board. Most of this was run, with indefatigable enthusiasm, by Staff Captain Meredith and the purser's staff, aided and abetted by Aymes who avoided as many calls on his professional ability as possible by occupying his time in such frivolous activities. To some extent Palmer dodged involvement by being on such an unsociable watch as the 12–4, both in the early hours of the morning and of the afternoon. He had made sufficient of an impact to discharge whatever obligation he thought he owed the passengers by lecturing the young people on the navigational methods and systems of the ship, digressing readily into past methods and the history of voyaging in a more heroic age. To some extent this popularity combined with its vaguely intellectual content to further irritate Meredith.

But, as yet, such things were not intrusive and Palmer was content to be on watch, almost alone with the night, the great ship humming beneath him.

"Have you ever considered how many people are actually fornicating on board at this very moment?" DeAth said, suddenly joining him and leaning, bare armed, on the teak rail that curved round *Adventurer*'s bridge wing.

"No, Simon, I can honestly say that the thought had not entered my head. I should have thought yours would be occupied with the purer considerations of an azimuth."

"Well I've resolved that problem, but I always feel randy at this time of night, particularly when I know there are several hundred people down below. . . ."

"All right; shut up! This whole bloody ship is devoted to sex when you analyse it; the eating and drinking are incidental. . . ."

"The eating and drinking and dancing and gambling are all jolly well part of it, Mr Palmer, sir," DeAth said mockingly, "as is the earnest jogging in the morning, the squash and deck tennis and swimming, a desperate attempt to re-establish a healthy body before the noon chota-peg encourages the dirty mind to reassert itself."

"D'you enjoy living by such a philosophy?" Palmer said suddenly, taking DeAth by surprise.

"Is there any other?"

"No, I suppose, given the evidence, there isn't," Palmer said shortly and straightening up, crossed through the wheelhouse, checked the automatic pilot, the Minerva Fire Protection system, rang the master-at-arms's office and spent the rest of the watch pacing the port wing of the bridge on his own.

He was relieved at four by the chief officer. After fixing the ship's position he handed over and went below to make his own rounds of the ship. In the complexities of the cruise liner's internal organisation the ship was policed during the night by the master-at-arms and his regulators, a kind of para-military police force answerable directly to the Captain. A member of the purser's staff was always on duty in the central lobby as was a night steward on each deck. As a consequence it was only necessary for the deck officers to take a turn round the exposed upper decks as a precaution against nocturnal suicides by alchohol-induced depressives. More than one passenger had been prevented from committing such a rash act,

40

even in *Adventurer*'s short life. However, as far as Palmer's limited experience went, he had found the decks deserted at such an hour, the usual nocturnal trysting places under the davits long-since forsaken by lovers for more comfortable surroundings.

It was as he returned from the exposed after-end of A-deck, where the outdoor pool was situated, and climbed up the starboard ladders to the boat deck, that he saw the girl. She was standing directly beneath one of the emergency boat-boarding lights by No 5 lifeboat with her back to him. She seemed preoccupied and he felt a slight alarm, striding towards her as she suddenly began to run forward.

She stopped abruptly beneath No 1 lifeboat and Palmer saw her head bend and heard, quite distinctly, the 'peep' of the alarm of a digital watch. He did not recognize her at first, she was wearing jeans and a loose cheesecloth shirt, her feet noiselessly shod in trainers. She heard him coming and spun round. He saw it was Lila.

"Hullo," he said, frowning, "what on earth are you doing?" A dark suspicion was forming in his mind. She was panting heavily, presumably from her exertions, and her breasts, bare beneath the cheap cotton, rose and fell. Her face was expressionless.

"Training," she said.

"At this hour of the night?"

"Why not?" She moved, with almost studied casualness towards the section of rail between the davits of the two forward lifeboats. "I have little free time during the day, and this is not a part of the ship I can come to, except at night. And I like to jog." A slight, amused yet cynical smile moved the corners of her shapely mouth as she leaned back on the rail and looked at him.

"You would be better if you jogged, Mr Palmer."

"Better than what?" he smiled back, pleased at the mild flirtation.

"Better than you are now . . . it doesn't matter. . . ." She turned and gazed out over the dark sea. Eighty feet below them the sea hissed past, a slight phosphorescence turning the foam of *Adventurer*'s passage into a glowing milkiness.

"D'you like working on this ship?" he asked, aware that it was a lame and inadequate opening gambit, yet eager not to let the moment pass.

She turned back to him and he was struck by the regularity and beauty of her features, marred only by a barely perceptible hardness in her expression which he attributed to having too frequently to rebuff the clumsy advances of men such as himself.

"Tell me very honestly, Mr Palmer, do *you*?"

"Call me Tim."

"No, that is a foolish name, a very *English* name, besides you are an officer and I, well, I am a worker."

"I can assure you," said Palmer suddenly bristling, "that anybody wandering about this deck at 4.30 in the morning is a worker too!"

Her sudden smile surprised him. "Good. So you do not like working on this ship, but you came to join her in a hurry, yes?"

"Yes, I have not had any work for a long time and, whatever your opinions of officers, I am, first and foremost, a professional seaman."

"*Ecce homo*," she said drily and it seemed to him an odd remark for her to make. The suspicion in his mind began to melt. Circumstances make strange bedfellows and ships have always been full of misfits whose appearance could mislead if judged by shoreside standards.

"Would you like a drink?"

"I don't drink," she replied, then added, "and if you're trying to get me to sleep with you. . . ."

"I'm not," he interrupted, looking down at the returned hardness about her eyes and mouth, emphasized by the harsh light of the boat emergency illumination. "It's an insufferable piece of arrogance on the part of many beautiful women that they automatically assume every man wants to fuck them."

He was angry and turned away; it was time he was in his bunk and began to walk forward to the officers' accommodation beneath the bridge, so he missed Lila's valedictory smile.

"Time to get up, Anna." Lila bent over her sleeping cabin-mate, her heart torn with pity at the sight of Anna's scarred face, so pathetic in repose. The girl turned over slowly, almost liquid in her movements as she stretched with a feline grace until, as always happened, she rubbed her eyes and her fists rasped upon the scar tissue that masked her. Sleep made her forget her lost beauty; she could dream fantasies the way God had made her, but every morning she was compelled to wake to the reality of what men had done.

The burns had been caused by the fires ignited by incendiary bombs and Anna's escape from the burning shanty had cost her her looks. There were times when she had wished she was dead. But Lila had saved her, befriended her and, eventually, got her the job of linen maid aboard the *Adventurer*. It was subterranean employment, a task for an untouchable, a low minion in the hierarchy of *Adventurer*'s microcosmic society. She collected dirty linen, counted and laundered it, reissuing it to the cabin stewards and stewardesses so that the passengers might rest between frequently changed sheets, never knowing who it was that made such luxury possible. Anna blunted her intelligence with the heavy routine of her employment and waited, waited for the moment Lila had promised. In that fact lay her only contentment.

But, at the daily moment of waking, Anna needed consolation and relied upon Lila, whose arm about her shoulder enabled her to face the coming day.

"It's all right, Anna ... all right," Lila crooned until Anna signalled acceptance of her lot, and gently pushed her friend away. Sitting up, Anna took the offered hairbrush and vigorously brushed her dark hair. A few tears trickled across the ribbed ugliness of her battered face.

"Well? How did you get on?"

"Okay, it'll work, just as we knew it would. I've only one last section to do, but I nearly got caught this morning."

"Who by?" Anna asked in sudden alarm.

"Palmer, the new second officer."

"Oh, what did he say?"

"He's not bad really," Lila said, an idea occurring to her, "In fact I think that I can probably turn the meeting to our advantage...." She paused and looked at her friend. "Yes, I think I could, and it would be quite nice for you too, but I'll wait a day or so."

"How much time have we got?"

"We're all right for a few days." She pulled at the cheesecloth shirt and stepped out of her jeans. "I'm going to take a shower."

"Lila . . ."

"Yes?"

"D'you think it's going to work?" She watched Lila step naked into the tiny shower cubicle in the corner of the small cabin.

"Of course, Anna," she replied and turned on the water.

"You're a goat, Giorgio, but I envy you."

Rubbing tired eyes Giorgio addressed himself to preparing a dozen trays with silver coffee pots and looked at his fellow steward.

"Stephanos, are you telling me that you are still innocent with that schoolgirl bitch making eyes at you yesterday afternoon beside the pool?"

"Huh, she is a kid. . . ."

"*You* are a kid. . . ."

"I'm not, besides there is plenty of time."

Giorgio said nothing but began to fill the coffee pots from the big percolator nestling handily in one corner of the first-class pantry.

"There is plenty of time, isn't there?"

"Listen Stephanos," said Giorgio with the rapidly exhausting patience of an elder brother, "take advantage of your situation; fuck while you can. It helps you sleep. . . ." He swept up two trays and made to leave the pantry. "Take the radio man his coffee, and see what you can find out."

Stephanos, several years Giorgio's junior, but with the same swarthy good looks, did as he was told. The radio office was just behind the bridge chart room, the whole deck a humming section of control panels, lights and dials. Stephanos liked this part of the ship and stood in apparent wonderment of the complexity of it all.

"Hullo, Stephanos! Coffee time already? Jolly good; put it down, lad." David Gordon, the senior radio officer spun round

44

in his swivel chair and smiled amiably at the young steward. "Come to have a look at the space-age technology, eh?"

Dumbly Stephanos nodded, his eyes alight with enthusiasm.

"What d'you fancy this morning? We looked at the Satellite telephone yesterday didn't we?"

"I see passenger with newspaper. . . ." he said in halting English.

"Ah, you want to see our news service. Over here, computer printout. It's sent via the HSD facility of the Inmarsat system, using the same geo-stationary satellite as the Satcomm phone, transmitted from the earth station at Southbury to the ship-earth-station which is us, the *Adventurer*. See?"

"HSD?"

"High speed data . . . belted out at God knows how many symbols a micro-second, up to the satellite, bounced back to us. Our dome, the egg-shaped thing over the top of our heads here, that's trained automatically on the satellite, locked on it in fact. See, here are the read-outs, elevation is nearly 90 degrees as we approach the equator, so it doesn't matter much what the azimuth is, d'you understand?"

"Same as sun, overhead, so looking upwards?"

"Good lad, you're bright, aren't you? Okay, so signal comes straight down to us and anyone else who wants it, into our 2,000k memory box and weeee . . . out on the printer."

"Can you hold in memory?"

"Sure. I usually cancel it just before dinner, by which time no one is very interested, then it's all ready for the next day. D'you want a copy of today's news?" Gordon concluded indulgently, "it's American, mind, lots of Uncle Sam's jolly crap, but most is news from the international agencies . . . okay. . . ." He smiled at Stephanos's eager nod, turned to a keyboard and began to type instructions onto a screen. The printer next to the VDU began to brip and lines of neat type rapidly rose as leaf after leaf of paper folded itself out of the machine.

"Mr Gordon, you forget coffee."

"Oh, carried away for a minute." Gordon helped himself to a cup and, as the machine stopped, tore off the sheets. "Can you read that?"

"I try very hard."

"Good lad!" The bridge phone rang and Gordon answered it. Behind him Stephanos retreated with the booty of his raid.

"I think it's terrible," said Dr Galvin at dinner that night.

"I'm sorry?" queried Palmer, awkward in the unaccustomed splendour of tropical mess kit.

"John is upset at the collapse of the United Nations debate on the plight of the Palestinians," explained Margaret Allen.

"I suppose it was fairly predictable," Palmer said, nodding to the steward to remove his empty soup plate, and dabbing the chilled gazpacho from his lips with a stiff linen napkin, "the problem is an old and intractable one, sad though it is."

"Does it have to be insoluble, young man?" Galvin asked, leaning forward with a peculiar intensity that Palmer had come to know as characteristic of the man.

"I don't know, Doctor ... but surely had there been a solution to hand, it would at least have been mooted by now." It was impossible, Palmer thought, for Galvin to guess at the pertinence of his remark.

"The trouble," said Mrs Rebanowicz indicating to the steward that more buttered green beans were required to complement her Tournedos Rossini, "is that there are too many people in the world and they take up too much room."

"You have a point," remarked Galvin acidly, looking over his glasses at his ample neighbour.

"Of course I have. A hundred years ago you could migrate, like my Stanislas's grandfather. There was room in the world for a little –" she stuck out her elbows and settled herself like a voluptuous hen, "– expansion."

"That is true to a degree," agreed Margaret Allen, nodding her appreciation at Galvin's choice of claret, "but even so, I don't think the case quite applies to the Palestinians. Besides, there were a few Indians who had to be exterminated before the Europeans could spread across the American West. I think the support Zionism eventually received at the expense of the people of Palestine was followed by the false logic that, if one's case is strong enough, as I suppose the Jews' was after the Holocaust, then a tide of approval carries you over the opposition.

46

"In earlier times the previous inhabitants would have simply been exterminated and left for another age to weep over. That's happened before, but with the Palestinians we simply shoved them to one side and pretended the problem would go away. They paid the price for western guilt over the Jews. The whole international community are implicated really, although the historical ramifications are so horribly complicated and mixed up with imperial retreat and the national ambitions of emerging states, that it's not surprising the poor Palestinians feel that most of the world is against them."

"You think that justifies them making terrorist attacks on innocent people?"

"No, Margaret doesn't think that, Mrs Rebanowicz, she merely finds it understandable," put in Galvin. "You see, it doesn't matter much what has happened in the past. The past will always dog us, but a generation doesn't solve problems by paying it over-much notice. The real point at issue is that the Palestinians must be accommodated. Do that realistically and you render their indiscriminate actions morally insupportable and redress a massive grievance."

"Oh, sure, pie in the sky! How the hell are you going to achieve that?" remonstrated Mrs Rebanowicz.

"How are *we* going to achieve it, Mrs Rebanowicz? Perhaps *we* could start by discussing the matter with Dr Blumenthal."

They looked across the dining-room at the elderly statesman in earnest conversation with a pale, thin woman of great beauty who was barely recognisable as a famous ballet dancer lately rescued from alchoholic poisoning.

"Us?" Mrs Rebanowicz was shocked.

"Well, yes," said Galvin quietly. "The Security Council of the United Nations seem unable to grasp the nettle. Perhaps we might do better."

Mrs Rebanowicz's mouth dropped open with astonishment. "That's preposterous!" she said.

"Not necessarily," replied the mild and unruffled Galvin.

And Palmer sensed an uneasy feeling of foreboding creep along the hairs at the nape of his neck.

"My God, your lot were bloody morbid tonight! What on earth

47

were you talking about?" Aymes asked as he stopped by Palmer's cabin door. "No cosy chats with Auntie Margaret tonight, Tim, me lad?"

"No. I thought I'd get a little sleep before going on watch."

Aymes shook a finger at him. "Hey, none of those effete cargo-ship habits here. If you're not knackered, you're not doing the job. You haven't any of the Scotch mist, have you?"

"There's some Glenfiddich in the locker."

"Bless you, me lad, I knew that I could rely on you. You're not perfect, but next to the 'Morangie, this," Aymes held up the triangular bottle, "is the next best thing. It's certainly best for a greenhorn like you to begin on."

"Get lost. Tell me, are you ever bloody serious?"

"Only in the consulting room and then I can be deadly serious. Doesn't always go down too well; there are certain ailments people refuse to believe they've contracted. It should be borne on the company's brochure: 'Beware, a cruise on the *Adventurer* carries a Government Health 'Warning.' Screwing, drinking, jogging and over-indulging may permanently damage your health. Do you know I've had five cases of Athlete's Foot and three verrucas to treat in only two days. My God I've been rushed off my feet!"

"Is that all?"

"So far, thank God. I can always hold 'em off for a few days. Act the fool; be seen in the cocktail bar half-shot; indicate that I was drummed out of the BMA because of my being implicated in an abortion-clinic scandal, you know the sort of subterfuge these idiots swallow, but in the end hypochondria triumphs and I end up servicing all the octogenarian valetudinarians on the ship! Hey, what d'you think of that?"

"The speech was facetious, the whisky isn't bad."

"Sorry, Tim. I can see that the eighth course is being serious tonight."

"No it's my fault, I'm the one who's a pain in the arse. Sorry."

"Well, you can cheer up tomorrow."

"Tomorrow, why?"

"Crossing the line ceremony."

"Oh, bloody hell!"

48

"Will you be the barber?"

"God, no!"

"Meredith is head-hunting, Tim ... be warned."

"Bugger Meredith, why doesn't he be the bloody barber?"

"Because he's the staff captain, me lad, and staff captains don't play silly b's, they leave that to their juniors. Besides, Meredith reigns as Neptune."

"Good Lord, have you been sent up to persuade me, you rotten bastard? At least you might have brought your own bottle!"

"You'll do it?"

"Okay. But on one condition."

"What's that?"

"I want to get hold of that stewardess Lila's details."

"What, the severe and handsome dark one with the 36 D-cup top set?"

"I don't know about 36 D-cups, last night ..."

"Ahhh, Tim, the dark horse emerges; why the hell don't you mosey down to the purser's office like everyone else?"

"Because I don't want to run into that frosty, painted little tart Melanie Corbett."

"Hey, steady ...!"

"Oh, God, Doc, you're not ...?"

"Well, I'm trying. Trouble is, I think she's sweet on you."

"Rubbish! She profoundly disapproves of me."

"Tim, me lad, you are truly an innocent but," Aymes slapped him across the shoulders and held out a hand, "it's a bargain. I'll find out about Lila and you'll shave the victims tomorrow. I knew you would and told Meredith so."

"You bastard!"

"It's the bedside manner, mate." Aymes made to leave but stopped by the cabin door. "Oh, by the way, I shouldn't get too excited about what's-her-name."

"Lila?"

"Yes. Mitch, the chief queen in the glory hole, thinks she's a lesbo. She's over-familiar with her cabin-mate, a rather unfortunate creature with a badly burned face." Aymes was suddenly serious, "The poor bitch is a high-seas refugee. Perhaps there's nothing in it ... Good night."

49

Palmer stared for a moment after the doctor, then, finishing his drink, began to undress. His eyes fell on the photograph on his desk. It had been a long time since he had had a photograph of a girl on his desk. A long time since Rosie had . . . well, he did not like to remember that. He picked up the picture and looked at Kate, pretty and fair under her short cropped and business-like hairstyle. It was the only clue, and not a very positive one, that she was a woman police officer. He wondered if he really contemplated being unfaithful to her, indeed he wondered if he had ever contemplated being faithful to her. And was she being faithful to him? And if she was not, what the devil was the use of getting excited over Lila after he had so firmly slapped her down the night before?

He shoved the Glenfiddich into his locker and rolled onto the bed.

"And I'm going to be the fucking barber," he muttered, and shut off the cabin light.

"I've decided you were serious at dinner," Margaret Allen said as she and Galvin sat out on deck as the great ship glided, hissing through the dark sea.

"About what?"

"About solving the Palestinian problem single-handed by contacting Blumenthal. It's ridiculous but you were sincere."

"Why shouldn't I be?" Galvin was surprised, "stranger things have happened . . . but what convinced you?"

"Because, although you are not obviously similar, you share certain positive characteristics with my late husband. *He* had an answer for just about everything. It might not have been very moral, or acceptable, but he sure knew what should be done. I think you are rather like that except that I suspect your answer might be, well, perhaps more idealistic."

"What did your husband do, Margaret?" Galvin asked quietly.

"That's irrelevant," she said, evading the question deliberately. "You *have* got an answer, haven't you?"

"Well, yes . . . of sorts. But whereas your husband might have contemplated genocide or mass-sterilisation and been

50

misunderstood," Galvin said with heavy irony, "my own solution would be even less acceptable."

"Why?"

"Because it would mean a complete overthrow of all our dearly-held views; nothing less than a world *revolution*, in fact!"

"I thought as much," said Margaret Allen with quiet satisfaction, glad that tonight they were alone. "Please go on."

"Only if you promise not to laugh."

"On the honour of a girl scout."

"The nation state is out of date. It has been since the dropping of the atomic bomb on Hiroshima. In his desire to provide for material comfort, man has surrendered much of his independence to the state, thereby losing his freedom. The nation state, which is merely a defensive enlargement of the tribe, has taken on a specious significance of its own and provided a new, unexpected rationale for pushing mankind into an idolatrous unity of parts which militates against the true spiritual and personal unity of individual *people*.

"The state forms, or purports to form, a little Kingdom of God on earth in which the Godhead, the state's authority, stands for a unity of the whole. But this is not true, because next door there is another state, doing the same thing; the two are in competition and therefore inimical. I hated competition at school and I retain my hatred of it now. Those microcosmic doubts have become macrocosmic certainties. A Jew and an Arab could live in perfect amity as neighbours, providing one did not think of himself as an Israeli, the other as a Palestinian, and both did not covet the same piece of real estate. Ideally we would exchange the politics of envy for the politics of tolerance."

"It sounds rather too fantastic to succeed."

"So did Marx's ideas when faced with the apparently overwhelming domination of Victorian capitalism. It's perfectly possible." Galvin spoke with such compelling confidence that Margaret felt herself constrained to remain silent.

"It's too late, of course. Zelda Rebanowicz was quite right. There *are* too many people and it is far too late to educate them now, with their numbers growing. Like rats confined in a small, restricted space, we shall go on dominating and killing each

51

other, ensuring that a less and less philosophical type survives. It starts in the inner cities, spreads out from those chancres of our universal disease and will, in the end, corrupt us all. We have, by the miraculous development of our neo-cortex, been capable of the most fantastic progress. We have been able to devise, plan and execute the most brilliant schemes, pursuing the talents of the universal creator without once stopping to think that we are no more able to get on with our neighbour than were our cave-dwelling ancestors. And we don't really want to; in fact we didn't need to, because the termination of our race was unthinkable.

"But, since August 1945 we swept that check on our collective ambitions to one side. Just as we ran out of space in which to shove our unwanted populations (of which the plight of the Palestinian Arabs and the displaced victims of the Holocaust were the first and most significant victims) we discovered that we had also the means to truly emulate God. We no longer need to pray for the plague to destroy Sennacherib, we can lob an ICBM at him and, as long as we do it first, we retain the all-important upper hand." Galvin paused and looked at Margaret. She was quite silent, her face suddenly drawn, haggard and ill. Before he could speak she seemed to pull herself together and smiled, a brave, false smile.

"But you said it was possible . . . ?"

"*Was* . . . William Penn tried it; his 'Holy Experiment' worked after the fashion of his times, but I think it is too late now. We have reached our paracme, I'm afraid."

"I thought we both came on this cruise to escape such morbid preoccupations," she said in a low voice.

"To be truthful, I came as a piece of the selfish indulgence I have been ready to condemn in others. Knowing the sands are running out I wanted to see one relatively unspoilt part of the world. However, I gather the Straits of Magellan are already being prospected and exploited for oil."

"So you're too late."

Galvin nodded slowly. "Yes. Somebody once told me those were the saddest two words in the English language."

Margaret shivered.

"Cold?" he asked, suddenly concerned.

"No. A grey goose flying over my grave." She stood up with

52

sudden determination and held out her hand. Looking up and seeing the abrupt expression of forced enthusiasm in her face, he glimpsed the girl she had once been.

"I've had enough of your morbid pie-in-the-sky, John Galvin. You can take me dancing, you old charlatan!"

"I can't dance," he replied, looking up at the slim, tall woman in the blue dress, "and I'm too short for you."

"The world's full of imperfections, Doctor," she said with a mock severity, "and fools will ever try to change it, so come on, let's dance."

Zelda Rebanowicz was already in the ballroom. It had become her established nightly ritual to sit alone with a bottle of Veuve Clicquot, to dance with whoever asked her, her heavily voluptuous figure accentuated by a glittering sheath dress that exactly fitted both her vintage and her shape.

Her partners were usually ship's officers and she took a detached delight in arousing them, to disappoint them as she waited for the hour of her rendezvous with Giorgio.

She was not entirely devoid of a certain grace. The determination of an American matron to keep fit had delayed the inevitable loss of muscular tone and this active prophylaxis, combined with the advantages of her style of dress, the champagne and the ballroom lighting, to give Zelda an attraction that was not all illusory. Her liaison with Giorgio had infected her with a light-hearted joy, a fact that was only heightened by the knowledge of the delights in store for her later in the night. She was thus a candle for the lusting moths in their white mess jackets, cummerbunds and bow ties, as they indulged in a good-natured competition to score.

Zelda enjoyed herself. She teased and taunted them, enjoying their ill-concealed response and delighting in this wanton, yet amusingly acceptable propinquity. It struck some note deep in her immigrant-American heritage to reject these British popinjays and forsake them for the almost brutal lusting of her beautiful Giorgio. There was a ruthless insistence in Giorgio's love-making that she could only express to herself as the epitome of virility and it was a matter of pride to her that she was the recipient of such a demanding passion. She took an immense care over her response, matching him mood for mood, demand for demand, so that the pace and activity of their passion debased and elevated her through sensations she would have blushed over six months earlier. The peccant quality of the *affaire* added an excitement that she had never thought it possible to enjoy, and the unashamed luxury of her first-class apartment, the result of the labours of her late husband, added a Hollywood glitter to the Arcadian perfection of Zelda and her Greek.

In such a frame of mind she was able to watch with secret amusement the clumsy dancing of Dr Galvin and Mrs Allen, to regard them indulgently as an adult might see the first clumsy gropings of two adolescents. Smiling, Zelda accepted the bowing Meredith's arm and walked out with him onto the floor. Facing him she slid her arms about his neck. The band struck up the languid chords of 'Moon River' and she felt his hands slide from her waist over the pert shelf of her buttocks. She thrust her pelvis forward and smiled up at him. It was nearly midnight and soon she would be with Giorgio. And there would be many, many more midnights on this wonderful cruise.

By three in the morning Palmer was finding his watch tedious. Pacing the bridge wing he found himself wondering how frequently Lila rose early to do her circuit training on the deserted boat deck, and whether he would see her this morning. He badly wanted to, partly to remedy her opinion of him, and partly to rid himself of the irritating anger that had overcome him after the ridiculous charade of the Crossing the Line Ceremony that had taken place the previous forenoon.

He found it difficult to explain to himself why he had been so annoyed, or why the annoyance had persisted so long. On the face of it the episode was designed to be a piece of slightly salacious fun, but Palmer was suspicious of 'fun', despite the fact that he had enjoyed it. The barber's task was usually given to one of the stronger members of the ship's company, for he had to wrestle with the half-unwilling victim, deploy the ancient skills of a barber-surgeon to shave and purge the guilty party for venturing unasked into Neptune's

Kingdom. Neptune was played by Staff Captain Meredith with unprecedented condescension; his queen, by tradition a male, the outrageously camped-up steward Mitch, a young American gay with a pro footballer's physique to which he had added mammarian glands of preposterous size and a green and shimmering mermaid's tail, a towering blonde wig and sufficient make-up to equip a dance troupe. Jonathan Aymes was the judge, black-gowned and white-wigged, while Palmer, uneasy in a scarlet mantle and wearing a false nose and fez, bore a huge plywood razor and a jug of 'medicine' from which protruded a wooden spoon.

There was also a flying squad of policemen, four of the ship's most muscular crew members, headed by the purser who seemed to spend most of his off-duty time working out in the *Adventurer*'s health spa. The remainder were Jim Barclay, the Second Engineer Officer, a hard-bitten Glaswegian with the build of a sumo wrestler, a young German seaman named Dieter Schmidt and an engine greaser with an unpronounceable name who answered to the cognomen of 'Zig'.

It was their task to capture half-a-dozen specified passengers and bring them before King Neptune. The king's court duly arrived on board and ascended with formal and hilarious pomp from the after mooring deck to the waiting throne set ominously beside the open-air swimming pool. Sheltered from the wind by high, transparent screens, the sun blazed down on this arena and the excited passengers of all classes watched from the sides and from the ascending terraces of the decks above.

The principals of the court made some show of their arrival with the 'Queen' camping it up to the delight of all. She was surrounded by her 'handmaidens', a motley collection of the purser's female staff led by Melanie Corbett who wore, as chief mermaid, a long tail and a bikini top in flesh pink that was intended to suggest she was bare-breasted.

When Neptune had at last seated himself and his consort, the hidden policemen attacked the crowd from forward, pushing in among them with great noise and frolic. A certain latitude was taken by these men as they sought their victims, several women were rudely handled and several men dragged forward before Judge Aymes who, to the victims' obvious relief, waved them away contemptuously. But at last, after a good deal of high-spirited and good-humoured scuffling, three males and three females were selected. Among them were a pair of the schoolchildren and their senior teacher, a man in his late thirties named Holton.

The schoolgirl was dragged forward first, giggling and screaming, only to be displayed to Neptune before being forced to her knees while Barclay read out the charge. This process was interrupted by frequent protestations of comparison and jealousy by the Queen, but at last the girl was pronounced guilty and passed over to Palmer.

Feeling irredeemably foolish, Palmer forced some of his 'medicine' down her throat. It consisted of yoghurt, whipped cream and brandy into which had been stirred chopped prunes. While the poor child choked on this mixture he belaboured her with a large paintbrush, smearing foam on her hair and elaborately shaved her with some inexpert play from his plywood razor.

Covered in both of the revolting mixtures she was promptly grabbed by two of the policemen and hurled into the pool while attention was focussed on the next candidate. The process was repeated with much ad libbing from Aymes and the Queen, both of whom made the show and attracted the cameras of the delighted passengers. Finally they came to Holton, a fit man who, with that slight superiority of the professional teacher, was prepared to resist. It was exactly what Neptune's court had been waiting for.

Holton succeeded in thrusting Zig into the pool before he had been made to kneel to Neptune. The outraged King ordered Zig to remove his 'uniform' as a symbol of his disgrace and the Pole removed his trousers, to hoots of delight from the crowd. Holton was forced to bow and accused, not only of entering the southern hemisphere uninvited, but of bringing with him numbers of children, a species that the Queen could not tolerate. With an elaborate and scarcely concealed mime full of dubious double-meaning Mitch reached new heights of extravagance and impropriety. Neptune, exasperated by his partner's delays in the administration of justice, ordered her to be charged with contempt of court. Wriggling ecstatically in the enormous embrace of Barclay, the Queen was triumphantly shaved of her blonde wig, divested of her bosom, which preceeded her into the pool, and flung after it with an enormous splash. Thereafter Holton was quickly despatched, a mutiny of handmaidens suppressed by the wholesale transfer of them into the pool. Wrongs were righted: the ducked wreaking vengeance on the duckers by clambering out, inviting the assistance of the crowd, and sending Neptune, Judge, Barber and Policemen in as well. During this *mêlée* a few of the assisting passengers inevitably got caught up in the horseplay. There was a general free-for-all in the pool and the Ceremony declared at an end by the appearance of Captain Smythe himself who graciously gave out the elaborate illuminated certificates that proclaimed the victims duly prepared for whatever might befall them in Neptune's Kingdom.

In remembering the morning, Palmer had been unable to forget the clinging body of Melanie Corbett, who had flung herself enthusiastically at him in the pool. She was, as usual, waspishly abrasive, but there was no denying her obvious charms and the way she cavorted led Palmer to the conclusion that the young woman was either a particularly persistent prick-teaser, or, as Aymes had suggested, genuinely fancied him. But, in the reflective isolation of the middle watch, he had to admit that Melanie's successful attempt to arouse him was not what had annoyed him. His lust had subsided in the cool of a shower, and, as he had stood under the hissing rose, Aymes had come into his cabin.

"You did bloody well, Tim, me lad, even the odious Meredith was complimentary. Here's a bottle of the glorious 'Morangie to bring you cheer!"

Palmer stuck his head out of the shower. "You only brought me that so that you could come and indulge yourself, you bugger!"

"True. But here's something for yourself alone. I'll stick them under your pillow. . . . Cheers, see you later," and he had gone.

When he had emerged from the shower Palmar had recovered two pieces of paper from their hiding places. They were photocopies of crew identity papers.

57

Lila Molina, he read, *born Mayaguez, Puerto Rico, 6.24.1962.*
She had been employed before at sea, though this was the first
voyage she had made in a ship of this company. Her previous
ratings had been as stewardess and she had been engaged in
the Panamanian Embassy at San Juan. Palmer congratulated
himself at his having deduced her origins correctly and looked
at the photograph. As was common with such 'mug shots',
it did not do her justice, recording the regularity of her
features and her practical, tight-drawn hair. There was an
almost androgynous quality to the picture and the only thing
recognisably Lila's that prevented the photograph from being
entirely anonymous was the look of hardness about her eyes
and mouth. It was curious the way the exact arrangement
of those subconscious little muscles could convey such an
impression. But here, in this harsh-lit tonal drop-out he fancied
it was not so much the hostility that she seemed to convey in
life, but a sternness of purpose that came through. Had she
not been so beautiful, Palmer thought, such an emanation
would possibly have transformed her. It was an odd, quirky
thought and it reminded him that his interest in her was either
excessively cautious or verging on the obsessive. He distrusted
his own motives.

His eyes flickered guiltily to the photograph of Kate Meldrum
on his desk and he turned hurriedly to the second photostatted
sheet. He had assumed it would contain additional documenta-
tion of Lila but it came as something of a shock to see a second
face staring up at him. At least, he supposed it *was* a face, for
it had eyes where the eyes should be and a mouth where the
mouth should be, but it was an ugly gash dragged to one side
by waves of scarring that ribbed across the face, contorting
the eyes, pulling the nostrils to one side and baring one side
of the forehead, so that the hairline rose over a great smooth
bight of scalp.

"Jesus!"

Palmer remembered what Aymes had said of Lila's friend
and the innuendoes supplied by Mitch.

"Bloody hell!"

*Anna Josephina Robles, born Aguadilla, Puerto Rica,
10.9.1964.* There was no clue as to the cause of her sickening

disfigurement, only the intelligence that this was her first voyage as *Adventurer*'s 'linen maid'.

Yes, it had been that photograph of Anna that had made him angry, angry with himself, reproaching him for his folly, accusing him of having betrayed his own instincts of revulsion at *Adventure*'s hedonistic purpose. Yet he was the Queen's man and had taken the Queen's 'shilling'; *Adventurer* even as she provided employment for him, also provided a troglodyte existence for Anna, somewhere deep in her steel bowels.

"Mr Palmer. . . ." he spun round. The voice came from the outer bridge ladder which led up from the boat deck. He could see the outline of a head and knew at once that it was Lila. He crossed the deck.

"Hullo. What do you want? I'm afraid you can't . . ."

"Yes I know it's forbidden but I want you to do something for me."

"What?" he cast a look across the bridge wing. DeAth was out of sight on the port side, although he could see the quartermaster in the wheelhouse.

"My friend, the girl I work with, she could not sleep; she works below all the time and never gets out of the air conditioning; could she come up here for a few minutes, please . . . let her see what it's like, it's her first time to sea . . . please. . . ."

She was illuminated partly from below by the lights along the boat deck, but the ship was darkened here, to preserve the night vision of the watch on the bridge. He looked beyond Lila and could make out the shape of a girl, jeaned and shirted like her friend, one hip stuck out and shoulder-length hair completely shadowing her face. Even the glabrous patch on her head was indistinguishable in the darkness and Palmer felt a great sorrow welling up within him. Here, at least in part, he could make an act of contrition.

"Yes, of course, come up."

He drew back to the rail and waited for them, leaning his forearms on the smooth teak, staring forward into the night, the ship's wind ruffling his hair as the dodger scooped it up and over the bridge in an aerodynamic curve. He felt Lila join him, the warm scent of her body alongside him, and beyond her another, hidden, half-furtive.

"Hullo Anna," he said, "I'm Tim." He did not turn his head, but heard the sharp indrawn breath of surprise.

"How did you. . . ?" Lila dropped the question as he turned to look. His extra height enabled him to see the other girl and his acute night vision showed him what the photograph had prepared him for. He smiled. "I'm glad you came up. We won't be disturbed at this time of the night and neither of the other men up here with me will say anything."

"How many of them are there?"

"Only two, the fifth officer and the quartermaster."

"What will they think?"

"That you are my girlfriends," he replied grinning, so that the remark contained no offence.

"Thank you," Anna said, and it was odd her voice seemed unaffected by the distortion of her mouth, though her accent was thicker than Lila's.

They looked forward again, over the sharp fore part of the ship where the capstans and cables led along the deck to the pointed bow. Ahead, the sea lay dark and the wash, emerging from *Adventurer*'s sleek cutwater, only fell back in their view just forward of the bridge. A few wave caps danced to the light wind that ruffled the surface of the sea and these glowed with a slight phosphorescence. Away to port, perhaps 12 miles distant, the lights of another ship could be seen, and overhead the great arch of the heavens spread, brilliant with stars.

Suddenly the two girls drew in their breath and Palmer smiled to himself. It seemed as though some vast conjuring trick had been played. The wake glowed with light and every wave top broke with a flash of white fire so that the sea seemed alive with illumination from its depths. Then, as if for them alone, streaking in from either side, pale ghostly green-white slashes in the depths, came the racing dolphins, tearing through the milk sea like torpedoes, arcing in to leap under the bow, dark shadows at the end of their suddenly abbreviated trails which gambolled and slapped back into the water, to resume their fire-trailing again as they plunged down and away.

It was all over in minutes.

"What was it?" asked Lila, breathless with wonder and Palmer, turning towards her with his dry explanation, caught his breath at the expression on her shadowy face. Had Anna not been there he would have kissed her, but instead he swallowed before speaking.

"It was a milk sea; phosphorescence caused by small, luminescent organisms in the water called dinoflagellates. Probably the tiny, plant-like *Noctiluca*, judging by the ecstasy of the dolphins, but there are others. Most notably sinister is the poisonous *Gonyaulax*. If the lobsters that make tomorrow's thermidor have any of that in their livers, our first-class passengers will show similar symptoms to having been poisoned by strychnine. But whatever it was, it is very beautiful."

"Would you like to give our first-class passengers *Gony . . .*?"

"*Gonyaulax*? Yes, sometimes, Anna, but really I'd rather just stand here and watch, and forget all about passengers."

"Mr Palmer is a dreamer, Anna," Lila explained, a certain note of archness in her tone, "he likes the *status quo*."

It was the second time she had used a Latin expression and again the incongruity of it struck him, but it was swiftly displaced by the reaction to defend himself that she provoked by her implied disapproval.

"Not so," he said, "in these very waters the sight which you have just seen made Charles Darwin think of chaos and anarchy."

"Would you approve of anarchy, Mr Palmer?" asked Lila sharply, the old harshness back in her tone. He felt wearied and disappointed by the probing and sought to turn it with good humour, for he had no wish that the moment should turn sour.

"If it was, in truth, as beautiful, then yes I would approve."

"Have you read Proudhon?" asked Anna.

"No," he confessed lamely, feeling the irritation that the arrival of the two girls had banished begin to regain a hold over him. A certain peevishness tempted him to terminate their visit, but it did not seem fair to penalize Anna for Lila's tartness.

"I told you he was a dreamer, Anna," Lila said.

"Perhaps he is a poet," said the far girl, "Surely only a poet would have let us come up tonight."

There was a movement and a warning cough behind them.

"Coming up for one bell, Tim," said DeAth from the wheelhouse door and Lila took the hint.

"We must go, Anna." She turned for the ladder.

"Thank you." He was face to face with Anna and could see her quite clearly now. It was impossible to guess at the extent of her ruined beauty but she was shorter than Lila. Palmer suddenly did not want her gratitude.

"Any time," he said.

"I will be able to sleep for a little now."

"Good." He watched them go then turned to write up the log in the chart room.

He heard DeAth's tongue clicking its mock disapproval.

"Fuck off!" he snapped.

"He is nice, Lila."

Lila looked at the mask peering upwards from the bunk and shrugged.

"I can see you want him."

"No!"

"I can see it . . . and he wants you."

"No," she said again, "Stephanos says there is a picture of a girl in his cabin. It will not be like that."

"There is no rule that says you cannot enjoy it. Look at Giorgio."

"Giorgio's an animal. And I don't want to talk about Palmer."

"He was kind."

"And I don't want to talk about people's kindness," she said sharply.

"No," said Anna, "no . . . that is always a danger." She watched Lila from the bunk. The older girl stood rigid with tension. "Lila," Anna said, "you can if you want to. It doesn't matter."

"It *does* matter."

"No. Do it . . . do it now. You'll feel better."

"How do you know?" Lila rounded on her friend and instantly regretted her action, kneeling beside Anna who threw her arms about Lila's neck.

"I know . . . that's all."

Lila drew back and looked at her. "How?"

"Giorgio's an animal."

Lila stared, like one stupefied, then very slowly she stood and turned to the mirror. Her right hand slipped the elastic band from her hair and she shook her dark mane out, watching herself for a moment. Then she made up her mind, pulled her shirt off and exchanged it for her cheese cloth blouse. When she was ready she slipped from the cabin.

She dodged the master-at-arm's patrolling regulators with ease, knowing, from her midnight forays, every predictable patrol they made in the name of good order and chastity. She reached Palmer's cabin undetected and was slightly relieved that he had not yet arrived. The light was on from his rousing four and a half hours earlier. She switched it off and sat on the settee, pressing herself into its cushioned corner, her heart hammering painfully in the brooding darkness.

She did not hear him approach along the alleyway. His shape was abruptly in the doorway and he reached for the light switch. He was already naked to the waist before he noticed her. She saw him pale, then flush, his pink skin reacting with amusing swiftness to his nervous response. It made her smile and he covered his confusion by turning and locking the door.

Without a word he slipped off his trousers. She was disappointed that he was unaroused. He crossed to the locker, reached in for glasses and the bottle of malt Aymes had so thoughtfully provided and held up an empty glass. She shook her head. He poured himself a drink, put back the bottle and the unused glass and sat down, turning the upright chair at his desk to face her. He swallowed some of the whisky and rested his chin in his hand. She sensed he was no longer nervous and began to feel she had lost the initiative. She turned her head and caught sight of the photograph. She reached forward and picked it up.

"Who is she?" she said, breaking the almost intolerable silence.

"A girl I know."

"You know her well?"

"Intimately."

"What is her name?"

"Kate."

"You are married?"

"Not to her, no."

"To somebody?"

"Divorced."

"Oh."

"Why do you want to know?"

"Because you must have found out about Anna and me . . . you knew her name."

"The doctor told me you had a friend named Anna. He also said that she was badly injured."

"You feel sorry for Anna?"

"Yes, of course."

"Why were you talking about me to the doctor?"

"Why not? You must have talked about me to Anna to have come up to the bridge this morning."

Silence fell between them again. Palmer sipped his whisky slowly, feeling it relaxing him. Lila was less hostile and he began to feel a slow engorgement. They exchanged smiles, slow uncertain smiles that, at last acknowledged an intimacy between them. She reached for the belt of her jeans. "I think I would like that drink."

He rose and fetched the glass, filling it as she stepped out of her jeans. Apart from her briefs she wore only the transparent blouse. As she looked down to take the glass, she saw he was tumescent. She swallowed the unaccustomed spirit; as it hit her stomach she shuddered involuntarily. He took the empty glass and looked down at her. The slight covering of her full breasts accentuated the erect nipples, the sinuous smallness of her waist swelled out over her hips and the flat expanse of her belly disappeared into the curve of her loins and parted the long smoothness of her thighs. His aroused mind had a sudden image of the erotic paintings in the caves of the Sigiriya rock, and his senses were pervaded with an intuitive oriental image.

Palmer was huge in his arousal; he could barely contain himself as his arm wound round her slender waist and he bent his head. He thrust aside her reluctance and felt her relax. Her own arms embraced him as he kissed her,

64

moving down her neck onto her shoulder. He could feel her nipples against his chest and the helplessly lubricious reaction of himself.

He lifted Lila onto the bunk, pulled off her briefs and tossed them with his own. She stared down at his inflamed phallus as he moved awkwardly above her. As he ran his hands over her he felt the desiccation of her tension and restrained himself, lying alongside her, petting and whispering until she signalled her willingness. He mounted her with a breath-taking thrust and she pushed back so their bodies sucked at each other and they gasped at the suddenness of their climax.

They did not pull apart but rolled onto their sides, looking at each other as only people in their situation can. Nature withdrew him, asserting its hold over them as separate beings.

"D'you have a cigarette?"

"Yes." He reached for the packet of Benson and Hedges and the lighter. "I didn't know you smoked, but then there's a lot about you I don't know, isn't there?"

She nodded, puffing the smoke out of her mouth. Taking the cigarette from her lips she lay back and stared upwards and he knew that the remark, meant flippantly, had dropped a veil between the two of them.

"I wasn't much good," she said in a tone suggesting it was she who was disappointed and no mock admission that she had failed on his behalf.

"I didn't notice."

"*Post coitus omnes triste est* ... isn't that how it goes?"

"I don't know ... I only know that *I* am not sad. Will you come here again?"

She looked at him and then, seeing he had not noticed the pun, asked, "Do you want me to?" She stared at the deck-head again, drawing on the cigarette.

"Yes, of course."

"I'm only a stewardess."

"Lila ..."

She turned and stared at him properly. Her expression softened and he melted at her beauty. "Lila ..."

"Poor Tim, what about Kate?"

"What about Kate?" He fished in the packet for a cigarette himself.

"What do you think she's doing at the moment?"

Chapter Three

Kate Meldrum was just closing the door of her flat in Hendon when the telephone rang. It was eight o'clock on a Sunday morning and it could mean only one thing.

She hesitated on the threshold, wondering whether to emulate Nelson and ignore the call of duty, but she knew that if it was important enough they would pursue her and she had nothing much planned for the day. She turned back and picked up the telephone.

"Hullo . . . ?"

"Chief Inspector Meldrum?"

"Speaking."

"Morning Ma'am, Sergeant Wallace. We've got something big, ma'am, I'm sorry to say. Your speciality and the Commissioner's involved."

"You want me to come in?"

"Not to the College, Ma'am, no. New Scotland Yard."

"All right. I'll be on my way in ten minutes." She put the phone down and turned to the bedroom. Changing quickly into uniform she felt her pulse racing with the old excitement. Wallace's understatement was well-known and he had obviously been instructed to be discreet. Kate's 'speciality' was unusual and she owed her rank and her present appointment lecturing to the Metropolitan Police College at Hendon to the studies she had made of the psychology of a variety of extreme human behaviour. 'Something big' usually meant an incident with sensitive political implications and the mention of the Commissioner, the chief of London's police force, made that doubly probable. She put on her tie, kicked her feet into her shoes and rapidly transferred the contents of her handbag. For the second time that morning she passed through the front door and made downstairs for the street. Five minutes later she swung the Ford Escort XR3 onto the A41 and was racing over an empty flyover at Brent Cross. She put on the radio, hoping for a news bulletin that would give her a clue to the nature of the flap that had intruded upon her personal life, but all she could receive was a concatenation of church bell peals. She switched off and tried to think of what the College staff had been talking about on Friday. But they tended to regard secondment to the college as a rest-cure from the constant pressure of police routine and the intelligence reports were often ignored. Like troops taken out of the front line for recuperation, the battle front was, at least temporarily, someone else's problem.

She tried to think of the recent news, but the last week had been a period of confusion and emotional upset so that she had taken little interest in the outside world. All she recollected was a particularly unpleasant child murder, a sex-and-drugs scandal involving staff and pupils at an exclusive Scottish school and the application of a veto after a particularly recriminatory debate at the United Nations, but she was hazy about the details. She changed into third and beat the lights, swinging the nippy saloon round the corner into the Finchley Road. London roads were remarkably pleasant to drive on when empty, she thought, passing the Camden Arts Centre and catching a red at Swiss Cottage.

The enforced idleness swept her thoughts back to Tim. He had been gone over a week now and she missed him more than she was prepared to admit. She knew her superiors disapproved. Kate Meldrum could have married almost anyone in the Met; she was very pretty, popular and had a sufficiently distinguished record to attract plenty of attention, as this morning's summons illustrated.

"Damn you," she muttered and let in the clutch. The thought of Tim upset her. "I wonder where you are now, you bastard," she said out loud, swinging the car round the one-way system and accelerating recklessly through St John's Wood. The long wall of Lord's cricket ground threw back the noise of the exhaust as she swung the wheel into the roundabout circling the statue of St George and headed for Park Road.

She felt helplessly confused by Palmer's departure, instrumental as she was in his going. She knew he was desperate for work, that her hold over him was not strong enough to prevent his departure, but she wondered if he even began to guess at what her part in his new job had cost her emotionally. Of course the circumstances were too odd for him not to have been told that she had recommended him. Gossip within the Met was usually a destructive force but just occasionally it worked to someone's advantage.

Chief Inspector Kate Meldrum was known to have been sleeping with a sailor, not a sailor, an officer, a master mariner, no less.... It had fallen on the right ears at the right moment....

Or was it the wrong moment, Kate thought as she swung out to overtake a group of fanatical cyclists bent low over their bright and gleaming bicycles, legs pumping the pedals with an almost audible snap of muscle and tendon.

It was odd how these things came together. It had been Chief Superintendent Alex Martin who had raised the subject. They had known each other since Kate entered the Force.

"I understand you're co-habiting with a Merchant Navy officer," he had said casually as they had shared a pot of coffee on one of his periodical visits to the Police College.

She had said nothing, only blown smoke into his face to match his own impertinence. He was, after all, her superior.

"And that he's unemployed ... is he looking for work?"

"Of course he's looking for work," she had snapped. "Look, is this a friendly enquiry or a Gestapo re-run?"

"Steady, Kate...."

"Well, to be frank, *sir*, if it was a Commander in the Met I was shacked up with, it would be fine, but as it's..."

"He's a bit leftish, isn't he?" asked Martin, ignoring her outburst.

Kate frowned. "Look, sir, the poor devil feels an understandable sense of having been abandoned by a somewhat callous Tory government. His whole profession is regarded as a sunset industry. Yes, he's a bit left."

69

"Well we've got rid of the 'callous Tories' and new brooms are sweeping clean. Maybe there'll be something for him."

"Look, I don't understand what the Metropolitan Police have to do with an unemployed master mariner. If you must know I've already asked in the Thames Division ... what's this all about?"

"Well, Kate, to be frank I can't really tell you."

"Can't or won't?"

"Can't. But I've a friend who works for a cruise line, he's in personnel, maybe he could help." Martin had paused. "You've come a long way, Kate, don't prejudice your career. He hasn't proposed marriage, has he?"

"No," she had said, taking the hint from her avuncular superior.

The flags on the Cenotaph lifted languidly as she passed into Parliament Square. Statues, trees and the towers and turrets of the Palace of Westminster, the Abbey and little St Margaret's nestling in its shadow, spun past as she entered Victoria Street, watching for the turn into Broadway and the entrance to Scotland Yard.

Showing her identity documents to the security guard she parked the car. A police officer was waiting for her in the glass-and-chrome entrance. She followed him to a lift and in silence they ascended for some time, emerging into a long corridor. At last she was shown into a briefing room fitted up with the usual equipment and looking like a cross between a lecture room and a private cinema.

"Coffee, Ma'am?"

"Please." She sat and waited, sipping the coffee from a plastic mug. Suddenly the door opened and a group of men entered the room. She stood up, recognizing the Commissioner immediately. He was accompanied by several uniformed officers and two civilians with the small-knotted ties of top civil servants. One of the police officers approached her. It was Alex Martin.

"Kate. Good of you to come." A suspicion crossed Kate's mind and she frowned. "This is very top-drawer," Martin muttered as the party milled about finding seats, "you'll be taken off whatever you are doing at Hendon; we may need you for a while. I'll introduce you in a minute."

"Does this have anything to do with that other business?" she whispered.

Martin looked at her. "What other business?"

"You know what I mean ... your interest in Tim Palmer. ..."

The Commissioner had finished talking to the civil servants and turned round. Martin rose and spoke to the Commissioner in a low voice. The Commissioner smiled at Kate.

"Chief Inspector Meldrum, I'm sorry to have to summon you like this on a Sunday. Gentlemen, may I introduce to you Chief Inspector Meldrum, a senior lecturer in anti-terrorist studies at the Police College." The other men murmured politely but were not introduced. The Commissioner smiled again, "We aren't asking for miracles, Miss Meldrum, but your special knowledge and perhaps a little feminine intuition may help us."

"I'll do what I can, sir," Kate replied mystified.

They settled themselves as the Commissioner offered the floor to one of the civil servants. He began to speak immediately in an ice-shattering accent that Kate thought had been reserved for theatrical pastiche. He stood with his hands behind his back, aiming his words over their heads and staring upwards. Every now and then he swivelled his body oddly, to give emphasis to some point. As he braced his shoulders he conveyed a ludicrous impression to Kate of being a small, uncertain boy. From what he was saying Kate judged him to be some sort of Foreign Office intelligence officer.

"At 2200 GMT last night our embassy in Athens received a typed letter delivered by a taxi-driver. The letter was opened after the standard anti-personnel device procedures had been followed. It contained a warning to the effect that large-scale 'freedom offensive' operations were about to take place on an unprecedented scale. It was not made clear by whom or upon whom. The message was, in accordance with standing instructions, accorded a priority grading and forwarded to us in London. An enquiry as to the identity of the taxi-driver elucidated the priceless information that he was Greek and drove a battered grey Mercedes saloon.

"The duty officer at the FO, in accordance with standing

orders, passed the message to Downing Street and the PM was informed. Two hours later our Washington embassy notified us that a similar message had been received, addressed to the United States government. This information was exchanged under the provisions of our Special Relationship Agreement and, whatever we decide, the American press will be running this as hot news a few hours from now. A discreet enquiry was initiated in the direction of Paris. The Elysée were cautious, but admitted a threat had been made in similar terms to their embassy in Athens. They indicated Bonn had already been in contact and they too had been visited by a taxi. . . ."

"Beware Greeks bearing gifts," said the Commissioner drily.

"When this information was collated and passed to the PM, this meeting was ordered. It has been given a top priority rating. Thank you."

Kate thought the speaker dreaded applause, so quickly did he duck into his seat, folding his considerable length into the chair and making way for his colleague who began to speak without introduction or preamble. He spoke with a cold authority that Kate found intimidating.

"Intelligence reports from all available sources, bearing in mind the provisions of the SRA and our exchange arrangements with Paris and Bonn, are unable to throw any real light on the subject. However, the confidently expressed view is that the very lack of action following the recent collapse of the United Nations debate on Palestine is significant. It is felt that the statement of outraged protest on the part of those legitimized to express a pro-Palestinian view at the Security Council was no more than an unavoidable token in view of the nature of the breakdown of the dialogue. . . ."

"I'm sorry but if only for my benefit, can you be a bit more explicit? I don't know if I'm the only one," the Commissioner looked round at Kate, "but I don't know what the devil you're talking about."

Kate smiled her agreement.

"I'm sorry Sir Charles, but certain governments express the Palestinian view at the Security Council, by tacit acceptance they are assumed to speak for the so-called leadership of the Palestinians."

"If you mean Libya and Syria, why the devil don't you say so?"

"Because I also include Costa Maya, whose ambassador to the UN actually made the statement."

"Costa Maya?"

"Yes, Sir Charles, it's the recently established Central American Republic. . . ."

"I know, and its a *People*'s Republic, a difference that electrifies your chums in the CIA, but please go on."

"Well, in view of the collapse of the talks some sort of protest had to be made. The Costa Mayan ambassador made it but, in the intelligence agencies' view, the lack of response was surprising. The matter warranted outrage and this was expected from several sources; it did not materialize and this is regarded as significant."

"I think Miss Meldrum and I understand now. You think that these notes are perhaps the real response?"

"At a guess, yes."

"A *guess*?"

"A hunch."

"That's language a policeman understands."

"Forgive me, Sir Charles," said Kate, "but what exactly happened at the UN? I'm afraid I have missed much of last week's news due to pressure of work," she lied, but the civil servants looked at her in a kind of dumb horror, as though she had confessed to having been an officer in the KGB.

"It won't hurt to remind us all," put in the Commissioner.

"Briefly then, and for Miss Meldrum's benefit, the deteriorating situation in the Lebanon emanating from the continued fighting there between rival factions has resulted in the capture, by the insurgent Palestinians, of the port of Sidon and the Sidon Declaration. This statement said that the Palestinian people were no longer prepared to live in their camps, that the time for the final fight for a homeland had come. In simple terms the Lebanon is about to metamorphose into a new Palestine. Support for this will come from several sources and can be supplied from the north and east overland, and from the sea via Sidon. "Cynically, it is expected that the Israelis will tolerate this, at least for the present, though the declared aim of the Palestinians is to recover their original homeland. With foreign backing they could roll up the map of Israel, having first asserted their full national identity in the Lebanon. To paraphrase another well-known terrorist with territorial ambitions, it would provide 'a final solution'. The matter thus came before the Security Council." The coldy authoritative civil servant paused and resumed.

"The Costa Mayans, whose long guerilla war has resulted in the overthrow of a military junta and the re-establishment of an ancient people as their own masters, have both inspired and assisted the Palestinians. Their causes have been united, the Palestinians have, effectively, a chair at the UN.

"But the proposed motion, to recognize Sidon as *de facto* Palestinian territory, was vetoed by the US in support of Israel and has caused the impasse. It is interesting because the ancient right of conquest might be thought to have given the Palestinians a powerful moral card as well as bringing a much needed ceasefire to the beleagured people of the Lebanon. All these reasons were, of course, deployed in favour of the refugees and as an inducement to the West the tantalising offer to cease all 'sorties and offensives', in other words terrorist attacks, were also put forward. In view of these factors the defeat of the motion might have been expected to attract more opprobrium than it did."

"Then you deduce the Palestinians expected the opposing veto?" asked the Commissioner.

"Yes."

"And had a contingency plan?"

"Yes."

"And this is it?"

"That's the hunch, Sir Charles?"

"Mmmm ... before we get down to specifics, has anyone any comments?" The Commissioner glanced round.

"Yes sir." They looked at Kate expectantly. "Listening, from my position of relative ignorance, I would say that, on the face of it, the Palestinians had a pretty good case. Even supposing they expected an opposing veto, shouldn't they have capitalized upon what was, after all, a propaganda victory of considerable magnitude?"

74

"You mean it doesn't make sense to let the matter lie?" asked Sir Charles.

"On the face of it, no sense at all, sir."

"Miss Meldrum has an excellent point." He of the folded limbs levered himself up in his chair. He was, as behove his profession, cautious. "But it is a point that is only valid if the two things are connected. If the notes are a hoax, or were initiated by, say, the IRA, her point is invalid." He sank again in his seat.

"True, but let's pursue Miss Meldrum's argument a little further. We have little enough to go on and I suppose we may at least suppose Athens is a more convenient post-box for the Palestinians rather than the IRA." Sir Charles turned to a silent, uniformed commander beside him, as though for confirmation. The man was dark and broodingly handsome. He nodded agreement. The Commissioner turned to Kate. "Do you want to say anything else, Miss Meldrum?"

Kate flushed. She was having trouble holding the thread of her hypothesis, vaguely aware of the faint aroma of male prejudice and the yet more exciting feeling that she might be onto something.

"I think that what is being suggested is that, if the notes and the failed UN motion are connected, the failure of the Palestinians and their allies to go on and gain at least a propaganda coup argues that their 'freedom offensives' are of long planning. . . ." She had their full attention now, especially that of the silent commander. Martin was watching her with the pride of an indulgent parent.

"To have made a big propaganda scoop would have invalidated a big campaign of terrorist attacks. . . .", she went in with a beating heart.

"*Ergo*" the dark Commander interrupted, "the terrorist attacks were already planned and should go ahead."

"If the motion failed at the United Nations, yes," Kate replied.

"That's very good," the authoritarian civilian said. "If the motion succeeded, then obviously the terror offensive could be cancelled, indeed the event would receive such worldwide publicity that it would be virtually self-cancelling."

75

"Exactly," said the Commissioner with evident enthusiasm.

"Was it only the Costa Mayan spokesman who made any comment?"

"More or less," explained the bleak-eyed civil servant, "I believe a couple of Arab chappies were interviewed by a West German TV team and clammed up after expressing their disgust."

"Could we get a video?" Kate asked, "to look for body language, that sort of thing. . . ."

"Good heavens, Miss Meldrum, d'you comprehend the Arabic version of that?" Sir Charles jested.

They laughed, a tight little laugh that expressed their tension.

"What I don't quite follow," the tall, rangy civil servant said, "is why mute the propaganda trumpets, even supposing you've a terror campaign planned?"

"So as not to alert us as you infiltrate your agents," Sir Charles said, as though explaining something simple to an obtuse pupil.

"I see that, Sir Charles," the man said, stung to a tone of asperity, "but the clarion call quickly followed by a strike. . . ."

"Would have been self-annulling," put in Kate, suddenly visualizing the whole scenario. "The value of the legitimized claims is immensely enhanced by the UN rejection only if unsupported by renewed terror attacks. To aspire to legitimate nation-status they have to put terrorism behind them; today's terrorist is tomorrow's statesman, but note the shift in timetable and see Israel for confirmation.

"I'm sure the notes are linked to the Palestinians and that there is no immediate link with the UN rejection."

"Why not?" asked the angular Civil Servant.

"The Palestinians are planning a final bid for the homeland," Kate explained. "It is immensely expensive in men and material. Their traditional allies are wearying, their traditional enemies have struck back, remember Tripoli and Benghazi last April? They wouldn't abandon their known methods of attack, the random terrorist bomb, the hijack and so on, but they need to augment that by solid conquest so they plan a major attack on Sidon to secure a port. They've never done anything quite like that before and," she paused, "they are never likely to be able to do it again if it fails. Gentlemen, I don't think they expected the attack on Sidon to result in its capture. They were prepared for defeat; they took a massive gamble, a last ditch attempt to prove the validity of ageing leadership and it worked. The terrorist offensive, planned as a continuation, admittedly an escalation, but nevertheless a continuation of their old tactics, suddenly assumes a new and critical reality. If it works it may indeed be their final solution. On such a gamble it must be worth sacrificing a few days of propaganda, however valuable."

Her exposition was greeted by a long silence.

"I think Chief Inspector Meldrum is right," It was the dark commander who spoke and Kate was impressed by the weight his opinion clearly carried. There was an expression of deference on the faces of the Commissioner and the two civil servants.

"I think Miss Meldrum has demonstrated her ability to think clearly, sir," he said to the Commissioner. "I'd like to apply formally for her immediate transfer to my section."

"Yes, yes, of course," Sir Charles smiled at her.

"Kate, this is Commander Ian Nicholas." Martin bobbed up, cast in the role of procurer, Kate thought. "He is in charge of an anti-terrorist section. . . ."

Kate sat in Commander Nicholas's office and smoked a cigarette. She was not an habitual smoker but, at such moments she enjoyed the nicotine and dragged greedily on it. It had proved a long day and she remembered she had not phoned her mother to explain why she had failed to turn up for the Sunday lunch they had arranged.

Curiosity made her stare round the office. Nicholas's reputation as a terrorist hunter was legendary and, such was the quality of the man's character, that even in his absence she felt compelled not to pry any further. Not that there was anything to see. The office was clinically bare, consisting of a desk, a large, lockable, filing cabinet, a glass-fronted bookcase and an incongruous metal coat-stand that reminded Kate of a Miro painting. On the desk was a keyboard and VDU, a single document tray in which, as far as she could see, only two pieces of paper lay, and three telephones. Two chairs, one of which Kate occupied, faced the desk and the room might have been unoccupied but for the chequered banded and silver-laced peak of the cap which perched atop the Miro structure in the corner.

Kate was suddenly desperate for an ashtray. In the end she used the flip-top of her cigarette-packet and relaxed, thinking over the long meeting. There had been a very tedious discussion about the likely nature of a terrorist offensive. The civil servants had spun out a long thesis based on 'probability factors' in which they sought to tease a great deal out of the bare wording of the Athens despatch. There was some trans-Atlantic telephone calling which produced the news that messages had been received by the Japanese and Indian governments, delayed by the time difference; and the Italian government who had delayed confiding in any foreign ally as they were currently engaged in a huge trial of alleged Mafia members and had assumed the threat had originated from the Cosa Nostra.

"At least we've got company," Sir Charles had said as they moved on to discuss the likely targets. As co-ordinating officer, Martin took copious notes. The Immigration Service was to be alerted through the Home Office, airport security was to be tightened up and all government offices, Ministry of Defence establishments and associated contractors put on Red Alert. Screened information was to be passed to selected executives in the transport systems of the major cities and, of course, all chief constables were to be informed.

"I think a conference of the chief constables should be arranged PDQ at Bramshill," put in the Commissioner and Martin nodded. It was all according to standing instructions. But Kate, her mind wandering to thoughts of Tim suddenly said, "What about ships?"

"Good point! Those in port are covered by the chiefs of port administration," explained Commander Nicholas, "but there's no provision for ships at sea . . . we'd better get the Department of Transport to promulgate a general security warning to all British ships through Portishead Radio. . . ."

"Very well, sir, I think that MoD may already cover that." Martin made another note.

"Won't hurt to fasten belt and braces, Chief Superintendent."

"No sir."

It had broken up at last, petering out into the vague speculations of worried and responsible men. Nicholas had ordered her to wait for him in his office so she sat and smoked her cigarette and cursed a man whose self-discipline was so severe as to deny even his guests an ashtray.

"I'm sorry to have kept you." Nicholas swept into the room. He had changed into a worn sports jacket and grey trousers. "The ashtray's in the second drawer on the left, help yourself." He began to take a few papers out of a file from the cabinet and locked it with a key held to his waist by a chain.

"I'm going to take you to dinner, Chief Inspector. Nothing's going to happen tonight and you deserve it."

"But I'm in uniform, sir."

"Got any kind of a coat?"

"In the car."

"Swap it for that tunic and lose the hat and tie. White shirt and navy blue skirt – very smart. . . ."

She avoided his scrutiny in the lift, rather in awe of him. In the car park she slipped into the Escort and took off her tunic and tie. Like most uniformed police she always carried a garment with which to conceal the more obvious indications of her job. In the pocket she found an orange square and wound it round her neck. Fortunately her rank allowed her to wear high-heeled shoes and she did not feel too awful as she relocked the car and crossed the partly empty space to where Nicholas's Rover waited.

"Orange and blue . . . very nice . . . !"

The security barrier went up and the duty officer saluted as the car swept up Broadway and into Victoria Street. They passed the piazza in front of the campanile of Westminster and Kate noticed it was raining.

"Going to be a wet night." Nicholas switched on the windscreen wipers as they swept past the equestrian statue of Marshall Foch, along the rear wall of Buckingham Palace then left towards Belgrave Square. The rain was pelting down and the flags drooped outside the white facades of the foreign embassies. Nicholas cut through Sloane Street and pulled into a parking bay in a backstreet just north of the King's Road.

They got out and he grabbed her arm as they ran stumbling along, pausing under the small canopy outside Daphne's. Inside, the restaurant was pink and cheerful.

"No shop," he said as they sat down and the waiter brought the menus. "D'you mind if I call you Kate?"

"No, of course not." She bit off the routine-conditioned 'sir' and thought of asking him what she should call him, but he was studying the menu and it was clear that although rank might be unacknowledged, it was not to be unrecognized.

"What would you like?"

"I don't know, these things always confuse me."

"D'you like fish?"

"Yes."

"Sole?"

She nodded. "We'll have the sole, please," he ordered, "and a bottle of Chateau d'Or." When the waiter had gone he leaned forward. She tried to guess how old he was and whether he was married or not. She could easily find out, but it amused her and somehow made him less intimidating.

"Thinking about your Palmer when you mentioned the ships, eh?"

"You know about that?"

"'Fraid so. Unemployed seafarer, very bad image, especially for a bright career girl."

"There are rather a lot of them," Kate said, "I seem to recall the country's gratitude is always expressed in times of national crisis."

Her tone contained some of the bitterness she had absorbed from Tim. "Besides, he's not unemployed, he went back to sea the week before last."

"And left you alone. I'm only joking, besides, I want you to come and live with me."

"I beg . . ." She choked on the words as he held up his hand.

"In a manner of speaking. There'll be about half a dozen of us to cover this thing, all living in. Bring enough clothes tomorrow. I'll give us a 48-hour hiatus and then, bingo. In the meantime you run computer models on all available information, collate any material initially deriving from your basic hypothesis." He paused as the waiter brought the wine and nodded his approval. "Your good health. I'm afraid it'll be burgers and ersatz coffee for the next few days."

"It doesn't matter." The Muscadet was deliciously sharp on her tongue, cleaning off the dull taste of the cigarette.

"How were you going to spend the day?"

"With my mother," she laughed.

"Oh."

"And you?"

"With mine!"

"Really?"

"Yes. I suppose I should have said 'Snap!'"

They laughed together as the fish arrived. For a few moments they tucked in in companionable silence. He was about to say something when he was prevented by an insistent bleep.

"Damn!" He cancelled the radio-pager, ignoring the inquisitive glances of the other diners and put down his knife and fork. "Please go on, I shan't be a minute." He rose and asked a waiter for a telephone. Dialling he put the receiver close to his face.

"Yes?" There was a pause and then he said, "All right," and returned to the table. "Sorry Kate, bit of a demand on doctors, I'm afraid. . . ." He looked apologetically round at the other diners whose curiosity seemed assuaged by this titbit.

"Finish off while I pay the bill."

He paid in cash and five minutes later they were in the Rover and heading for the King's Road. For a while he said nothing, dodging the traffic on the wet street and forcing the pace across Sloane Square.

"I'm guilty of an error of judgement . . . there's been a bloody nasty big bang at the Savoy, the Dorchester, the Grosvenor and the Hilton Hotels!"

"Oh God!" She could hear the noise of ambulance or police sirens.

"It looks like war, Chief Inspector."

"Yes." She paused. The suspicion still lurked in her mind,

despite the sudden change in circumstances. "How *did* you know about Palmer?"

"Is it relevant?" asked Nicholas, a faint note of irritation in his voice as he swung the car round a corner. "I don't know . . . pity about the dinner."

"Yes. The sole was lovely."

He turned to her and smiled briefly, his mouth illuminated by the lights of the shop windows. "We'll finish it another day."

"That would be nice, sir."

DOWNING STREET, LONDON

"Very well, Sir Charles, it wasn't entirely unexpected. So what actions have you taken . . . Good . . . fine . . . what was that? Portishead Radio? No, I'm still here . . . yes, yes, of course . . . very well . . . in the morning. . . ."

"What's the matter, darling?"

"Terrorist attacks all over London."

"We knew that 20 minutes ago, sit down and have some coffee, that Scotch won't do you any good at all."

"For God's sake, Jill, I've barely got my feet under the desk and this has to blow up in my face!"

"You said it wasn't entirely unexpected and assured the American Ambassador that you could handle the matter."

"I'll tell the American Ambassador to go to hell if he patronizes me any more."

"Perhaps he was used to patronizing your predecessor."

"All right, you win, pour me some coffee . . . and thanks. . . ."

"I believe it's what wives are traditionally supposed to be for. What's Portishead Radio?"

"What? Oh, the long-distance radio station for commercial traffic. It's run by British Telecom and used to send messages to merchant ships."

"What's that got to do with poor Sir Charles?"

"Sir Charles? Oh, nothing, nothing at all."

"I assume I'm only supposed to be supportive, not consultative."

"Let's just say there are straws in the wind, darling. I'm sorry I can't say more."

"That's all right. I suppose I shall get used to it. Will you let me choose the new wallpaper?"

NEW SCOTLAND YARD, LONDON

"Paris is the same, so is New York and San Francisco . . ."

"All set to go off simultaneously irrespective of time zones."

"Yes sir. That's a nice touch of power," put in Kate.

"Any more?" asked Nicholas.

"Not yet," replied Martin, "but we haven't . . ."

A telex machine in the corner of the room bleeped and chattered into life. Pulled by the same reflex they all crowded round it. It was a repeat terminal to that of Reuter's and bore the sinister news that a large hotel had been devastated in Tokyo with the loss of many lives. The building was still on fire at the time of despatch.

"All hotels, eh!" Nicholas looked at Kate, "That gives you something to start on."

A telephone rang and Martin answered it. They saw his face go white and he motioned for a pad and pencil. Kate pushed one along and held the pad while Martin scribbled. She saw his firm hand jot down the details of disaster. Cathay Pacific flight CP 319 had exploded shortly after take-off from Kai-Tak, Hong Kong. Japan Air Lines flight JL 32 had disappeared from the radar at Tokyo when making her approach on a scheduled flight from Washington. She had been 20 miles out over the Pacific Ocean. Five minutes later they heard that a Canadian airliner on a short-haul flight had disappeared from the radar even as an air traffic officer had called it.

"None British," said Nicholas suspiciously. He sat in the stunned silence for a moment and then said sharply, "'Priority, to all airline operators: Cancel all flights out of British airports pending full bomb searches.' Circulate copies to all constabulary bomb squads and let the Ministry of Defence alert their own teams. Get me a line to Sir Charles, we must get immediate Home Office sanction for a general alert to all chief constables and a cancellation of all police leave. Message to all ferry ports, Chief Superintendent, you've got the distribution list?"

"Here sir."

"Good. 'To the Chief Immigration officers: a priority alert for terrorist suspects.' . . ." He raised an eyebrow at Kate, "Anything? Any intuition?"

She looked at her own notebook when it struck her: "Yes, sir, the nationalities . . . this has got to be a co-ordinated attack. This isn't just the Palestinians, they couldn't have carried this out. This is an allied attack, all minority terror groups co-ordinating a single attack."

Nicholas nodded. "All for one, eh?"

"It's got to be!"

"I'll get the gist of that circulated on the B-list," volunteered Martin.

"No. On the C-List, the lower the security screening with this one the better. We won't catch anything except a cold any other way . . . now I'd better talk to Sir Charles. . . ."

"Here's the line now, sir."

As Nicholas spoke, the second telephone rang and this time Kate answered. "Hullo?"

"Call here Ma'am, from RUC headquarters in Belfast," said the switchboard operator and then she heard the broad, flat nasal accents of Ulster.

"We've a major incident here, the new Type 23 'Duke' class destroyer just ready for launching at Harland and Wolff's has been destroyed by an act of sabotage."

"Can you tell me whether it resulted from a bomb explosion?"

Silence greeted the question and she heard, in the background, the voice say, "I've got a bloody woman on the other end. . . ."

"Hullo. . . ."

"Hullo. I'm a Chief Inspector if it helps. You said it was sabotage. What makes you so sure?"

"Because, Ma'am, it usually bloody is when there's a bang in Ulster!"

"Have the IRA claimed responsibility?"

"Not yet, but it'll be them all right."

"But what was the cause of the explosion? You're sure it was a bomb?"

"Yes Ma'am," the voice was weary.

"Thank you. Please keep us informed, especially if there's a claim. It's important to us."

"That makes a change."

"You haven't heard the news?"

"I've just come on duty; walked into this lot."

Kate looked at the clock. It was a minute after midnight. "Well, just for once you're not centre stage. Good night." She put the phone down and caught Nicholas's eye. "I think I know why we haven't had an airliner hit yet."

"Oh? Why?"

"There were easier pickings in Belfast. . . ." she explained and Nicholas whistled. Kate lit a cigarette; she had a headache and realized that the ashtray in front of her was full of stubs.

One of the telephones burst into life again and Martin picked it up. There was no surprise in his voice now. He wrote slowly and read out the message after putting the receiver down.

"That was the MoD; air traffic control at RAF Leuchars have just intercepted a civilian helicopter of North British Helicopters flying between the oil rigs in the Gannet Field. They report sighting explosions from one of the rigs . . ." he looked up, "it could be coincidence."

There was a brief silence as those in the room digested the news.

"No," pronounced Commander Nicholas, "I think we now know why none of our airliners has been hit. . . ."

HMS *ORFORD CASTLE*, NORTH SEA

Lieutenant Commander Tiplady was called to consciousness by the insistent ringing of the telephone beside his head. With one hand he reached out and pulled the receiver down to his pillowed ear.

"Captain, sir? Officer of the watch, Lieutenant Tillotson, sorry to disturb you but there's a major incident in the Gannet Field, sir. The Yankee Zulu complex has just put out a Mayday and there's a lot of VHF traffic on Channel 16, civvie helicopters, Lerwick Coast Guard and Stonehaven Radio, it sounds like an explosion, sir."

"Distance?"

"Only 22 miles, sir, I took the liberty of bringing her round. . . ."

"Well done . . . best speed and I'll be up in a few minutes. Get some coffee organized and call the first lieutenant."

"Aye, aye, sir."

Tiplady put the phone down, rolled on his back and rubbed his eyes. Judging by the motion of his ship the weather was being seasonally bloody. Holding on he threw his legs over the edge of the bunk and staggered across the cabin to dash water in his face, rubbing his beard with a towel to stimulate his laggardly circulation. Not for the first time he blessed his decision to grow a beard and after scouring his teeth, dressed with practised speed.

Coming onto the bridge in the penumbral gloom of dimmed lights he heard first the soft hum of electronic instruments, the twin radars and the gyro compass, but then he noticed the whole enclosed space, maintained at a steady temperature by ducted air, vibrated to the roar of the gale outside. His eyes fell on the anemometer dial: 45 to 50 knots: Force Nine to Ten. Instinct took him to the forward window where the short point of the bow rose from the sea. Water cascaded aft, over the capstans and the bitts, to stream over the side as a great gulf opened out beneath her dripping forefoot and HMS *Orford Castle* suddenly tilted and dived forward.

Tiplady felt her stern shudder as the racing screws came up into the aerated water and the little ship plunged downward. Ahead of her the grey sea rose in a wall, its huge face streaked by spume clearly visible in the gloom. As the ship slid forward he sensed the sudden lack of wind in the lee of the great wave and then found himself looking upwards as the foaming crest appeared. *Orford Castle's* bow slammed into the rearing face of the sea and her whole fabric protested at its own buoyancy as she strove to lift herself from the abyss.

With a bang the port wheelhouse door slid open and shut

quickly. It was Tillotson, dodging in from a vain search of the horizon.

"Hold on ... morning, sir. . . ."

He got no further. The sea broke against Tiplady's ship, thundering down over her tiny hull, engulfing her wheelhouse in solid, green water. She struggled under the immense weight of it and, only as her momentum carried her forward and the storm-driven wave swept astern, felt the burden ease. Sluicing the inhospitable North Sea from her trembling hull *Orford Castle* emerged again into the windswept darkness.

"Coffee sir?" asked the duty signalman, trying to keep the relief out of his voice.

"Please." he exchanged greetings with Tillotson.

"It's been quiet for the last few moments, sir, but I should think that things are pretty serious."

"I suppose these accidents are to be expected from time to time," Tiplady said trying to be philosophical, "and Sod's Law guarantees that if anything's going to go wrong it'll be on a night like this."

He broke off as the VHF loudspeaker burst into life.

"Lerwick Coast Guard this is helicopter Romeo-Whisky . . . over."

They were too far to the east to pick up more than a garbled syllable of the coastguard's reply.

"That's the civilian helicopter, sir, he reported the incident first."

"I see."

They heard the pilot again. "Roger Lerwick, this is Romeo-Whisky. Present Sitrep: I have lifted two men, repeat two men only from *accommodation* rig. It is now burning fiercely, I repeat burning fiercely . . . over."

There was another pause as they imagined the scene. Used to such clipped and formal speech, they could discern the tension in the pilot's voice and they knew that in such weather flying would tax his ability without the added complications of a raging inferno beneath his machine.

They were joined by the figure of the first lieutenant. "Morning."

"Morning Neville."

87

"Hullo Lerwick, this is Romeo-Whisky, by all means, but I cannot remain indefinitely, my fuel situation already critical. I repeat that chances of further rescue by air hazardous due to fire and risk of further explosions . . . over."

"His fuel consumption'll rise significantly if he spends much time in hot air. . ." volunteered the first lieutenant.

"Yes." Tiplady picked up his own handset and waited for an obvious gap in the dialogue. Romeo-Whisky was talking again:

"No chance, Lerwick, but men have been seen jumping into the sea, over."

"Bloody hell!" whispered Tillotson.

"Roger Lerwick, understood, I have already been in touch with rescue ship *Northern Virtue* and they are moving into position but the chances of picking anyone up are not good . . . roger, Lerwick, wilco. . . ."

"Tiplady pressed the transmit button. "Romeo-Whisky, Romeo-Whisky this is Warship *Orford Castle*, do you read me, over?"

"*Orford Castle* this is Romeo-Whisky, loud and clear, go ahead, over."

"I am seventeen miles from the Yankee Platform. ETA . . . ?"

"Oh-four-hundred, sir."

"Oh-four-hundred and I have helicopter flight deck. Are the two men you rescued in need of medical attention? I have a doctor on board. Over."

"Romeo-Whisky. Affirmative. One badly burned and liability aboard me. Stand-by."

"Roger." Tiplady tried to imagine what it was like for that dispassionate voice. The man was probably consulting his flight engineer and calculating fuel and flight times while trying to hold his helicopter in a wind now gusting to 55 knots. Somewhere behind him the burned oilman might be writhing in agony and Lerwick was a long way to the west.

"Warship *Orford Castle*, this is helicopter Golf-November-Sierra-Romeo-Whisky, I intend to land on the unmanned production platform Zulu One and await daylight and your arrival. Will attempt emergency touchdown on you at first light. Seems to be oil slick developing from Zulu Platform, sea much flatter there. Will need instant lashing on touchdown. Can you oblige?"

"We will do our best Romeo-Whisky. Over."

"See you later. Out."

"Roger and out."

"Poor devil sounds exhausted," said the first lieutenant.

"He's probably been flying for hours before this lot happened. It's not going to be much fun for him sitting on top of the production platform."

The two men bent over the chart. The small squares of the oil platforms dotted the sea to the east of Shetland, magenta lines, the umbilicals of a nation's economy, stretching for mile after mile across a sea known only a generation before for its desolation and its cod. The Zulu and Yankee platforms were well away from the other rigs in the same field. The Zulu platform was the oil producer, bringing up the crude from the porous rock hundreds of feet below within a radius of half a mile around it. Just too far to be incorporated in this complex pumphouse another group of well-heads were tapped by a smaller platform, a mere pump which gathered in the pipes from its family of wells and boosted their flow a mile or so across the ocean floor to Zulu platform where it joined the main pipeline to Shetland. Next to the Zulu Platform stood Yankee, the accommodation rig, a dozen floors of utilitarian construction containing the cabins, kitchens, and life-support systems for the 224 men who worked, day and night, to keep the gas turbine pumps pushing the unrefined, high-quality North Sea crude to the cracking towers, tank farms and shipping terminal of Sullom Voe.

Plunging wildly, staggering with the impact as her bow thumped into heavy seas and shuddering as the racing screws lifted from the water, the little warship ploughed north-west towards the Gannet Oil Field. During the next hour Tiplady and his first lieutenant speculated upon what they would find when they arrived and the preparations they should make to meet such circumstances as they found. Chief among their problems was that of getting the helicopter Romeo-Whisky safely secured on deck.

"He sounds pretty desperate to me," Tiplady said.

As they closed the scene of disaster they spoke to the grandly named *Northern Virtue*, a former North Sea trawler that had been converted as a rig stand-by ship, a mandatory safety provision which had, in the event, been quite unable to prevent the multiple explosions ripping apart the twin platforms.

"I can see it, sir." Young and enthusiastic, Lieutenant Tillotson had been dodging the worst of the weather and peering through powerful binoculars at the horizon ahead. He stuck his head into the wheelhouse from the tiny bridge wing as sheets of spray hissed aft. Tiplady picked up his own glasses and raised them to his eyes, waiting for the ship to climb over the next sea.

On the horizon the pinpricks of light were dotted across ten degrees of the horizon, the scattered platforms of the Gannet Field. Among them the bright orange flames of the flare-offs streamed to leeward in the gale. But ahead of them lay a prominent mass of red and yellow, full of a powerful and numinous energy.

"I thought that they made those things fire-proof," muttered the first lieutenant beside him, "specially constructed of non-flammable materials with fire doors and what not."

"No machinery's ever really 'safe'," said Tiplady, still staring through the binoculars, "nuclear reactors were pronounced safe until Chernobyl. . . ."

Behind him someone came on the bridge and gave a discreet cough. "Captain, sir. . . ."

Tiplady turned: "Yes?"

"It's Pike, sir. Signal just come in, sir, classified 'Most Secret'."

Tiplady groaned inwardly. Just when they were committed to a serious incident which would demand his utmost concentration, their Lordships had different ideas and they sounded important. He moved across the wheelhouse beneath the dimmed light over the chart table. 'Sparky' Pike's face was abominably solemn. Tiplady took the folded slip of paper and opened it. It was already in plain language and he skipped the preamble:

... INTELLIGENCE REPORTS INDICATE POSSIBILITY EXPLO-
SIONS GANNET FIELD YOUR AREA MAY HAVE TERRORIST

90

He read it through a second time, folded it and put it in his pocket.

"Thank you." He turned back to the window. Two and half hours to dawn. Looking ahead at the raging inferno blazing above the sea he wondered what on earth there would be to 'investigate'.

It was a bleak, grey dawn such as only the high latitudes know; a gradual change, uninspiriting after a night of little rest and much worry. The wind had moderated slightly, but the seas were still huge and hoary, a waste of tumbling crests that thundered into long streaks of spume streaming downwind, marbling the surface of the sea with an unregarded beauty. In and out of the wave-troughs the sabre-winged fulmars glided, their motionless wings slicing the wind and impelling them inches from the wild surface of the water. Tiplady caught a glimpse of the fulmar's tiny cousins, dabbling their dark feet in the crashing waves in search of the tiny organisms that sustained their delicate lives. The storm petrels seemed oblivious of the chaos surrounding them and Tiplady, tired in the dawn, took encouragement from the thought that they might be the *zeitgeist* of the morning. But it was not to be; as *Orford Castle* drew closer to the blaze the stench of oil came down to them, overwhelming in its power, seeping into the ship through every air duct.

There was little left of Yankee Platform. It stood on vast legs, braced from the seabed fathoms below and was, basically, a great box of accommodation. Whatever its non-flammable properties in theory, there had proved much to burn. True, the shell was still discernible, but the steel was devoid of paint and had buckled crazily in the tremendous heat. Much had burnt out and only an occasional flicker of flame showed now from its interior as a watery sun shone out, sparkling the sea with a pale silver light. But fire still raged undiminished on Zulu Platform and Tiplady knew he was watching the substance of the very planet consuming itself in a mighty roar that could be heard three miles away. From time to time it seemed to set fire to the sea itself and strange licks of dull red flame spread across the surface of the smooth water that trailed away from the burning wells.

Above the platform, like some vast, hellish cumulonimbus cloud, rising hundreds of feet into the air the red flames turned to jet-black smoke, dense and choking, to be forced horizontal as the wind caught and the heat spread it upwards. Within this massive rolling cloud sudden recombustion took place, the hot gasses reignited and flashes of orange veined through the pall.

"It's a gigantic cock-up," remarked someone in the wheelhouse, seeking a facetious release from the overwhelming sense of helplessness that seemed, like the stench itself, to engulf them.

Tiplady eased the ship's speed back and as she slowed, her motion became easier. He had no wish to do more than take advantage of the slick to land the helicopter, not push his ship into the dangerous fumes that might explode on board, for all he knew. More than that he could not do for there was nothing more to be done. *Northern Virtue* had recovered two bodies, but that was all. Tiplady picked up his binoculars and swung them round, looking for the outwork of Zulu One. It was due north of him and he caught occasional glimpses of its legs beneath the pall of smoke and fire.

"Call the men to Flying Stations, Number One," he ordered, hoisting himself up into his chair. The atmosphere in the wheelhouse changed and he sensed the ship come to life around him. This was something they could do, a contribution, no matter how pathetic, to change the circumstances that faced them.

While he waited for his men to report themselves ready at their stations, he stared at the two rigs. What was there left to investigate? All he could say was that both were damaged beyond repair, that the well was burning fiercely and would require the services of an experienced trouble-shooting team to stop it doing irreparable damage. He thought of the storm petrels and the effect the slick would have upon a vast tract of their wild habitat. And then he sloughed off his bafflement; he had to snatch something from the situation, like those tiny birds snatched their food from before the onslaught of the breaking seas. It came to him as blindingly obvious that there was no 'possibility' that the fire had been started deliberately, for the wind was blowing across the catwalk that ran between Zulu and Yankee; no chance spark, no random gas emission could cross that gap. Even now the fires sent up twin columns of smoke and only downwind, as they spread, did they mingle and become one. If accident had set fire to one platform it was doubtful if coincidence could have ignited the other simultaneously. Such a thesis argued arson, and arson on the grand scale, arson so deliberate that it had destroyed the living quarters of 200 men, perhaps arson enhanced by some form of sabotage that minimized the inherent fireproof quality of the hotel accommodation. There were few bodies; men dying of toxic and inflammable gas poisoning would not rush out to jump 80 or 90 feet into the cold North Sea. They would simply roast where they were while explosions ripped through the rig, rolling a fireball along the corridors which would be full of the deadly fumes, just as *Orford Castle* was filling up with the stench of crude oil.

"Ship's at flying stations, sir, closed up to X-ray status."

Tiplady acknowledged Tillotson's report and reached for the VHF handset, cocking an eye at the anemometer. He ordered a minor adjustment in their course and speed.

"Ask the first lieutenant what the rise and fall is."

"Aye, aye, sir." Tillotson turned to the PA mike and Tiplady pushed the transmit button on the radio-telephone.

"This is Warship *Orford Castle*, *Orford Castle* calling helicopter Romeo-Whisky, come in please, over."

"Glad to see you *Orford Castle*, this is Romeo-Whisky, I'm warming up now and can be with you within five minutes, over."

"Roger. How is your patient? Over."

"Full of morphine, one of my reasons for wanting to touch down here, over.

"Roger, what kind of chopper are you? Over."

"Mike Bravo Bravo 105 Delta, three on board and ready to lift, over."

"Bloody hell, he's on his own!" Tillotson exclaimed and then, remembering himself reported, "First lieutenant says it's bumpy sir, four to five metres but eases down to one to two for short periods."

Tiplady passed the information to the helicopter pilot.

"All in favour of short periods," he replied, "I'm on my way."

The helicopter came in low, a small white dot with the morning sunshine glancing off the perspex bubble of its nose, as the pilot slipped beneath the great black cloud billowing to leeward.

"Tell the first lieutenant it's a Messerschmidt-Bolkow-Blohm one-zero-five."

Tiplady walked out onto the bridge wing. The smell of oil was overpowering but the sea, though it tossed the ship up and down, was smooth under the layer of light crude that damped down the effect of the wind.

The cloud was clearing and the sun was breaking through a heavy veil of altostratus, giving the day a different complexion. Patches of blue sky were more frequent and he had to shade his eyes as he looked aft, over the bare patch of deck with its nets awaiting the gallant attempt of the helicopter to land.

Tiplady could take comfort from one thing; quite by chance providence had provided *Orford Castle* with the unusual luxury of a doctor, a young and rather supercilious young man, recently qualified and more recently commissioned, on board for sea-going experience and complaining daily of *mal de mer* and inactivity. This would give him something to occupy his time with, Tiplady reflected, as the white Bolkow came to the hover off the warship's stern. He watched the pilot synchronize his motion with the ship's rising and falling as *Orford Castle* pitched in the swell. Beside him Tillotson whistled in appreciation.

Suddenly the Bolkow was descending, landing and skidding slightly as the pilot killed the turbines and the flight deck party ran forward, at considerable risk to themselves, to catch rope lashings round the helicopter's skids.

Tiplady breathed a sigh of relief and watched the first lieutenant walk aft to shake hands with a tall, rangy figure who seemed too big for the machine.

"Thank God for that," Tiplady said to no one in particular.

"How is he, Doc?" Tiplady looked at the pale face of Surgeon Lieutenant McLeod.

94

"Bad, sir. Third degree burns. . . ."

"Can you save him?"

"I'll do my best."

"Yes," Tiplady smiled reassuringly, "I'm sure you will."

He found the other man with the pilot enjoying coffee in the wardroom. After the introductions and congratulations to the pilot who seemed to want to do little more than close his eyes, he turned to the other rescued man.

"Can you try and tell me what happened?"

"I'd gone to the radio room. I'd come off shift at midnight, had a shower and just finished my dinner in the mess hall when I got the message. My wife gave birth in the Royal Infirmary at Edinburgh tonight. I went up to the radio room to telephone back, tell my parents and so on, like we'd arranged, even though it was pretty late. . . .

"I was actually talking to my father when I heard the first bang."

"How loud was it? I mean, was it unusually loud?"

"No . . . no, it wasn't, but you get to know when to expect bangs, like. I mean if a delivery's expected you switch off to the noise if you're not on shift, you know. This bang was unusual, but not so unusual that it alarmed me, like. You know, it was someone else's problem, I was off shift and talking on the phone."

"I understand. Any idea at all where it came from?"

The man shrugged. "I think . . . I mean I had the feeling that it was on the rig. . . ."

"You mean Zulu Platform?"

"Yeah."

"Go on."

"Well, there was a few seconds and then another bang and the alarms started going. That in itself isn't that unusual, except that by the look in the radio operator's eyes, and he wasn't over the moon about babies, I knew that something was really wrong. A moment later the whole bloody platform rocked and the shit hit the fan! I couldn't believe it. The operator pushed me out of the way and he was just about to send out a Mayday when . . . well, I don't know what happened. The whole bloody place was full of noise and smoke. . . ."

"The radio room?"

"Yeah."

"Was the door open?"

"No . . . they all spring back into the closed position, you know. . . ."

"So you think the last explosion could have gone off in the radio room itself, do you?"

The man shrugged again, a look of helplessness on his face. "I don't know, I just remember this hot wave pushing me and the noise and things. . . ."

"What happened next?"

"I . . . I don't really know . . . I found myself outside. The radio room's on the top level, you see. Everything was blazing, bloody great flames pouring up from below and I just went upwards. . . ."

"Upwards?"

"Yeah. Onto the helipad. . . ."

"What happened there?"

"My feet got hot and then there was this light . . . I thought I had had it and I went to the edge of the helipad. I caught the wind and it forced me to kneel down . . . then there was this chopper and I realized the light was from the chopper. I shouted out something and another man came up. He was very badly burned but I recognized him as a bloke named Hinton, a roustabout from the opposite shift, like . . . the shift that was on duty. Somehow we got in the helicopter." He looked at the pilot, who was fast asleep, "That lad's a fucking hero. I couldn't have done what he did. We got off just in time . . . it was a bloody miracle . . . I passed out for a bit in the chopper, and came round when he was landing on the Zulu One pad . . . I couldn't believe I was still alive. . . ."

The man was shaking. His skin was dark with oily filth and tears flowed slowly down his cheeks. He did not seem aware of them and was smiling at the open-mouthed face of the snoring pilot.

"A fucking hero," he repeated almost reverentially.

"What's your name?" Tiplady asked gently, "We don't want your wife thinking the worst when the news gets out, do we?"

"Mayhew . . . Tony Mayhew. . . ."

"Thanks Tony, you've been very helpful. You sit there and

rest. I'll have the doctor come and give you something to help you sleep as soon as he's finished with Hinton."

"Okay, thanks Skipper."

"And congratulations about the baby."

"Yeah."

"Keep a good eye on them," he said to the wardroom steward as he left.

On his way back to the bridge he looked in again on the doctor.

Surgeon Lieutenant McLeod shook his head and Tiplady stepped inside the cabin. He had been in the presence of death before, in San Carlos water. He had seen burned men in plenty then, and this one was no different, except that he seemed to be fighting through the veil of drugs in an exertion that was clearly too much for him.

"I've done all I can," McLeod said.

Hinton's eyes were fixed on Tiplady and the Lieutenant Commander had the strange sensation of somehow being recognized. As *Orford Castle*'s captain he was used to a mixture of wariness, effacement, recognition or occasional hostility in the eyes of officers and men aware of his rank. Something of this seemed to emanate from Hinton, some inner desire of the stricken man communicating itself through the pain and the drugs and recognizing Tiplady for. . . .

For what? He could not answer the question, except by obeying an impulse to bend over the man's blistered face.

The noise of Hinton's breathing was filthy, the burnt muscles dragged air into his scorched lungs instinctively. But his lips, huge and puffy, were forming words and Tiplady strained to catch them.

"Gate Six," Hinton said, and repeated quite distinctly, "Gate Six."

Tiplady straightened up and looked down. Hinton was nodding, a barely perceptible motion of the empurpled head on the white pillow. And his eye, Tiplady saw, burned with a strange and terrible fire that seemed to the naval officer ineluctably defiant.

Three minutes later he was dead.

Chapter Four

NEW SCOTLAND YARD, LONDON

Kate Meldrum discovered that Nicholas had a lot of clout. The arrangements that he had put in hand for the establishment of his incident room were completed by breakfast time and it was rapidly manned as the regular 'office-staff' police came on duty and found themselves seconded to the task. But there was more to Nicholas's influence than the mere collection of additional telex and telephone facilities, the marshalling of some desks and two dozen police officers of both sexes. Nicholas's very name seemed to cut across departmental barriers and open doors that were normally only accessible through 'proper channels' which meant, effectively, not at all.

As the hours dragged by she found herself talking on his behalf to such diverse and influential figures as the Commissioner, half a dozen county chief constables, the Prime Minister's personal private secretary and a man in Washington who insisted on being called Dave because, he said, he thought by her voice she must have nice legs and he could not be formal with a dame who had nice legs.

This elevation to playing word games with the mighty was carried out from a windowless room within the complex of New Scotland Yard, a hermetic box whose dry air-conditioning made the eyes water and in which even the clock confused you as to precisely whether it was day or night.

Kate was beginning to feel very jaded when her telephone rang.

"Kate? Nicholas, no, no more messages for a moment. I want you to come in here."

She crossed the corridor to his own office. It was regulated by the same air-conditioning plant as the incident room but it seemed to contain a cooler, more controlled atmosphere, perhaps because the telephones were silent, or perhaps because Nicholas was one of those rare people who gave off calm, as some give off the unpleasant scent of exertion.

"Sit down." He nodded at one of the telephones. "I've just had the Ministry of Defence on. One of their ships on North Sea patrol has the survivor from the Gannet Field tragedy on board. The other died but the captain says he has some circumstantial evidence to confirm our theoretical explanation for the disaster."

"You mean a terrorist attack, sir?"

"Specifically an act of sabotage, rather than an attack."

"I see." Kate frowned, too tired to worry about splitting hairs over such niceties as exact phraseology.

"The point is, the captain also thinks he has evidence to suggest that the contrary is the case, that the disaster was a genuine accident, unconnected with what's happened elsewhere." Nicholas paused. "You're as aware of the situation as I am . . . what's your opinion?"

Kate stirred her sluggish brain and expelled her breath resignedly.

"Do we know anything about what this 'contrary evidence' is?"

"Only that the fellow who died mentioned something . . . he was badly burned, drugged, and barely conscious at the time, I understand."

"It could be a coincidence, sir," she said doubtfully, frowning. "In fact it was the only incident that doesn't fit the others. . . ."

"What d'you mean?" Nicholas asked sharply.

"Well, sir, the others all happened within a fifteen-minute span. Given the time differences and the difficulties of absolutely simultaneous detonation we can reasonably assume that they were planned to be coincidental. Also observer's and reporter's timing might have varied a few minutes either way in each case. But the Gannet rig explosions took place nearly forty-five minutes later. Now that *could* argue natural accident."

"You don't sound very convinced."

"I'm not."

99

"Neither am I, that's why I've asked the Commander-in-Chief, Naval Home Command to relieve this captain and fly him and the survivor south, so that we can interview them here." Nicholas smiled. "The admiral's scrambled his private helicopter. I don't know why, but he called it his 'green parrot'."

"Good Lord."

"Now you must get a couple of hour's sleep, because after the interview you and I have got to do some hard thinking."

The debriefing of Lieutenant-Commander Tiplady and the roustabout Mayhew lasted less than two hours and was inconclusive and disappointing. In the scenario that Nicholas and a handful of close assistants put together, there remained two tantalizing options. The disaster was a circumstantial accident, the case for which was the survival of a duty roustabout who, despite terrible pain, desperately wanted to convey the information that 'Gate Six' was somehow to blame; or the multiple explosions on the Gannet Field Platform were the result of devices planted by terrorists. How and when were going to be difficult to establish, that was a matter for Nicholas's boffins. What preoccupied Kate was the why, and it was for this that she had been drafted into Nicholas's command.

Kate Meldrum had joined the force as a school leaver faced with unemployment. Despite uninspiring academic achievements she had displayed a natural empathy with suspects, a curious ability to break them down without undue pressure which in certain cases made her valuable as an interrogator. It was a flair, a gift of imagination, enabling her to get into another's skin, to probe outwards and establish likely patterns of behaviour, and to supply possible leads for enquiry. Irritated by senior officers who frequently passed her own deductions off as their own, she had been drawn to the complex psychology of rape victims and then, by a logical extension of her natural progress and her professional interest, to that of their tormentors. From this point Kate's obsession with the darker sides of male libido touched other cores within the dimly perceived recesses of the human brain. She probed the labyrinth by instinct, aware of the danger of her assumptions, but slowly achieving results that seemed borne out by successful prosecutions obtained largely from confessions. It was a lugubrious subject but she found one generous and high-minded patron in Chief Superintendent Martin. Her promotion was rapid and it was Martin who suggested that she extended her studies further. If rape was based on the savage infliction of violence as an expression of power as much as a response to lust, were there not similar springs to the behaviour of terrorists?

Initially, Kate had thought not, but time, given her by her lecturing appointment at Hendon, was leading her to other conclusions. Already a paper on the subject originally drafted by her was privately circulating among chief constables under Home Office approval. Her co-opting into Nicholas's anti-terrorist think-tank had, therefore, a degree of logic behind it. While Nicholas and his other assistants investigated what evidence was available from the foreign incidents in addition to those at Gannet and Belfast, she retired to her desk to tease her tired brain into the *ne plus ultra* of fantasies; she tried to become a terrorist, to seek the means by which the Gannet platform had been blown up and to await the inevitable claim by the IRA for the attack at Harland and Wolff's.

Hours passed, but nothing came from the Provisionals for the sabotage in Belfast. There was no claim from the FLQ for the crash of the Canadian airliner, none from the Japanese United Red Army for that of the JAL Boeing, nothing for the near destruction of three of London's most prestigious hotels. In fact the silence was deafening, so deafening that its very significance ate its way remorselessly into Kate's reasoning. Motives, methods and the staggering impact of simultaneous timing became for her less important. She left the why, how and when to the painstaking research of detectives who could think of nothing else; who could only, like good and faithful hounds, sniff out trails that were already old and cold. For her the flights of the imagination were leading in a more sinister direction.

As Kate recalled incident after incident out of the index displayed on her desktop VDU and had sheet after sheet printed out, she searched for the fall-off of endeavour, the failures of purpose, and the eventual lack of achievement that always marked every phase of warfare as it reached its point of effectiveness, after which it declined in the face of counter-reaction. The hijack and political assassination had passed beyond this point, they were no longer effective in the manner they once had been.

The visiting of death in this massive and outrageously indiscriminate offensive against the world had stunned governments and peoples in a paralysis of fear. As yet, its effects were incalculable; yet a model of predictability could be argued to demonstrate its potential effectiveness. The disastrous results of the threat to tourists in the summer of 1986 had been brought about by the air strikes made by the United States against the Libyan cities of Tripoli and Benghazi. Was this a re-run on a more massive and effective scale?

Yet, once again, the propaganda initiative seemed to be thrown away. A conspiracy of silence frustrated the media markets of the world. The makers of influential news were cheating the avid televiewers of Europe, Japan and North America of their most fascinating image: the death of others.

To Kate Meldrum, sitting in the artificial atmosphere of the incident room, tired and frustrated, the silence was a most insidious form of terror.

Kate had not realized Tony Nicholas wore glasses and somehow she was disappointed by this dent in his superman image. He was the only person in the incident team who did not look exhausted. Kate wondered if he had slept secretly, or whether he popped pills to keep him going. He needed something, for the hours of concentrated police work had produced virtually nothing. The intelligence releases from foreign agencies, which all were swapping like dirty jokes in the hope that somewhere, something would gel into a lead, were scarcely helpful. There was some evidence from regular suspect surveillance that 'something was going on'. Had *this* information been shared as a matter of course then its global significance might have been more obvious. But national security agencies have their own reasons for keeping their own secrets. Those suspicious of Britain had good reason, and the British maintained their own shibboleths in defiance of the passage of time and the march of history.

Some forensic evidence had been recovered from two of the airliners to suggest that similar long-fused bombs had been used. These were now common enough and the pattern for all the attacks was against people, designed to cause horror and the kind of outrage that provoked a reaction which would say 'enough is enough' and send the politicians back to the debating chamber where they belonged. All that is, except the Belfast and the Gannet attacks, and it was still by no means certain that the latter was not an incident in isolation. Both of these were aimed specifically at Britain, her power and her prestige. It was true that the Gannet explosions had cost many lives, but its true target had been to pinpoint the hopeless vulnerability of the platforms to a dedicated attacker. By an irony that went unperceived at the meeting that morning, the very presence of *Orford Castle* as a form of protection was not even noticed. It was merely stated that it was lucky she had been on hand as a glorified lifeboat.

Fact after fact was brought up. Evidence sifted from the ruins of the hotels was discussed; IRA and UDA moves considered. Nicholas himself had pursued a line of enquiry along the 'Gate Six' lead. The complex was fitted with hundreds of gate valves and its electronic circuitry, its control systems, monitors, sensors and varied instrumentation contained thousands of electronic 'gates'; but nowhere, the experts had assured him, was there something specifically called 'Gate Six' that could have materially contributed to the explosion. Nicholas, in a moment of rare exposure, said all he could suggest was that the poor man had been saying something else, something that had seemed like 'Gate Six' to Lieutenant Commander Tiplady's ear.

"And now," Nicholas concluded, looking in Kate's direction, "I should like to call on Chief Inspector Meldrum to give us her prognosis for the most likely scenario to come. There will probably be little we can do until those responsible for these acts reveal themselves, and likely little enough even then, whenever that is, but our political masters demand something and it is as well we have a formidable expert on the terrorist psyche in our midst and do not have to call in outside help . . . Chief Inspector Meldrum."

103

She stood up and peered at her notes. Distilled from hours of painstaking work they were pathetically small. She took a deep breath.

"I have to emphasise at the start that this is an exegesis, an interpretation based on observation, parallel incidents, comparisons and likely trends. Like weather forecasting it is easy to get it wrong and the consequences can be quite other than either expected or wanted. What I have to say is offered for your consideration and is open to your modification."

Nicholas smiled, concealing it behind his hand. It was all true; it was also devilish clever to preface her 'exegesis' behind a disclaimer, particularly when the majority of her listeners were experienced and hard-bitten coppers to whom a young, pretty female chief inspector was an affront.

Kate continued: "I think it is common knowledge to you all that we have reasonable grounds for supposing that this worldwide series of attacks has been co-ordinated, employing a network of differing minority groups who, on this occasion, are acting in concert on behalf of the freedom fighters of Palestine, for so you must think of them for a moment. . . . This is in itself an unusual departure. Certain states have given support, tacit and active help before, but concerted action on this scale is, so far as we know, unique.

"We also believe that this action represents a major push for final victory by the current Palestine leadership. CIA reports indicate a fall-off of support and the emergence of splinter groups. I imagine this information derives from Israeli intelligence and can be relied upon.

"The Palestinians passed up the opportunity to score a major victory in the propaganda war after the UN veto. This was undoubtedly to cover the final preparations for the advertised terror offensive that we have just witnessed. You are probably already drawing your own conclusions for the reason for the present silence. The lack of claims for responsibility for the recent attacks is very unusual. This *could* be because some groups may lose local ground support for admitting they are operating on behalf of someone else. There is quite a strong case to be made on that basis; on the other hand that does not prevent the Palestinians from claiming they were *solely* responsible for *all* the attacks. Such a claim, true or not, unchallenged carries its own implicit authority.

"But they chose not to do so for quite other reasons."

Kate paused. Their prejudice had evaporated in an intense concentration and interest in what she was saying. She could see it had the effect of clearing their own minds and confirming their own thoughts.

"For many years the terrorists' most effective universal weapon has been the international hijack which reached epidemic proportions at Dawson's Field in the mid-seventies. Since then a number of hijacks have gone wrong; being faced with counter-attacks as at Mogadishu for example. The storming of aircraft and embassies and so on, the so called pre-emptive attacks made on certain cities, the bizarre circumstances surrounding the arrest of the *Achille Lauro* hijackers, have all rendered the hijack a most risky and desperate venture, possibly counter-productive. Recent events have shown, as they did with the Air India plane that blew up south of Ireland, that devastating loss of life can produce a change of public will which in turn can influence governments or produce significant political change within a country. These new outrages meet the criteria of success now required by freedom fighters but, good though they appear to be for securing success, our hypothesis suggests this is a *final* attack. However, there is no guarantee of clinching the matter. You stake all on a single hazard, and single hazards can go wrong.

"What, for instance, if the abused nations take it into their heads to emulate the United States and launch punitive strikes? This is a good reason for keeping quiet about responsibility, incidentally. If this is the case then the hazard has failed. The good general keeps something in reserve, something to plug the gap in the line or to toss into a faltering attack . . . I think we can expect something more, something with a very high emotional effect, heightened after such a period of silence and possibly supported by a series of minor sporadic attacks in various places which will demonstrate the vigour of the revolutionary movement, distract governments, disturb populations to the point of capitulation and secure for the Palestinians their final victory.

"I can see only one activity that currently offers them that kind of advantage, one that was tried with some success some years ago. It does have logistical disadvantages, but I imagine the present target was selected some time ago and these will already have been taken into account. I think the terrorists will capture for hostages either a hospital or a school, some semi-disciplined relatively self-contained place, full of people who are vulnerable and therefore emotive. I believe they will put forward their demands and I do not believe they will tolerate extended deadlines, that is a lesson they have learned from the past. What I cannot say is where that act will take place. Some well-organized groups have *not* been involved. This may argue their unwillingness to participate on behalf of others; they are, by definition, formed for a single purpose. But it may be true that they are to carry out this second phase. For example ETA, the Basque group, are not obvious perpetrators of the crimes we have considered to date, but Spain would be a likely target for a massive hostage-taking operation and the Basques are ruthless or dedicated enough to carry it out.

"The peculiar concentration of attacks on Britain, our proximity to the centres of activity of several groups and our special relationship with the United States, argue very favourably in selecting this country as the most obvious place, given the general unrest from which we are currently suffering."

She sat down. An uneasy silence filled the room.

HENDON, NORTH WEST LONDON

Kate woke from a disturbed sleep feeling terrible. Her exhausted body had demanded rest, her stimulated mind refused its permission. She had slipped quickly into an hour's deep sleep, woken from it as abruptly, and spent a miserable, restless night slipping fitfully through varying shades of consciousness, dreaming, worrying and imagining in a kaleidoscope of images so that, in the waking dawn, she could not distinguish fact from fantasy, nor fantasy from phantasmagoria.

In the hiatus following the outbreak of terrorist outrages she had crept home to her flat to sleep, and as she lay twisted in the bedclothes she recalled only the nub of the dream. It was of a man ascending from flames; as he climbed a ladder on what, in retrospect she supposed was an oil rig, he tore at his body which blistered and erupted in tiny explosions. His bare hands pulled aside layer upon layer of flesh, so that they became great iron claws. Yet the body did not diminish, but grew in size so that the popping explosions grew too, bursting around her and forming their own centres of maimed bodies. And over all a voice thundered with a terrible tone of accusation 'Gate Six! Gate Six!'

Shakily she got up and staggered into the kitchen to make some coffee. Her beating heart calmed and the pale daylight filtering reluctantly through the curtains reassured her. Sitting at the table she shook off the gloomy images that were the inevitable consequence of stress and overwork. But still she could not shake off the feeling that, if Lieutenant Commander Tiplady's intuition was right, great significance lay in those two words. While Nicholas and his team had questioned Mayhew and the helicopter pilot, the only two witnesses to the actual destruction of the Yankee and Zulu platforms, Kate had had a long talk with Tiplady. Probing, leading and, ultimately confusing the poor man, whom, she thought, probably felt he had been crudely psychoanalysed, she had established the reality of those unspoken communications between Hinton and Tiplady. With unerring skill and a practised confidence she tapped Tiplady's intuitive recognition of an ultimate defiance in Hinton, a defiance carried to the point of death.

She rang the incident room. Chief Superintendent Martin was put on.

"It's Kate, sir . . ."

"I thought you'd still be asleep. . . ."

"Have you run a check on Hinton?" she interrupted, her heart once again pumping adrenalin round her body.

"Well, a routine one, why?"

"Never mind why sir. I'll be there in an hour, in the meantime would you oblige me by repeating it, and this time making it a bit more than a routine check?"

She could almost hear Martin pausing. "Okay, Kate, for you I'll *kill* the bull. . . ." It was an old joke between them.

"I think you'll get more than the ears this time," she said, her tired face smiling. A few minutes later she was in the shower, and it was here that something else struck her.

NEW SCOTLAND YARD, LONDON

Kate was met by Martin on arrival. His eyes were shining with admiration for his protégé. "How the hell did you know?"

"Know what?"

"About Hinton. . . ."

"Feminine intuition. Now what is it I'm supposed to know?"

"Well, he's only been on the platform a comparatively short time, three months. He came with good character references and was well thought of by his seniors, in his last report the production engineer in charge of his shift spoke very highly of his above-average ability."

That man was dead now, Kate thought, as Martin turned over the page of his notes.

"He was a bit of an oddball then," she said, "round peg in a square hole."

"Yes. He had lodgings in Aberdeen, was quiet, didn't seem to have much of a social life but took off in his car quite a bit during his time ashore."

"Sex?"

"Nothing on that . . . we traced him back to Cardiff, his landlady at Aberdeen thought he had once mentioned his mother lived in Cardiff, but the trail went cold. That's as far as we'd got before your phone call this morning."

"I was with the Boss when you phoned. Old Nick said he thought you might be onto something. Mayhew's escape was explicable, he was less happy with Hinton's, though it had clearly gone wrong if it *was* an escape bid. And Hinton alone of the roustabouts on duty made the helicopter platform which was on the accommodation rig, *not* the production platform several hundred feet away. He argued that despite the delays available to the devisers of such bombs and what he quaintly called 'infernal machines', the complexities of guaranteeing the utter destruction of the Yankee/Zulu platforms argued the need for a man on the spot. . . ."

"Hinton."

"Yes."

"And did you get anything more on Hinton?"

"Yes. Nicholas suggested running through the incidents involving Welsh nationalists. In 1979 a young man was questioned in connection with the burning of a cottage near Porth Dinllaen, in North Wales. He was never charged and he came, not from Cardiff, but from Barry in the south. But the cottage was owned by a Brummie doctor, a man named Hinton."

"So he takes it as a *nom-de-guerre*. Which argues the collusion of the helicopter pilot."

"We're picking him up now."

Kate was pleased with the hunch that had led them to Hinton. He might be dead, but he had died fighting for a cause and that made the destruction of the two Gannet platforms an act of terror. But there was something else she wanted to pursue now, something that had come to her in the shower and stirred her sluggish body with a new excitement.

She reached for her pc, typed in the security code that gave her access to the desk menu, selected and punched in her priority rating for high-grade security access.

It was refused. Cursing her carelessness she repeated the command, carefully inserting the semi-colon without which knowledge of the codeword was useless. Again it was refused. She frowned; surely she had not been taken off the case? Suppressing a mounting anger born of over-tiredness and frustration, she carefully typed in the request for 'Help'. The sub-menu appeared and she typed out the request for the list of personnel at her security level.

Her name was not on it.

"What on earth . . . ?"

She recalled the basic menu and called up her own file. She saw the change immediately. Her security clearance rating had been altered. Somebody had moved damn fast, but encouraging though it was, she had to get the password, and that meant a personal interview with the Boss.

She had no trouble getting into Nicholas's office, but she had to wait another quarter of an hour before he finished a tedious phone call.

"Sometimes I wonder whose side the politicians are on," he said, putting down the telephone. "They want cake as well as a tea party . . . you've come for your new password." It was a statement, not a question.

"Yes sir."

"You did very well, Kate. I only wish it was giving us a positive lead by which we might pre-empt any further death and destruction. I've had a man from Britoil on this morning cataloguing the effects of the destruction of the Gannet platforms as though I can wave a magic wand and turn the clock back." He smiled. "Feel better after that sleep?"

"Much," she lied.

"Good. Your security rating's cleared to the top on this project. We're using 'Garibaldi', you'll find you'll be able to access everything with that and it'll avoid a lot of tedious cross-briefing. Are you hoping to pull another hunch?"

"Hoping, sir," Kate said cautiously.

"Good! By the way, that's 'Garibaldi' the freedom fighter, not 'Garibaldi' the biscuit."

"I'm glad to hear it, sir," she replied smiling back at him.

Returning to her desk she typed in the password, 'Garibaldi', and studied the menu. Then she selected the file on the Canadian airliner. It was painfully thin and she had already seen most of it. Whereas the other aircraft had simply blown up, air traffic control at Seattle had been in the act of talking to Algonquin Airways' short-haul flight AQ 32 when sudden silence and the loss of the plane's echo from the radar had given the alarm. She had seen the gist of the conversation in a transcript, but now she wanted to hear that conversation. There was also a new item filed on the menu. She put in a call to Nicholas and asked for special clearance to obtain a copy of the tape recording of the air traffic control conversation.

110

"All right," he replied, "it'll take a while, they're still in bed over there, but I'll get someone onto it."

She stared at the file and selected out the new item. It was the list of the missing people, the crew and passenger list of flight AQ 32; 85 persons, 3 of them children. They offered no clue beyond being casualties in a vicious skirmish in a dirty and protracted war.

Lighting a cigarette she felt hunger gnaw at her. She had had no breakfast. Closing down her desk VDU she went in search of something to eat.

She had only been back at her desk five minutes when Nicholas sent for her. He was rubbing his chin and with him were two civilians, Martin and another police officer whose name she did not know. They had obviously been listening to a tape, for a cassette recorder lay on the desk.

"Sit down, Chief Inspector," Nicholas said formally. "We would like to know why you asked for this," he tapped the cover of the cassette recorder. "It's a copy of the conversation between Seattle air control tower and Algonquin Airways flight AQ 32 sent via satellite link. Why did you ask for it, you'd already seen the transcription?"

"Just following a hunch, sir. . . ." She looked round at the circle of men. There was a distinct lack of cordiality in their eyes.

"It's all right," Nicholas said, "I've explained the unorthodoxy of your methods; please explain."

"Well, sir, in front of such witnesses, the explanation of a hunch seems rather trite. I would rather have had time to explore it a bit first, but if you insist. . . ."

"Yes, I do."

"It's just that I thought that something, I don't know what, might come out of the conversation . . . you see the only things we have to go on are the statement of Tiplady about a dying oil man and this conversation. There is no forensic evidence available yet beyond the statement that preliminary findings from the hotels indicate a second generation, long-fuse bomb such as the IRA used in the Brighton bombing. That's all really, sir. It sounds pretty lame when put like that." She paused, then added, "D'you mind if I ask why you think it's significant?"

"Because you've opened a can of worms, Miss Meldrum," put in one of the civilians.

"Listen to the tape first," said Nicholas, "I don't want you distracted at this point, we'll explain later, listen. . . ."

He switched on the tape recorder and there were some indistinct noises, then: "Hullo Seattle, yeah, this is AQ 32 on one-two-nine decimal seven, do you copy, come back." The voice was mellow, relaxed and there was a pause on the tape.

"That frequency," one of the civilians said, "One-two-nine point seven megaherz is a chat frequency, used for 'domestic' not flight information. Getting an engineer ready to look at a malfunction when the aircraft arrives, that sort of thing." He spoke with a mid-Atlantic accent.

"I see," said Kate, waiting for Seattle to reply.

"Okay AQ 32, understood you require two wheelchairs on arrival. That you Charlie?"

"Sure, Frank," said the mellow voice.

"Hi! Good flight?"

"Yeah, got a Quebequois pissed out of his mind out back, giving the stewardesses a bad time, come back. . . ."

"You got Avril with you? Come back."

"Yeah, complete with hot pants for you, Frank. Come back."

"Tell her I'm off at midnight."

"Okay . . . she's having a hard time with this drunk. Says he's mad to ball anyone called Avril . . . suppose it reminds him of his wife. See you, Out." The pleasant, mellow voice ended on a chuckle.

There was nothing else.

"Thirty seconds later the plane disappeared. They've found the wreckage but not the black box," said Nicholas pressing the stop button.

Kate stared about her. "It's just a bit of male chauvinistic repartee," she said somewhat archly, "I can't see where the can of worms comes into it. . . ."

"I telephoned an officer in the RCMP an hour or so ago, Miss Meldrum," said Nicholas formally. "He sent the tape over via satellite. The reason I got him in the middle of the night was because the Mounties are in a similar ferment to ourselves. But they've got more to go on. You see, on the passenger list of

112

Algonquin Airways flight AQ 32 was a certain Hubert Vauclois, a native of Quebec and formerly an activist in a breakaway group formed from the French-speaking minority.

"Vauclois had had a row recently with the group's leadership, that much was known to the anti-terrorist section of the RCMP. During the row Vauclois had flirted with a journalist, trying no doubt to secure a big pay-off for his story when he split. He had made arrangements to meet this journalist in a Seattle hotel and was on his way there when his aircraft exploded. The RCMP linked the two incidents when they found the journalist dead in his hotel room. In his diary was an appointment with 'H.V.' for the previous evening." Nicholas paused, "It looks as though the FLQ killed two birds with one stone."

"Yes," said Kate flatly, "but it doesn't get us very far, sir." She looked round at the men's faces.

"No," Nicholas said, a rueful look on his face, "we thought you might have been able to help."

She shrugged. "Sorry."

"So it's back to the waiting game, is it, Commander?" asked the older of the two civilians.

"Well, we do have the forensic evidence to come from the hotel bombings, sir," said Nicholas deferentially.

"That sounds like a bloody politician's answer, not a policeman's."

Kate stared after the man as he impatiently quit the room.

"You should bloody well know . . ." someone muttered.

"Steady, the Buffs!" said Nicholas, "I'm afraid he's right."

Kate played the tape again on headphones in the incident room. She went over it three times before the idea occurred to her. She looked again at the passenger list. Vauclois's was not the only French name on it, but it was the only French name that fitted Vauclois's sex and age. The others belonged to a woman and her two children, a teenage student and an elderly lady. Vauclois was the drunken Quebequois, that much must have been obvious to Nicholas and his hatchet-faced gang. Perhaps she had disappointed Nicholas in not pointing that out. But she had bought herself more time to think.

113

She went over the tape again. Frank, the air traffic controller, was obviously having an *affaire* with the hostess Avril. Vauclois, drunk as a lord for obvious reasons, was – how did the pilot put it? – giving her a hard time saying 'he's mad to ball anyone called Avril'. She frowned, perhaps the pilot had been called back into the aircraft and witnessed this charming little incident, but drunks did not say they were mad to ball people, though she knew well what the American-style slang meant. No, the pilot Charlie, had bowdlerised the drunken words. Vauclois had been using a different expression. She slipped on the headphones again and played back the phrase, over and over.

"I'd like to fuck Avril," she said, conviction entering her mind. Yes, that's what Vauclois, on his way to betray his comrades in the FLQ and anaesthetizing his conscience with booze, had exclaimed to the hostess when he knew her name. "I'd like to fuck Avril!"

Kate turned scarlet when she realized everyone in the incident room was staring at her and she was almost shouting the phrase out. She whipped off the headphones and apologized, picked up a telephone and spoke to the information section.

"I want to know whether the hostesses on Algonquin Airlines wear their names on their uniforms, got it?"

She put the phone down and ignoring the sniggers returned to Nicholas's office. One of the civilians was still there. This time he was introduced as someone from the Canadian embassy; she guessed he was probably the military attaché.

"I would like information on Vauclois sir. I want to know whether he associated with any girls, prostitutes or whatever, called Avril."

Nicholas looked up at the Canadian.

"That's smart, Miss Meldrum," the Canadian said, "and the answer's 'no', we've already checked."

Somewhat crestfallen Kate returned to her desk. There was a fresh burst of sniggering in the incident room but she ignored it again and sat down. Drawing her notebook towards her she wrote the phrase, underlining the name 'Avril'. Did Vauclois simply express drunken lust at the prospect of the now dead hostess Avril, who was clearly desirable enough to keep Frank

114

from Seattle on tenterhooks? No, the pilot had not suggested that, so whatever Vauclois had said it seemed certain that his implication had not been quite so simple; and that, Kate thought, was in accord with the likely state of his mind, given his intention in Seattle.

She underlined 'Avril' again, laid down her pencil and lit a cigarette. Expelling the smoke, she had to confess she was going nowhere fast. She reached out her hand and lifted the previous page. There, at the bottom, she had underlined something else, another blind lead, the two words 'Gate Six'.

So, the sum total of five day's work was three words, two uttered by a Welsh nationalist dying of third degree burns aboard a British warship, one by a drunken defector from a French minority group dedicated to the secession of the Canadian province of Quebec a few seconds before his treachery was punished by sudden death.

Kate sighed. A Welshman and a French-speaking Canadian, somehow implicated on the fringes of the most concentrated terrorist attack the world had yet seen with a death toll totalling thousands.

She sat up suddenly. *French* speaking . . . !

She crossed out 'Avril' and translated it: April.

April. Gate Six. . . .

"God!"

She crossed out a letter, stared a moment, tested the idea and then re-spelt it:

'April Eight Six.'

In April 1986, carrierborne bombers from the United States Sixth Fleet had bombed Tripoli and Benghazi, two Libyan cities. The act was aimed as a punitive strike at a state alleged to have patronized international terrorists. Vengeance for this act had long been promised.

Kate's hand was shaking as she picked up the desk telephone and punched Nicholas's number.

"Yes?"

"Chief Inspector Meldrum, sir."

"Oh . . . yes . . . ?"

She knew she was bothering him, that he was losing patience with her at her frequent interruptions.

115

"I'd like to see you again, it's important, sir."

"All right."

She rose and the phone on her desk rang. Standing, she picked it up.

"Yes?"

"Your query about the Algonquin Airlines, Ma'am. Yes, the hostesses wear their names embroidered on the left lapel of their uniform jackets. It's part of what the airline calls 'Good, old-fashioned Canadian hospitality', Ma'am."

"Thank you." She put down the telephone and went to see Nicholas. Kate could see he was tired, not just of her, but exhausted.

"I've got an ID, sir. . . ."

"*What?*" Nicholas snapped.

"I think that very soon we are going to hear that the terror campaign is being waged by an organisation, or rather an alliance of organisations known collectively as 'April 86'"

Nicholas leaned back in his chair and expelled air. "Query any information under that name known to the CIA, French, Israeli, Indian, Italian, Japanese and West German agencies. If they clamp down let me know."

"Yes sir . . . you look as though you could do with some sleep."

Nicholas leaned forward on his elbows. "Kate, you've done wonders, but it's not game, set and match for me. Whatever they're called they haven't finished yet. What I really need to know is – where next?"

"But what about the helicopter pilot, sir?" she asked frowning.

"Vanished, Kate, disappeared, and to think we had him sitting here in the middle of us!"

Nicholas sat late in his office, half waiting for the news he knew must come eventually. If Chief Inspector Meldrum's theories were right this offensive would only succeed on momentum. He looked at his watch. He would watch the news shortly.

He ought also to have some response to the enquiries he had initiated into the make-up of the April 86 Group.

But mostly he was dominated by his failure to have held the

helicopter pilot. Wrapped in an heroic aura it seemed inconceivable that the man had been involved with the roustabout 'Hinton', he had seemed so confident, so sure of himself. But then of course he would. Hinton had died, that much of the plan had misfired, but in picking up Mayhew the heroism of the pilot found an advocate.

Nicholas slammed his hand down on the desk in self-disgust, got up and began pacing the office in silent fury. After a few minutes he sat down, drew open a locker door and pulled out a small, coloured television and switched it on. The BBC news was just starting.

"Reports are just coming in that Israeli air and armour strikes have failed to penetrate the outer defences of Sidon today, despite a massive and unprecedented build-up of Israeli forces. . . ."

There was shaky, hand-held video film of crumbling masonry and a tank moving ponderously through the falling rubble of a collapsing building. A steadier shot of a field gun crew labouring in brilliant sunshine panned round to white roofs, green trees and a distant brown hill dotted with the dark spots of an olive grove.

"Claims from Radio Sidon stated that two Israeli Kfir fighters were shot down by SAM rockets. . . ."

An elongated silver triangle trailing wing-tip vortices sliced across the blue sky ejecting a puff of yellow into which a second streak ran before exploding. The screen threw up the legend: *Library Pictures*.

"We hope to bring you a full report from our correspondent later in the programme. Meanwhile," went on the newscaster, "The Prime Minister, facing a crucial first week in office, has been touring the shattered streets of London this afternoon. . . ."

A trail of media cameramen jostled about the posse of rain-coated figures that walked across the ruins of London's Dorchester Hotel. The famous facade had crumbled into the street. A frock-coated commissionaire stood among the rubble.

The camera homed in on the face of the new Prime Minister. He was asked for his reactions. He paused and turned to face batteries of cameras, his eyes reflecting the popping bulbs of the fill-in flashes.

"My reactions are those of horror, over one hundred people have been killed or injured in this building alone. . . ."

"What is the British Government going to do to stop these outrages?"

"The British Government will do everything in its power to stop all outrages against innocent people."

"What does that mean, prime Minister?"

"It is essential that answers are not just found to the prevention of terrorist outrages in the United Kingdom, but answers found to the causes of the acts themselves."

"Bloody cant," said Nicholas, his mood unmollified by the news. Reaching forward he pressed the off button.

Chapter Five

ADVENTURER, SOUTH ATLANTIC

Stephanos entered the radio room of the *Adventurer* with the morning coffee. The right hand of the two bulkhead clocks registered the ship's local time as 10.00.

"Good morning." He was smilingly cheerful, despite the fact that it was not David Gordon who was on watch, but the Third Radio Officer, a fat slug of a man named Crabtree who suffered from boils on his neck and gave off a strong scent of musk. Stephanos concealed his dislike and put the coffee down on the wide desk.

Crabtree turned in the swivel chair, took his feet off the desk and unhooked one earphone of the headset.

"Ta." The monosyllabic courtesy of West Yorkshire went unrecognized by Stephanos, whose eager and curious gaze raked the cabinets of dials and switches, and came to rest on the VDU of the Satcomm system. Crabtree knew that Gordon gave the steward a daily news round-up, but was of a less obliging nature. As far as Crabtree was concerned Stephanos could go and screw himself.

"You go ashore in Rio, Mr Crabtree?" Stephanos asked pleasantly.

Crabtree looked at the steward over the rim of his coffee cup.

"Yeah. Met the girl from Ipanema."

Stephanos grinned. "You have good time, eh, Mr Crabtree?"

"Yeah ..." Crabtree looked at the steward and wondered whether to boast a little, but he rejected the idea, preferring another game. He put his headset on properly and turned back to his MF radio. There was a friend of his on a homeward bound

119

Blue Star reefer and the greasy wop could go and whistle for his news printout.

Stephanos hesitated. It was important that he got the news today, but Crabtree's attitude only hardened the steward's resolve. As he turned to the door, Gordon walked in.

"Morning. Ah, Stephanos, want your newspaper?"

Stephanos switched on the smile immediately. It was easy with a man like David Gordon. Stephanos liked Gordon; the 'Sparks' was a kind and considerate man, the antithesis of his obnoxious colleague. "Oh yes, please."

"I had one printed earlier. When you're a rich Greek ship-owner you'll be able to have a Saturn terminal on your yacht and get the New York stock exchange news while sunning yourself in the Aegean."

"Oh yes, Mr Gordon," Stephanos said, his eyes narrowing slightly, "when I get a big yacht. . . ." He broke off, laughing, and taking the sheets of paper left the radio room.

"I don't know why you make such a fuss of that bloody wop," grunted Crabtree, acknowledging the presence of the senior radio officer.

"Because he's interested, which is more than I can say for some people."

"Hey, what the bloody hell is that supposed to mean, eh? He's a bloody steward and it's his job to bring in my coffee when I'm on watch and then sod off. You know it's against regulations. . . ."

"Oh, for Christ's sake! All he wants is the news, and he's interested in the radio equipment, he's only a kid, there's no need to treat him like a leper."

Crabtree pulled the headset down and affected to ignore his chief, while Gordon left the man to his pathetic prejudices and began to leaf through the day's paperwork already mounting up on his desk.

On the top was a telegram to be sent on behalf of one of the first-class passengers: Mrs Rebanowicz wished to book a double suite at the San Francisco Hilton when *Adventurer* disembarked her passengers at the end of the cruise.

Gordon raised an eyebrow and filed the message for transmission.

*   *   *

Captain Smythe glanced up from his own papers at the knock on the cabin door. He looked at the clock. It was far too early for a drink, but he wanted one before the coming interview. Sighing he turned to the intercom.

"Come in."

Palmer entered the cabin. It was thickly-carpeted, furnished in light oak and the bulkheads were fabric-covered. Only the barograph and barometer indicated the traditional décor of command, although Smythe himself sat at his desk, his beard and his high colour the familiar hallmarks of his trade. Men changed much slower than their environment, Palmer thought.

"You sent for me, sir."

"Yes, Mr Palmer, I did."

Smythe leaned back in his chair and looked the tall young man up and down. Palmer guessed the visit was not going to be pleasant.

"You didn't go ashore in Rio, Mr Palmer?"

"No sir." He had nothing to go ashore for; Lila was on board.

"Mr Palmer," said Smythe, leaning forward and seemingly reading Palmer's mind, "if you want to sleep with stewardesses you should hire a hotel room ashore. You don't do it aboard any ship I'm in command of!"

"How the . . . ?" Palmer choked off the angry response he was about to make. "With respect, sir. . . ." he began.

"With respect, Mr Palmer, an order is an order. Your duty is to keep the passengers happy, not to give trollops a good time."

"Miss Molina is not a trollop, sir."

"She is as long as she's sleeping with one of my officers."

Palmer paused. He would do little good in riling Smythe and at the moment it looked as though Smythe was going to let him off with a warning.

"Do you mind if I ask how you know, sir?"

"No. I don't mind you asking. But I don't propose to answer and I think less of you for doing so."

Palmer frowned. Up to this point he had enjoyed a good relationship with *Adventurer*'s captain. Smythe was a good man, a little addicted to drink, perhaps, but that was quite usual; certainly his professionalism was well past muster. But there was something implied in his remark that irritated Palmer. Smythe had clearly been considering his second officer, presumably as a result of the information laid against Palmer. Somebody had been attempting to prejudice Captain Smythe's opinion of him.

"Sir, if I am the victim of some malicious . . ."

"Mr Palmer," cut in the captain, "you've as good as admitted that you and Miss Molina are fornicating. . . ."

"Sir, I object! I'm not a married man, I was off duty, I had done everything required of me. I don't see what business it is . . ."

"Damn you, Palmer!" Smythe's fat but powerful fist crashed down onto the desk top, making the malachite pen stand jump. "I know what you're thinking. This isn't a British ship and maybe I'm a trifle old-fashioned, but *I'm* British and I'm not having you fraternizing with the bloody crew to the extent of fucking them. D'you hear me, sir? I command here and it's your job to obey. It's bad for morale and it's bad for you. You should be taking more interest in the passengers with whatever spare energies you've got. That's what they pay you for. I know you've been skulking around after dinner with that queer fellow Galvin, but you're supposed to take a full part in the social life of the ship."

"I took part in the Crossing the Line ceremony." He wanted to tell Smythe that he loved Lila, but the power of his passion was not to be trivialized in such mean self-defence. Instead he took refuge in an equally justified anger. "What was wrong with my performance, sir? Do I lack the theatricality of Captain Meredith, sir? Because if I do, perhaps I should remind you that I'm a seaman, not a gigolo. . . ."

Smythe had opened his mouth to speak, but when Palmer mentioned the staff captain's name he had hesitated and Palmer had spotted the hesitation

"Yes, I thought so. . . ."

A silence fell, briefly, between them, then Smythe rallied. He was a man to whom command now came as habit. In such circumstances judgement was not entertained. It had been the same with the Yankee pilot.

"Mr Palmer, I am not interested in your opinions or in prolonging the present interview. I have made known my orders to you. That is all."

Palmer stared down at the captain as he bent to the papers on his desk. He was almost choking with a furious emotion.

"Yes sir." He spoke through teeth clenched with the strain of keeping himself under control. As he closed the cabin door and stood for a long moment outside in the alleyway, he slowly expelled his breath.

"You old *bastard*!" He hissed, while beyond the door Captain Smythe reached for a bottle of gin.

Palmer lay on his bunk, staring up at the deckhead. He had half an hour before he must go onto the bridge for his afternoon's watch. The choking lump was still in his throat. There was no doubt that he would disobey Smythe's order. He was involved too deeply with Lila now even though she remained enigmatic. Palmer was no novice with women and he forbore to enquire into her past life. She would eventually tell him all there was to know about Mayaguez and the convent school where she had picked up Latin along with a fair education and a smattering of socialist dogma as a necessary antidote to a surfeit of nuns. Palmer was too intoxicated with the power of her love-making, for she seemed more self-contained than any woman he had known previously. The fact vaguely disturbed him, except that its satisfaction wrapped him in waves of a perfection he had never thought existed.

If Kate Meldrum had repaired the damage of a failed marriage, Lila Molina had effaced all previous sexual experience and replaced it with something quite unique. He was damned if he was going to let it go in obedience to some outdated, misguided code of suspect ethics!

He knew Meredith had shopped him; but how? Surely DeAth had not ... but no. Simon was a dirty little devil who played his own games, but shopping Palmer was not his style. Not Aymes, surely?

"Bloody hell!" Palmer sat up just as the cabin door opened

and, as though conjured up by some diabolical mechanism, the surgeon walked in. He carried a bottle of Glenmorangie and two glasses.

"The Doctor's here, Tim, me lad, and it's time you had your medicine . . . I've heard all about it on the jungle drums."

"*You* didn't shop me, did you?"

Aymes poured the whisky and raised one eyebrow. Passing a glass to Palmer he looked the second officer in the eye. "Don't be stupid, Tim. Why the hell would I do that? I got the photostats, remember."

"Look, I'm pretty sure Meredith told the Old Man, but I can't work out how Meredith knew and why the bastard's got it in for me. I mean he could have come and had a quiet word with me."

"And what would you have said to him?"

"I'd have told him to mind his own business."

"Bad for Big Chief's dignity. Lose plenty face. Better see Bigger Chief. Bigger Chief chop unruly Brave down to size." Aymes drank the whisky, making a gesture of notional toasting in Palmer's direction. "And what did Bigger Chief say? Don't touch Blackfoot squaw? Mohawk Brave not sully himself with Blackfoot squaw?"

"Something like that," replied Palmer, smiling despite himself.

"And what are you going to do about it, Tim?" asked Aymes seriously.

Palmer felt the raw malt whisky uncoil its warmth in his belly. He looked at the doctor. "Nothing."

Aymes made a face. "Have I got a case of true love on my hands?"

Palmer turned away and stared out through the cabin window to the hard blue line of the distant horizon. He said nothing for a moment, then: "Look, Jonathan, I know you don't approve and I know you think it's stupid. . . ."

"How d'you know I don't approve? And why should you suppose that I should think it's stupid?"

Palmer turned. Aymes met his eyes for a few seconds and then dropped his own to the empty glass he held. "It is, of course, quite preposterously bloody stupid, Tim, me lad, but

124

if it's *love* . . ." he refilled his glass and held the bottle out to Palmer who shook his head, "if it's love it's incurable. Medicine Man recommend strong firewater only cure, but cure worse than disease . . . SNAFU. . . ."

"SNAFU?"

"Situation normal, all fucked-up, story of human race, epic tragedy, don't know why the bloody hell I ever went to medical school."

Palmer smiled again. "I'm sorry." Aymes's raw nerve lay exposed like the anchor cables on the fo'c's'le.

"There's no reason why you should be, Tim, me lad. It's me that's sorry for you. After all, I've got used to it."

Palmer knew by the middle of the afternoon watch. Somehow Aymes's half-confessed, half-sympathetic gesture switched him out of the narrow channel of morbid introspection. His mind was still full of his rupture with Captain Smythe and the unwitting enmity he somehow aroused in Staff Captain Meredith, but he was calmer in himself, more detached and objective about the incident. He was turning his mind to the practical ways in which he could continue to see Lila without arousing further suspicions when DeAth approached him.

"Tim. . . ."

"Aren't you supposed to be working out a compass error?"

"The sun's still too bloody high . . . look, I heard about what happened. . . ."

"Bloody hell, does the whole ship know?"

"Of course not. It's just that I thought, with my being on watch with you and you having the girls up here on the middle watch . . . well, that you might draw the wrong conclusions."

Palmer stared at his watch mate. DeAth was shorter than himself and, he realized, was painfully aware of their difference in rank. He was not a bad fellow and was obviously showing his sympathy.

"As if I would . . . I just wonder how the Old Man. . . ."

"Don't you know?" DeAth said with such asperity that Palmer, in the act of turning away, looked back at him.

"No."

"Melanie. She's got hot pants for you, she's absolute dynamite Tim, bloody exhausting, but dynamite . . . didn't you know? She gives your bit of stuff a really rough time. Did you really not know?"

"No."

"Yes, she came snooping around up here in Rio, I told her you had done all your chart work and gone below."

"Oh, hell!" Palmer had a vision of the purserette outside his cabin door and he recalled Lila making a reference to having been in some trouble for not being 'available'.

"But you were off-duty," Palmer had said to Lila, annoyed.

"Workers are never off-duty," Lila had snapped back in a rare moment of uncontrolled anger. He had forgotten the incident, reading into it no more than the passing spitefulness of normal ship-board human relations.

"If it's not romance its a fucking feud," said DeAth philosophically, recalling Palmer to the present.

"Thanks for the warning," said Palmer, "it looks as though it's going to be one of those voyages."

DeAth brightened at the tone of cynicism in Palmer's voice. "It's always one of *those* voyages. Why don't you try knocking off Zelda Rebanowicz? That'd *really* have old Meredith climbing out of his pram."

But Palmer was thinking more about what the man in London had said.

Zelda Rebanowicz had been 'awkward' since the *Adventurer* had been in Rio de Janeiro. The great white ship had steamed slowly into Rio Bay with the dawn, early sunlight gilding the statue of Christ. The Sugar Loaf and the surrounding mountains were dramatically highlighted in pale gold with purple shadows. The sands at the water's edge had fallen back to the white monoliths of the city's tower blocks which also gleamed in the dawn's freshness.

Zelda had stood at the picture window of her first-class suite situated just behind the bridge but discreetly screened from the rest of the ship. Behind her in the cabin Giorgio had been dressing and, as she pulled back the curtains and stood, arms outstretched and naked, she felt a great peace and happiness at the beautiful view.

She had turned briefly back into the cabin to speed Giorgio about his day's duties, pulled a satin wrap about her glowing body and returned to the window. Sliding it open she stepped out onto the small verandah that belonged exclusively to her cabin.

The moist warmth of the tropical air caressed her sensuously as she stretched herself. At his most unfaithful, her husband could never have felt like this, she thought, for her revenge now seemed complete. Zelda's Greek god was wonderful and had enraptured her, releasing her from her past when she could respond at the height of her powers. She looked up at the benedictory Christ and felt a sweet and pagan defiance fill her.

But her mood did not last. As the *Adventurer* glided to her berth and the waking city enveloped her, the ethereal quality of the day faded. The small attentions Giorgio customarily paid her during the course of a day at sea vanished; she was bundled off ashore by the purser's staff to see the sights, to swing up the Sugar Loaf in a cable car and toil up the hill where the mighty statue revealed itself as a cracked and man-made image, to gaze in frustration at the beautiful bodies of Brazilians idling the day on the beach at Copacabana while an irritating tape on their air-conditioned coach played *The Girl from Ipanema* with a monotonous insistence that only increased Zelda's edginess. She found her fellow-passengers equally annoying and longed only to return to the ship, her bath, and a lubricious preparation for the ritual of the night.

In the event, that too disappointed her. Giorgio was too busy and did not come to her. She saw him briefly; he seemed preoccupied and, to Zelda's expectant mood, off-hand. She felt spurned, simplistically attributing Giorgio's indifference to the attractions of the shore. She had seen the lithe and lissom girls on the Copacabana. . . .

Rio had disappointed her, but her 'awkwardness' had begun when the ship sailed and she still had not seen Giorgio. She had kept the service bell in continuous use, making impossible and excessive demands upon the stewards and stewardesses who came to answer it. But Giorgio was not one of them, nor was Lila, by whom she might have passed a message to her lover.

In the anger of her frustration, Zelda Rebanowicz saw only the rejection of her ageing body and seemed to hear, in the loneliness of her luxurious apartment, the laughter of the stone Christ.

Margaret Allen had not joined the tourists. She had been to Rio de Janeiro before, many years earlier, with her husband. She had sat with Galvin on the almost deserted deck, reading one of several books she had purposely brought with her. She had lent another to the doctor. A portable radio had been playing, the property of one of the deckhands who was cleaning up a patch of scaled rust, industriously covering the primer with white paint while the passengers were ashore. Neither Galvin nor Margaret minded the rhythmic background music, nor took much notice of the punctuations of the disc jockey's Portuguese.

Margaret knew a few words of the language and was distracted only once when a news bulletin announced the disappearance of two airliners and some hotel bombings. The news had impinged on her peace, turning up memories and awakening old fears, but she calmed herself. The incidents were a long way from Rio de Janeiro and the fear was no worse than that of a half-forgotten nightmare. She had returned to her novel, not troubling Galvin with the news.

Lila had missed the news of the terrorist bombings due to the opportunity she and Palmer had taken to make love in his cabin. Anna, alone in *Adventurer*'s linen room, amid the mountains of dirty laundry which it was her task to sort for the wash, had heard on the transistor radio she habitually worked with. She had looked at her watch when she heard, pausing hardly at all as she threw towels and sheets into separate piles, but her twisted face bore the grimace of a smile.

Giorgio knew at Rio and despite the sustained fire of his lust for Mrs Rebanowicz, was too busy to see her until some time after the ship had left the Brazilian port. While

Tim Palmer pondered on the undeserved treachery of Melanie Corbett and the unprovoked dislike of Staff Captain Meredith, Giorgio slipped into Zelda Rebanowicz's cabin. He had seen her briefly during the morning, pleading the distraction of work and passing the news that he would be free of the ship when it reached San Francisco.

"Can you please find me some place to stay? With your friends perhaps, even ..." and his eyes had been eloquent of unsatisfied passion in the public place of the arcade, while his voice dropped to a whisper "... with you."

Hardly daring to breathe, Mrs Rebanowicz had enquired from the purser's office how she might make a reservation in the San Francisco Hilton. It presented no problem to the ship's staff at all, she was informed.

When Giorgio came to her in his off-duty period after lunch, their love-making was as if after an absence of weeks.

Lila heard of the bombings from Giorgio and waited for the confirmation that Stephanos brought in the news printout from the radio room. In the evening, when she knew Palmer was dressing for dinner, she telephoned his cabin. They had not seen each other since Rio.

"It's me...."

"Hullo, have you had a bad time? I heard that that bitch Melanie ..."

"Never mind. It doesn't matter. It is better we do not see each other, just for a day."

"Yes," Palmer said, surprised at the prescience of the girl, "let the hue and cry die down."

"I don't understand that expression."

"No, of course, I'm sorry. Lila.... ?"

"Yes?"

"I can't wait very long."

"No ... I ..." She hesitated, as though making up her mind to something. "I cannot either. You have been in trouble too?"

"Yes. Big trouble." There was a pause.

"I'm glad." she said, and hung up. Her heart was pounding as she turned from the telephone on the bulkhead. Melanie Corbett was bearing down on her and she picked up the bucket.

129

"One of those bloody kids has thrown up all over the carpet in 5224, for God's sake get down there, I sent for you ages ago!"

Lila brushed past the neatly dressed and pretty woman. Melanie Corbett stared after her, utterly at a loss to see the attraction of such a severe person as the stewardess. The dark stain of perspiration on the back of Lila's overall failed to give Melanie any satisfaction. It only served to confuse and anger her.

NEW SCOTLAND YARD, LONDON

Kate Meldrum was the only senior police officer left in the ops room that evening. She was looking over the notes she had made after watching the TV video recording of the Palestinian observers and their reaction to the news of the United Nations débâcle.

How much was she trying to fool herself? There had been all the classic Arab gestures of resignation, the eloquent submission to the will of Allah, a readily recognisable piece of 'body-language' to anyone with only the sketchiest knowledge of the Middle East. But she had been looking for less obvious signs. Tiny symptoms of triumph or of something rather like the triumph that might come to desperate men to whom an unwitting world had, by their own standards, just given *carte-blanche* to launch their own brand of ultimate sanction.

She had studied the corners of mouths, the tiny, reactive muscles surrounding the eyes, the gestures of hands. At first she had had all her suspicions confirmed. But her confidence had evaporated by the time she had looked at the thing for the twentieth showing. She sensed the psychiatrist's compulsion to make the case facts fit the theory. In the end she knew only that she had smoked too many cigarettes and she wanted a shower. It was an irritation to remember that her Escort was off the road having a new exhaust fitted. She turned a page in her notebook, lit a final cigarette and sat back.

The pot had gone off the boil. Had they had a trail, that

130

would have run cold, but they had been deprived of that false satisfaction by the disappearance of the helicopter pilot. It did not do to dwell too much on that episode. She knew Nicholas blamed himself for letting the lead slip so easily through his fingers. They had traced the man back to his home. His bank account was untouched, his ex-wife knew only that he had said he would not be around for a bit. Twenty-four hours later immigration at Dover had turned up the fact that a male foot passenger had left on the *Free Enterprise VII* on a non-existent passport. They apologized for letting the matter slip their attention. Nothing had been seen on the French side. The following day, via a circuitous route that was surprising with the promptness of the intelligence, a report arrived on Nicholas's desk indicating that an Audi Quattro had been parked for two days in Abbeville. It bore West German plates but had vanished while the local police were pursuing routine and rather dilatory enquiries as to its ownership. Comparing timetables it had gone within four to seven hours of the *Free Enterprise VII*'s crossing.

It was cold comfort to Nicholas.

"You hungry?"

Kate looked up. Nicholas was haggard and she felt an instant sympathy.

"Yes, but I must shower and I'm not going out dressed like this."

"That's all right." He seemed utterly beyond argument.

"My car's in dock," she said lamely, standing and picking up her handbag.

"I'll drive you."

They were half way up the Finchley Road before either of them spoke.

"They found out I let the helicopter pilot slip through our fingers."

"Who's 'they'?"

"Home Office."

"Oh."

"I wish," he began and then subsided into silence.

"If only something would happen, it would end this bloody suspense." He half turned and smiled at her.

"That's not what you should be thinking, Kate," he admonished gently. "According to your theory, it might be schoolchildren next time."

"I know." She paused, tired herself, though mercifully free of the recriminations of those with power. "You don't seem too keen on my theory."

"No, nothing personal. It was argued with cogent logic and your paper was first class. You drew attention to the growing respectability of the terrorist organisations, how they are battening on Western capitalism to generate funds for their campaigns. I especially liked your elucidation on their involvement in the new national airline of Costa Maya, but somehow a school did not ring true. . . ."

She was disappointed, but after having studied the faces of the two Arabs in New York she shared his own scepticism.

"I expect there'll be questions in the House tomorrow. Somebody will have leaked something by now." He fell silent again. They crossed the flyover at Brent Cross and she directed him for the last mile.

Her heart was fluttering slightly as she showed him into the flat. She found half a bottle of Scotch that Tim had left.

"Help yourself to a drink. I won't be long."

"Thank you." Uncuriously he sank into the settee. He was fast asleep when she came out of her bedroom. He had not touched the whisky. She stood looking at him. Relaxed, his face was smoother; one would not dream of calling it boyish, but sleep robbed it of influence from his powerful personality. It was a pleasant face; the face of a man of dedication, neither fanatical nor brutal. Kate knew she was weakening towards him and hurried into the kitchen, her hair still damp. She had the double pack of 'Gourmet Spaghetti Bolognaise' slowly turning under the microwave before she recalled they were supposed to be eating out. Somehow it had seemed quite natural to cater for him. The double pack of convenience food was a remnant of Tim's occupation of the flat.

"Nice flat, Chief Inspector."

His voice startled her as she was dishing up the meal. He stood in the doorway of the tiny kitchen, the glass of whisky turning slowly in his hand. "I'm sorry I fell asleep."

She smiled up at him. "That's all right. I thought this was a better idea than traipsing round Hendon."

"Yes, that's very kind of you."

"I'll bring it out if you don't mind eating off your knees."

He was looking at the photograph of Tim that she had tucked in the bookshelf when she carried the two steaming plates through.

"Oh, God . . . I'd forgotten about that."

He seemed surprised at her confusion. "You don't have to apologize. He looks a decent enough man."

"I'll get some Parmesan cheese." She fled to the kitchen, furious with herself, reappearing with the cheese and half a bottle of white table wine.

He had put the photograph down, but was standing, looking at the spines of the books.

"You don't see hardback books around these days. My father had shelves of them."

"Some of those are Tim's."

He sat down again and took the offered glass. "So I gathered. I didn't recognize Danton's 'Seamanship' as essential reading for even the most ambitious women police inspectors."

The joke killed the spectre of Tim Palmer and for a moment they ate in companionable silence. Then quite suddenly, Nicholas stopped masticating. He stared into the middle distance, his fork poised, the snakes of white spaghetti trailing ignored from its tines. He looked as though he had had a seizure.

"Are you all right?" Kate asked sharply.

"Yes . . . a ship . . . that's it . . . a bloody ship! We've virtually ignored the precedent of the *Achille Lauro.* . . ."

Kate frowned. "No sir, it was mentioned, you sent out a warning via Portsmouth Radio."

Nicholas looked at her as though from a distance. "Portishead . . ." he corrected. "Yes, I know, but we've never followed up the idea."

"There's been no report. . . ."

"There might not be with a ship. It would explain the delay, perhaps the April 86 people have to wait for something. I don't know much about ships. It's a pity your Tim can't help us."

Kate felt her heart thump. "Did you know that Alex Martin asked me about Tim, helped to get him a job? The only thing I ever got out of him was that he had a friend in shipping, but he was hedging . . . at the time. . . ." She paused, flushing with embarrassment.

"Go on . . ." Nicholas was suddenly attentive. "Go on, Kate."

"Well, I thought, to be quite honest and knowing that certain parties didn't approve. . . ."

"That the promising young and beautiful Chief Inspector Meldrum shouldn't be seduced by a drunken sailor . . . should be kept in the force, so to speak."

"Yes. I know it sounds conceited, but it did cross my mind."

"I wish it had crossed mine." He reached a hand across the table. She put down her fork and took it.

"It didn't, but it does now."

She could not remember afterwards how she capitulated so easily or how they reached the bedroom. What lasted beyond the last flickerings of a protracted climax was the memory of his slow and delicate love-making rolling them gently together through the long night.

Chapter Six

Simon DeAth was the first to die.

Plotting the 0200 Magnavox Satellite Navigator fix on the chart, Palmer heard the single staccato cough of the silenced Makarov and thought it was DeAth himself.

He was aware of someone blocking the port chart room door, shutting out the noise of the sea and the night wind. He turned. If he had been some way prepared for what might possibly happen aboard the *Adventurer* he had not expected what now confronted him. He gasped with horror and shock at her face.

Anna stepped into the chartroom, her eyes chips of coal. In the light from the chart table the ribs of scarred flesh showed with startling clarity, some trick of the dimmed light reflected back from the plane surface of the chart. The sight shocked him more than the dull gleam of the snub-barrelled gun pointed at his belly.

"Keep still!"

He had half turned, aware that someone else was on his other side. Lila, a machine-gun at her hip, came into his line of vision.

"Lila. . . ."

Her eyes were impassive. "Be quiet. Do *exactly* what we say. *Exactly!*"

Palmer felt sweat breaking out, prickling the surface of his skin. Despite the knowledge he had boarded the ship with, despite the precautionary nature of his shopping trip in Charleston, he had been caught unawares. These were the last two he had marked down as suspects and yet, as he felt his knees shake, he realized how stupid he had been. The evidence had been screaming at him. Lila's nocturnal jogging, the brief revelations of her socialist sympathies and the strange allusion to anarchy she had made the night they saw the milk sea. Then there was Anna's reference to Prudhon, Lila's Latin and the glimpses of both girls having been educated far beyond the requirements of a stewardess.

Some of these things could be explained by the false assumption of Puerto Rican nationality and the oppression of the Catholic convent. But Palmer realized that Lila had betrayed herself to him alone in the hardness of purpose he had found so erotic in the desperation of her sexual passion. He remembered with chagrin his own intuition at the sinuously oriental waist that had first aroused him to a peak of lust he had never before experienced. He had been gulled, duped for a cunt-struck fool.

"Let me see the chart." Lila jerked her gun barrel and he moved aside. Anna's eyes never left him as he watched Lila manipulate the parallel rulers and the dividers. He noticed the practiced ease with which she marked a position and measured the distance. She looked up at him. Staring back at her it seemed impossible that he had seen that mouth moan in ecstasy beneath his heaving body.

"Telephone the engine room. Order them to make the maximum speed possible. Say the captain orders it."

He swallowed. The man in London had told him what to do, but not how to do it. He felt his heartbeat subside. They were not going to shoot him. Yet.

He moved across into the wheelhouse proper. In the faint light from the console LEDs he saw the body of the quartermaster slumped in a corner. A similar heap lay out on the grey planking of the port bridge wing: Simon DeAth. The fateful aptitude of the fifth officer's surname struck him. He picked up a telephone and dialled.

"MCR. Third speaking . . ." Palmer could hear the faint whine of turbo-blown machinery.

"Morning Charlie, Tim . . . the Old Man wants her wound right up, full throttle."

"Nothing in my night orders from the Chief."

"No. Bad forecast just come in. If we push ahead a bit we

might dodge round a depression. Got to look after the cargo, no spilled Martinis, eh?"

"Okay Tim, it's some time since we opened her up." There was an appallingly gullible enthusiasm in the third engineer's voice. Palmer hung up.

"Good," Lila said, then added in a lower, more intimate voice, "No trouble, Tim, please no trouble from you."

He could not reply, only aware of how easy it had been for her, and how bloody ironic it was for him.

"Giorgio baby, stop that thing!"

The insistent 'peep' of the digital watch alarm interrupted the last rapturous waves of love and Giorgio pushed himself to a furious climax before rolling off the still-shuddering body of Mrs Rebanowicz.

"Giorgio ..." she protested. The Greek's exhaustion was usually total, temporarily at least. Tonight's behaviour was uncharacteristic. He pulled on his slacks in haste, making ready to abandon her. One hand reached out to tickle her crotch.

"Giorgio got special job to do tonight."

"What special job?" A dark and terrible doubt crossed Zelda's brief and curtailed ecstasy. "Are you two-timing me?"

Giorgio stood, unzipped his fly and looked down, then zipped up. The shrivelled wreckage of his manhood was unimpressive. He grinned without saying anything and pulled on his shirt.

"See you tomorrow. You got Giorgio place in San Francisco?"

"Sure honey. I've got the biggest double bed in the 'Frisco Hilton."

"Giorgio not two-time you."

She saw he was serious and smiled up at him, unashamed in her naked abandon. He had forgotten how many women he had had, but it was strange that this great Yankee she-goat should be of them all the most erotic. "You trust Giorgio, eh? Trust Giorgio?"

Zelda frowned. "Yes ... yes, of course." She was uncertain what was required of her.

"Okay. We come together soon, eh? Now I go."

And Zelda was staring at the closed door. Five minutes later Giorgio, armed with a Kalashnikov machine-gun, had reached the rendezvous in the upper engine room, three levels above the engine room entrances, with a commanding view of the access to the machinery control room and an ascending ladder to the inside of the funnel, the fiddley and from there, the bridge.

The greaser Zig was already there.

"*Jihad*," hissed Giorgio

"You're late coming," replied Zig.

"Will of Allah!" grinned Giorgio. He cast a look round the area obscured from all but the most assiduous inspection. They were hidden behind auxiliary generator settling tanks and the exhausts from the main Sulzer diesel engines. On either side, similar pipes conducted air downwards from the upper levels to the greedy turbo-blowers. The last person inside the area had been a United States Coast Guard Inspector and he would be the last until the *Adventurer* reached San Francisco. Since the night's events put that beyond the bounds of likelihood Giorgio expressed his satisfaction.

"Good work, Zig."

Peering downwards Giorgio could just see the distant figure of the third engineer inside the MCR. As he watched, the noise of the screaming engines increased in pitch. The two conspirators exchanged smiles of congratulation.

"You tell Lila now?"

Giorgio patted his comrade's shoulder and nodded, slipping upwards via a steel ladder that led towards the funnel and a door onto the fiddley just abaft the bridge.

Stephanos stood for a moment in the alleyway outside the radio room. His body felt as though it weighed nothing; he was vibrant with life. It was his first active mission. He smiled slowly as he cocked his pistol then, holding it as he had been taught, he poked its ugly silencer round the corner of the door and moved inside.

Crabtree did not hear the intrusion. He had the headset on and was reading a book. The centre boil on his neck above the less-than-clean shirt looked like a target to Stephanos, but the young man resisted the temptation to blast the 9mm slug through its purulent head. Instead, he made the hole in the back of Crabtree's head. It was a neat hole, opening the skull just above the joint with the spinal column, but the slug's exit

138

from the front was less so. Crabtree's face, reduced to a mass of blood, mucus, bone, hair and glutinous matter, splattered onto the facing bulkhead and slid slowly down it.

Grabbing a towel from the adjacent lavatory, Stephanos wrapped it round the wrecked head. Gagging, he began to drag the body out along the route defined by Lila. It rolled overboard quite easily from under one of the starboard lifeboats, hitting the water with a perceptible splash, followed by a violent eructation of vomit from Stephanos.

The young man felt better after voiding his stomach. He returned to the radio room and began to clear up the mess, glad that Crabtree had been an indolent and unpleasant man. Had the radio officer on duty been sitting properly, Stephanos's shot might have damaged the equipment. Equally he would not have enjoyed shooting David Gordon, even in the line of duty.

When he was satisfied with his cleaning operation he telephoned the bridge. Lila answered.

"*Jihad!*" he reported.

"*In'sh Allah!*" came back the response.

Able Seaman Dieter Schmidt walked casually along the luxuriously carpeted first-class alleyway. At intervals, elaborate mock baroque sconces illuminated the passage. Between these, prints and paintings decorated the bulkheads. The unashamed luxury acted like a spur to Schmidt.

In the interests of chastity and security, the regulator's staff patrolled the ship during the night hours. They were theoretically empowered to inform on anybody visiting passengers' cabins. Officers caught thus were banned from the passengers' company, kept 'off-decks' by the captain's decree. It was company policy, despite the accepted need for the passengers to be kept happy. Officers and others engaged on assignations were expected to obey the eleventh commandment and avoid being caught.

'Ginger' Marshall had done this kind of thing in the Royal Navy, but there he had had to police a ship full of men. Now his work had the added attraction of the occasional sexual adventure. He was whistling quietly under his breath as he came up to the first-class accommodation. There was a nubile teenager with the body of a depraved angel whom he had been initiating into the joys of mutual masturbation. The sight of Schmidt coming down the alleyway forced him to stop.

"Hey, Dieter, you shouldn't be up here." It crossed Marshall's mind that he was not guiltless. "Piss off quick before the master-at-arms catches you."

Schmidt seemed not to hear, continuing to approach, one hand behind his back as though scratching his behind.

"Schmidt?"

They were five yards apart when Marshall sensed something was wrong. He stopped. "Schmidt . . .?"

The slugs punched into Marshall's belly, doubling him and sending him backwards. He was still alive as Schmidt dragged him out on deck, his head bumping over the low sea-step, and rolled him over the side. You could see little of Marshall's blood on the deep-piled crimson of the rich carpet.

In the entrance foyer Schmidt found several of the night staff gossiping over a cup of tea.

"Hi, Dieter, what are you doing?"

He did not answer, merely brought the machine-pistol up and fired from the hip. He emptied the magazine into their bodies as their jerking dance subsided, the muffled and rapid thunder of the silenced reports absorbed by the carpets and the hangings. Dispassionately he dragged them to one side to be dealt with later, an untidy heap of lolling limbs and tangled hair.

He found the master-at-arms moving up a lower alleyway. He was conveniently near a door onto the upper deck. The winded man followed Marshall over the side, dazed, but still breathing.

When he had finished his alloted task, Schmidt telephoned the bridge. It was just after 0300.

Stephanos had unlocked the *Adventurer*'s satellite dish aerial from its azimuth and altitude settings. By keeping itself trained on the equatorially geo-stationary Inmarsat communications satellite over the Atlantic, *Adventurer* was ready to send or receive a telexed message or a telephone call. There was an emergency device on the set which enabled a Mayday distress call to be transmitted automatically and for the encoded information of the ship's approximate position to aid a search. By unlocking the dish aerial this facility was removed. *Adventurer* was isolated and almost impossible to locate by standard search and rescue methods.

Disconnecting all other main and auxiliary aerials Stephanos further isolated the ship. When he was satisfied, he left the radio room and moved smartly along the alleyway, turned to descend a single flight of stairs and made for the cabin door at the end of the passageway. He had forgotten his nausea.

As he paused to check the pistol, Stephanos noticed the ship was trembling more than usual. He reached out his hand and turned the door handle.

Captain Smythe, like every shipmaster, was a light sleeper. Command never rested easily on any man and many anaesthetized themselves from its most insistent worries with alchohol. Captain Smythe's subconscious had noted the increase in engine revolutions and the list as the ship swung to the alteration of course. It had only been slight, perhaps half a degree or so, but it was enough to thrust its irregularity into his mind and stir him to wakefulness. He switched on his bunk light and looked at his watch. It was 0305. Palmer was on the bridge.

Smythe swore and reached for the telephone. Who the hell did Palmer think he was? He heard the door of his day cabin open and let the telephone fall back on the hook. This would be young DeAth with a verbal explanation of the alteration of course and increase in speed. It was probably in response to a Mayday signal for which every ship was both duty-bound to listen for and duty-bound to assist.

"Yes? What is it?"

The Captain could see little beyond the brightly illuminated area of his bed. The bunk light was designed to allow a man to read in bed. It spot lit his upper body as he propped himself up. It made Captain Smythe a perfect target for Stephanos's gun.

"Captain?"

"Yes? Who the hell are . . . ?"

The noise of death was unspectacular; a tribute to the efficient genius of inventive men.

Captain Smythe's body was too heavy for Stephanos and he left it where it was, only pausing to switch off the

141

bunk light and lock the cabin door before returning to the radio room.

He checked all was well with the bridge and reconnected his main receiver aerials. His fingers rolled the variable tuning knob with practiced ease. He could hear the stutter of distant morse in his headphones and he lifted his eye to the left hand of the two clocks on the bulkhead. It was just after 0600 Greenwich Mean Time. Too early yet for his own transmission.

Suddenly he froze. His fingers moved and he reversed the large knob. The digital frequency readout flipped back. Seizing a pencil he began to scribble on a pad. It was impossible, absolutely impossible!

Not yet, at any rate. They had barely accomplished the hijack!

His heart was beating and he felt sweat breaking out on his forehead and beneath his armpits. The morse ceased and he looked down at what he had written:

CQ CQ DE GKA PAN PAN PAN BEGINS ALL BRITISH SHIPS WARNED POSSIBLE TERRORIST THREAT EXISTS ENDS STOP CQ CQ DE GKA.

He was on the extreme range of the transmitting station, the main British W/T station at Portishead, near Bristol. A repeat of the same signal would soon be sent out from the new British station on the Falklands.

Stephanos swore, tore off the message and stared down at it again. He had missed the date and time group, but it scarcely mattered. What mattered was that the bastards *knew*. He did not know all the details of their mission, but he knew the co-operation of at least a dozen other freedom fighting organisations across the world had been asked for and had volunteered their assistance. Now they had fallen victim to treachery.

Stephanos swore again. His people were desperate to regain their homeland and such treachery only increased his own determination to succeed, or to die in the attempt, for this was a *jihad*, a holy war.

He went in search of Lila on the bridge. He was no

142

longer queasy or sweating with anxiety; he was frigid with anger.

Palmer stood uneasily in the chartroom under cover of Anna's gun. For the last few minutes Lila had answered, in Arabic, calls on the internal telephone system.

Even now she was talking, then she slammed down the phone and turned to Stephanos who had just made his report. There had obviously been something wrong. Stephanos was agitated and Lila shocked at first, but then soothing. It was clear to Palmer that Lila was the group's undisputed leader.

When she had calmed Stephanos she rapped out some new instructions. Stephanos appeared to query them and Palmer thought he heard the name 'Blumenthal'. Stephanos hurried off.

"Keep a watch in your radar set, Palmer," said Anna and he crossed to the Racal-Decca ARPA to do as he was bidden.

"Are there any ships?" Anna asked. Palmer looked up from the blank screen and ran a practised eye round the horizon.

"No."

"Keep watching."

"Do you know what the time is Dr Galvin? It is more than past three o'clock."

"Mr Blumenthal, what does time matter to us? Old men do not need much sleep."

"That depends upon how they have spent their lives, doctor. . . ."

"Do you make this voyage for your health?"

The old Jewish statesman chuckled drily. "Oh, yes, for my health. It is for my health that I come to the United States. There are good Jewish doctors in the United States."

Galvin smiled in the darkness. He recognized the humorous self-mockery of the Hebrew.

"But not good enough, eh?"

"What is your diagnosis?"

"Carcinoma."

"It was that easy to tell?"

"Yes." They both sat in silence, occupying two deck chairs

143

on the deserted after verandah of the sun deck, muffled up against the night air. Under the deck lights of the great ship the abandoned sun deck and its chairs had the look of an area littered with sticks. On either side of them the Perspex windscreens threw back the dull glare of the deck lights. Above them the black night sky and the oily upwellings of the sea as it roiled astern of them, reflected their illuminations as *Adventurer* pitched into the darkness. Overhead an overcast sky obscured the stars. The slurp and splash of the water in the pool could be heard as the water slopped back and forth under the influence of the pitching ship and, at either end of the pool, the deck was wet and shiny where it had overflowed.

"I remember," said Galvin after a long silence, "when I was a young student I had a difference of opinion with a friend. We began the argument, which was about appeasement or opposition to the Nazis, with a reasonable exposition of our points of view. We argued with increasing vehemence for five and a half hours, by which time both of us had forsaken our civilized standpoints and retreated to the polar regions of utter bigotry. Both of us felt justified, but both of us knew we had lost the debate. You and I have avoided that."

"But we have not solved the problem, even in theoretical debate. Israel is a fact, my friend. It is absolute."

"And it did not scruple to use violence to become absolute. You yourself have admitted your part against the British occupying forces who were in Palestine to prevent your people entering the country. You cannot blame those you displaced for doing the same. He who sows the wind reaps the whirlwind. . . ."

A shadow fell across the two old men, two shadows. In the gleam of the deck lights they could see the sheen of metal. They both twisted round and looked up.

"What is this?" asked Blumenthal.

"Nemesis," said Galvin quietly.

Palmer recognized the two old men as they were brought to the bridge. He could sense the satisfaction among the terrorists

144

at the capture of Blumenthal. His attempt to intercede for the harmless Galvin was cut short. He watched them led off.

He looked at the chartroom clock. The light-emitting diodes registered 0340 ship's time. The new watch was due on duty in 20 minutes. He looked at Anna. She was leaning back on the control console, one elbow taking her weight, one hand about her gun.

"Lila wants to trust you." Her voice, though he had heard it before seemed strange now that he had seen that trap of a mouth. She must have sensed his revulsion. "You will get used to the way I look. I had to. For you it will not be so difficult."

"I'm sorry."

"Of course you are. You are a decent man, but you are the enemy, whatever Lila says." The low light showed a slight movement in the gun barrel. Oddly, he gained composure from that sinister act of menace.

"I meant it, Anna."

"Yes. That is what Lila says. She is a good judge of character, but she has not had to judge a lover before. If you betray us, I will kill you."

It was so coolly said, so matter-of-factly spoken that he had not the slightest doubt of it.

"What happens now?"

"This is not a movie, Palmer. I am not going to explain our policy for you. What happens now is that you watch the radar."

"There are no ships ..." he paused, oddly happier that Lila had not totally abandoned him. It seemed, from what the implacable Anna said, that she had not forgotten what had passed between them. The slight reassurance emboldened him. "You are Palestinians, not Puerto Ricans?"

"Yes. We are part of a large group called April Eight Six. What were you doing on April 15, 1986, Palmer, the day when the mad dog Reagan bombed Tripoli and Benghazi?"

"I was looking for work in London."

She had not expected that. It made them a little more equal in the matter of deprivation, but not much.

"Look for ships now."

Patiently he stood over the radar. He felt her move closer

145

beside him. The screen was empty, the sweep of the S-band scanner revolving every three seconds, lighting up the heading marker that glowed out from the centre on their chosen course, the abruptly altered course that Lila had selected on the auto-pilot after she had usurped the bridge.

"You see," he said, "empty. . . ."

He could feel the muzzle of the gun barrel touch his ribs as she peered into the orange after-glow of the sweep. He looked at her as she raised her head from the visor.

"Keep looking." She smiled, a terrible twisting of facial muscles that actually looked painful in the bizarre light. Palmer was touched by a ridiculous desire to help her, to ease the bitterness that ate her as much as the patriotism she felt for her distant, occupied homeland. He wanted to think of her as he had first known her, her face hidden in the darkness, her mood light and almost buoyant.

But it was too late for all that.

Chapter Seven

SUBMARINE *LIBERTAD*, SOUTH ATLANTIC

"Three miles to go, Comrade Adviser."

Captain Sergei Korolenko put down the old copy of '*Morskoi Sbornik*' and switched his mind from his native Russian to Spanish.

"Good, thank you." He flung his legs out of the bunk and hoisted himself to his feet, bending with the ease of long practice in the cramped space. He felt the plane of the submarine's deck alter as Vega, her commander, brought her to periscope depth. Instinctively he looked at his watch. The timing was perfect. Korolenko rubbed his face vigorously with a dry towel. It saved water but made him alert and awake; an old submariner's trick. Then he stepped through the open watertight door and into the control room.

The submarine was called *Libertad* now, but Korolenko remembered her having a different name. She had been his second command and he had commissioned the Foxtrot-class patrol boat from the Soviet building yard at Sudomekh as long ago as 1969. Like all new boats, she had had her problems and he recalled, almost with affection at this distance in time, those nail-biting incidents that were now mere memories, redolent with the bitter-sweet sadness of past youth.

In some ways nothing had changed, he thought. From the engine room astern came the hiss and growing thunder of compressed air starting the diesels. Vega was already at periscope depth, his snorkel up to suck air down for the three oxygen-hungry diesels that, in a few moments, would take over *Libertad*'s drive to her triple screws. Korolenko was pleased with Vega's initiative. A familiar disciplined order reigned in the control room. The sonar operators sat at their control panels, their sets passive, listening to the myriad sounds of the ocean received in the sensors, arrayed in a vertical pod on the round bow of the *Libertad*. Technicians monitored the boat's internal systems and, at that moment, Vega's second in command was overseeing the trimming of the submarine, adjusting the degree of water in her tanks to maintain her at periscope depth. In the centre of the control room rose the gleaming columns of the periscopes and the housings of the snorkel and aerials. He resisted the temptation to take over. *Libertad*'s deck canted uncertainly as the trim was established, but it was a creditable effort and Korolenko was pleased with the way in which his trainees overcame their difficulties. He reminded himself that *Libertad* was no longer his ship.

Some things had changed. The faces in the half-light of instrument dials were not those of Russians, they were Hispano-Indian faces; and the smells that pervaded the boat, the stale cooking, the mephitic air filled with the scent of unwashed men were not Russian in origin. He realized he had scarcely noticed until now, when the snorkel was sucking in cool fresh air and the pockets of staleness seemed almost tangible by contrast.

He smiled at the young watch officer who made way for him. *Libertad* might be long in the tooth, but years of service in the Soviet Navy had honed her to a lean perfection. And she still had her fangs, her six bow and two stern-mounted torpedo tubes were still capable of dealing a devastating blow.

He watched Vega, his hat reversed in the time-honoured tradition of submariners, complete his horizon sweep with the attack periscope. He would have trouble seeing far until his officers had mastered the art of trimming but, Korolenko looked at his watch again, they still had some time in hand. Vega clapped up the handles and gave an order. With a smooth hiss of hydraulics the periscope lowered into its pit. The Costa Mayan turned to the Russian.

"We are on station, Comrade Adviser, nothing in sight, but Garcia here reports he has a sonar contact."

"Signature?"

Vega shrugged, assaying a half-smile. "We do not yet have your expertise. Garcia . . . ?"

The operator turned. "Certainly diesels, Comrade Adviser, like that ship off Recife."

"Good." There was no point in listening himself with the diesels hammering within the boat's hull. "We will know soon enough."

Turning to the chart table Vega joined him, watching the Russian as he plotted their position from the read-out of the SINS. Vega did not know if all the Foxtrot-class were fitted with a Ship's Intertial Navigation System but after years of nursing merchant ships about the globe with a sextant and chronometer, the box of tricks in the *Libertad* was magic.

"I will elevate the receiving aerial then?" A hint of uncertainty had crept into Vega's voice. Korolenko hoped it was not because he was overawed.

The Russian captain liked his colleague. Manuel Vega had converted from a merchant shipmaster to command of a submarine in a very short time, but he was not over-confident, particularly given the delicacy and importance of their present mission. It was not surprising. Soviet advisers were not always tolerant or easy to get on with, but Korolenko hoped he did not intimidate Vega. It was quite possible that, with Korolenko gone, Vega and his scratch crew would contrive to drown themselves. Vega was seaman enough to sweat at this prospect. Korolenko smiled encouraging-ly.

"You are in command Manuel. . . ."

Vega nodded and turned to give the necessary orders. Korolenko looked up at the bulkhead clock. It was registering Universal Co-ordinated Time. It showed 0658.

Unobtrusively, Korolenko moved through to the radio office, a small space at the after-end of the control room. Its worn chair was empty. He swung back.

"Captain!"

Vega's anxious face appeared. "What is the matter?"

"Where the hell is your radio operator?"

"I am here."

The man was pushing past the ratings at the 'planes, pulling at his fly.

"You make sure you piss in good time in future. D'you have the frequency?" Korolenko's tone was sharp enough to make the man aware of his stupidity.

"All ready, Comrade Adviser. I'm sorry."

"Never mind!" snapped Korolenko. The time on his digital watch was past 0659 UCT.

The rating settled himself and pulled on the headphones. Korolenko leaned on the bulkhead and waited. The young officer handed him a plastic mug of coffee. He grunted his appreciation. That was one advantage of his present assignment. The home-grown coffee was magnificent.

Korolenko sipped contentedly as the seconds ticked by. Seven o'clock came and went. It was quite possible that the group had failed to make the attack. In that case *Libertad* repositioned and postponed everything for 24 hours, but Korolenko did not want that. A second position would be too bloody near the hunter-killer submarine the British now kept on station close to the Falklands. They would not know the *Libertad* was full of sailors in nappies. If they came screaming along in one of their nuclear-powered *Swiftsure*'s to play catch-you-fuck-you he did not rate Vega's chances very highly. Such a game of nerves would probably ruin the poor fellow's burgeoning aptitude forever, and it was not Korolenko's brief to frighten Vega or his ship's company shitless. Besides, this was Korolenko's last assignment before he retired. It had let him escape a desk and he wanted his unblemished record to stay that way.

There was a dark patch of sweat on the operator's shirt. Had his overwhelming desire to pass water made him miss the vital signal? Korolenko felt his own stomach tense in the contraction of anxiety. It was 060057z.

The clocks could be well out of synchronisation, but supposing the other was ahead? They would definitely have missed the transmission and the group would not know. There was nothing in the plan to offer an acknowledgement. Korolenko felt the sweat on his own forehead. They would not like a cock-up at Northern Fleet headquarters at Severomorsk.

150

Stephanos knew he was late. The need to assist Giorgio in detaining the two old men had put him behind his schedule, for they were not to be killed wantonly. He rushed into the radio room aware that he had only seconds to spare. At any moment Crabtree's relief might walk in. David Gordon was a conscientious man and probably programmed an alarm to wake him.

The Greek connected the aerial, swtiched on the transmitter, selected the frequency and sat at the morse key. It was a few seconds past the correct time of 0400 ship's time, 0700 UCT, when he tapped out the morse letters of an Argentine naval cryptogram. The code group had been obtained through a revolutionary cell in Buenos Aires. It was a procedural instruction to Argentine surface warships and if intercepted by British operators on or around the Falklands, would fix their attention to the westwards. In the unlikely event of any wide-awake Brit actually getting a DF fix on the brief transmission, their present position was sufficiently close to the River Plate to make them look for an Argentine warship.

He only sent the group once and did not expect an acknowledgement. Those that were waiting for it, he knew, would not miss it.

EAST GERMAN REEFER *THEODOR KAST*, SOUTH ATLANTIC

Konrad Lenz, radio officer of the motor reefer *Theodor Kast*, peered through the cigarette smoke that rose in front of his face and stared at the piece of paper Captain Otto Müller had just given him.

Lenz had expected something ever since the man in the grey suit had boarded them in Paranagua. Ship's business had taken him to Müller's cabin at the wrong time. The man in the grey suit had been sitting on the edge of the armchair with the air of a man giving orders. Müller was a good Democratic

German but at heart he was first a seaman; he did not like politics. Neither did Lenz, for that matter. But Lenz did not like smoking either, yet he was rarely without a cigarette between his lips. He kidded himself he never inhaled, he just let them burn away and breathed round them. He avoided nicotine with the same success that Müller avoided politics.

Lenz twirled the tuning knob on the MF receiver, looked at the bulkhead clock then down at the frequency again. Satisfied that he had tuned in correctly he looked up at Müller's face.

"I've got it."

Müller nodded his appreciation. He was a spare, taciturn man with a beautiful wife. You always thought of Müller's wife when you looked at Müller, for they were an incongruous pair. Annelise was devastatingly attractive, too attractive to let a sailor sleep soundly at night, Lenz thought. Still, that was no more his business than the present matter. He slipped the phones over his head and leaned back. The cigarette smoke coiled upwards.

He heard the three-letter group six minutes later, turned the tuning knob and grimaced at the cacophony of morse that was jamming up the ham frequency. Very deliberately he began to send. Lenz was a skilled operator, his wrist the most supple joint in his body, but for this he was deliberate and positive. There were no prizes for speed tonight.

It took him ten minutes to get through. The amateur in Florida was being bloody slow, but eventually they exchanged call signs. Lenz began to send, a slow grin on his face as he did so. He was sending in English, the international language of the sea. It was a gossiping message, the sort that hams send for the pleasure of contact across hundreds of miles of aether.

... ON OUR WAY HOME NOW STOP GOOD TO SEE THE FAMILY AGAIN STOP NICE TO TALK TO YOU HOPE YOU ARE OKAY YOUR TRANSMISSION IS GOOD TONIGHT STOP OVER.

The response came quickly:

... GREAT TO HEAR YOU AGAIN STOP HOPE

*YOU HAVE PLAIN SAILING ARE YOU TAKING
ANY PRESENTS HOME FROM SOUTH AMERICA
STOP OVER.*

"That's him," said Lenz to the captain, happy to know that he was transmitting to the right person. He began to send again.

YES SPECIAL SOUVENIR CHOCOLATES STOP OVER.
LUCKY LUCKY LUCKY STOP HAVE A NICE DAY
OVER.

Lenz took the headphones off and looked up at Müller. "Well Captain, whatever it is he's supposed to know, he knows it now."

Lenz left the question hanging and Müller shook his head. "I don't know, Konrad, and I don't particularly want to know."

Müller withdrew. "No," muttered Lenz, his cigarette bobbing up and down as the heat of it burned his lips, "but I bet you want to know what's happening back home in Rostock tonight. . . ."

He reached up and switched off the transceiver. Looking up at the clock he jotted down the time. In column for zonal time he noted '0420' for they were still on Brazilian East Coast time. Finally he removed the cigarette from his mouth and ground it out into a tin ashtray.

CAPE PEMBROKE LIGHTHOUSE, EAST FALKLAND

One wide-awake Brit on the Falklands intercepted the three-letter group transmitted by Stephanos. He was an amateur radio enthusiast, a 'ham', and busy twiddling his dial in the lighthouse at Cape Pembroke. Billy Pugh was fed up with his present station. He had enjoyed his hobby far more in the Smalls lighthouse off the coast of Pembrokeshire, but since Trinity House had decided to automate the rock tower he had transferred to this Austral Pembroke and was beginning to regret volunteering.

He heard the three letters clearly, so clearly that he thought

153

they must have come from the Argentine. It would have amused him to have a ham contact in Argentina; to break down the barriers imposed by the politicians and the military, and to enjoy a simple mutual interest with a kindred spirit. But the signal was not repeated and he heard nothing further. Besides, it was time to go up and attend to the light. Random signals were not unusual hereabouts, although this one was well away from the naval, air and military frequencies used by the forces guarding Fortress Falkland.

He stood and stretched, ignoring the three letters scribbled on the piece of paper, and made his way up the curving stone staircase from the watch room to the lantern above.

CHILEAN FRIGATE *BERNARDO O'HIGGINS*, DRAKE PASSAGE, CAPE HORN

Operator First Class Arturo Hernandez heard the signal clearly and knew exactly what it meant. He was pleased with himself having long nursed a private opinion that the Argentinians transmitted instructions to their forces on odd frequencies, a theory whose confirmation now gave him a reason for justifying breaking orders and scanning unofficial wavelengths. Still, his watch officer was very young and he could bluff his way out of trouble, confident that the captain would not ask too many questions when he knew the nature of the intercept. The only thing that puzzled Hernandez was the station of origin. He did not recognize the transmitting touch and, though Hernandez did not know it, it was a sheer fluke of atmospheric ducting that had enabled his private theory a gratifying, though specious, validity.

He turned to the watch officer in the radio section of the operations room. A few minutes later the watch officer rang the bridge and asked for the captain.

Captain Enrique Soto stood happily on his bridge awaiting the dawn. It was one of his chief joys when at sea, a habit formed when he had been the first lieutenant of his country's fine training ship, the four-masted barquentine *Esmeralda*.

It had been his last sea-going appointment before he had been compelled to lecture in the Chilean Naval Academy at Valparaiso. The Academia Naval Arturo Pratt was not to be compared with a sailing ship, nor to his present vessel, the British-built *Leander*-type frigate *Bernardo O'Higgins*.

Soto gazed happily down at the lean hull as it rolled easily, crossing the long, low swells of the Southern Ocean as they forced their way across Drake Passage, the gap between Cape Horn and Antarctica. Today, crossing the dirtiest bit of ocean in the world was a pleasure, a yachting excursion on a delightful summer morning. All in all, Captain Soto was delighted with his transfer to the Third Naval Zone which stretched south towards the pole. His frigate, with its general-purpose capability, had a roving commission and was returning northwards to Punta Arenas after landing men and stores at the Chilean stations in the Antarctic.

"Sir. . . . ?"

The officer of the watch stood beside him. "Yes?"

"Radio office have intercepted an Argentine TX, sir. Three-letter group meaning 'Proceed as per my instructions'. Signal strength three; formulation of the cryptogram was very positive."

Soto frowned. "Who is the duty operator?"

The lieutenant bit his lip and returned to the wheelhouse to find out. Putting back the telephone he reported again. "Hernandez, sir."

"Ahhh . . . he's good . . . what about direction?"

The lieutenant turned back to the telephone.

"Never mind, Lieutenant, I'll go down. Just remember that you're no longer in the academy . . . you're at sea now and those Argentinian bastards may be up to anything."

His hands on the handrails and his feet clear of the steps, Soto descended to the operations room with practised skill. His sudden arrival caused a stir.

"Well, Hernandez, what d'you make of it?"

"Difficult to say, sir . . . but it was distant . . . didn't get a DF, sir, it was too quick. . . ."

"Pity. . . ."

"Yes sir."

155

"Was it from the Tierra del Fuego area?"

"I don't think so, sir ... more like the east coast. ..."

"Malvinas?"

"Yes, I think so."

"Makes more sense ... perhaps they're going to rattle the British defences. Keep guarding the frequency. ..."

"It wasn't one of their usual ones, sir."

"Oh? What were you doing scanning it then?"

"I was just moving along the band, sir ... returning." Hernandez lied.

Soto gave him a long look and saw the sweat break out on Hernandez's forehead.

"Good work, Hernandez. I like initiative ... occasionally."

"Thank you sir." Relief was plain on the man's face. Soto turned to the watch officer. "Encode that for the information of Talcahuano and get it off at once."

SUBMARINE *LIBERTAD*, SOUTH ATLANTIC

Captain Manuel Vega watched the seconds pass on the clock. He hoped his operator had not missed the vital signal, but Jose had been his own 'sparky' when Vega had commanded a cargo ship. His other operators, however, were little more than trainees, despite their period under the expert tutelage of Russian instructors who had brought the *Foxtrot* over from Severomorsk six months earlier. Vega was still in awe of the vessel he commanded. Caught up in the violent revolution in Costa Maya he and a group of his cargo-ship crew had boarded and captured the fast patrol boat sent to the anchorage of San Niccolo to escort them safely into port where they could discharge their cargo of arms from the United States. None of Vega's men wanted the rockets, shells and napalm bombs dropped on their own homes.

Vega landed the arms to the insurgents and took a small group of volunteers away in the patrol boat to beat up government forces wherever he found them. The consequence of his daring was to ensure him a captaincy in the new navy of the

People's Republic of Costa Maya. Vega found he was a hero of the revolution and commander of his country's first submarine. There had been months of training then, quite suddenly, the Russian instructors had gone, leaving only Captain of the First Rank Korolenko and the special orders of the Chairman of the People's Republic.

"Got it!" Jose, the Costa Mayan radio operator, tore off the phones, grinning. Both Vega and Korolenko almost collided in their eagerness to peer over Jose's shoulders.

"Very good, my friend," said Korolenko.

"Well done, Jose!" added Vega.

"I will go and prepare our guests." Korolenko smiled again and ducked forward, disappearing through the small doorway into the maze of piping, wiring and the resting places of men. Vega looked at the read-out of the SINS. He knew the co-ordinates of intersecting meridian and parallel by heart. Three minutes later he telegraphed the engines to stop.

"Prepare to surface."

Korolenko pushed forward. The Costa Mayan sailors drew aside for him as they made for their stations in response to Vega's orders. They were very respectful and Korolenko liked them. They had the enviable zeal of first-generation revolutionaries. It was a heady wine.

He entered the torpedo space. *Libertad* was carrying only a few of the 533-mm torpedoes she was capable of storing. The torpedo stowage space was occupied by two dozen men and women. Already alerted, they were pulling on clothes. Flak jackets, pouches of ammunition, belts of grenades, Kalashnikov rifles and smaller hand-guns were being checked and water bottles filled from a large plastic container. The place was a riot of preparation.

"Comrades. . . ." He drew attention to himself. "Comrades, we will be surfacing in a few moments. I want to wish you luck. What you are doing is historic in terms of the World Revolution, what you will achieve for the oppressed people of Palestine you all know. You are going to attack the ancient enemies of your class in a cause as just as any in human history. I wish I was coming with you."

He smiled and they grinned back, the Costa Mayans and the Palestinians, the men and the women. Korolenko longed to be young again. He withdrew to the control room.

"Comrade Adviser!" Vega's tone was sharp and his eyes bright with excitement He was motioning Korolenko to the periscope.

The Russian had no need to swivel or focus the optic. He needed no time to accustom his eyes to the difference in light. Pale in the South Atlantic dawn, her huge hull grey in the half-light, her decks still ablaze with lights, the shape of a great liner bore down towards them. He could see the brighter twinkle of her two white masthead lights and the ruby glow of her port sidelight. His face triumphant he turned to Vega.

"Take her up, Comrade Captain."

ADVENTURER, SOUTH ATLANTIC

Palmer leaned his tired head against the glass of the wheelhouse window. Routinely, he relied upon the period between 0400 and noon to sleep, for social duties took up most of the evening. And lately there had also been Lila.

But he did not want to think about Lila.

Behind him, in the captain's chair, sat Anna, a machine-gun across her lap. Ahead of him, stretching out in a long grey dart, the bow of *Adventurer* rose and fell gently as the ship breasted a low swell that indicated heavy weather somewhere to the south of them. A faint glimmer of daylight was trying to squeeze between a lead-coloured sea and a heavy overcast. It was going to be a watery, uninspiring dawn. He wanted to sleep and he wanted to talk to Lila. Above all he wished they had not made him help throw the bodies of DeAth and the quartermaster overboard. In London he had not bargained for that.

"You watch the radar, Palmer."

He turned wearily to the girl terrorist. "I can see the horizon is clear."

"Radar!" The gun jerked and he reluctantly obeyed.

He looked up from the screen. "Nothing."

Anna looked at her watch. "You are sure?"

"Of course I'm bloody sure," he said, suddenly tired out, and wondering how much longer he was expected to stand watch. The new watch was almost an hour late coming on duty. Palmer wondered if any of them had woken up themselves or what the terrorists could do about it if they did. He did not know that, down below in the engine room, the changeover had gone with routine precision, watched by Zig and the gun of Schmidt. The third engineer and his greasers had innocently gone back to bed, creatures of habit at such a graveyard hour.

Anna looked at the radar beside him again. He saw the orange light on the glabrous patch above her forehead and again wished he could turn the clock back. The tension of uncertainty was beginning to play on his nerves.

"How did it happen?" he found himself asking abruptly and indicating his own face.

"You want to know? It was a simple thing . . . a fire started by rockets launched from Kfir fighters of the Heyl Ha'Avir, the Israeli airforce. Did you know, Palmer, that the Israelis obtained the design of the Kfir by stealing plans from France and that the Mirage airframe has a United States jet engine? I tell you this, Palmer, to help you understand why we Palestinians feel we are victims. We are angry, Palmer.

"The Kfir fighter-planes attacked my home, a shanty in the Shatila camp, in the Lebanon, Palmer, a country at peace with Israel. We were supposed to be the headquarters of a unit of the PLO. Perhaps some of our young men had weapons; but young Israelis have weapons too, the difference is they carry them under the flag of a country that is legitimate, civilized.

"We have no country, no flag. The Israelis stole it from us and then they bomb us while we try to live our lives in some other country.

"It was a bad raid. My family were all killed. I was burned. . . ."

Suddenly she took his hand from where it rested on the side of the radar and pulled it up to her face. The grip of her wrist was strong. The palm of his hand felt the dry, ribbed tissue, scarred across the bone of the skull. In the faint dawn he

159

could see small patches of unhealed flesh which suppurated slightly.

"Don't try anything, Palmer, my gun is pointing at your balls."

There had been no thought of such an action in his horrified mind. Anna's face was so sadly hideous that the blank look that greeted her new aggression told Anna that Lila had been right. Palmer *was* a dreamer, as Lila had said, but not all dreamers were supine. What had that great British charlatan Lawrence said? That most men dream, but not all equally and those that dreamed by day, dreamed dangerously. . . .

She could not recall the quotation exactly, but it did not matter. Palmer might prove useful, certainly Lila was banking on his expertise.

"We are just people, Palmer, not terrorists, not bandits, just very angry people . . . now check the radar again."

He turned slowly from her face and watched the orange sweep of the scanner.

"Christ!"

Just beyond the dapple of the sea-clutter that bounced back from the wave crests close in to the ship was a persistent glow: the echo from another ship. He grabbed his binoculars from their box beside the radar and raised them.

The sea was grey in the dawn, faintly streaked with white and furrowed by the low shadows and undulations of the swell. But there was no mistaking the dark shape that wallowed in the troughs of the seas less than a mile ahead. The rounded black hummock of a conning tower, topped with an array of irregularities that were her aerials, antennae and periscopes; the long cigar of her hull appearing occasionally as she rolled, the water streaming greyly from her casing; the slightly higher bow with its stepped vertical sonar pod.

"A submarine!"

Beside him Anna showed no surprise. "You must stop the ship now, Palmer."

The brief moment of intimacy was gone now. Again he was staring down the uncompromising barrel of her gun.

Korolenko and Vega stood side by side in the narrow deck atop

160

Libertad's fin. Through binoculars they saw the great ship was even more impressive than they had guessed. As they gasped at the cool fresh air of the southern dawn they saw the bow wave under the high flare drop away and as the liner lost steerage she fell off the wind, forming a natural lee into which Vega began to turn the *Libertad*.

The ship began to loom over them as she lay-to across their bow. The white hull with its severely raked stem and long cruiser stern seemed to rear upwards like a cliff, pierced by row after row of cabin windows. Only at the stern did the slab sides relent in descending steps of sun decks, shielded from the wind by gigantic side screens of transparent Perspex. Above her wedding-cake superstructure and her navigating bridge, rose her masts with their turning radar antennae, the dome of her satellite communications dish and the huge blue and orange funnel with the logo of her capitalist owners.

Black snakes appeared down her white sides, her lifeboat-boarding ladders thrown down her topsides. Through the glasses the two seamen could see a pair of dark figures hurling them over. They moved with the lean economy of well-trained men, their backs disfigured by jutting machine-guns slung there to leave their hands free.

Vega slackend the *Libertad*'s speed and the Atlantic ceased to wash over her bow and sluice past the passive sonar array that rose like a tiny phallus from the bow. Shouting his orders below, Vega swung the submarine parallel with the liner and stopped her, the triple screws threw a white and green marbling of stern-wash up alongside her casing. Between the two vessels the sea ran dark and shining in the lights from the liner. *Adventurer* loomed over them, her hull silhouetted against the rapidly growing daylight, Goliath to *Libertad*'s David.

There was a banging from forward and the torpedo loading hatch was thrown back. Dark shapes emerged, glanced briefly at the towering liner and assembled in a disciplined group on the casing. Seamen followed, dragging up strange bundles and a compressed airline from the engine room. The hiss of air soon unrolled the bundles to reveal inflatable boats. In minutes they were being pushed down the casing where the sea sucked and gurgled along the steel flanks of the *Libertad*. The flak-jacketed and accoutred shock-troops began sliding down into them. Two went into the sea but were hauled aboard none the worse for their ducking. From right forward a hiss and cloud of bubbles showed where four pods of equipment were vented through the torpedo tubes to be taken in tow by the inflatables. Within half an hour of surfacing the neoprene boats had reached the side of the *Adventurer* and Korolenko watched anxiously as the first of the freedom fighters began to scale the swaying ladders. Swiftly he recorded the moment with his Zenith SLR camera.

Above them, on the port bridge wing a figure waved. It was a girl. Both men waved back.

"*Viva la Revolucion!*" bawled Vega beside him, his eyes shining with excitement.

It was heady wine, thought Korolenko.

ADVENTURER, SOUTH ATLANTIC

"Here they come, Palmer, come and look!"

Palmer did as he was told, joining Anna and Lila on the bridge wing from where, only a few days earlier, Captain Smythe had taken revenge on the Yankee pilot, Hansen.

He could see . . . who? Schmidt, yes, Schmidt and Stephanos and Giorgio the steward, leaning over the rails below the lifeboats. Were they all Palestinians? Schmidt certainly wasn't, and neither was that bloody submarine. From her rounded shape Palmer knew she was a Russian-built job, but surely the Kremlin was not so unsubtle?

"Our Costa Mayan allies, Palmer, showing solidarity to the people's cause." He saw the inflatable boats crossing the narrow gap of water between the two ships and heard the revolutionary battle-cry in Spanish. The degree of planning that had gone into this raid began to dawn upon Palmer. And yet it was not quite totally secret; something had leaked and London had known. He began to see his own position in its true perspective and, as the newcomers scrambled over the boat-deck rail, fear uncoiled itself in his belly.

A figure appeared on the bridge ladder. The man was heavily

162

armed, his waist slung about with ammunition and grenades, his figure bulky with flak jacket and bulletproof vest. Around his head was wound the chequered *kaffiyeh* of the PLO. "Lila? Anna?"

"Jamal?"

The cavalry had arrived.

A telephone began to ring in the wheelhouse. Instantly, Anna was alongside Palmer. "Answer it," she commanded.

She was close to him, so that she could hear, her gun in his ribs.

"Bridge. Second Officer."

"Tim? What the hell are you still doing up there?" It was Jim Barclay the second engineer. "Someone's just reported we've a submarine alongside. Has that got anything to do with why we're stopped? Charlie said earlier he'd had orders to crack on at full speed . . . hey, what the fuck's going on . . . ?"

Palmer heard the roar of idling diesels suddenly increase. He knew someone had opened the MCR door. Presumably the cavalry. . . .

Anna grabbed the phone from Palmer. For a moment she listened and then he heard the faint sound of a voice. Anna spoke a few words of Arabic and then handed the telephone back to Palmer.

"Tell Barclay to go full speed again," Anna snapped. "As fast as he can, and quick!"

He took the phone. "Jim . . . Jim?"

"Tim?" Barclay's voice was shaken. "Tim, I've got the place full of soldiers or something . . . there's a gun in my gut . . . !"

"Same here, Jim. We've been hi-jacked."

"Oh fuck . . . !"

"They want full speed, Jim, and fast."

"Where are we going?"

"Tell him," said Anna leaning close, "tell him Antarctica."

Zelda Rebanowicz woke before dawn, her bed lonely, her body aching for the passionate thrusts of her Greek. She heard the engines slow, but paid no heed. The amount of engine vibration in her luxurious suite was minimal, but she stirred when the ship began to wallow slightly in the trough of the sea. Still she thought little of the matter until intrusively unfamiliar noises occurred somewhere outside her cabin.

Drawing a thin wrap about her she slid back the double-glazed balcony doors and stepped into the dawn. She felt the chill air strike her warm flesh, stirring lascivious longings for Giorgio, but the noises continued and she moved forward to peer down onto the boat deck.

It was alive with dark shapes moving urgently. They wore dark, blotchy clothes. More of them were coming over the side, rising out of the sea as in a dream of rats infesting a safe place. Then she saw the gleam of the light on automatic weapons and the chequered headresses some of the moving people wore. At the same instant as she saw the submarine the doctrine of reprisal struck her like a blow. This was anti-American revenge for the bombing of Tripoli and Benghazi!

She retreated to her suite, slamming the glass door and pulling the curtain across the great picture window. From inside, the cabin looked no different, yet outside it was as though wolves prowled. She was trembling uncontrollably.

What would become of her and her lovely Greek?

SUBMARINE *LIBERTAD*, SOUTH ATLANTIC

Korolenko saw the swirl of water under the stern of the *Adventurer* as her screws began to turn. Next to him Vega was shouting orders to his men on the casing. They disappeared below and the torpedo hatch closed behind them. A few moments later the call came up from the control room that the boat was resecured and the *Libertad* ready to proceed.

"We are ready, Comrade Adviser."

The two men watched the liner, her hull foreshortened as she turned away, heading southwards, her white side pale yellow as the first gleams of the sun broke over the horizon.

"Call me Sergei, Manuel. Let us go below and have a little drink, eh?"

"Yes, thank you . . . Sergei, of course."

"I think Tequila."

164

They took a final look at the fast disappearing liner and began to scramble below to the control room as Vega gave the order to dive. Vega secured the hatch then lingered in the control room as the deck tilted and he saw his boat sink safely to 80 metres. Entering the curtained space that passed for a cabin, Korolenko brought out the bottle and a pair of vodka glasses. Vega joined him, taking off his stained cap and wiping his forehead.

"Course set south, Comrade . . . Sergei."

South.

Korolenko smiled as he poured the spirit. He felt at home in high latitudes.

PART TWO

HUNT

'They change their sky, not their mind,
who scour across the sea.'

Virgil

Chapter Eight

DOWNING STREET, LONDON

"It's late David. Are you coming to bed?"

"Er, no, darling . . . I'll be a while yet."

"Are you expecting someone?"

"Well, yes."

"Men's talk?"

"Actually yes . . . I'm sorry."

"Not the American Ambassador?"

"No, not the American Ambassador."

"The White House are really worried about this Sidon business. The BBC news reported Russian warships moving out of the Black Sea."

"Yes, the carrier *Borodino* escorted by two *Krivak*-class destroyers. The President is moving the Sixth Fleet east from the Gulf of Sirte."

"Oh."

"I'd rather meet in here, darling, if you don't mind."

"Of course. I've a good book to read."

"What is it?"

"You're not really interested are you, but it's called 'The Painted Cage,' by Meira Chand, all about a woman who is accused of murdering her husband."

"Ouch!"

"Night."

"Goodnight, darling."

"Prime Minister?"

"Eh? Oh, John, come in . . . I must have dozed off. Any news?"

"None, I'm afraid."

"That's bad . . ."

"It may not be, sir, they would never commit themselves to a timetable."

"I can tell you're worried though, you're too bloody formal for once. Pour us both a Scotch. This thing's got to come to a head before the Sixth Fleet gets into the Levant . . . you heard about the Russians?"

"The ships from the Black Sea? Yes. Could foul the nest . . . cheers."

"Next few hours could be crucial."

"Next few *days*, Prime Minister!"

EAST COAST HIGHWAY, FLORIDA

The battered Pontiac was through Vero Beach before dawn, heading north on the coastal highway towards Daytona Beach and Jacksonville. The hood was down and the man driving beat with one hand on the wheel as an old Beach Boys tape mixed with the wind. His hair was thinning but he wore it long around the back and sides of his head and a once-fashionable Zapata moustache drooped alongside his mouth. To his right the blue Atlantic combers crashed onto the white sand which stretched northwards before bulging outwards to where, on the skyline, the lights of gantries and the metallic sheen of launching towers indicated Cape Canaveral.

By nightfall he would be in Atlanta. He had to lay low for a couple of days. Plenty of time to ball some and maybe mainline a little. That was another secret, one that the Comrades did not know about.

They were more interested in chocolates.

HENDON, NORTH WEST LONDON

Nicholas stirred and woke in the unfamiliar bed. Beyond the

curtain a sleeting wind slashed at the window. The events of the previous evening returned to him and he eased himself onto an elbow and looked down at Kate.

She lay with her lips parted, a lock of hair across her brow. Her unremoved eyeshadow was smudged slightly, giving her even features a waif-like appearance. One arm and breast lay exposed, the coverlet thrown back to expose a gently undulating pink nipple. Her hand was curved beneath it, thumb and forefinger touching in a curious, unconscious gesture that suggested excellence; or was it a lotus signal from some half-learned yoga fad? He could not make up his mind, except that it implied the nipple was being offered to him. The wanton innocence of her sleeping figure reminded him of an erotic Renaissance painting by some obscure Venetian master and hung in a mouldering Italian church.

He lay back on the pillow and stared at the ceiling. Further sleep eluded him, his active mind roved back and forth over the present crisis, spun inconsequentially to thoughts of Kate beside him and then, insidiously to Tim Palmer, her last lover. What did she really think of him? Why had she let herself be so easily taken by another?

There was something intrusive about this notion of Palmer, Nicholas thought, digging in his memory. It was worrying him, and not merely because the man had occupied this bed first.

Suddenly he sat up, his mind whirling. Beside him Kate stirred, turned over and subsided into sleep. The long delicate curve of her spine ran into the warm recesses of the bed beside him.

No, it was a ridiculous fantasy, mere supposition. He dismissed it and closed his eyes. He was drifting off into a doze when his radio-pager began to bleep from the other room.

She was awake when he came back from making the phone call. She smiled at him. "What was it?" She stretched.

"The West German police have picked up the Audi Quattro. The plates were false and it was found in a back street of the St Pauli district of Hamburg."

"Audi Quattro?" Kate frowned, "St Pauli?"

"The helicopter pilot's car, remember? And St Pauli's the red-light district of the German city."

"And the pilot himself?"

"Dead inside. Gunshot wounds from close to. He was carrying the false British passport that Dover Immigration let through the other day."

"Going to collect his pay-off, d'you think? And liquidated for knowing too much?"

Nicholas nodded. "Yes, I should think so. He was only wanted for his aeronautical expertise."

"And the very good cover of appearing a hero."

"Good point. Coffee?"

"Yes please."

She joined him in the little kitchen as he waited for the kettle to boil.

"Last night was pretty bad . . . from the professional point of view," she said.

"Yes."

"We both have other people."

"You have Tim."

"You have your wife."

"True; but I have not seen her for two years. She thinks I'm obsessively work-orientated and care for nothing but my career in the Met. I am not a promiscuous man but she was too stupid to see any virtue in constancy, either for my work or for my family. Perhaps she was just too blind."

"I didn't know you had children."

"I had one. He was killed in a road accident when he was twelve."

"Oh, I'm sorry. I didn't know."

"No reason why you should . . . it finished any pretence at a relationship between me and my wife."

He poured the water onto the instant coffee in the two mugs, then asked; "And Tim?"

She paused before replying. "I don't know. He wanted work badly, and I know he was a sailor, but somehow I didn't think he'd actually go. I mean, he used to say the Merchant Navy was finished, that there was no future for him. He was pretty bitter about it, actually. A bit leftish was how Alex Martin unkindly described him."

"Martin?" Nicholas frowned.

"Oh, Alex has been rather a Dutch uncle to me. He didn't think I should be living with an unemployed merchant seaman. Tim's a perfectly respectable professional officer but," she shrugged, "you know the way these things look. Tim used to say that the British considered the Merchant Navy was the pickings of the prisons officered by the sweepings of the public schools."

"He *was* bitter. Odd Martin should be *that* interested, though. . . ."

"Well, as I said, he's always had a bit of a soft spot for me." She sipped the coffee then said, "Have a shower while I get some breakfast."

ADVENTURER, SOUTH ATLANTIC

Lila was worried and stood in the radio room looking at Stephanos. They spoke in Arabic. Her hold on the liner complete, she had time now for other considerations. "You're quite sure?"

"Yes . . . but I don't see how they could possibly know." Stephanos was young to be on such an important *fedayeen* mission, but his expert knowledge of electronics was vital to the success of their task and Lila knew she had relied on him for much acquisition of knowledge since they had infiltrated the crew of the *Adventurer*. Ever since he had intercepted that 'all ships' call from the British radio station at Portishead, warning of a possible terrorist attack on a British ship, she had been worrying. The hijack of the *Adventurer* was the nub of a vast international plan that relied on a complex, interlocking timetable. The offensive would free Palestine.

If the British knew of this threat, where had the knowledge come from? How much of the plan was already disrupted, perhaps irreparably ruined by treachery, discovery or plain bad luck?

On the other hand, she reasoned, their rendezvous with the *Libertad* and the reinforcement of *fedayeen* and Costa Mayan

173

guerillas had been faultless and the liner *was* in their hands. At this moment they still held most, if not all the initiative. She smiled reassuringly.

"I think we are worrying unnecessarily. The British have had long experience against such activists as ourselves. Strikes have been made against them and this may be just part of a routine and co-ordinated precautionary measure. They are warning their ships just as they have warned their airports."

"But they would have warned them as soon as they received the initial threats of our original strikes, that was the whole idea, to build up a dread of terror, to paralyse the running dogs, then to strike here. . . ."

"Yes," she agreed, disturbed by his logic, but aware that she must soothe his fears, to keep his mind on his own tasks and to take upon herself the burdens of command. "But they may have been putting out that message for some days, you wouldn't know. They repeat those things don't they?"

Stephanos nodded. "Yes, I hope that you're right."

"I am certain of it," she said as she left him.

Stephanos prepared to send the liner's routine morning position. He had learned the frequencies, the format and the relevant details, including Gordon's morse 'signature' and the characteristics of his sending, from the obliging chief radio officer. It was a simple task, but as a piece of deception this was its very foundation.

Their 0600 position was reported to the owners' offices in Miami and London as 41° 01.5' South, 54° 50' West. No one bothered about the office in Panama City. It was a simple room and bore the name of eight other shipping companies on its door. The ship was as mendaciously positioned as the location of her owners. In fact she was already many miles to the south-south-east.

Jonathan Aymes woke with his usual headache. He ran a professional hand down over his belly and palpated his liver, raising a forlorn eyebrow in token of acceptance. Slowly he eased himself out of his bunk and slid his feet into the worn red-leather slippers beside the bunk. At the first movements of his body the trembling began, sometimes in violent spasms. He

174

reached out for the bottle and leaned blissfully against the cabin washbasin as the first whisky of the day uncoiled its steadying warmth in his stomach.

With a crash the cabin door burst open. He dropped the empty glass and it shattered in the sink.

"What the hell . . . ?"

The man in the doorway was dappled in camouflage. Over his head and across his face was drawn the black-and-white chequered *kaffiya* of a Palestinian *fed'ai*. He held a machine-gun of some sort and the sinews and tendons of his hands as he cradled the weapon betrayed his tension.

"Hijack?" Aymes fired the question with a dawning conviction. The merest flicker of acknowledgement showed in the man's dark eyes above the mask. The *fed'ai* jerked the gun-barrel.

"You. Come."

Aymes turned. "My clothes. . . ."

"You! Come!"

He was ushered out into the officers' alleyway. It was seething with pajamaed and saronged men interspersed with the raised barrels of machine-guns and the uniforms of the PLO.

Melanie Corbett had the advantage of being dressed, but the surprise of meeting three armed men in the passengers' lobby turned from shock to terror when one of them twisted her arm behind her back and forced her forward. Her cry of pain was muted when she realized it was a woman who held her pinioned. She was thrust forward to join an increasing throng of people, passengers, catering staff and crew who were converging with a frightened shuffle in the vast space of the ship's cinema where Palmer had addressed them about the ship's itinerary. A low rumble of half-voiced fears stirred the downcast mass. She could see, at intervals above the heads of the hostages the raised barrels of the terrorists' guns. From time to time they called to each other, or shoved someone forward. She saw Aymes and tried to push nearer to him. He gave her a half-smile, divining her intention, and began to do the same. Ahead of her someone was starting an argument. She heard

Meredith's voice and the word 'demand' and then 'outrage'. The slow-moving flood of people flowed round the staff captain like a turgid stream negotiating a rock. Melanie was almost level with him. He was remonstrating with a small, dark, masked man in a plain beret, not a *kaffiya*. The man clearly did not understand and kept pushing Meredith back into the throng with his gun, the Kalashnikov across his chest.

"*Adelante!*"

Then Melanie saw something else, something that turned her legs to jelly so that she staggered. Aymes caught her, but he too had seen it and she could hear him swearing.

Anna, the linen maid, her ghastly scarred face borne proudly against the flow of shuffling prisoners, appeared above the now-familiar gun. Around her Melanie heard the gasps of horror and disgust that turned to fear as she dealt with Meredith.

The staff captain had not seen her. He had began to rage impotently to the patient Costa Mayan who still pushed him back.

"Hey!" Anna's voice cut like a whip cracking the air. Meredith turned, his face going pale, though whether it was disgust or recognition at the sight of this menial empowered with a gun, it was not clear. "Move with the others!"

"This is an outrage. . . ." Meredith never finished his sentence. Suddenly people were pushing into Aymes and Melanie, stumbling as Meredith was thrust backwards by the violence of the blow from Anna's gun butt. They drew back, then shuffled forward again, a space opening up around Meredith as he lay, his legs drawn up in a foetal position, his hands clutching his bruised genitals. Anna stood over him, her gun-muzzle pointing at them all, sweeping round them. They shuffled forward faster at the arcing movement.

At the entrance to the cinema Melanie recognized Lila. Aymes still clutched her arm and she looked at him. They exchanged glances, both were thinking about Tim Palmer.

"The bitch!" whispered Melanie, already convinced that Lila had seduced Palmer to further her terrorist aims. Palmer was probably already dead, shot on the bridge in the middle of the night.

Lila was watching them individually as they filed into the

176

crowded space of the cinema. Melanie saw one of the women passengers dragged out of the crowd. She was pale and drawn, her eyes large with fear and with only a dressing-gown pulled round her. It was Margaret Allen and Melanie watched a gunman lead her away.

As Melanie and Aymes approached the doorway she thought Lila might wreak some petty revenge upon her, but Lila's eyes merely raked her face, no trace of recognition manifesting itself. Melanie felt a stab of pure fear at the lack of response. It was as if she did not exist.

Palmer was almost asleep when Lila returned to the bridge. Her expression as she greeted Giorgio, his guard, was one of obvious triumph. He had heard a few shouts and cries from below. At one point, Palmer saw, one of the first-class male passengers from Aymes's table had obviously broken away from his captors. He ran up onto the long forecastle head, as though the bow of the ship offered some refuge from what was happening elsewhere. Two gunmen pursued him, one wearing a *kaffiya*, the other a beret. They were enjoying themselves, playing the man in a grim game of 'he', as he dodged round the great capstans and the self-tensioning mooring winches. Twice they fired, their slugs whining off in ricochet so that the passenger cowered in mortal terror, but it was clear they had no intention of killing him. In the end the poor man tripped over the long expanse of the starboard anchor cable as it led from the capstan to the hawse-pipe. Before he had time to recover himself the two gunmen were standing over him. Even from the distance and height of the bridge, Palmer could see him shaking.

As the terrified victim lay there *Adventurer* dipped her bow into a heavy swell, snorting two white columns of water up her hawse-pipes, one of which sluiced coldly over the passenger. He was led dripping away.

Lila's arrival revived him. She was in conversation with Giorgio but after a few minutes the man left and they were alone on the bridge.

Below, in the captain's cabin, Dr Galvin finished laying out the

177

corpse of Captain Smythe. Beside him a reluctant Blumenthal was helping.

"I did not think you would be a squeamish man, Mr Blumenthal. You have seen dead bodies before, I believe."

"Yes. And I have handled them. It is not the same."

"No, but it is what people like you leave for people like me."

Blumenthal turned away and lowered his ancient frame into one of Smythe's comfortable and clubby armchairs.

"I have lived my life according to my sacred beliefs, doctor. It is not for you to judge," Blumenthal said slowly.

"Indeed not. . . ." Galvin plugged the last orifice and bound up the jaw, "I was just surprised that you baulked at this task."

Blumenthal remained silent. In their present circumstances he had a lot to think about. Galvin seemed monstrously unruffled by the terrible events that had happened on board.

"Why," asked Galvin, wiping his washed hands on Smythe's towel, "aren't you terrified? I seem to remember reading in *Time* magazine that you had been a member of the Stern Gang."

Blumenthal looked up. "The Irgun . . ." he corrected.

"Ahhh. . . . It looks as though, from the way that they've locked us up here, that we are special cases."

"We are hostages, Dr Galvin, hostages of Fatah. I was warned by the Mossad of this possibility, but a man in my condition does not worry exactly when he meets his maker."

Their conversation was abruptly interrupted by the cabin door opening. Margaret Allen was pushed roughly inside.

"Margaret. . . ." Galvin stepped forward as the door closed and the lock turned upon the three of them.

"And what have you done, dear lady," said Blumenthal, "to incur the displeasure of our new hosts?"

Giorgio slipped along the wide and luxuriously carpeted alleyway of *Adventurer*'s most prestigious accommodation. Above the level of the boat deck the half-dozen penthouse suites opened onto balconies overlooking great vistas of the ocean. He was pleased with the bargain he had driven with Lila. Giorgio was Lila's lieutenant, the brawn to her brains, and he knew she relied upon him to buttress her with his experience and skill. A fighter since the age of eight when the *Ashbal*, the Lion-cub movement, had given him his first gun, violence had become as much a part of his life as meat and drink. He had graduated to become a part of the Fatah organisation, operated on the fringes of Black September and devoted the energies of his life to the anti-Zionist campaign to free his homeland. He was just old enough to remember another Palestine, before the Israelis came.

But he was ageing, past 40 now, an old campaigner who was privately aware of his own failing powers. The speed of his reflexes, the dexterity of his aim were declining and he had lived too long on the unfulfilled promises of his leaders. He knew, too, that the fates of such operations as they were engaged upon so often ended in disaster and death for the operatives. Zelda Rebanowicz was his insurance policy.

It had not been hard to convince the preoccupied Lila that he wanted the fat capitalist whore left for his own pleasure. She would cause no trouble, she was compliant to his every wish. Besides, he had nodded in Palmer's direction, Lila had her own amusements.

"We need him for the ship," Lila had replied, "to navigate."

"I need my fat whore" replied Giorgio, "for myself."

Lila had shrugged.

Giorgio had reached Mrs Rebanowicz's cabin. Without ceremony he slipped inside.

For a long time Zelda Rebanowicz had cowered against the padded satin covered headboard of the bed, straining her ears for noises of approaching doom. She had heard some muffled shouts and a noise from the adjacent cabin, but no one had come to her door and after what seemed like a long time she had fallen asleep in an armchair. She woke to find Giorgio standing over her. Smiling with relief she thought at first she had been victim of a dream.

"Giorgio. . . ."

He grinned at her, a savage smile, and laid the Kalashnikov on the elegant mock Louis Quinze dressing stool beside her.

"Oh. . . ." She drew back into the recesses of the winged chair. A terrible comprehension was breaking through her confusion.

179

"Giorgio?" she frowned, "you are not . . .? You have hijacked this ship?"

He was still grinning. "How did you know? Ah, yes the window . . . you saw the deck. You could not sleep because Giorgio was not with you, eh?"

He leaned over her. "Now Giorgio come back. Now we stay together. You do what Giorgio say and you are safe."

She was not listening. "Get away from me you Commie bastard!" She thrust against his chest.

"Hey! Giorgio is not a Communist. Giorgio is a Palestinian."

"Oh my God!"

He took her by the shoulders, pulling her to her feet. "Come, we make love now, eh? Then get some sleep. We are still friends. Nothing change between us. . . ."

"No!"

She brought her knee up as they had told her in the anti-mugging, self-defence teach-in. He was too quick for her and her head reeled from the stinging blow he fetched across her face with his open hand. She fell backwards, oversetting the chair and crashing against the bulkhead, subsiding into a heap, burying her head in her hands, her shoulders heaving with sobs.

He looked down at her. She looked her age now, round lumps of flesh crumpled into an unlovely pile. He was pleased, it would make the discarding of her easy when the time came. But he felt a surging power over her and unzipped his slacks.

The movement made her look up.

"No!" She cowered.

"I try to think of you as not American woman, but as person. We are good together . . . very good. . . ."

He was rigid with excitement and bent down, grabbing her by her upper arms. She could have kicked him then but he pulled her close, forcing his mouth on hers. One arm snaked round her back, crushing her breasts painfully against his chest, the other reached into her groin, forcing her open while his weight thrust her back against the fabric-covered bulkhead. She felt her resistance weaken; there was a lubricious response from her treacherous body.

"You bastard . . . you bloody bastard!" she gasped, the

180

tears streaming down her face to be kissed and licked by her panting lover.

"Anna says we cannot trust you."

Palmer wearily looked at Lila. She was severer even than when he had first seen her. The heavy jacket, the bandolier, belt and gun turned her from a woman to an androgynous instrument of intimidation.

"Trust me to do what? I was not aware that you were trusting me anyway."

"You are still alive."

Palmer looked at her. There was no sign in her face of their former intimacy. He remembered feeling like this once before, desolate and bereft, chilled by a kind of neglectful cruelty. He had met Rosie at a party months after their divorce. They had acknowledged each other but so frigidly that it seemed impossible that they had ever known each other. He forced his mind to think. He too had his orders.

"What do you intend to do?" he asked.

"With you?"

"With me, with the ship."

"I need you to navigate and to mediate, Palmer. In the engine room I have some people but I need some of the engineers as well. They are co-operating now, but in case of trouble. . . ."

"I'm a hostage then?"

"Yes. Of a kind."

The irony of his situation struck him even more forcibly. He was a hostage indeed, but different from the mewed-up passengers in the cinema who were negotiable. He was, like DeAth and the others of *Adventurer*'s crew, expendable.

It was such a reasonable, logical word. So, he was expendable to Lila too; the man in London had implied much the same.

"We will leave you up here. You can sleep on the chart room bed."

"Thank you."

"It is better than being dead." Their eyes met then and Palmer read something in hers; perhaps regret, possibly some residue of love. "We do not live forever," she said.

181

It was a cold crumb of comfort, but at least it was something more than had passed between him and Rosie.

THIRD CHILEAN NAVAL ZONE HEADQUARTERS, PUNTA ARENAS

Captain Henrique Soto put down the telephone and stared out of the office window, a smile of satisfaction playing about his mouth. He watched a Bell 206A Jetranger helicopter come to the hover and then touch down. He rose and picked up his hat. Rear-Admiral Aguirra was absent at a meeting at Talcahuano, but he was a hawk who hated the Argentinians and Soto's intercept had come at a propitious moment. There had been some Argentinian movements at Ushuaia, opposite the Chilean naval base at Puerto Williams on Navarino Island, and Aguirra, always hating to be absent from his post at Punta Arenas, was only too happy for Soto to make a sweep down through the Beagle Channel and out round the eastern end of Navarino Island.

"Those bastards go ashore on Lennox and Nueva to piss like dogs marking a telegraph pole," Aguirra had said, referring to the Argentine claim of ownership of the Chilean flyspecks of Nueva, Picton and Lennox Islands north east of Cape Horn. "Go and chase them away."

It was all Soto wanted. He walked across the dockyard, casually returning the salutes of enlisted men. The Jetranger's turbines dropped in pitch and the rotors swished to a halt. He could see the masts of his ship above the sheds. She would be refuelled by now and he watched the curious, eccentric revolutions of the angled cheese-shaped 965 air-search radar revolving in its constant quest for aircraft. On the after-mast the big bedstead of the guided weapons GWS 22/MRS3 turned with a ponderous motion, warming up. Soto was enthusiastic about his ship, regarding the *Leander*-class frigates operated by the Chileans as being superior to those used by the British Royal Navy. Due to the huge Pacific swells they experienced, the Chileans had heightened their masts and gained a few extra miles of radar horizon. More important than that, they had not sacrificed the twin 4.5-inch gun-mounting to carry Exocet. They carried both, mounting the Exocets aft, behind the flight deck. It made flying a chopper a little difficult but, hell, he thought, the helo boys could handle that!

Soto admired the British nevertheless, applauded their stand against the Argentinian generals, for their tradition ran strongly in his own service. Lord Cochrane, the disgraced British admiral who had founded the Chilean navy, was reputed to have had a hand in founding the naval tradition in Soto's own family and the Marine Brigade stationed here, at Punta Arenas, was named in his honour.

It was one of the regrets of Soto's life that the Falklands War had not escalated and allowed the Chileans to clear the arrogant Argentinians out of the Magellanic Archipelago altogether.

He reached the foot of the brow and looked at his long, grey ship with pride. He saw the fluster on deck as the duty officer mustered the guard to greet him. They exchanged salutes as he stepped down onto the deck.

"Pass word we sail in one hour."

Four hours later the *Bernardo O'Higgins* was steaming south, the Paso Ingles opening to starboard as she headed for the cluster of islands that littered the entrance of the long, narrow strait of the Beagle Channel. On every hand, long fingers of water, blue, grey and silver stretched into the hinterland, dividing the dark slopes of evergreen beech trees into thousands of islands, lined by narrow strips of beach set in tiny bays. The whole area was swept by frequent squalls, katabatic winds of brief and terrible fury that slid down from the mountainous summits rising black and jagged above the beech woods. And over all, dominating the whole land of Tierra del Fuego, high above the narrow straits and fiords, the mighty shoulders of the snow-capped Cordillera Darwin touched the clouds.

On the bridge of the lean, grey frigate, Captain Soto smiled to himself, hoping to catch an Argentine pissing against one of these Chilean rocks.

NEW SCOTLAND YARD, LONDON

There was no doubt in Kate Meldrum's mind that her relationship with Nicholas was unprofessional, for it had decidedly unprofessional results. The Commander's section of the Metropolitan Police's anti-terrorist branch was chiefly concerned with dissemination and liaison. Operating on the fringe of C13, Nicholas's responsibility was primarily to the Commissioner, but he had close links as a co-ordinator with military intelligence, particularly insofar as IRA activities might affect the capital and with the various intelligence agencies of foreign, friendly governments. In the main his work dealt with the movements of terrorist suspects.

The section was a somewhat elastic sub-group of the Met, bloating itself to full strength according to the scale of terrorist activity that it was currently engaged against. In the hiatus following the so-called 'terror-offensive', it wound itself down by a natural process; other incidents demanding redeployment of its seconded staff, reducing it to its core of full-time officers.

With one exception: Chief Inspector Kate Meldrum.

Her continuing presence showed the extent to which Nicholas's judgement had been clouded by their affaire. Or did it?

"I want you to stay on for a while, Kate," he had said over breakfast three days earlier. "Let's play that nautical hunch out."

Well, that was his excuse, she privately thought, and she was reluctant to return to the mundane lecturing job at Hendon. Although Alex Martin and his few remaining sleuths were busy following a few cooling trails, the origins of the much advertized 'terror offensive' had grown cold.

When the telex chattered into life it startled her. She got up and walked over to it. P and O Cruises Ltd were informing Scotland Yard that *Canberra* and *Oriana* had reported their positions satisfactorily. An hour later the Cunard Line had reported the *Queen Elizabeth 2* quite safe, the *Cunard Countess* and *Cunard Princess* likewise. Reports from the *Vistafiord* and *Sagafiord* were expected at any moment.

The routine reports were about the sum total of Kate's contribution to the whole matter. On impulse she rang Adventure Cruises Ltd, in Berkeley Street.

"Oh yes, *Adventurer* reported her position as usual this morning. No, there are no problems."

So Tim was all right then. She cleared her desk, wondering how much of her concern was transferred guilt, and disliked herself for the thought.

The VDU flickered its relentless 'ready' signal at her and, almost idly, she tapped in the top security password 'Garibaldi'. It would not hurt to go over the files again.

She began to access them, her mind slipping away from its personal preoccupations, matching the computer with the speed of its impulses and exceeding it with the speculations that went far beyond logic.

Nicholas sat in his office and studied the daily intelligence reports. It was routine stuff, mainly concerned with the movements of IRA suspects in and around London.

He was still smarting from the drubbing the Commissioner had given him. He knew Sir Charles appreciated the difficulties of his section, but it was inconceivable that he should have let the only positive contact in the whole disastrous matter of the destruction of the Gannet Oil Platforms slip through his fingers. That the man had actually been in the building was a cruel irony. Alex Martin had said he never suspected a thing, that the man was cool as a cucumber.

It was no comfort that the pilot had been shot dead in the whores' quarter of Hamburg. That simply sealed off the only lead they had.

The dead ends and the fizzling out of the 'terror offensive' worried him. In his business no news was not necessarily good news.

His desk intercom buzzed.

"Nicholas."

"Chief Inspector Meldrum, sir. May I see you?"

She was formal. He hoped to God she was not about to take advantage. "Yes, of course."

She came in, trim and crisp in her uniform.

185

"Sit down, Kate." He smiled, permitting intimacy this far. "What is it?"

"I've been doing some analysis, sir, and I've come up with some odd bits of evidence. Circumstantial, of course, but worth knowing."

"Go on." He pushed the pile of message forms and telex printouts to one side and watched her face as she expanded her notes.

"Some of these things may seem a bit irrelevant, sir. . . ."

"I'll bear that in mind . . . have you cooked up a scenario?"

She frowned. "Well, no, sir, not exactly, but I feel . . . well, I lack the imagination for that, but I've a hunch I'm on the right track."

"You sound like Barlow, or whatever his name was."

She laughed at the allusion to the television series.

"I started with the primary attacks, the hotels, the air crashes, the oil platforms, the ship at Belfast, then I analysed the death tolls. All the attacks were made against nationals of countries within which there are terrorist cells sworn to bring down the established governments. FLQ against the Algonquin Airlines flight, the Japanese . . ."

"Yes, I'm with you."

"Most of the dead were nationals of the country of ownership. In the case of the Canadian airliner they also killed a defecting operative. . . ."

"Who nearly gave the game away."

"Yes. Same with the hotels. The San Francisco hotel was filled with Americans, same in New York, while in France a business convention in Paris caught a lot of Frenchmen, but that was not the case in London. In London the hotels happened to be largely filled with foreigners and the staff are not overwhelmingly British."

"What are you trying to say?"

"That analysis of the dead shows relatively few British compared with the numbers of other nationals." She held out a computer printout.

"What about the Cathay Pacific flight?"

"Largely Japanese and American passengers. Further, the Belfast bomb might have destroyed the Royal Navy's latest

186

Type 23 destroyer, but no one was killed, while in the Gannet Oil Platform disaster the polyglot nature of the offshore industry has resulted in fewer British lives being lost than one might have supposed. In fact only 57 per cent were British."

"Yes, I recall those pictures of the funerals on television which the new Prime Minister attended as showing a lot of Dutch and Norwegian flags. Overall then, these are the figures here . . . and we're well down the list of victims numerically speaking."

"Yes sir."

"And what do you infer from that circumstantial statistic?"

Kate opened her mouth to speak, thought better of it and blew out her cheeks. "Well, sir, nothing as yet. Perhaps you'd like me to go on a bit first."

"Okay."

"I remembered the Canadian official I met here. The Mounties had the best lead after our helicopter pilot, with their dead FLQ man. I put through a request for follow-up briefing. It was denied. Not refused on the basis that there was no information, but denied. I checked back through the signals files and found that the information petered out the day after the 'terror-offensive'. It not only petered out from our Commonwealth cousins, but also the Americans . . . so much for the Special Relationship. Most significant was that the routine Mossad information usually relayed by the Deuxiéme Bureau also faded at that time. But, yesterday, MI6 put through a routine 'inward' report of two Israeli Mossad agents; nothing sinister or unusual about that, except that they sometimes let us know . . . apparently . . ."

"Now that *is* interesting . . . but go on, what's your exegesis, Chief Inspector?"

"Well sir, despite the apparent damage to British hotels, oil platforms and military targets, we appear to have been treated rather leniently. The reactions of our friends and allies suggest they've noticed."

"But that hardly explains their isolating us like this."

"No, I agree, although it does explain why we've not had a single lead, particularly on the April 86 thing."

Nicholas smiled wryly. That had been Kate's own baby and she had hoped for great things from it.

"I mean," she went on, "the Israelis must have known something."

"So?"

"So, sir, I reason it out something like this. . . ."

Nicholas sat for a long time after Kate had gone. He considered everything she had said and at the end of his deliberations he was a worried man. He picked up his secure telephone and rang his contact at MI6, asking for a tail to be put on the two Mossad agents.

It was nothing like enough, but it was all he could do. He found himself praying for the final strike by the Palestinians, surely then the curtain would be rent asunder. For the time being London seemed to be under an intelligence blackout for which there really was only one credible explanation.

Kate Meldrum's.

GAINESVILLE, GEORGIA TO FAYETTEVILLE, NORTH CAROLINA

The battered Pontiac convertible pulled out of Gainesville and crossed the Chattahoochee River. By lunchtime it had reached Spartanburg, slowing in the traffic while an old Beach Boys tape played amid the growl of idling engines.

The balding driver with the dark, drooping moustache had a short stopover at a diner and by early afternoon crossed the second state boundary into North Carolina. A few miles farther on he swung right, heading for Fayetteville.

TAIWANESE DEEP-WATER TRAWLER *NIGHT OF THE BRIGHT MOON*, SOUTH ATLANTIC

Wang Lee Foo was the toughest kind of seaman on earth,

a deep-water fisherman. Hardship had been his lot in life since, as a baby, he had been bounced upon his mother's back, his head lolling violently as she ran screaming from the exploding bombs dropped on their village by Japanese aircraft. His father, a Nationalist soldier in Chiang Kai Chek's Guomindong army had been killed in an obscure skirmish and, after many wanderings, Foo's mother had arrived penniless in Taiwan. Foo had begged scraps of food from the fishermen of Chi-lung and, as he grew old enough, shipped out on a fishing junk. In those days they had fished the near Pacific or the Taiwan Strait, risking strafing by the Chinese Communist airforce.

Forty years later he commanded his own diesel trawler and roamed the high seas on behalf of the population of his over-crowded and increasingly beleaguered island. This morning he was some 360 miles south-east of the estuary of the Rio de la Plata, and the *Night of the Bright Moon* was rolling abominably as she had been rolling now for the two months she had been fishing these waters. He had just given orders to haul the pelagic trawl.

Foo leaned from the window of the wheelhouse and yelled orders at his crew in a harsh, cracked voice. His deeply lined face was moon-round beneath a beret pulled squarely down over his head, his tiny eyes peered keenly from the folds of his eyelids. His gnarled hands with the split, claw-like nails suddenly clenched. The cod-end of the trawl was suspended above the deck. In an assortment of hats his crew stared upwards at the bulging net. It was bloated with silver fish, a marvellous catch, but there was something else, something less welcome.

The cod end was loosed and a cascade of twitching fish flooded the deck, slithering between the wooden baffles as his crew waded among the dying mass. Among them were four human bodies.

Foo was no stranger to untimely death, nor to the tattoo on the muscular arm on one of the corpses. His feelings about the Union Jack were decidedly ambivalent, but he knew enough about what had happened in these waters a few years previously to know that recently dead British sailors could spell trouble.

189

RFA *TIDESTREAM*, ON PASSAGE ASCENSION TO PORT STANLEY, SOUTH ATLANTIC

Third Officer Robin Bush stared through his binoculars from the bridge of the Royal Fleet Auxiliary *Tidestream*, a naval supply tanker taking diesel fuel to the British forces based in the Falkland Islands.

Through powerful binoculars, Bush, the officer-of-the-watch, was watching the bucking and rolling fishing boat with pity. He was an imaginative young man and it defied him to visualize how one could live for a week on such an oscillating platform. How some poor bastards had to work to earn a living!

Taiwan was a very long way away.

He was very surprised when a morse light began blinking at the *Tidestream*. Fishing boats rarely communicated with passing ships. This one was winking away the dash-dot-dash code of the morse letter 'K'. In the International Code of Signals it meant 'I have something important to communicate'.

A mine in his nets?

"John Chinaman's really on the ball," Bush muttered, summoning the *Tidestream*'s master, pulling the engine telegraphs to 'Stop' and establishing VHF radio telephone contact with the trawler.

It was a bizarre conversation, Foo's English was poor and the *Tidestream*'s master spoke only a few words of Cantonese, but they had a Hong Kong laundryman on board and an hour later, after the sea-boat had been launched and recovered, the bodies had been transferred to the *Tidestream*'s fridge.

Both vessels parted company and were soon separated by the vast spaces of the South Atlantic.

ADVENTURER, SOUTHERN OCEAN

They were walking in a long crocodile, two-by-two, round the boat deck. At intervals above them on the penthouse and fiddley decks were posted the ubiquitous gun-toting figures of terrorists, well swathed against the chill wind in which the exercising party of hostages shivered dolefully. Margaret Allen leaned on Galvin's arm; ahead of them the bent back of Blumenthal was alone, an isolation that was more than symbolic. In the past few days of incarceration Galvin had realized that he was selected as a 'special prisoner' because of his profession. It was his job to keep the old Jewish statesman and former terrorist alive. The Fatah people had done their homework well; he wondered if they knew Blumenthal was dying of cancer.

Beside him, Margaret was shivering. The perceptive Galvin sensed it was more than a reaction to the cold. He looked sideways at her. She looked tired and drawn, her skin shrunk round her bones, her lips bloodless. He recalled thinking as a student how similar skulls looked when compared with the faces that had covered them in life. He had not yet discovered what made Margaret special to the hijackers but, from her state of nerves, she knew.

It was not difficult to work out why half-a-dozen of the teenage schoolchildren had also been singled out from the great mass of *Adventurer*'s passengers. Galvin had discovered they were being kept in one of the penthouses a few feet abaft the captain's accommodation in which he and his two companions were mewed up. They all had surnames prominent in the international field of politics and industry.

A movement above them caught his eye and he looked up. Higher than the watching guards, swaying from gantlines, a dozen of *Adventurer*'s intimidated seamen were swinging slowly down the ship's huge funnel in bosun's chairs. They wielded paint rollers, loaded with white paint and were drawing a descending veil over the bright orange and blue colours of the *Adventurer*'s owners. The great ship was donning camouflage.

"I think I know where they're taking us," he muttered in a low voice.

"Where?" Blumenthal's voice came back to him, though the old man did not turn his white-haired head.

"We're heading south . . . towards the Antarctic."

He felt Margaret's grip on his arm tense. Beyond the limits of the boat deck the sea was grey, streaked with white, leaden under an overcast sky. Occasionally the pale disc of the sun showed briefly and could be stared at without discomfort.

Galvin trudged on, turning as instructed and breathing in the cold, damp air, trying to fight off the crushing inevitability that was stifling him with its suffocating fatalism at the way things had turned out. He was distracted by a second squeeze on his arm. Beside then as they marched past a door into the accommodation, stood the figure of the hideously disfigured young woman. Of all the terrorists, she alone scorned the anonymity of a mask.

Galvin saw her watching Blumenthal, but the old man did not look up at her. A grimace of satisfaction was playing about her lipless mouth. This time he could not resist a shudder of foreboding.

In the engine room Jim Barclay wiped his sweating forehead for the hundredth time and stared the length of the machinery control room. There were two engineers down there, together with two greasers. There were also three gunmen. One was his own former greaser, the man they had known as Zig. Whenever their eyes met, Zig's became blank, the eyes of a complete stranger. Barclay swore under his breath. He was outraged that the ship had surrendered without a fight. His own unwitting complicity did nothing for his mental turmoil. He had come below God knows how long ago, come on watch as routinely as on any other morning, called by telephone by the third engineer and seeing only his mustering watch as he slid with easy practice down the steel ladders to the MCR.

Seconds later the engines had stopped and the nightmare had begun. Zig had started it, Zig and some complete strangers in head-cloths and berets that had seemed initially like a practical joke in bad taste. They had not long been left in doubt as to the seriousness of Zig's purpose. Barclay had the bruises to prove the uselessness of resistance. Now he glared at Zig.

"I'll get you, you bastard," he muttered. Zig returned the hostile look with the patient observation of a watching hawk, but the gun moved imperceptibly, a slight gesture that indicated relative status.

192

"Prick . . ."

Far above Barclay's head the exhaust pipes, flues and uptakes rose gleaming into the funnel casing. Its exterior had undergone a transformation. Barclay did not know it but, from a distance the ship was almost indistinguishable from an iceberg.

Palmer picked up the first iceberg 15 miles on the Racal-Decca radar. It gave off a response exactly like a small island with a cliff facing the observer. Half an hour later he saw it emerge through the veil of mist that obscured the horizon, not more than three miles away. It was undramatic, an average-sized tabular berg, calved from the ice-shelf of the Weddell Sea. It loomed insubstantially through the poor visibility. Its bearing opened on the port side and it passed about seven cables away, an oddly regular almost man-made iceberg welcoming them to the Antarctic. *Adventurer* would have to reduce her speed now, to avoid striking any of the partially melted bergs that floated too low in the water to be detected by radar. Palmer recalled the ill-omened jest of the American pilot at Charleston; perhaps they were another *Titanic*, destined to founder after contacting another kind of sea-borne danger. He moved to the chart table, the masked gunman keeping him company, and stared down at the British Admiralty chart of the Antarctic Peninsula.

The pencil line of their intended track, leading down from a position miles east of the Falklands, disappeared into a welter of tiny islands that fringed the long, northward-poking finger of the Antarctic continent reaching up towards the salient of Cape Horn. The pencil line stopped just short of a small curl on the chart, a curl of high-peaked rock neatly hachured by the painstaking hand of an Admiralty cartographer thousands of miles away in England. It looked like the letter 'C' which had been rotated clockwise through 90 degrees.

Destitution Island rose to nearly a 1000 metres above mean sea level and enclosed a lagoon formed by the crater of a volcano. It had once been a whaling station, but was now uninhabited by man and lay off the beaten track of the support ships that might be encountered on their annual summer voyages to the British and American survey stations on the peninsula.

Palmer shook his head, aware that this operation showed the hand of genius in its conception. Secure inside that innocuous curl of ice and snow-covered rock, *Adventurer* would be utterly lost.

Palmer wondered how what had seemed so reasonable in London could possibly be made to work.

Chapter Nine

DOWNING STREET, LONDON

"You can hear behind me the concussion of the Israeli guns and see, on the horizon, smoke and dust rising from the Lebanese port of Sidon. There is a news blackout here, neither side allowing foreign correspondents near their front lines. There is a story circulating here that so fierce is the resistance put up from the defenders of Sidon that the Israelis are embarrassed by their failure to take the port quickly, despite the presence of tanks and strikes by rocket-carrying fighter aircraft.

"Lying off the port are a number of merchant ships, caught in the crossfire of this, the most serious crisis to be posed for some time by the Palestine question. This is Brian Lord, News at Ten, Sidon."

"It is serious, isn't it, David?"

"Yes, very . . . Admiral Backhouse's Sixth Fleet is already in the offing and the Russian helicopter assault ship *Borodino* with her task force is only a day away. Frankly it's as serious as the Cuban Missile Crisis of '62."

"Have you heard anything from the American Ambassador?"

"No. He's been strangely quiet now for a couple of days."

PORT STANLEY MILITARY HOSPITAL, EAST FALKLAND ISLAND

"Fucking arseholes!"

Surgeon Lieutenant Commander Morrison looked up at his Sick Berth Attendant with a jaundiced eye.

195

"That is scarcely a formal description, Hunter, whatever the sexual proclivities of the poor fellow."

"But I know him, sir, it's 'Ginger' Marshall, sir. We were muckers on the old *Torbay!*"

Morrison looked at his assistant sharply and then both stared down at the corpse. It was white and wrinked from loss of blood and immersion, but the ginger hair and the unmistakably naval tattoos stood out like colours on paper. It lay naked on a slab in the wing of Port Stanley Hospital reserved for service use. 'Wing' was, perhaps, too grand a word for a room that was now crowded with the inert figures landed earlier that day from the RFA *Tidestream*. Morrison's task of autopsy was relatively simple. All the victims had died from gunshot. One had his face missing. But the matter of identification was something else; something else until SBA Hunter's crude outburst.

"Are you sure?"

"Positive, sir. The tattoos. . . ."

"A lot of sailors have Union Jacks and 'I love Mum' on their arms, Hunter," Morrison said drily.

"Look on his arse, sir."

"What will I find?" The body was the last they had examined. Apart from the faceless man all the others had had gunshot wounds in the thorax. Entry and exit holes, though leached of blood, were hideously obvious. This man had been shot from the front; they had yet to examine his back. Morrison had asked the question deliberately, before turning the cadaver over.

"He's got two bloody great eyes. . . ."

"Dear God . . . !"

They rolled the corpse over. On each buttock an eye, neatly done in black, green and red, focussed its pupil on the cleavage of the seaman's buttocks.

"It's a seaman alright," observed Morrison.

"It's 'Ginger' Marshall, sir."

"Mmmm . . . so how does your messmate come to be picked up in a Taiwanese trawl, Hunter, eh?"

"I dunno sir."

"Well, is he still in the Andrew?"

"No, sir. He left the navy in '84." Hunter frowned in recollection, "He was going to join the Merchant Navy, but I lost touch."

Hunter looked down at the bloodless corpse. "He was a good lad."

There was no trace of the bullet. No matter; he had extracted a pair of 9mm slugs from the others. Morrison paid only cursory attention to the huge exit wound and began to peel off his gloves.

"That's not a bad epitaph for a man."

BRITISH NAVAL HEADQUARTERS, PORT STANLEY, EAST FALKLAND ISLAND

Captain Crosby-Milne, Royal Navy, holding the temporary appointment of Commodore and currently the Senior Naval Officer commanding Her Majesty's ships and vessels in the Falkland Islands Area looked at the messages on his desk. Next to them lay two 9mm slugs, blunt from impact.

He hated with all the passion of an active man the mind-clogging routine of paperwork. Since the British victory in the South Atlantic his command, the nearest to a front line he could hope to get in the last years of his service, had degenerated into a ceaseless stream of paperwork. Crosby-Milne was too good a professional to shirk this thoroughly irksome duty, but his dislike of it made him aware of one danger inherent in any 'system'. In coping with the mundane, the unusual or important could slip through unnoticed. But the messages had arrived as near simultaneously as was possible and the slugs had been dropped on his desk by Morrison like audible promptings.

The first message was a 'co-operative signal' from Rear-Admiral Aguirra of the Chilean Navy. Aguirra had just arrived back at his command post at Punta Arenas. He had been at a naval staff conference at Talcuahano when one of his best frigate captains had reported intercepting an Argentine code group which might be of some significance to either of them. It was known to mean the recipient should act on some previously given instruction. As it was transmitted on a random frequency, Aguirra thought Crosby-Milne might like to know about it.

They knew each other, Crosby-Milne having handed over the Royal Navy's former County class Guided Missile Destroyer *Suffolk* to the Chilean Navy. They had liked each other and such contacts transcended official channels. Crosby-Milne knew Aguirra's dislike of his neighbours was as much a spur to the Chilean admiral as his friendship with Crosby-Milne.

Aguirra thought the Argentine naval activity referred to was probably some incursion to Picton or Lennox Island, but it did no harm to be vigilant. Crosby-Milne's relief was due imminently. He did not want anything to go wrong now.

The second message was from HMS *Stupendous*, one of two nuclear-powered hunter-killer patrol submarines whose deterrent presence theoretically kept the Argentine Navy mewed up. *Stupendous*'s commanding officer had routine ship contacts. Several merchant ships of no significance plus a Russian '*Foxtrot*'-class submarine, tracked on sonar heading south. *Stupendous* thought her too noisy to be Russian operated. The Libyans, Cubans, Chinese and now, thought Crosby-Milne remembering the intelligence reports, the Costa Mayans, all possessed *Foxtrots*. That was, nevertheless, a piece of information that should be forwarded to Northwood, the British Fleet Headquarters.

As for this other matter, the body of ex-Leading Seaman Marshall and the corpses brought in by *Tidestream* from Skipper Foo's trawler, that too ought to be forwarded. It was very odd, but piracy on board merchant ships was on the increase and one of the bodies, a headless cadaver, had been wearing the shoulder epaulettes of a radio officer. He would forward the autopsy reports too. It would clear his in-tray.

Curiously he rolled one of the 9mm slugs under the ball of his right forefinger. Such a little thing.

NEW SCOTLAND YARD, LONDON

"I think you'd better come in a moment." Nicholas's voice was chill with foreboding. When Kate reached his office he dismissed his shorthand typist and asked her to sit. He waited for the girl to go, pushing an ashtray across the desk top. She lit a cigarette.

"No, go ahead," he said as she hesitated.

It was obvious to Kate that something had happened. "What is it, sir?"

"It's not good Kate, I'm afraid." There was an inexplicably personal edge in Nicholas's voice. She blew the cigarette smoke out and attempted professional detachment. "I presume you mean the main strike?"

"It looks like it," Nicholas nodded.

"Ship or school?"

"Ship ... actually Kate, although there's no confirmation, it looks like being the *Adventurer*."

She sat quite still, letting the information sink in, testing her true reaction to it. At least it ended the uncertainty and, she told herself, she had known all along it was going to touch her. She could not explain that to a man, least of all a man like Nicholas, but she felt calmer; somehow you could be positive about facts. Even when you were quite unable to act on them.

"Would you mind explaining, sir."

"Two days ago a quite routine military intelligence enquiry started in London as a consequence of some news from the Falklands. The enquiry set out to discover the movements of a former British naval seaman named Marshall. His body, together with several others, as yet unidentified, was picked up in the South Atlantic. They had all been shot. Marshall had left the Royal Navy in 1984. For a while he was unemployed and lived with his divorced mother in Reading. In mid-85 he registered on the International seamen's 'pool' at Rotterdam, apparently it's the only way our merchant seamen can get work. Two months ago he succeeded; he signed on the Panamanian-registered ship *Adventurer*."

". . . As yet unidentified . . ." Nicholas had said. Did that mean Tim's body was lying on a slab in distant Port Stanley?

"There was one other thing. MI6 were unusually communicative, probably because they're starved of information," Nicholas put in drily, "but I elicited the information that a '*Foxtrot*' submarine had been tracked in the area east of the Falkland Islands."

The statement jerked Kate's introspection back to the present.

"What on earth made you ask that, sir?"

"Your Costa Mayan link theory. I simply asked if any Costa Mayan ships had been in the area and they came up with the possibility that this submarine might be Costa Mayan. Apparently the Russians let them have one after the success of their revolution."

"But we don't know for certain that it was Costa Mayan, do we? And if the Russians give them to the Costa Mayans, doesn't that mean that they give them to others?"

"Or sell them, yes, India, Cuba ... but if it *was* Costa Mayan. ..."

"It was a bloody long way from home," Kate finished with sudden vehemence. Then her voice fell. "But we don't know for sure."

"No."

The tone of his voice said he was hedging.

"But, sir?"

"But I turned up a report from the CIA that the Costa Mayan submarine *Libertad* hasn't been seen in home waters for some time."

"Circumstantial."

"Very."

"But it's nice to know the Yanks are passing the information across again."

"They're not, Kate. This news is weeks old."

The significance of that time-lapse was also circumstantial, but it allowed the submarine time to cross the Atlantic Ocean.

"What made you think a Costa Mayan ship might be involved?"

"Well, the breadth of your scenario argued massive collusion focussed, outside Palestine, on the Costa Mayans. I argued that their assistance might prove more active than mere fronting at the United Nations. As soon as I began to think about your ship theory I perceived its ease of execution, but also its difficulties. Okay, you get the wooden horse into Troy, but then you need reinforcements, guards, reliefs, watchmen and so on. Quite a lot of people, especially on a big boat like *Adventurer*."

"Ship, sir, not boat."

"Sorry. Well the only way is to rendezvous ... open the gates as it were, and let in the Greeks, only for Greeks, read Costa Mayans."

They were silent for a while, digesting the implications of this complex guessing game. After a pause Kate said, "But no one has officially admitted that the *Adventurer* has been hijacked, or that they've hijacked the *Adventurer*...."

"No, but the first is easy to explain. The company is continuing to receive daily positions. It will be easy to check them by air from the Falklands if she's bound through the Strait of Magellan, but it's my guess they're completely spurious. As for the second point, they won't claim anything until they're ready. It's my guess they're going to hide her. I should think that's not difficult among the islands around the coast of Patagonia."

Kate took that assertion on trust. Geography had never been a love of hers at school. But Nicholas had not yet finished.

"Knowing it's the *Adventurer* before it's admittedly so gives us a small edge of initiative."

"It's still only a hunch, sir. I mean can we act on it?"

"We can and must, Kate, I think I've enough clout to frighten a few people into some sort of reaction. That's what they pay me for ... and there's another thing...."

"Oh, you mean Tim?"

Nicholas's face clouded. "No ... sorry, I didn't mean Tim." She could see he was disappointed, even slightly angry.

"What was it then?"

"Well," he said, the enthusiasm less warm in his voice, "the reaction to such a request will be rather interesting. I mean that it will either confirm or disprove your outrageous theory."

"Yes," said Kate, "yes, I suppose it will."

After Kate had gone Nicholas telephoned the Commissioner and reconvened the security committee with its representatives of the Home and Foreign Offices on the promise of revealing a lead. He wondered if the Foreign Office would admit their intelligence starvation and whether they had found the two Mossad operatives. He was about to place another call when Chief Superintendent Martin requested a brief interview. Nicholas called him in, half expecting Martin to supply another piece of the rapidly filling jigsaw.

Instead Martin asked for a transfer.

"Why Alex? And why now for God's sake? I think we might have something on the Gannet Platform attack."

Martin did not look surprised at this, merely doggedly insisted that he intended making a formal request in writing, but wanted to tell his chief first.

"Damn it Alex, you're assured of a good future, you're a key man in my section, you can't just bugger off in the middle of things like this. D'you want to go back to wheel-clamping?"

"No sir. I don't want to leave at all."

"Well, the matter's settled, then, you don't have to."

"I do, you see it's my wife . . . things have been a bit strained, you know, the hours, sir . . . I haven't seen too much of her and the lad lately. You know how it is."

Nicholas bit off his retort. Yes, he knew exactly how it was.

"You'd better let me have it in writing then, Alex."

"Thank you sir."

When the Chief Superintendent had gone Nicholas finished his phone calls. A few minutes later Martin's formal request arrived. It must have already been written out. Nicholas looked at his watch. He had over an hour until his meeting, an hour of possibly lost initiative. He was wound up tight as a clock spring. All his instincts told him that Kate's analysis was correct and reaction to his proposal would surely settle the matter. He would have to distract himself for that hour, force his mind into a different track. He pressed the intercom.

"Sally?"

"Sir?"

"Be so kind as to bring me in Chief Superintendent Martin's file."

HENDON, NORTH WEST LONDON

Kate did not know how long Nicholas's meeting had lasted, for she had seen nothing of him for the remainder of the day. More than ever the hours at her desk had dragged and she viewed her continuing presence at the Yard as pure self-indulgence. Whatever the result of the security committee's deliberations, it was certain she was out of it now. She mooned dispiritedly about the flat. Without thinking, she stood Tim's photograph up again. The thought of the unidentified bodies occurred to her. They would have hijacked the ship in the middle of the night. She knew Tim would be keeping the midnight-to-four watch, for he had told her as much. It was almost certain he was dead.

She tried to weep, out of love, or out of guilt, she was not sure which, but she remained stubbornly dry-eyed. Staring past his picture she saw the glossy brochure he had posted to her from Charleston the same day he had joined the ill-fated *Adventurer*. It had a photograph of the ship on the cover and inside were pictures of the luxurious public rooms and a penthouse cabin. There were some words in Tim's hand too, a quick valedictory scribble.

Arrived safely, ship looks like a wedding cake, wish you were here, all my love, darling, Tim.

He had obviously picked up a standard Adventure Lines publicity brochure and used it as a grand postcard. From the words *'wish you were here'* an arrow pointed at the unimaginably luxurious acreage of a penthouse bed.

Kate felt a lump rise in her throat. Despite herself she read it again, something stopped her and then made her turn and look at the picture on the front.

'Ship looks like a wedding cake. . . .'

Or an iceberg, she thought.

Nicholas phoned at eight.

"Kate, it's Ian . . . Ian Nicholas."

The use of his Christian name threw her aback, but the enthusiasm was in his voice again.

"Have you got any more of that Spaghetti Bolognaise?"

"No," she said smiling, despite herself, "only two tins of ravioli."

"That'll do . . . be with you in three-quarters of an hour."

They augmented the ravioli with toast and graced it with a bottle of St Emilion Nicholas brought with him. By unspoken

203

consent they ate first then took the rest of the wine through into the living room.

"Well," she asked, "right or wrong?"

"Too early to say . . . but don't be discouraged. I had almost no trouble convincing them of the circumstantial evidence supporting the *Adventurer* theory. Circumstantial evidence is something peppery admirals see as trivially equivocating. Admiral Blacklock couldn't get a signal off fast enough. Initially a search and locate operation. He was absolutely right; any initiative we can seize off the terrorists is worth a lot, nullifies that 'reactive-disadvantage' status most governments find themselves in the grip of."

Kate smiled, recognizing a phrase from her own paper on terrorism.

"He wanted to get his ships and planes going at once. . . ."

"So we don't have sanction from the top?"

"Not yet, but the Prime Minister was closetted with the American Ambassador so there's still time. Anyway, for what it's worth, the Home and Foreign Secretaries weren't seen as great obstacles by their representatives on the committee."

"I should think not. They've only been in office for ten days or so; if this thing is pulled off they'll have the Falklands Factor squarely dumped in their political laps without lifting a finger."

"If. . . ."

"Yes . . . if. . . ." Kate refilled their glasses.

"I also got a few other bits of information today, all of which make me even more certain that you are right. Here's the passenger list from the *Adventurer* obtained from the cruise line." He handed her a long computer printout running to several pages. "You don't have to be a policeman to know some of those names."

Kate whistled. "Blumenthal . . . I'll check the others tomorrow, especially these. They're only children, though."

"Very emotive."

"And the crew list."

Palmer's name was four down from the top. "Yes."

"And something else, Kate, probably the oddest thing of all and I'm convinced it fits in."

And he told her what he had found in Alex Martin's file.

204

DOWNING STREET, LONDON

"Prime Minister, the President has personally, *personally* mind you, called me to determine your attitude to co-operating with us in this matter. Now let me be specific, Prime Minister, this is a courtesy. If we have to we will use our air bases, your non-co-operation notwithstanding, sir."

"That's a very high-handed attitude Mr Ambassador. Drink?"

"This is a very serious situation, sir . . . yeah, Scotch, please . . . on the rocks . . . very serious. The Soviets . . ."

"Are exercising their right to use the high seas, Mr Ambassador."

"Your predecessor didn't see things like that, this is a situation where the Western Alliance must stand firm against Soviet intimidation, you haven't been in office too long, sir, if I may say so; these things are a matter of pragmatism ultimately, not party policy."

"Frankly, Mr Ambassador, my predecessor's methods do not interest me any more. I expressed my opinion of them from the opposition benches at the time. As for the delicacy of the situation in the Lebanon, I really do advise the President to allow the inhabitants to settle the matter for themselves. If the Palestinians gain Sidon it will be by right of conquest which is, I believe, as ancient and Biblical as the claim of the Israelis on Palestine."

"Then you are not concerned with the Israeli position?"

"Mr Ambassador, my chief preoccupation at the moment is ending social deprivation in the north of England. As for your unrestricted use of East Anglian air bases, I must warn you that you do *not* have *carte-blanche* to do what you like."

"Then your answer's 'No'?"

"Yes, Mr Ambassador, my answer is 'No'."

"Prime Minister?"

"Ah, John, come in, come in. . . ."

"I saw the American Ambassador leaving. He looked pretty angry."

"Yes. I expect he did."

"The Palestine business?"

205

"Yes. Admiral Backhouse has got the *Brandywine* and a supporting task force big enough to blast the whole of Sidon off the face of the earth but is worried about resupply. He wants support from the East Anglian bases. The Russians, being more cunning, have fielded a smaller force, puny by comparison with Backhouse's fleet, a helicopter landing ship and some destroyers, but big enough to pack a sizeable punch ashore. It's a clear case of sabre-rattling with the Kremlin acting David to Washington's Goliath."

"Sabre-rattling and potential loss of face, eh?"

"Yes. Bloody stupid from any point of view!"

"And you vetoed the use of the bases?"

"Yes, of course. Surely you're not surprised?"

"Well, Prime Minister, no, I'm not surprised, though I admit to being worried. I've just had the Home and Foreign Secretaries on to me. They wanted you but I explained you were tied up. It seems there have been some developments on the other front. In short, it looks as though the 'terror offensive' is about to enter its climactic phase."

"Go on."

"Delay not being to Admiral Blacklock's liking, he has, as Chief of the Defence Staff, initiated a sea-search from the Falklands. He's looking for a liner called the *Adventurer*, British owned though Panamanian registered. Due to some brilliant sleuthing by Commander Nicholas's special anti-terrorist section it appears that there is evidence the liner has been hijacked. At the moment we have a slim initiative."

"They've got to find her first."

"And then refer the matter to you."

"Yes."

GREENSBORO, NORTH CAROLINA

The man with the Zapata moustache thrust against the quivering buttocks of the girl crouched on the bed. A bead necklace bumped on his chest and he panted with mounting despair, his mouth twisted in a rictus of frustration. Reaching down he tugged at her pendulous breasts, gasping for air.

"You comin'?" she asked, tired of the abuse for so paltry a fee. "If ah'd have knowed it'd take this long ah'd have charged you double!"

He threw her sideways and twisted round, his lean body sickly pale in the early light. Lifting her heavy leg over his head he pushed her on her back. Her breasts rolled lasciviously across her torso, the dark nipples diverging and trembling as he renewed his effort to climax.

Bracing herself on her elbows she raised her head and looked at him. "Honey, for Chrissakes come! Ah ain't made of Firestone, man!" Her weary lack of response failed to arouse him; he performed a joyless mechanical act, and that imperfectly.

"Oh Christ!"

She saw the blue marks on his inner arm for the first time. She had not seen them in the darkness last night.

"You're all shot too full o' shit, honey."

"Come on you bitch!"

She rolled her eyes with professional distaste. She could feel him wilting within her.

"Jeesus . . . !"

She began to simulate orgasm, contracting the muscles of her belly. He fell across her soaked in sweat, angry and dissatisfied. She stopped and extricated herself from his exhausted body and padded across the floor of the hotel room to squat over the washbasin.

"Ah sure hope you ain't done me no damage, honey."

He was incapable of reply, laying almost asleep as she completed her douching.

A fly buzzed against the window pane, a sizzling noise against which she dressed, watching him for signs of dissatisfaction and violence. His heaving chest subsided as she slipped on her shoes. She made sure she had the money, took a look for his wad, thought better of it and slipped out of the room.

He came to half an hour later, sore and irritated. Dressing, he went downstairs and paid his bill. As he pulled out of Greensboro he stopped the Pontiac by a mailbox and posted a brown envelope. It began to rain as he headed south-west alongside the railroad, towards Winston Salem.

PORT STANLEY, EAST FALKLAND ISLAND

Captain Crosby-Milne swore with all the venom of an articulate sailor. His Dartmouth elocuted accent gave the crude words a peculiarly acid quality.

London were meddling. They had given him instructions to search for a cruise liner at the same moment as he was worrying about a possible movement of Argentine warships. His anxiety had not been mollified by the failure of his radar pickets or the Royal Air Force's Phantoms to detect the slightest irregularity within the defence zone. It was all bloody irritating, particularly as his colleagues in the RAF and Army were inclined to pooh-pooh his concern.

He looked at the signal again. He was instructed to commence a search across the wastes of water around the Falklands and report the location of the cruise liner *Adventurer*, a possible hijack victim.

"That's all I bloody well need. . . ."

His relief would be arriving shortly and he needed time to prepare the paperwork for the handover. Oh, well, he would do what he was told. As bloody usual. He had already warned his vessels to make ready to proceed, now he began to draft his operational order when an idea occurred to him. He paused in his writing and stared out of the window.

The bight of Port Stanley harbour lay before him, a windswept sheet of water fringed with the grey-green of sheep-cropped grass moorland, rock outcrops and patches of purple heather.

'Benbecula in winter,' was how one Pongo major had unenthusiastically described it. And it was high-fucking summer!

He made up his mind and reached for the telephone.

"Get me Rear-Admiral Aguirra at Punta Arenas."

Ten minutes later he was feeling more cheerful.

CHILEAN FRIGATE *BERNARDO O'HIGGINS*, ESTRECHO DE LE MAIRE

Captain Soto handed the radio-telephone back to Operator First Class Arturo Hernandez. The rating disconnected the scrambler and wondered why the captain was smiling. He had been sent from the W/T office for a few minutes and had been unable to eavesdrop. He reseated himself in his chair and resumed his routine listening duties, aware that Soto remained in the office. He felt Soto's fingertips rest on his shoulder and turned.

"Captain, sir?"

Soto's eyes were slightly narrowed, deep-set behind the great bulbous nose. He had obviously been considering something in his recent telephone conversation and had reached a decision.

"Hernandez, I want you to use your initiative, as you did the other night. Scan as many frequencies as you can, listen for odd signals, bursts of coded groups. They will probably be on, or near, the merchant ship frequencies, between one and two kiloherz . . . anything Hernandez, understand?"

"Yes, Captain, sir."

"Good."

Hernandez grinned to himself. His watch officer was being spoken to by the captain. He was pleased to be selected. It would kill the boredom.

Soto climbed to the bridge. He was still smiling. Away to port the blue coast of the Mitre Peninsula terminated in Cape San Diego, the toe of South America, Tierra del Fuego, Argentine territory. Much closer to starboard lay the football, the rugged Isla de los Estados, Staten Island. Soto was intending to round the island before turning back towards Chilean waters. He had swept down the impressively narrow Canal Beagle, to demonstrate off Ushaia. A flotilla of Israeli-built gunboats had joined him from the base at Puerto Williams and they had enjoyed an afternoon of high-speed manoeuvres, running down to Gable Island. The Argentinians had sensibly stayed in port. There had been a lot of *pisco* drunk in *Bernardo O'Higgins*'s wardroom that night with the young gunboat lieutenants. More than one of them was blond and Aryan and all of them lean and fierce as wolves.

Now he was making this sweep up through what the *gauchos* thought were their own waters. He could still hear Aguirra's chuckle through the scrambler. "Good, good, my friend. . . ."

His only disappointment was that, apart from the anchored and moored ships in Ushuaia, they had not seen a single Argentine ship, despite the fact that they had run down through the strait to the west of Picton and Lennox Islands to the lonely marine outpost on Cape Horn itself. But his disappointment was short-lived. Aguirra had told him not to turn back, but to take his departure from Cape San Juan and head out towards the Islas Malvinas and rendezvous with the British Royal Navy. They were looking for the large white cruise liner that had been expected at the eastern end of the Straits of Magellan in a few days.

Nothing could better please a man who claimed Lord Cochrane's blood in his veins.

HENDON, NORTH WEST LONDON

"Okay," said Nicholas, passing the palm of his hand over his face,

"Let's have the exegesis."

She looked at him over the top of the typed sheet. He was spread-eagled across her settee, one long leg dangled over the arm, a glass of wine in his free hand. She was facing him, briefing him, having worked all day, preparing the paper for his meeting tomorrow. Tomorrow these ideas of hers would go to Sir Charles Oldham, the Commissioner, to the Home and Foreign Secretaries and possibly the Prime Minister himself.

"We must take as our precedent the *Achille Lauro* hijack. This was seen as a failure, but the terrorist organisations learn as much from their mistakes as their successes, despite the fact that the hijackers ended up being tried in Italy. I think the hijack paid dividends through its *lack* of success," she said.

"By this I mean that in their desire for revenge upon the

captured hijackers, so-called friendly governments were brought to a state of dramatic confrontation. It proved the potential disruptive power of such an act, leading the planners to consider the ultimate hijack.

"The aim of any terrorist organisation is the acquisition of power, political power. By using sudden, shocking violence, terrorism forces its opponents to operate under duress, in a non-rational environment at, as the phrase has it, a 'reactive-disadvantage'. This gives the minority terror-cell an almost permanent initiative, forcing its opposition to largely reactive processes which are sometimes outside its own laws. Sometimes these are successful, such as the SAS storming of the Iranian embassy in London, but the irony of even these successes is that it does not usually transfer the initiative. The terrorist organis-ation can strike again at a time or place of its own choosing. Analysts call this terror-inspired advantage *metapower*, because it actually changes human interaction. To use a military analogy, it radically re-arranges the rules of engagement by one side. It is a tactic of total war."

Kate paused and sipped her wine.

Nicholas nodded and refilled both their glasses. "Good solid stuff, go on. . . ."

Kate lit a cigarette and continued.

"The situation in the world has deteriorated in recent years and terrorist activities have increased as terrorist organis-ations have proliferated. But that section of it devoted to revolution has largely failed because it has been unable to exploit this initiative. Threatened governments closed ranks and we have been treated to the spectacle of governments which developed out of terror campaigns themselves, join-ing hands with their former enemies. As we have seen, the *Achille Lauro* episode brought about a full-scale confrontation between the armed forces of two allies, the United States and Italy. In the case of the former they claimed the right to try the alleged murders of one of their nationals on the ship, in the case of the latter the Italians argued the crime was on their nominal territory, the ship being registered in Italy. . . ."

"Hang on, Kate. If we're right, then this weakens our case, the

211

Adventurer is registered in Panama, although we know she's owned and officered by Britons. . . ."

"Yes, but you've seen the passenger list and we already know the relationship between the security agencies of our friends and ourselves is chilly. Any strain imposed on the Western Alliance, any rift in the solidarity of their governments in the United Nations, in the diplomatic or military fields elsewhere would give a smokescreen to powers sympathetic to a cause such as that of the Palestinians. The events at Sidon have destabilized the balance of power in the Middle East. A territorial acquisition by right of conquest or with popular support will mean an enormous access of power to Fatah. Israel will feel increasing isolation and fall back on her powerful ally, the United States.

"The effect of the hijack of a liner with a passenger list like that of the *Adventurer* will first shift the axis of media attention, secondly it will put enormous strains and limitations on the political and military response options open to world leaders, specifically our own Prime Minister and the President of the United States.

"Finally all the evidence that we have indicates this hijack to have been well-planned, carefully co-ordinated and is far more than a murderous piece of theatricality."

"Very good, Kate, you should go into politics. Now, what about the prognosis?"

"Two things, sir."

"Ian."

"Two things," she smiled. "One, from what *we* surmise, our reaction may not be so predictable."

"If we *are* right," Nicholas interrupted, "the process of – what did you call it – Metapower, may already be at work."

"Yes, and second, the next phase will undoubtedly be the hijack demands."

"Which leaves only two questions in my mind."

"And they are?"

"Will those demands be ransom or coercion?"

"You haven't been listening!"

"Yes I have and I'm going to have to increase security round our man. The Mossad boys have gone to ground."

CHILEAN FRIGATE *BERNARDO O'HIGGINS*, SOUTHERN OCEAN

Captain Soto stared ahead through his Zeiss binoculars, holding the horizon level while his long, lean frigate pitched into the seas and sluiced tons of green water over her bow where it crashed off the breakwater and the gun turret to pour over either side as the battered ship rose to the next wave. Perversely, the Great Southern Ocean, which was as every cadet at Valparaiso knew, the kingdom of the west wind, was hurling a north-easterly gale at them. Soto saw them before the lookout. The two grey hulls were much like his own, except one still bore the wide black vertical paintmark of identification to denote her British nationality. It was a relic of the Falkland conflict, a signal to friendly aircraft and ships that the Type 42 destroyer was British and not one improvidently sold to the Argentine. He read her pennant number.

"Delta Nine One." He called to the officer of the watch.

"*Nor-wich*, Captain," the officer replied.

"*Norrich*," Soto corrected, proud of his arcane anglophile knowledge.

"He is calling on VHF radio, sir." Soto turned. The first lieutenant handed him the VHF radio handset.

"Chilean warship on my port bow, this is British warship *Norwich* calling you, come in please, over."

"*Norwich*, this is *Bernardo O'Higgins*," Soto replied in good English, "Good morning, I hear you loud and clear, over."

"Good morning *Bernardo O'Higgins* I should like to speak with your Captain, over."

"This is captain speaking. I have received instructions to co-operate with you from my admiral. You have not found the ship *Adventurer*? Over."

"Negative. Understand you are under orders to assist. Is that correct?"

"Affirmative. I can launch helicopter and commit my ship to area of your choice. Over."

"Good. Many thanks. Suggest you might make sweep east-south-east towards South Orkney Islands. Intelligence indicates possibility of ship being east of Falklands. Over."

"Roger. Understood. Wilco. Out."

Soto put down the radio-telephone and raised his binoculars. The *Norwich* was just forward of the beam, running fast with a stern sea and scending through the combers. She was lit by a patch of sunlight which sparkled off her aerials and armaments, her great bedstead radar antenna flashing with every three-second revolution. He could see a figure on her bridge waving his white-covered uniform cap and he responded. Just astern of *Norwich* came a smaller ship, with a lower profile and lighter look to her. She seemed to be making heavier weather of it than her larger consort, rolling and corkscrewing in the following sea.

"Type 21 frigate ... Foxtrot One Nine Five." He read the pennant number and received the prompt answer from the JOOW reading the fleet list.

"British Frigate *Alert*, Captain ... newest addition to the class."

"Thank you, Lieutenant, now come right and steer one-zero-five."

The *Bernardo O'Higgins* turned away and left the two British ships to sweep farther north, closer to their vulnerable cluster of islands.

ADVENTURER, WEDDELL SEA

"I wonder why she wears no mask, like the others do?" Margaret Allen asked as the door of the captain's cabin shut. She stared at the food Anna and a *fed'ai* had brought; cheese, bread and cans of beer. It was a sharp contrast with the former cuisine of the first-class passengers, designed to keep them alive but little else. They already huddled in blankets to keep out the cold for the air-conditioning had been turned off.

"I don't know," replied Galvin, non-committally.

"It's a terrible disfigurement."

"It's a burn."

"How horrible ..." Margaret paused, for she had found it difficult to take her eyes off Anna's face and the image lingered

214

unbidden on her retina. The face had been fascinating in its obscene distortion, compelling pity, too, a pity that was mixed with repulsion at finding a young woman engaged in an act of such uncivilized barbarity. Margaret tried to excuse Anna's involvement on the grounds of embitterment caused by her injury, but she was aware that there were other women in the terrorist group on board. A mild, theoretical feminist, Margaret nevertheless found this display of arrogant female-machismo profoundly frightening.

"Why do you suppose she doesn't care if she's identified? No one could forget a face like that."

"Perhaps, my dear," said Mr Blumenthal looking up, "because she does not expect to get caught."

There was such a terrible note of resignation in the old man's voice that she found his remark inexpressibly chilling.

"Come," said Galvin patting her hand and holding it gently in his own. She had aged years in the last few days, he thought; it made the three of them more nearly equals in the matter of infirmity. "Let us just sit quietly."

She watched him out of the corner of her eye, envying him his ability for quiet reflection at such a time. He did it often, she had noticed, a curious quirk of his odd religion.

Nobody touched the food. They were not hungry. *Adventurer* was rolling and scending as she raced southwards, rolling in the low, relentless westerly swell of the Southern Ocean while a north-easterly gale blew over her port quarter, making her long hull corkscrew with a ponderous and sickening motion.

Palmer had passed beyond the mere physical exhaustion that follows lack of proper sleep. He was functioning mechanically now, catching catnaps on the chart room settee, drinking endless cups of coffee and eating toast. These he shared almost fraternally with whatever guard had been detailed to cover the bridge, though Lila had left him in no doubt that they had orders to shoot him if he behaved with the least suspicion.

He walked out to the starboard bridge wing. The north-easterly had cleared the air and the visibility was good. A few large bergs were strewn away to the southwards, but since that first sighting the sea had been relatively clear of ice. He felt

215

someone watching him. He was used to being spied on and for a moment did not react, then he looked up. Floating not 10ft from him, ridge soaring on the air currents forced upwards by the motion of the ship's mountainous bulk through the air, a huge wandering albatross flew on motionless wings alongside the bridge wing.

Palmer watched the bird. Its wing span must have been 10ft across, a great grey-white bird with the fluted beak of a gigantic petrel and an eye as yellow as a buttercup. It seemed to be watching him then quite abruptly, it dipped its wings and slipped sideways and down in a long graceful curve which took it half a mile from the ship to curve round in a great circle and quarter the wake far astern of them.

Despite himself Palmer smiled, drawing the invigorating air through his nostrils. It reminded him of a happier time here on the bridge of the *Adventurer*, when he had explained the milk sea to Lila and Anna.

He looked at the horizon to the southwards, then straightened up and reached for binoculars. Away on the starboard bow, lifting above a low blur on the horizon he could see the jagged peaks of distant mountains, blue white in the clear air.

Nearer, the indistinct blur lay along the rim of the world, right across the southern arc of the skyline. He knew what it was and what it meant.

"Ice blink," he muttered to himself, "The edge of the pack."

Aymes was shaking. It was a disgraceful, disreputable quivering; quite uncontrollable and easily taken for fear in the stinking congestion of the cinema. In fact, he told himself with easy self-contempt, it *was* fear, but an addict's more than that of a hostage.

He looked around. He was not the only one. Men and women were shivering from the cold or from fear and possibly some, like him, from want. There was hardly any talking now: there was rarely any food, or drink or warmth except for what they exuded themselves, and that was done with the sickly-sweet smell of anxiety.

A lot of people slept uneasily, in huddles or with their heads thrown back, ugly in their refuge of unconsciousness. Melanie's head stirred in his own lap. He stroked her hair and hoped she was oblivious to his shivering. Calming her had done much to ease his own worry; now she slept while fear and the want of whisky kept him awake. He saw the gunmen, recognized the crew members Giorgio and Stephanos, the supposed Greeks. He wondered what their real names were. Then there was Dieter Schmidt, the man he had cavorted with when they had crossed the equator. A hard-line German, Aymes presumed, ruthless bastard anyway. And Anna, Anna the Disfigured, a character from another age, with an almost Messianic quality ... but perhaps that was lack of booze, a fantasy that went with pink elephants, which God forbid. ...

And Lila, the girl Tim Palmer was crazy about. He looked down at the sleeping Melanie. He could scarcely be judgemental. La Corbett was little better than a whore and his own feelings for her were stupidly excessive, but Lila. ...

Poor Tim.

Aymes wondered if he was already dead. "Best thing for him," he muttered, much, much better than this awful sitting about dying for lack of the 'Morangie.

Zelda Rebanowicz fared better than the rest. Warm and well fed, she ate the same hot food as the *fedayeen* and their Latin-American allies. Isolated in her locked penthouse stateroom she was visited periodically by Giorgio. She could not think of him otherwise, although he had told her his Arab name was Yusuf. They had done little during his visits except talk and eat. He had done most of the talking, slowly suborning her with the story of his life so that she generously over-reacted to the lack of opportunity, the squalor, the death and the deprivation that haunted the valleys of the Lebanon and the camps of Shabra and Shatila.

Her sympathies shifted and she began to see his point of view, to share his aspirations and his outrage at the treatment meted out to his people.

"The Israelis say there are many Arab states, but only one Jewish state; they took Palestine as the Russian Tsars had taken their homes, as the Nazi Germans had taken their factories. My father was a shepherd, we lived as my people have always lived.

He died when the Jews came. *They* have their Exodus story. *We* must pay for the guilt of Europeans."

She did not argue, could not, for she knew little about it all. Giorgio did not blame America, it seemed.

"America? No, good place. We go there one day, eh?"

"Together?"

"Of course, yes, together. Make love in San Francisco hotel, yes?"

"Yes."

Giorgio rose, for they had been squatting Arab-fashion on the deep-pile carpet. He smiled down at her.

She would be his camel for crossing the desert, if there was a desert to cross. If not, well, it did not matter.

Palmer eased the pitch control and *Adventurer* slowed. He felt immensely detached and strangely elated. The air was invigorating and he had the hunger and excitement-induced feeling of living for the moment a sensation heightened by his long, sleep-deprived days. Uncertainty about the future was not a new feeling to him, he had lived with its confidence-eroding effects for long enough. But this was something different, this was a wildness, a strange fulfillment absent from the steady, time-serving world of the Western wage-slave. He was, though he did not know it, experiencing the elation of battle madness. He had forgotten the man in London, though part of his sentient faculties acknowledged the moment of culmination was not far distant. What filled him most was something beyond all moral considerations which embraced altogether different, more primitive values.

Adventurer cut through black water dotted with small lumps of ice. The sea was calm, a smooth mirror which ran deep and narrow in the strait. On either side of the ship enormous, towering black cliffs reared upwards, their heads lost in folds of heavy, towering cloud. The near-vertical rock faces were too steep to retain any snow or ice beyond what had secured itself in the myriads of thin, vein-like fissures.

Files of penguins waddled with military precision along the flat ice floes, Weddell seals were abundant both lying on the ice and peering curiously from the sea. The air was full of

218

birds of every description, gulls, terns, boobies and dark, marauding skuas.

Adventurer brushed alongside a floe, rolling it down her side with a sharp, grinding noise. She moved into clearer water and Palmer edged the controllers forward a little, increasing speed through the dark sea.

A puff of wind sent flurries of wavelets across the sea's surface and suddenly the cloud lifted from the mountain tops, a startling and dramatic change in which the scene altered with an almost magical rapidity. As the alteration in air temperature consumed the cloud, the sun broke through the overcast. It burst on the waters of the strait like some gigantic theatrical effect.

The sea took on a hue of deep blue, its edges fringing the ice a limpid green. The ice sparkled, a million points of light dancing from its infinite reflective surfaces. The reverse slopes, crevasses and shadowed areas appeared of a different material so blue were they to the human eye. But other colours abounded, for the old floes were rimed with algal growths and the black rocks, now a dark and sinister grey in the sunshine, were marked by patches of light green and ochre lichen, and veined with thin lodes of contrasting deposits.

The sunlight must have penetrated below the surface, for Palmer was suddenly aware of movement on the starboard bow. A small school of whales suddenly rose, the shiny black curves of their backs appearing in a gap between the floes less than half a mile away. They spouted and six vee-shaped clouds of mist snorted from their spiracles as their backs humped over and they fluked briefly before diving again.

"Right, whales." he whispered to himself, half in awe of the splendour of the scene. So absorbed was he in conning the ship through this wonderland he failed to hear the first shot.

Jim Barclay had had enough. The pugnacity of his Glaswegian heritage rebelled against supine submission, the reversal of order in his engine room was an affront to his professional sensibilities and he was plain bloody sick of the treacherous bastard Zig holding a God-damned gun at his head.

He had had to leave the MCR to check a bearing that the sensors indicated running hot, a routine job that had been put off for some time. Inactivity was a trial for Barclay at the best of times, inactivity when something needed doing in his engine room was purgatory.

"Look," he shouted at the ubiquitous gunman, "if ah dinna hae a fucking look at the fucking thing, you'll no be going anywhere . . . !"

In the end, escorted by Zig, he had left the MCR and made for the shaft tunnel. He knew what it was.. The enforced neglect of the simple routines of engine maintenance had caused overheating in a bearing on the port propellor shaft. The clearances had never quite satisfied his exacting standards and the constant running of a variable pitch system gave the coupling no chance to cool. Now some swarf or accumulation of muck and waste had starved the bearing of oil and the bloody thing was red hot. The neglect made him angry, angrier than he already was.

"This is your bluidy fault . . ." he said to Zig, "I'll get the greaser's oil can."

Zig stepped back to let him retrace his steps. Just inside the watertight door was a shelf on which the oil can was stowed. Beside it was a red button and a warning notice.

An impulsive idea occurred to Barclay. He picked up the oil can and as he did so he pushed the red button. His body shielded the movement from Zig and he spun round.

"This is your bluidy fault, fucking about with your damned games, any fool knows an engine canna work by itself, it's only a fucking machine!" he railed, holding Zig's eyes as he went to push past and squirt the oil in the top of the bearing, anything to keep the terrorist from noticing the result of pushing the button.

Barclay had hated that bloody watertight door. He had hated anything on the *Adventurer* that did not work properly. It was just another item of 'builder's bullshit'. The damnable thing was so slow you were persuaded it would never work. The alarm never did anyway. Just when you passed back through it to get to the manual control the thing would grind into gear, its supposedly 'automatic' motor responding slowly to the switch. Barclay had piously hoped that the sea would hold off long enough for him to get it closed if it ever decided to breach the hull. Now he was thankful for that providential delay. By the time the door began to slide across the small opening to the engine room he was almost level with Zig.

He squirted the oil into the terrorist's face and grabbed the gun. Even in the one-second burst Zig fired Barclay felt the heat of the barrel. But by then he had thrown his whole weight into the chest of his enemy and sent him crashing backwards. The handrail that ran down the starboard side of the tunnel caught Zig in the small of the back and Barclay turned, smashing his knee upwards into Zig's groin. The hot air in the confined space was filled with another cacophonous burst of gunfire and the shrill scream of ricocheting bullets sounded off the steelwork. Barclay drove the oil can forward, mad with blood-lust, bending the thin spout as it entered the terrorist's eye. The searing pain made Zig jerk backwards and let go of the gun. Barclay had picked it up in a trice. There was no safety catch on and the magazine was not empty. The briefest squeeze of the trigger was enough. Zig's bloody body folded, then slumped and slithered off the plating into the bilge beneath the port propellor shaft.

Barclay wiped his face, set down the machine-gun, picked up the oil can and tended the bearing. When he had replenished the oil he sat for a moment. All that he could see of Zig were his boot soles. Barclay began to shake with reaction. Now what?

They could not have heard the bursts of fire beyond the heavy steel watertight door and, mercifully, the slugs had flattened themselves against the internal steelwork of the ship. They were soft-headed anti-personnel bullets. Nasty if they slammed into human flesh but otherwise harmless to thick steel plate. Barclay was an engineer. It took him about two minutes to work out how to remove the magazine. A few minutes fumbling in the bilge beneath the revolving shaft and he had removed more cartridges from Zig's body. He loaded them carefully into the magazine and stowed the remainder in his boiler-suit pocket.

The macabre nature of this act began to unnerve him. He was sweating and shaking.

"Remember Jeannie and the kids." he muttered to himself. His drying sweat felt clammy on his skin. He made up his mind. To go back to the MCR where the second gunman was on watch risked damaging the controls. But there was an alternative course of action. Barclay knew his way round the engine room better than almost anyone on the ship. He knew of the ladders ascending into the funnel casing, of the door onto the topmost deck. He knew how he could get up there without being seen from the MCR. His heart beating painfully, he pressed the red button again. After an age the door opened. Keeping low he slipped out and behind the huge, hammering bulk of the port Sulzer diesel. He ascended the first ladder, which terminated on a long platform running forward. Moving low he edged along, keeping his body hidden by the horizontally gleaming cylinders of the two big calorifiers. A battery of pumps and a compressor gave him less cover but he reached the second ladder and began to ascend it. It came up alongside the MCR door but he could just remain hidden as long as no one came outside.

He froze as a *kaffiya* moved across the small window. The instant it had vanished he turned swiftly aft again and ran upward as fast as he could.

He made it to the fourth ladder. The most dangerous part was over now. He began to feel a surge of confidence and pressed on. The great pit of the engine room began to open beneath him, while alongside his climbing figure the huge lagged uptakes rose in confluence towards the aperture of the funnel. He could feel a downdraft of air as he passed the settling tanks where Zig had hidden, awaiting the moment for attack.

A few minutes later he stood in the base of *Adventurer*'s funnel. He paused to catch his breath before emerging on deck. When he was ready he checked the gun. They must be getting suspicious in the MCR as to his whereabouts. They would not have heard the shots, not the far side of the watertight door in the thundering cacophony of the engine room. Besides, the MCR was conveniently lagged against sound.

He must remember to confine himself to short bursts of gunfire. And to keep in cover. The longer he deceived the bastards as to how big was his one-man insurrection, the better.

He eased the dogs of the small steel door in the base of the funnel.

"This is for you, Jeannie. . . ."

Chapter Ten

ADVENTURER, WEDDELL SEA

The first thing that confused him was the light. Heaving his bulk through the small door onto the fiddley he had expected it to be dark. He had been confined for days and had no notion of *Adventurer*'s whereabouts, but instinct suggested it was late evening and he had expected a measure of protection from darkness and shadows. The virtually perpetual daylight of the high Antarctic took him by surprise.

He recovered quickly, closing the door behind him and feeling the air cold on his sweating skin. He looked forward and aft. The fiddley was deserted and so, it appeared, was the boat deck below. Its long expanse terminated at the ladder to the port bridge wing and was quite empty, a perspective of teak planks and pitch seams which ran under the arches of the davit trackways. He began to move forward cautiously, cradling the machine-gun, sure that on the bridge he would find the core of the terrorist hold on the ship.

Above him the fiddley, the casing that surrounded the funnel, gave way to the individual open verandahs of the luxury penthouse staterooms set between bridge and funnel. Each was screened from its neighbour by a Perspex shield, opaque and private, like a horse's blinkers. Pressed against the bulkhead, he passed below them dropping to deck level as he worked forward of the radio-room windows.

Barclay's heart was beating like a drum. He had reached the point of no return. He was on deck with a gun; he had killed a terrorist and any second now he expected to hear the noise of alarm raised in his pursuit. He had no time to lose.

He was about to ascend the ladder when a shout of alarm

caused him to turn. He saw the terrorists behind him. They must have emerged onto the boat deck through one of the doors abaft the officers' accommodation. There was no doubt that he had been seen.

A harsh childhood in Greenock had taught Barclay the rudiments of guerrilla tactics, a street-wisdom that knew the virtues of speed and cover. He was the other side of the forward boat winch before the alarmed gunmen had time to fire at him. He paused only an instant. With a savage satisfaction Barclay stood at the same second as his pursuer loped forward. He kept the burst short and saw the slugs pulverize the head of the leading gunman. His lips drawn back in a snarl he hit the second, uncovered by the collapse of the first. The impact of the bullets thrust back the rash advance and there was a clatter of falling weapons and two inert shapes were laid out on the planking.

"Fucking hell!" At the moment of death Barclay saw he had killed a young woman. He began to pour out a stream of obscene filth, a torrent of words that kept his courage and his mettle up while he reloaded. Behind him a burst of fire made him spin round as the whine of ricochets sparked off the vertical plating of the boat winch. Barclay crouched, clicking in the refilled magazine, his body partly shielded by the bow of the forward lifeboat that masked him from the bridge wing.

Palmer looked round at the second burst of gunfire from the boat deck. His guard was moving at a stooping lope towards the top of the port bridge ladder. Looking aft he shouted something. Another gunman appeared in the wheelhouse from below and took up a covering position while the first man began to descend the ladder.

A telephone rang and Palmer answered it. The voice, which he guessed came from the MCR, was saying something in Arabic. Palmer heard the line click dead. He had no sooner hung up than it rang again. He picked it up. This time a voice was speaking in a language he thought sounded vaguely familiar. It was not Arabic and it took a few seconds to realize it was Spanish. It was too garbled for him to understand. Again he hung up, aware that something was very wrong.

224

There was another burst of fire from the deck below, invisible from Palmer's position in the wheelhouse, but the gunman giving cover from the bridge wing suddenly opened up, firing down at the deck below. Even as Palmer watched, his heart in his mouth, it seemed as though an invisible boot hit the *fed'ai* in the pit of his stomach. Palmer saw the force of the impact double the man, thrusting his viscera through his body. The small of the man's back erupted into bloody rags as he crashed against the forward bulwark of the bridge wing.

A second later Barclay appeared at the top of the ladder. He was almost unrecognisable. His eyes were staring and his overalls were torn, showing blood in several places where he had been grazed.

"Jim!"

Barclay bent and picked up the gun dropped by the dead *fed'ai*. With the easily acquired expertise intended by its designer, Barclay fitted a new magazine and held it out to Palmer, standing shocked and surprised in the wheelhouse doorway.

"Here, Tim, take this!"

"Don't touch it, Palmer." Her voice was low and her gun in his back pushed him forward. He could see a frown of uncertainty on Barclay's face as he held out the Kalashnikov. "Walk slowly forward. . . ."

Barclay could not see Lila, hidden behind the bulk of the tall second officer.

"The gun, Tim," Barclay hissed, "be quick . . . what's the matter?"

Barclay sensed Palmer's hesitation, taking it for fear, perhaps, and sought persuasion. "They've killed God-knows how many. . . ."

Palmer shook his head. Something communicated itself to Barclay's feral instincts. He began to back off. Perhaps he saw Lila, but whatever the cause Barclay moved with a rapidity surprising in so large a man. Palmer felt Lila shove him aside and revulsion made him lean backwards. Lila's shoulder drove into the small of his back and he felt the searing heat from the blazing muzzle of her stuttering gun sting his arm, but she had lost valuable seconds, failed in the accuracy of her aim. Lila broke cover, moving out from behind Palmer as he grabbed sideways at her.

"No, Lila, no!"

But Barclay was unaware of Palmer's predicament. All he could think of was Palmer's ambivalent hesitation and the rumoured relationship between the second officer and the girl with the gun who had emerged from behind him.

"Bastard, bastard. . . . !" he swore to himself as he stumbled along the boat deck in search of a door below.

Palmer tried to prevent Lila raising her gun again but she strained round and drove the butt of it into his belly. He doubled with the pain as she swore in Arabic and ran for the top of the ladder.

But only the bodies of her dead *fedayeen* lay on the deserted boat deck.

Two more of the terrorists had arrived on the bridge and she gave them both orders. Through a mist of red-rimmed pain, Palmer saw her look once, briefly, in his direction. He lay in the foetal position, gasping for breath, and then closed his eyes. When he had recovered a little he opened them again. He seemed to be alone. Raising himself above the level of the rail he saw that the ship had traversed the length of the strait on automatic pilot and was clear of the immediate ice. The morning was still lovely, but Palmer's eyes were no longer seeing it.

Barclay descended two decks by the forward ladders. He met no one. He knew the alarm was raised all over the ship, but she was huge and the humans on board were so concentrated into easily guarded ghettos that most of her was an empty shell. He moved with the instinctive caution of an animal. All the street-wisdom of childhood, the ability to run and twist and turn corners without being seen or surprised had once been nothing more than the simple avoidance of a pursuing bully; now it was put to a more deadly use. His mind was working on two levels. Something had been wrong with Palmer's reaction. The man must be cunt-struck; the bloody bitch Lila had suborned him. Barclay guessed Palmer was an easy pushover for a determined woman. He had no hope of the bridge so must get back to the engine room. Without the engines the terrorists could do nothing.

He paused a moment to get his bearings. A man crossed the end of an alleyway and instinctively Barclay flattened himself against the bulkhead. The man disappeared and Barclay drew breath. As he paused he heard noises. They came from the cabin behind him. He knew immediately what the noises were.

Flinging open the door he brought his gun butt up and crashed into the cabin.

He could see the pain on the girl's face and her hands clawing at the bare buttocks of the man who rode her unwilling body. He was in the last throes of the sexual act.

"You bastard!" bellowed Barclay.

Stephanos, snarling with rage reached for his gun, twisting off the girl whose abused body was rigid with fear and unable to accommodate the movement. Barclay watched her convulsion, her reaction of pain, shock and outraged sensibility. His foot stamped down on the terrorist's machine-gun.

"Bastard!" he repeated, jerking his own gun so that Stephanos cringed back, clear of the girl. Barclay thought again of Jeannie and the children. The girl was not much older than his own daughter, Fiona. She had drawn her bruised legs up in a terrible gesture made with her whole body.

"Bastard!" Barclay levelled his gun at the terrorist and squeezed the trigger. The roar of the exploding shell cases filled the cabin and they shot from the breech, catching the light so that they danced before the shocked eyes of the girl.

Barclay blew out Stephanos's loins and pulverized his body with a burst of fire. Long after he was dead his body twitched and disintegrated under the relentless hail of lead. Beside him, watching in horror, the raped girl crouched shuddering, a pool of blood spreading beneath her on the rumpled bedclothes. Her mouth was open and she seemed to be screaming, but she could not be heard above the noise of Barclay's gun.

Stephanos's body was reduced to a shambles of red meat.

Anna found Barclay.

She killed him with a single shot as he backed out of the cabin. He was still firing and he never knew what hit him. The last image on his retinae was the face of the terrified girl, the last thought in his head was of his wife and family.

*　　*　　*

227

Giorgio stood smoking calmly. Somewhere in the distance the sound of firing died away. In front of him over a thousand people huddled into the seats of the cinema or on the steps that led between them and tried, individually, to efface themselves. He felt his authority absolute. The gun ensured it.

His eyes, sharp as a desert falcon's never wavered as it quartered the rising tier of seats. One move, one suspicious gesture would result in a hail of bullets. They all knew it; they would remain quiescent. He resisted the nervous impulse to shiver. Cold was seeping down into the ship despite the numbers of people in the great space. Terror made body temperature drop; so much the better, chilled and inactive people were less likely to take it into their heads to do anything fool hardy.

Anna came in through the swing doors.

"It's over," she said, "Lila said to tell you."

"How many?"

"Only a handful of them . . . a few officers led by the Second Engineer."

"Barclay?"

"Yes."

"And us?"

He heard Anna sigh, "I'm not sure, maybe seven or eight, mostly Costa Mayans," she added hurriedly, well knowing Giorgio's jealous conservation of his own cadre of *fedayeen*. "Except Stephanos. . . ."

Giorgio swore. "What happened?" He looked at her, his eyes blazing with anger and pain.

"The little fool was screwing one of the young schoolchildren. . . ." She looked at Giorgio and saw the pain cross his face. The muttered obscenities were meaningless but Anna knew that Giorgio was deeply touched by their loss. Stephanos, was Giorgio's sister's son. Since his sister's death in an air raid Giorgio had felt responsible for his nephew.

"We will make reprisal, eh?" he said venomously, waving his gun so that hostages near him cringed back with fear, not understanding the reasons for his sudden and obvious anger, but well aware of what its consequences could be for them.

"Lila says not yet . . . maybe not at all."

"Damn Lila!"

228

"Don't let this cloud your judgement," Anna said sharply, putting her hand on his arm. "Go, I will relieve you, go to your whore."

Giorgio looked at her for a moment and his brow cleared. He snapped the safety catch on his gun and slung it. He was too preoccupied to see the tears in Anna's eyes.

The mute hostages watched this change in their guard. There were others about the cinema, but either Anna or Giorgio or the severe-faced woman with the drawn-back hair were the obvious leaders from whom the others took orders. They were watched by the hostages, who considered the disfigured woman the most threatening. She stirred a primaeval fear of the abnormal in them and the small slits in her ribbed face through which her eyes regarded them were capable of a savage and merciless glitter.

"Why did you do that, Palmer, why?"

Palmer faced Lila as she returned to the bridge. Without asking he knew that Barclay's revolt had been crushed. There was a weariness to Lila's voice that told him the crisis was past.

"Why did you try to stop me?" she asked.

"He was my friend."

"Am I not your friend, Palmer?" She ran a desperate hand through her hair and, for the first time, Palmer detected a note of hysteria in her voice.

"I could not stand and see him die."

"He is dead anyway. Had he not been so foolish he might have lived."

"But *you* did not kill him. . . ."

"No." She suddenly looked up at him, her eyes full of renewed vigour. "He is dead. He killed Stephanos. I have no radio operator."

It was a confidence and the knowledge struck him like a blow, reminding him, if he needed reminding, that their relationship was so complex, so convoluted, that normal standards of behaviour had ceased to exist. She stood with a bowed head, downcast at the loss of Stephanos. Yet she was a murderess, a purveyor of terror, a pirate.

Despite the bruising in his belly he reached out and took her shoulders. He felt them shake as she relaxed into his embrace.

He felt the hard pressure of her gun along his thigh. She was also a freedom fighter, a guerrilla, a patriot.

She mastered her momentary lapse and he stood back. What did that make him? A great lover? A traitor? Or merely a fool?

She pushed him away, brushing the gleam of tears from her face. She brought up her gun, a black, steel phallus between them.

"Take us to Destitution Island, Palmer, as quickly as you can."

ALOUETTE HELICOPTER FLOWN OFF FROM CHILEAN FRIGATE *BERNARDO O'HIGGINS*

Lieutenant Clausen pulled the lever controlling the collective lift and felt the airframe of the Alouette helicopter tremble and become airborne. A single glance down showed the diminishing rectangle of the *Bernardo O'Higgins*'s flight deck shrink rapidly and then slide out of view as he lowered the helicopter's nose and sped off in forward flight. He climbed slowly until he reached 2000ft.

From this altitude the view was spectacular and Clausen smiled to himself. He was flying solo to conserve fuel, making his third sweep of the day, eastward from the frigate in the hunt for the missing liner *Adventurer*.

"We know what we're looking for, Lieutenant," Captain Soto had said, "We have seen her passing Punta Arenas before. I think we will concentrate our search to the east of the Antarctic Peninsula. Between here, at Signy, the Bransfield Strait and on down the west side to Palmer Station, she would have been too conspicuous. Try the far side of the island, Lieutenant."

Clausen did not know why he was looking for the ship, but it did not bother him. His chief joy in life was flying, reasons for doing so were convenient excuses for his own indulgence.

Lieutenant Clausen had his mother's dark Hispano-Indian good looks, except for his eyes. These were a clear blue, inherited from his father, a Luftwaffe officer who had settled to farm the remote Patagonian hills of southern Chile. But the subtle influences of parental inclination, stories and mementoes, the half-secret gathering of old comrades and the singing of strange and romantic songs, had led young Clausen to aspire to an aviator's career. He had two brothers to run the farm and, at the age of 17, had joined the Navy as a cadet officer intended for flying. There was no doubt as to his eventual appointment, provided he passed his examinations; his father saw to that through the self-help organisation of old comrades.

Lieutenant Clausen had been flying from the deck of his frigate for three years now and the Antarctic waters still touched him with awe. The beauties of the Chilean archipelago were too often mist-shrouded to stun him with their beauty; flying amid such hazards as their fiords and mountain peaks was exciting, but a man could never relax, particularly as one was so often on anti-bandit patrol. But here, in the high summer, when Captain Soto wanted a reconnaissance flight in near-perfect conditions, a man might fly with a heart as light as feather on a bird's breast.

From 2000 ft the sea was ribbed in regular patterns not visible at sea level, where wave height differed. From aloft the mathematical relationship between wind speed and water reaction resolved itself into a simple equation of movement. He saw, quite clearly, the trails of dolphins and a school of whales. You could see the whole of the giant mammal, not merely a spouting hump as at sea level, watch it breach and fluke and dive, roll over and play in the horizontal rays of the midnight sun. Then there was the ice, dotted across the sea in all directions. To the southward he could see the white shadow of the permanent ice shelf and ahead the black and rugged teeth of the Antarctic mountains, reflecting the light of the crazy sun which dipped down, but did not disappear in the high summer of this weird region.

He was flying with his fingertips, barely moving the stick as the little machine roared over the sea, its blades flashing in the sunshine, while his clear blue eyes scanned the horizon and watched the black ridge of the distant mountains grow ever closer.

Lieutenant Clausen almost missed seeing the ship. He was

looking for a white liner with swept-back lines and a vast great raked orange and blue funnel. He had already seen several icebergs that reminded him of ocean liners and dropped to 800ft to throw them into a more recognisable silhouette. It would consume his fuel faster but he had only enough for a further ten minutes before he would be forced to turn back for the *Bernardo O'Higgins*.

He saw the wake, the tell-tale twin lines of disturbed water miles astern of the ship and there, at the end of the white scufflings on the dark surface of the ocean an odd, barely recognisable shape that swiftly resolved itself into the *Adventurer*.

"Alpha Charlie One to Mother, sighted stray sheep. D'you hold me?"

"Alpha Charlie One, negative. We lost you over the mountains, over."

"I have been steering one-zero-three since our last contact, speed 97 knots in . . ."

"Okay, Clausen, 14 minutes since your last, we can work that out. . . ."

Clausen grinned. The last voice had been that of Captain Soto. Enrique was always on the ball. Usually you did not want him to know exactly where you were all the time but there were occasions when the unsleeping bastard could be a comfort. Clausen wondered where the Captain had been when he had called in. Not far from the radio room, he guessed, probably went there the moment the Operations Room plot lost his radar trace as he crossed the mountains. He zoomed in low and fast, chuckling at the surprise he would cause.

"*Dios!*"

The view of the liner was suddenly criss-crossed by an opacity of white lines, jaggedly moving outwards as across his field of vision the machine shook. There was an implosion of Perspex shards that lanced past his face and hit his chest. The breath was knocked from him and he felt both a sudden fearful warmth spreading through his lower belly and the chill cutting edge of the Antarctic air searing through the shattered nose.

The Alouette began to dive as more bullets, their velocity enhanced by the forward speed of the aircraft, smashed into Clausen and his machine. Fired from below they hit him in the lower body, severing his spinal cord so that hardly a sensation of pain beyond that first, strange, inexplicable warmth, reached his highly-tuned brain. He was able to see what was happening, though powerless to avert it. He was unable to control the foot pedals and the encyclic lift and joystick control wires were ripped apart by the storm of lead flung up by the rapid-fire automatic weapons.

He was still perceptive as the Alouette hit the sea, bounced like a level-thrown stone and then slammed with disintegrating force against the small escarpment of a piece of welded and hummocked ice that floated innocently just off *Adventurer*'s port bow.

The machine blew apart almost instantaneously, exploding fuel tanks completing the work of oblivion begun by impact. The long-flung shadow of the ship passed over the briefly burning remains of the helicopter like a veil over the face of the dead.

CHILEAN FRIGATE *BERNARDO O'HIGGINS*, SOUTHERN OCEAN

"Dios!"

Soto, grinning at the badinage between himself and Clausen, froze the smile on his face. Clausen still had the headset switched on and the captain could hear the noises of destruction coming in a distorted but recognizable form through the throat-mike.

"Clausen. . . ! Clausen . . . ?"

The radio operators turned to stare at their normally imperturbable commander. His face was white, his mouth open from shouting his lieutenant's name.

"Mother of God!" Soto tore the headset off and flung it down, lunging for the door with a furious energy. "Keep calling him!" he ordered over his shoulder as he leapt for the bridge ladder to plot the position of Clausen's machine and to wind the turbines up to their 30,000 h.p. which would give him 30 knots to close the distance between him and his lost helicopter.

There was no doubt in Soto's mind: his helicopter had been shot down.

ADVENTURER, WEDDELL SEA

Lila stared astern where the pall of greasy black smoke rose and dispersed in the wind. She stood in a litter of spent cartridge cases and dropped magazine clips. From the moment Stephanos had told her of that intercepted broadcast to British ships from Portishead Radio, she had been worried by the possibility of such an event causing their discovery. Although she had soothed Stephanos's fears, the seed of doubt had been sown. This, and the death of her radio operator seriously compromised success. Had the helicopter reported their position? Where was it from? Had it discovered them by chance? So many questions without answers.

Now, more than ever, they must reach Destitution Island.

HMS NORWICH, SOUTHERN OCEAN

"Signal sir."

Captain Crosby-Milne took the piece of folded paper from the messenger and opened it. It was in plain language. Soto's *Leander*-class frigate had located the approximate position of the maverick liner.

Stiffly he eased himself out of the Volvo truck driver's seat that a thoughtful Admiralty provided for their commanding officers to occupy while at sea. It always struck Crosby-Milne as a great irony that a nation which, in decline, had earned itself a reputation for inertia, could not even design a seat for the recumbent arses of its sea captains. At that moment, however, such a thought was far from his mind. He moved towards the chart, staring at the co-ordinates of latitude and longitude on the message from Captain Soto.

By that magic telegraphy that works silently and is known in the Service as 'scuttlebutt', the navigating officer joined him. The young man leaned over the chart just as Crosby-Milne completed his almost effeminately neat cross and replaced the 2B pencil in its resting place between the two parts of the parallel rules.

"That's where the bugger is, Pilot," remarked Crosby-Milne.

"That's in the Weddell Sea, sir. What the devil's she doing there?"

"Search me . . . we'd better go and find out . . . give me a course and distance."

The captain turned back to stare at the horizon as though he would suddenly see his quarry appear on the grey line that encompassed their visible world. His mind began to consider fuel and endurance and how long he could justify being off station. He could recall *Alert* from her patrol area and refuel, then send her into Stanley to refuel herself from the providentially arrived *Tidestream*. That would free him for range and his obligation to the defence of the Falklands. Alternatively he could take *Norwich* back and sent *Alert* on by herself.

"How far is it, Pilot?" he asked irritably.

The navigating officer dog-legged the brass dividers round Joinville Island at the northern extremity of the Antarctic Peninsula. "Just a moment, sir. It's quite a long way . . . a bloody long way," he added under his breath.

ADVENTURER, WEDDELL SEA

Palmer had been dozing in Smythe's bridge chair when Lila had seen and shot down the Alouette. The sound of her Kalashnikov on rapid fire snatched him from fretful and unsatisfactory sleep. Leaping to his feet he had rushed to the bridge wing to see the helicopter hit the water.

She had come into the wheelhouse and given him a perfunctory glance. Her expression was clouded with preoccupation and she had almost lost her former beauty.

He turned to the radar and the chart. They were less than 20 miles from their destination. He peered forward, through the wheelhouse windows. The calm that had so swiftly followed the easing of the north-easterly gale was equally quickly about to be displaced. The horizon was no longer clear, but misty with ice blink and a thickening of the weather caused by a freshening southerly wind.

He crossed to the radar. The screen was glowing with the random yellow dots of sea-clutter round the ship. Someone, presumably Lila, had been fiddling with the controls and this was insufficiently suppressed. He instinctively adjusted the control which eliminated such extraneous echoes. The ice floes showed up better, returning persistent echoes to the aerial, though even these were sometimes difficult to see, depending upon the aspect of their surfaces to the radiating signals striking them from the questing scanner. An experienced radar observer could quickly distinguish ice from mere waves, even in a gale, but not all ice sent back a return. Some was too slushed, too smooth, or too low to bounce the signal back. But what Palmer was looking at was not ice. Ahead of them, lying athwart the heading marker, a solid echo lay curved round their track. The little black inverted 'C' on the chart had now assumed this concrete reality, this electronic response on the main radar display.

He was looking at Destitution Island.

DOWNING STREET, LONDON

"Mr Ambassador, this is an early and unexpected pleasure. You must have some coffee, I insist upon it."

"This isn't exactly a social call, Prime Minister, things have taken a turn for the worse."

"Yes, I heard it on the BBC news earlier. The Israelis have been pinned down, even driven back. . . ."

"It's not that, sir, there's a new factor in the game now."

"Oh?"

"The editor of the Washington Daily Post has gotten a letter that claims a British-owned liner called *Adventurer* has been hijacked by a METO organisation."

"A *what*?"

"A multi-ethnic terror organisational group. It's a new phenomenon, we've been studying it for some time, this one's called April 86."

"Never heard of it."

"It's Palestinian oriented. Tacit backing from the Kremlin, possible links with other organisations; FLQ, IRA, ETA, Red Brigade, Red Army Faction, the Nips, even the Costa Mayans, you can guess the kinda thing, Prime Minister. They've got this ship and hijacked it somewhere off South America's our guess. Point is, it has American nationals on board and includes a lot of kids from that school in the Hebrides, Castle Drumdhu. The passenger list reads like the next generation 'Who's Who.' They've also got Blumenthal . . . I see you're surprised. Of course there are British nationals involved, too. Point is, sir, you well know the President's no-deal attitude to hijackers, particularly this lot."

"April 86?"

"Yeah."

"That refers to your raids on Tripoli and Benghazi, I assume?"

"I guess so. . . ."

"And you say you've known about this April 86 Group for a while?"

"Uh-huh."

"Then why the devil weren't we told?"

"Oh, I expect you were, sir, at least I expect the British Government were informed as a matter of routine under the Special Agreement terms. You have so recently taken office, sir, that I suspect you haven't been fully briefed."

"Mr Ambassador, I do assure you that intelligence briefing was one of my first priorities after taking office and kissing hands. I assure you that the existence of April 86 was not made known to my intelligence chiefs via the good offices of your own."

"But you know about it?"

"I learned very recently, *very* recently mark you, of its possible existence, that it might possibly have been responsible for the destruction of the Gannet Oil Platforms and that a splinter group acting under IRA guise blew up our new destroyer building in Belfast."

"So what are you going to do about it, Mr Prime Minister?"

"Nothing, nothing until I am presented with demands, which I am sure I soon will be, but until I know what they are it would be foolish to speculate."

"Or commit yourself to the support of your ally, the United States?"

"Have *you* received demands?"

"Yeah. The murder of all American nationals on the ship within twenty-four hours unless the United States secures an immediate withdrawal of the Israeli forces around Sidon, guarantees the security of the Lebanon and recognizes territorial occupation of Sidon and its environs as forming an independent Palestinian State."

"You mean Fatah have *annexed* Sidon?"

"That's about the size of it, at least that's what they want."

"Then why not go along with it?"

"Prime Minister!"

"You lectured me on pragmatism the other day. With Backhouse's fleet out-gunning the Russian squadron, the President is not being intimidated. It might be regarded as a statesmanlike action."

"Hell, no! These bastards have got US citizens hostage! They've got Blumenthal. . . ."

"Mr Ambassador, Blumenthal was in the Haganah when he was eighteen. He transferred to the Irgun when he was nineteen. He's no stranger to the concept of dying for Israel; besides, I read somewhere he is believed to have cancer . . . as for your own citizens, their release can easily be secured."

"That's capitulation!"

"Washington thought it a splendid idea at Yorktown."

"Hell, Prime Minister, you're serious!"

"You bet your goddam boots I am, Mr Ambassador!"

"I sent him packing, Johnnie," the PM said.

"Was that wise, David?"

"'Son thou dost not know with what little wisdom the world

238

is governed', Oxenstiern, John, the great Swedish chancellor. Of course it was wise, whether it was politic is another matter, but I came to power on a platform dedicated to concentrate on internal problems and disentangle us from the coat-tails of Uncle Sam."

"It's difficult. . . ."

"Of course it's difficult, Johnnie, so is anything worth doing. In a minute I shall phone President Reilly. He isn't going to like it but I shall make it clear that I regard the Israeli incursion into the Lebanon as unacceptable; that'll find echoes of sympathy within Israel itself. I shall also complain of a lack of intelligence information pertaining to the April 86 Group which might have allowed us to prevent the attacks on the Gannet Field. It wouldn't, of course, but it'll take him time to work that out and secure me the advantage of righteous indignation."

"You're learning fast, David."

"Something to do with a week being a long time in politics. Was it Wilson who said that?"

"But there is something else."

"You've got that cautionary look in your eye . . . something to scupper my self-conceit?"

"Well, yes. They think they've located the *Adventurer*."

"What d'you mean *think*?

"Detail's a bit sketchy, but a Chilean helicopter on a routine reconnaissance flight appears to have been shot down."

"Argentinians?"

"Apparently not."

"Where do we fit in?"

"A Chilean ship is co-operating in the search for the *Adventurer*."

"Damn! Get Admiral Blacklock on the telephone . . . I'm due in the House at eleven. What time are we due at Nottingham University tomorrow?"

"Not until lunch at noon."

"I don't want to cancel that."

"There'll be a lot of coverage for such a major speech."

"Let's hope we can keep the subject to revitalizing our national sense of purpose."

"Unless other subjects obtrude."

"Yes. Now get Blacklock, I don't want him running away with

the idea that he has any kind of mandate for interfering with this damned ship."

"What about the Chileans? They won't be too happy if they've had a helicopter shot down?"

"No, Blacklock's man-on-the-spot will have to exercise some restraint. I wonder where, exactly, this *Adventurer* is?"

Part Three

SEIGE

'You know not, my son, with what a small
stock of wisdom the world is governed.'

Oxenstiern

Chapter Eleven

Shivering in the cold, damp air Palmer watched the summit rise out of the mist as the gale blew itself out. Gradually, more peaks were revealed as the mist dispersed to reveal a landscape of awesome beauty.

Destitution Island; its name inspired by deprivation, a name of heroic last resort and in the end, to the unknown explorer, a place of forlorn hope. Black cliffs rose sheer from the sea, almost surrounding the silent liner as she lay to her anchor under their beetling crags.

Streaking down from the remote summits dazzling white snow and sparkling ice filled in the irregularities of the volcanic rock faces. Here and there wind-scored caves of cerulean blue pierced the smooth slopes, their mysterious interiors polished like glass. In these places where ice and snow could find a lodgement, they sought out the fissures and faults of this stupendous upheaval of the earth's crust, working their eternal business of attrition and erosion upon its substance. But the gentler lower slopes, from which at this season much of the ice and snow had run off, turned to talus. A sloping declivity of broken rock and scree, patched here and there with the bright greens and ochreous yellows of mosses and lichens dropped to the sea.

This fantastic panorama almost encircled them, embracing them half in shadow and half in sunlight.

Within the lagoon the water was flat by comparison with that beyond the entrance to the bay. Its waters were almost free of ice, except for a few rotten growlers that bobbed about the opening, out of which the molten heart of the earth had once bled and through which, as it had eased, the boiling sea had surged in to cool and plug the ancient volcano. Palmer supposed that the waters of the bay were comparatively warm, heat-inducted from the still-hot core of the vent far below them. Looking up into the clear blue sky he could see a tall column of cloud rising above the island and, Palmer observed, this displacement of warmed air was supplemented by sudden, savage little katabatic squalls which slid off the mountain summits and screamed down across the flat water of the bay, raking it with spitefully vicious catspaws. These phenomena were of relatively short duration and had little effect beyond turning *Adventurer* slowly about her anchor cable.

On the small beaches of black laval sand penguins and seals abounded, while above the sea the air was dense with birds, the quick wing-beat of the auks, the white of gulls and the dark hawking shapes of the predatory skuas.

Palmer stood wide-eyed, a prey to conflicting emotions. He had brought *Adventurer* to an anchor, seeking out the only shelf of even seabed that extended far enough from the shore to allow them to moor. They lay beneath the almost sheer face of a 1000 m cliff, secure in the ancient crater of a volcano whose last eruption was unrecorded. The concentration this task demanded had slipped from him now. He could have gone below to sleep but he was keyed too highly and his mind was now open to the impact of the scene of wild beauty before him. It touched something deep within him, catching at his soul with a hint of the numinous of nature. As he stood there a strange change was wrought in him. The hijack, the promises of the man in London, even his own ambivalence in the whole matter, was swept aside as matters of relative triviality, to be replaced by a sense of completion, of elation, almost and his mind barely closed over the thought of satiety.

It was no more than a flash of insight, such as is given to solitary people in vast and lonely places, and it was gone, ripped from him almost before it had impinged itself upon his consciousness.

"Al Fatah, the Palestine Liberation Movement, is not struggling against the Jews as an ethnic and religious community. It

244

is struggling against Israel as the expression of Zionist racism and colonialism. Al Fatah proclaims the right of the Palestinian people to exist in an independent democratic state and the struggle of the Palestinian people, like that of other peoples of Asia, Africa and Latin America, is part of the historic process of the liberation of oppressed peoples from colonialism and imperialism. . . ."

The voice of Anna, haranguing the hapless hostages as they made their daily pilgrimage round the boat deck under the watchful eyes of their guards, brought Palmer back to the present. He could not see them from where he stood and he made no move to draw attention to himself. In the past few hours he had earned a measure of respite from surveillance and the close attention of the terrorists. *Adventurer* had reached her destination and there was so little her well-guarded, frightened, cold and half-starved passengers and crew could do.

Now Anna pressed home her psychological invocation of the sympathetic syndrome that would half-woo the most intransigent opponent to the objective of the *fedayeen*. The recitation of the Fatah 'Manifesto' was the latest bruising of their minds, for the afternoon had been filled with films of the desperate life in the camps of Shabra and Shatila, of the dispossession of the Arabs, of Israeli domination, of Christian massacres and of the hopelessness of the lives of two million refugees.

The first surges of sympathy had already begun and Anna had emerged as the demagogue of the April 86 Group, an orator of considerable ability. Because of her sex, she had turned a natural though unkind revulsion for her disfigurement into a core of understanding and tacit condoning of her group's desperate action. The enforced audience had begun to accept the West's burden of guilt, to comprehend through hunger and cold and fear, the need of a wronged people. They had only to do what they were told and they could play a part in liberating refugees from their plight. Surely, Anna declared, it would be an act of compassion compatible with the finest tenets of their Christian religion.

Palmer listened to the tramp of feet and the low buzz of voices as they died away. The hostages were being returned to their respective prisons and Anna ceased her strident indoctrination. Trying to recover his lost mood, Palmer stared at a Weddell seal as it pursued a fish along the ship's side. He was suddenly aware that Lila had joined him at the rail. They leaned side-by-side, much as they had done the night they had seen the phosphorescence in the sea. The loss of innocence in the intervening time bore down upon them.

"You do not sleep," she observed.

"No."

"Are you afraid?"

He shook his head. "No. Not any more. I'm afraid of the pain of dying, but not of death itself."

"That is how you feel on a good mission." He could sense the tension ebbing out of her. For Lila, Destitution Island was an oasis. She had time for more personal matters. "You are not on a mission, Palmer. Why should you feel like this?"

He shrugged. "I don't know. It's not easy to put into words, but I should not mind dying here. . . ." he gestured round the anchorage, "I should not mind being part of something so magnificent."

He felt the slightest pressure of her shoulder as she leaned against him. "Anna said you were a poet."

The low howl of a squall built up round them and they watched as a cloud of whirling snow rolled down a shallow valley in a white, misty swirl, watched as it flattened out across the surface of the sea and suddenly raced across the surface of the bay, tearing at the dark water, scouring it into slapping waves no more than a foot high. The whole thing vanished as it reached the centre of the bay and the ship twitched at her cable.

Palmer broke the silence. "There is nothing for us," he said slowly, his voice catching so that he had to cough to clear his throat. "You have cured me of ambition and we have had all that life can offer us."

Their eyes met. Her face was still pinched and hard, but her eyes were bright with tears and then she turned away and when she spoke her voice was shrill. "I have to do what I am doing . . . what is your English proverb? To be cruel. . . ."

246

"To be kind. Yes, I understand."

"It is to redress the grievances and misfortunes of a deprived people at the expense of those who have so much."

"I am not judging you, Lila. I know that you are different from me in that your sense of fighting for a future is so much stronger than my own."

"What about your girl in London?"

"Kate?" He shook his head, knowing that Kate and London were not reality. They existed on another planet, despite Lila's intention of coercing them from this distant place. Therein lay the false premise of politics. But he knew he could not expect her to understand, her world was drawn in absolutes of black and white. Odd that Kate would have understood immediately. "You forget, Lila, that your hostages are not only prisoners, here they are quite out of their element. I, on the other hand, am a seaman. If I have any personal attachment it must be to you."

"You are a fool, Palmer." Her voice was low, as he remembered it after love-making, but he made no move towards her, just stared out over the water of Destitution Bay.

"I have no illusions about you, Lila. I know what you are capable of. I know the hostages are quite incidental to the blackmail pressure you are applying for the recognition of your claim to Palestine. You would happily die, blowing this ship and all on board it to hell, if it liberated Palestine. I know that. So this is for us, the end."

"Is that why you have been thinking about dying?"

"We haven't come all this way to play games," he said with a sudden edge to his voice.

"And you, Palmer, would *you* die for Palestine?"

He raised his binoculars and stared through them. He had not noticed the buildings before. Some trick of the sun's movement had thrown them into focus. They stood at the head of the bay, partly hidden behind a spur of black rock, the rusty iron sheds of a deserted whaling station.

"No," he said slowly, lowering the glasses. "not for Palestine, Lila."

As he bent to kiss her he wondered what, on that other planet, the man in London would say.

247

HELICOPTER FLOWN OFF FROM HMS *NORWICH*, DESTITUTION ISLAND

The dark-blue Lynx helicopter with the Royal Naval markings and the white letters 'NH' that identified her as the advanced eyes of HMS *Norwich* dropped out of the cloud at 2,800ft. The relieved pilot, aware that he had cleared the jagged peaks of Destitution Island more by luck than judgement, dropped the machine's protuberant snout and zoomed down into a steep dive. The single patch of cloud that had caught him unawares seemed to form over the centre of the enclosed lagoon and trailed downwind above the island's rim.

Beside him his observer relieved his own tension with a wild whoop. The machine levelled off just above the corrugated and rusty iron buildings of the old whaling station, crossed the disused slipway and sped out over the dark waters of the bay. A katabatic tailwind suddenly boosted their speed in exhilarating acceleration and they scattered birds left and right as they headed for the distant opening in the mountains which gave onto the open sea beyond. Alert to the dangers of bird-strike the pilot eased the throttle back and momentarily consulted his instruments.

"Jesus Christ, it's the ship!"

The pilot looked up as his companion pointed. The unmistakable outline of a liner detached itself from the background. Both men knew the fate of the Chilean helicopter and the pilot reached down for the collective lift control. Gas turbines screaming, the Lynx banked and climbed in a rising turn that distorted the faces of the aircrew and caused the airframe to tremble with stress. Neither pilot nor observer saw the white faces of the startled lovers staring up at them from the ship's bridge.

ADVENTURER, DESTITUTION ISLAND

Palmer turned from staring at the helicopter. Lila's expression was aghast and she began to swear, a combined and ferocious mixture of anger, frustration and savagery. He felt suddenly moved to pity, feeling beneath her rage a deep despair. She was already hampered by the death of Stephanos, or whatever his real name was.

He was unsure if she had realized the nationality of the Lynx.

The fact that it was British seriously compromised him.

COSTA MAYAN SUBMARINE *LIBERTAD*, WEDDELL SEA

Captain Sergei Korolenko nodded his thanks to Captain Vega and peered through *Libertad*'s periscope. He shared some of Vega's apprehension, the ice was everywhere and the inexperience of the crew was showing up in these conditions. Korolenko had to admit that they had done well, not as well as a Russian crew, but better than anticipated. He had to remind himself that six months ago most of them had not seen the inside of a submarine and they had only the vaguest notion of what an iceberg was, let alone acquired the ability to gauge its size and depth from a few sonar responses. Vega was a good man, a seaman to his finger tips, but the length of the patrol and the strain of his new command combined with the undoubted irritation, necessary though it was, of having the Russian expert on board, was wearing his resilience thin.

Korolenko snapped up the handles of the periscope and nodded. Vega gave the order for its housing and both men crossed to the chart table. The spread chart was a Gnomonic projection of the Antarctic peninsula. Vega put his index finger on the neatly pencilled cross that marked *Libertad*'s position. Korolenko noticed the nail was bitten to the quick.

The nibbled fingernail trailed down, through a myriad dots of islands and islets, of fiords and broken mountain ranges until it stopped next to the curl of rock marked on the Russian chart as Lazarev Island, named after Bellingshausen's second in command during the Tsarist Antarctic expedition of 1819.

"On the British chart, Manuel," Korolenko said discursively, "it is called Destitution Island."

"Perhaps," replied Vega in a misanthropic tone that emphasized his apprehension which increased in the same proportion as their southerly latitude, "the British gave it the better name."

Korolenko laughed, though his shrewd eyes watched his colleague. "Well, you have not far to go now. Perhaps tomorrow, at dawn, you will be able to make your passage northwards."

"Yes, but when *is* dawn in these infernal parts, Comrade Adviser?"

The image of that black and white island with its faint plume of cloud trailing above it had not yet faded from his mind's eye.

"Come, we must wait a little, let us have a drink, my friend. This time not tequila. This time we shall drink vodka, eh?"

Vega relaxed. "Yes, we will drink vodka."

CHILEAN FRIGATE *BERNARDO O'HIGGINS*, WEDDELL SEA

Captain Enrique Soto leaned over the rail and gauged the moment. Ahead of him the sharp bow with its raised forecastle beyond the twin 4.5 inch gun mounting dipped and rose in the grey-green swell, slicing through a sea that was dotted with the low, rotting bergs of last year's ice, lethal masses that could rip open his ship with the ease of a can-opener.

"Right! Right full helm!"

The grey ship leaned to the sudden turn, the hull tremulous as her rudder bit deep into the water and drove her stern round in a rapid turn designed into her for the hunting of submarines.

"'Midships . . . steady. . . .'"

In other circumstances Soto would have delighted in driving his ship to the limits and revelled in the brush with danger that his pursuit had involved him with.

"Steady as you go . . . steer one six three."

But Soto had lost Clausen and his helicopter and the loss weighed heavily upon him, for he had failed to anticipate an act of hostility from the missing ship, had clearly briefed Clausen inadequately and was victim to the self-recrimination of a commander who has failed in his own conception of his duty.

Now he sought to make amends, to avenge Clausen. He had already dropped his speed to 18 knots, still too fast in such conditions and he peered with keen-eyed vigilance into the wind conscious that the visibility was improving. But this did not mollify his feelings.

"Left! Left full rudder. . . ."

From down below came the crash of breaking crockery that told where the wardroom steward had forgotten to fit the table-fiddles lulled by the lazy pitching that had suddenly given way to these tortuous twists and turns which rolled the frigate onto her beam-ends.

The low berg, its slippery smooth surface glinting with green algae, slid down the starboard side and astern. A second later he smelt the pungent odour of decay from the multitudes of tiny organisms upon it. He turned forward again, the ship's wind sweeping aft, keen on his face, alerting his hunter's instincts.

Though it had distressed Soto, the loss of Clausen had effected a transformation aboard. Their passage had suddenly become vital, a mission of revenge to break the endless monotony of routine patrol. Soto was no fool. He knew most of his conscripted crew wished they were back home or alongside at Punta Arenas at the very least. Loss of their helicopter was a personal matter, involving them all. Clausen had been popular and there was now an almost tangible air of purpose, one that infects a ship's company when they begin to act and think like a single being, conferring on their ship a corporate sentience for which she had been invented. Feeling this, Soto shook off his depression and conned his grey ship southwards, towards Destitution Island where, he knew from *Norwich*'s Lynx, the *Adventurer* had taken refuge. He consoled himself with the reflection that Lord Cochrane, his putative ancestor, would have approved his zeal.

251

Forty-one miles to the north and in contact with the *Bernardo O'Higgins*, Captain Crosby-Milne was equally unhappy. He had recovered his Lynx and was in the act of drafting a signal after debriefing its pilot when he was handed a message from Northwood. It was disarmingly inexplicit and he felt the weight of responsibility bear down on him. Its execution was complicated by Soto and the *Bernardo O'Higgins*, out of sight to the southward, close to Destitution Island.

Crosby-Milne entertained the uncharitable thought that he hoped the impulsive Chilean would dash ahead and take the matter out of his own hands but, like the well-trained naval officer that he was, Crosby-Milne re-read the message. There seemed to be some political implications to which he was supposed to conform, though what these were he had no idea except that it was up to him to work miracles. Their Lordships were less obfusc, they wanted the matter brought to a 'satisfactory conclusion' although he was urged to use the 'utmost caution'. He was also virtually forbidden 'to initiate any action which would precipitate counter-productive political repercussions elsewhere', but he was equally forcefully required to 'do everything possible to avoid embarrassment to Her Majesty's Government by appearing to negotiate' even though 'a degree of negotiation might prove of tactical advantage to the on-scene commander'.

It was a masterpiece of expedient politico-military double-speak, and Crosby-Milne swore with a quiet venom that was becoming habitual.

"I suppose," remarked his first lieutenant, handing back the signal, "that's what comes of voting in a wishy-washy radical with no ministerial experience." The first lieutenant regarded the grey waste with a jaundiced eye. His audible sigh declared his uninspired regard for the Antarctic Ocean. "Want to fly over and talk to this Soto, bloke, sir?"

"Thought about that, Number One; decided I'd fly over when we're a bit closer."

The first lieutenant looked at the Doppler log. Nine knots. "Be some time yet."

"Yes."

Cunning old bastard, thought the first lieutenant.

COSTA MAYAN SUBMARINE *LIBERTAD*, WEDDELL SEA

Korolenko tossed off the third glass of vodka as the cabin curtain was drawn back and the frightened face of an officer appeared. He spoke to Vega in a patois that Korolenko could not follow, but he knew alarm when he saw it in Vega's eyes.

"Noises on sonar!" Vega explained briefly as he rose, reached for his hat and made for the control room. These Costa Mayans were amateurs and the ocean, especially the oxygen-rich oceans of his beloved polar regions, were as noisy as Red Square on May Day. Slowly Korolenko followed.

Vega handed him a spare set of headphones, but Korolenko did not need them. The speaker was turned up and the ticking, rather like a child's toy heard from the next room, was clearly audible. Korolenko's heart gave a painful skip. It was still some distance away, perhaps 20 miles, but he knew instantly what it was.

"British *Leander*-class frigate," he said, watching the reaction of the news on the circle of half-trained faces in *Libertad*'s control room.

CHILEAN FRIGATE *BERNARDO O'HIGGINS*, WEDDELL SEA

Instinctively, Crosby-Milne ducked as he scrambled out of the dark-blue Lynx. Above his head the rotors whirled as the pilot increased pitch and lifted off the deck of the *Bernardo O'Higgins*, to wait for his commander while hovering over the starboard quarter of the pitching frigate.

The *Bernardo O'Higgins* was familiarly alien to Crosby-Milne as he was led through her towards the bridge. His own last command had been a *Leander*. The same narrow alleyways were lined with the same miles of piping, cabletrays and wiring; they were punctuated by the same doorways and hatches, bulkhead fittings, hydrants and fire extinguishers. Everything was much as it would have been on a Royal Naval frigate of the same class.

Men drew back or peered curiously at the foreign officer; the white-capped cook leaned as inquisitively from his galley door as any RN rating, and a dopey watchkeeper, just roused from his sweaty 'pit', stumbled along the alleyway half-naked and dangling towel and razor before jerking aside in recognition of Crosby-Milne's four gold shoulder bars.

But the *Bernardo O'Higgins* was Chilean, a fact that manifested itself in smells so different from those he was accustomed to; in stencilled warnings and instructions, in notices and labels in unfamiliar Spanish. Hispanic and Indian genes showed in her men's faces, so that it was a dreamlike series of slightly incongruous images that flashed past him as he followed the young officer sent to escort him to the bridge.

He emerged into the wheelhouse after a series of ascents by ladder and was confronted by the familiar control panel of a Kelvin Hughes KH 1006 navigational radar. Catching his breath, Crosby-Milne also recovered his composure and turned to face his host, a tall man with a lean, lined face, a pair of hard, dark eyes and an over-large nose.

"Enrique Soto, Captain, welcome on board."

"Peter Crosby-Milne, Captain Soto, how d'you do." They shook hands. Soto's English was good. "I know Admiral Aguirra."

"Yes. He tell me, and now we find this ship for you."

"I am very sorry about your helicopter."

"Yes. Clausen was a very good officer. These bastards in this ship, it is hijack, yes?"

"Yes. Has Admiral Aguirra sent you orders?"

"I am in what you call . . . hot chase?"

"Hot pursuit."

"Yes. Hot pursuit." It seemed Soto was acting on his own initiative. Perhaps Aguirra and General Pinochet approved.

"And . . . ?"

"When I come to this ship, I shall decide." Crosby-Milne studied the Chilean officer and recognized the symptoms of an impetuous character. Misgivings as to the inherent weakness of the Latin temperament sprang to mind. "I am descended from your Admiral Cochrane," Soto said suddenly, "like him I do not like to lose my men."

"I think we must not act hastily . . . too fast, you under-stand?"

"I have lost a good officer and a helicopter." There was a bristling undertone to Soto's reply.

"True, Captain," said Crosby-Milne, "but there are innocent people on board that ship and my government do not want any unnecessary force used. The matter has serious international implications."

"Certainly it does, Captain," said Soto drawing himself up, "the honour of my flag is insulted. . . ."

Crosby-Milne groaned inwardly. The words seemed oddly out of date and yet there was something very touching about them and he suddenly envied Soto his independence. The thought of what the Chilean might do, however, caused his stomach to churn with anxiety.

"I shall join you as soon as possible, Captain Soto. We shall remain in touch. There are British and American nationals aboard that ship. I should not like us to come to blows over the honour of *my* flag either." He had intended the remark to be a flippant reference to caution, but Soto remained rigid.

"I am sure we will co-operate," he said coolly.

Crosby-Milne held out his hand, but Soto saluted and nod-ded at the young officer to return the British captain to his helicopter.

ADVENTURER, DESTITUTION ISLAND

Lila sat on the edge of Palmer's bunk. She was alone in his cabin while he slept, rolled in a greatcoat on the chart room settee. She

255

lay back in the bunk, patiently waiting for the end of the deadline she knew would have been given to the British and American governments by now.

Twenty-four hours. No extensions. Only executions, beginning with Blumenthal, the dispossessor.

She wanted to sleep, to enjoy a few minutes of blessed unconsciousness but the image of that helicopter shattered her imagination, prompting her to worry. The hostages were utterly cowed now, half-starved, their pampered bellies protesting, each intent only upon his or her survival. No, it was that damnable helicopter that caused the fate of Palestine to hang in the balance. She stared at the deckhead, wondering what was going to happen, trying to divine the future. Giorgio had rigged Katyusha rockets on the bridge now. If the second helicopter came back it would find more than a pair of startled onlookers.

Where *had* it come from?

She knew from her briefing that the ice-patrol ship *Endurance*, the British Antarctic Survey ships *Bransfield* and *John Biscoe* were, with the supply ships of other organisations, within 1000 miles of them. But those two helicopters with a much lesser range had appeared from nowhere and located them without trouble.

How much longer would it be before the *Libertad* joined them at the rendezvous?

She was suddenly startled by the roar of an explosion.

Grabbing her gun and a spare magazine she was running to the bridge in an instant. Palmer was awake and stood behind Giorgio and Anna. Along the deck she saw the black dots of her gunmen, brought suddenly alert by the rolling concussion, dull echoes of which still reverberated from the cliffs. As the noise died away and the cries of thousands of startled birds subsided, a silence of profound expectation settled over the still waters of the bay. All around them the great split black crags rose, their surfaces sliced by ice-filled cracks and their summits sparkling pinkly from the low rays of the midnight sun which were reflected from the snow that lay there.

The second blast made them all jump.

256

COSTA MAYAN SUBMARINE, *LIBERTAD*, WEDDELL SEA

"What d'you make of her?"

Vega replied confidently without removing his eyes from the binocular eyepiece of the attack periscope. He could see the high, narrow hull end-on, a great bow-wave creaming out under the flare of a frigate racing through the low swell.

"*Leander*-class . . . British . . . seen the guardship off Belize."

"Good; pennant number?"

"Obscured by aspect . . . plot?" This last was addressed not to satisfy Korolenko's interrogation, for Vega was sure that he was being put through his paces, but to his own staff. The officer standing behind the row of operators at the control panels bent over one of the rating's shoulders.

"Course one-nine-two, speed 21 knots."

"Very good . . . he's confident. . . ."

"Or fool-hardy." Korolenko ruminated.

The atmosphere aboard *Libertad* was thick with more than the stink of men living cheek by jowl in a confined space. The last hours had sharpened nerves and brought *Libertad*'s company to a brittle state of readiness for almost any enterprise. Men who had overturned that much of the world that they could now call their own were in no condition to act with considered moderation, particularly as their present assignment had been advertised as advancing the cause of world revolution.

The men of the *Libertad* had taken their lead from Vega, but Vega had been seduced by the image of a glory peddled by Korolenko. Korolenko himself knew of the importance of this mission, understood its international implications far better than the Costa Mayans and was able to calculate the effects of his meditated action. Yet even he was misled, misled by the flaws in his own character. Trained for a never-fought battle, he had waited all his life for a chance that never came in the cat-and-mouse game of deterrence. Now it presented itself with irresistible appeal to his eager imagination. In the last hour, as *Libertad*'s control room echoed to the whirring of the *Bernardo O'Higgins*'s racing screws, the submarine crew had been preparing her upper bow torpedo tubes. They had done it

257

before and even now the very slow deliberation of Korolenko's patient coaching had had the quality of an evolution, for *Libertad* had only two 21 inch torpedoes and they had been stowed well down in her forward stowage space to make room for her complement of commandos.

Now they were ready for firing, almost without the crew knowing that coincidental with their exertions, Korolenko and Vega had brought *Libertad* into the very track of the speeding frigate.

"You must have the honour, Comrade Adviser." Vega relinquished the attack periscope to Korolenko who seized the twin control handles eagerly, a sense of exhilaration sweeping through him.

The image jumped into focus as he adjusted the ranging graticules. The narrow grey bow rose and fell with an easy motion, cutting through the grey-green of the sea. As the frigate plunged, he could see the details of her forebridge, a brief sparkle of light on wheelhouse windows, the flat side of her reversed 4.5 inch gun mounting and the tall foremast with its array of aerials and fire-control antennae. Twinkling with rhythmnic reflection, her radar scanners caught the light of the odd, cheese-shaped air-search 965 most prominently before it disappeared behind the rising bow.

Korolenko needed to see nothing else. He lay in the track of his quarry, the perfectly poised hunter.

"Fire!"

CHILEAN FRIGATE *BERNARDO O'HIGGINS*, WEDDELL SEA

Captain Soto lowered his glasses and gauged his distance from the opening point of the entrance to Destitution Bay. A moment later his query was confirmed by the officer at the navigational radar. In exactly six minutes he could turn into the bay.

"Action stations!" he ordered, his voice harsh with excitement. He was thinking of Lieutenant Clausen and the Communist-inspired shit on that hijacked liner. He was glad he had beaten the British ship to Destitution Island, glad for Clausen and the honour of his country's flag.

The next instant the deck beneath his feet buckled and his ship began to die with a roaring explosion that seemed to come from deep within her.

COSTA MAYAN SUBMARINE *LIBERTAD*, WEDDELL SEA

"Give her a second fish, Manuel," Korolenko said, relinquishing the attack periscope to Vega who was twitching with suppressed excitement next to him. What Vega saw as he bent to the instrument made him draw in his breath.

The frigate had slewed to starboard and was already listing over. Her momentum was still carrying her forward but clouds of escaping steam engulfed her waist and the neat line of her sheer was broken. The torpedo had done its work well but it was essential the target be sunk quickly, before she could transmit to the world the news that she had been struck.

"Right full rudder, come ahead flank speed!" Manuel Vega began a half-circle to reposition the *Libertad* to administer the death blow to the frigate.

CHILEAN FRIGATE *BERNARDO O'HIGGINS*, WEDDELL SEA

There was total confusion aboard the *Bernardo O'Higgins*. Her whole company had been caught in the act of running to their action stations and the sudden, shattering explosion of the Russian torpedo immediately below the ship's engine room had not only irreparably damaged her boilers and turbines but had put out of action her generators so that her warren of internal compartments were plunged into darkness. There was a brief surge of current as her emergency services stirred into life and then they too died and the constant hum of ventilation fans, of pumps and motors and electronic equipment which were like the surge of lifeblood in a warship, ceased. As the stricken and listing ship lost way, her back broken, the darkness was filled with the shouts and screams of men, the orders of superiors trying to combat the inevitable, and the pervasive sounds of fear as fires started, flickering into diabolical life where electrical shorts ignited flammable materials in the messdecks.

On the bridge Soto was stunned. He suspected sabotage, a nightmare with which he had lived for months. Around him the wheelhouse fell deathly silent and only the noise of the wind and sea came to his shocked senses, those and the white expectancy of the faces of the men about him.

COSTA MAYAN SUBMARINE *LIBERTAD*, WEDDELL SEA

"Any signal?" Korolenko barked the question at the radio operator sitting behind him.

"No, Comrade Adviser." They had hoisted their aerial after discharging the first torpedo and the Russian had instructed the operator to monitor the international distress frequencies to see if their target sent off a Mayday transmission.

"Fire!"

Beside Korolenko, Vega gave the order which sent the second homing torpedo hissing out of the bow tube of the *Libertad*. The Costa Mayan could see the broken sheer of the *Leander*, the clouds of steam darkened now by smoke and the shapes of men running hither and thither along the decks. A group were congregating by a motor boat slung in davits amidships when the second torpedo struck just below the bridge. Vega watched in fascinated horror at what he had wrought as the *Bernardo O'Higgins* blew apart.

"She is not British!" he said, his mind registering something that had been obvious to him some seconds earlier, "The Pennant Number is not painted in the British manner." He searched for an ensign and saw it as Korolenko edged him impatiently aside.

"Chilean!" snapped the Russian instantly, straightening up with a great grin on his grimy face. "A double blow for freedom, Comrade Captain, eh? Now we have avenged Comrade Allende. Come, take her up, let us ensure no one lives to tell the tale and the unfortunate loss is blamed on the inanimate ice."

CHILEAN FRIGATE *BERNARDO O'HIGGINS*, WEDDELL SEA

Soto regained his senses when the second torpedo struck and he realized that his ship was under attack. The unpredictable path of the blast swept over him, leaving him dazed but conscious on the starboard bridge wing where, what seemed an age ago, he had been making preparations to turn his beautiful ship into Destitution Bay. Now she lay dead in the water beneath his feet, the hiss of steam, the shrouding of smoke and the cries of wounded men coming to him through a mist. His powerful mind grasped one thing with the desperation of a man fighting for his life. He groped his way into the twisted remains of the wheelhouse and found the portable radio, lying on the forward bridge window shelf. He picked it up and adjusted the frequency.

Beside him the officer of the watch was whimpering, trying to pull himself to his feet. As Soto bent to the portable VHF radio he sensed the young man had not yet comprehended the blast of the second torpedo had destroyed his knees. The man slumped down again. Tears started from his eyes but he gallantly began to drag himself vertical once more.

"Mayday, mayday, mayday!" said Soto, transmitting on Channel 16.

COSTA MAYAN SUBMARINE *LIBERTAD*, WEDDELL SEA

"They're transmitting a Mayday, Comrade Captain ... weak signal."

"Portable set," snapped Korolenko after a moment's judgement. Then he hefted the Kalashnikov, looked at the group of Costa Mayans assembled beneath the conning tower ladder and grinned. They were all carrying automatic weapons.

"We'll soon stop that eh?"

They jumped back as water cascaded downwards. Vega's feet disappeared upwards, a shaft of light dropped through the opened hatch and a draught of cold but unbelievably sweet air rushed into the mephitic stench of the *Libertad*.

HMS *NORWICH*, WEDDELL SEA

"I've got a Mayday, sir!"

The sudden shout from the Operations room to the bridge shattered Crosby-Milne's peace of mind.

"Where from? Get a DF fix at once!"

"In hand, sir . . . one-seven-eight, sir."

Crosby-Milne spun from the loudspeaker of the intercom. The navigator was already bending over the chart.

"That's right ahead, sir, on the bearing of the *O'Higgins*."

"Jesus Christ!"

"Captain, sir. . . ?" It was the intercom again.

"Yes?"

"That's all, sir . . . nothing else but I'm almost sure that the voice was that of the Chilean captain."

"Yes. Thank you . . . keep listening . . ." Crosby-Milne replied flatly. He was recalling the proud Chilean and the impetuous speed with which he had been rushing to avenge the insult to 'the honour of his flag'.

"I expect the poor devil's hit ice," remarked Crosby-Milne switching his mind from the prospect of confronting a highly dangerous gang of international bandits to mounting an air-sea rescue operation in the freezing waters of the Weddell Sea.

"Yes sir." The navigating officer concurred, his face hidden in the radar visor, "I think you're right. There's a hell of a lot of it ahead of us."

Crosby-Milne lifted his binoculars and raked the horizon.

"Damn." he said.

WEDDELL SEA

Enrique Soto fought to stay alive in the freezing water. The hail of bullets from the casing of the submarine had missed him but he was aware that his survival was impossible. He was a brave man, not to have died well would have negated his existence and, although the seductive warmth of approaching death already permeated his lower limbs, he fought the inevitable with the courage he had hoped might one day be called upon to defend Chile.

All about him the wreckage of his ship bobbed to the surface. A few men floated in life jackets, freezing slowly to death like their commander. Some were drowning far below him, trapped in air pockets, possibly fighting their friends for the last of the oxygen. The lucky ones were already dead of gunshot wounds. Odd artefacts bobbed about them. A wooden chopping board from the galley, an unoccupied life jacket, a large wooden crucifix. A life-raft, its casing released by the hydrostatic device surfaced with a whoosh, bursting its cocoon and expanding in an untimely, automatic sequence. Those men left alive on the sea's surface were too numb to swim towards it.

It was to be the *Bernardo O'Higgins*'s gravestone.

The stink of oil hung heavily over the sea, slicked it and corroded the mouths and nasal passages of the dying.

Presently only the scream of the gulls could be heard, swooping down on the unseeing eyes of Enrique Soto.

ADVENTURER, DESTITUTION ISLAND

The explosions had woken Palmer from an uneasy, dream-filled sleep. The bridge was suddenly occupied by several of the terrorists. Giorgio and Anna and an unknown *fed'ai* were joined by two of the Costa Mayans and Lila. The *fedayeen*

263

were conversing intensely in Arabic, their eyes looking up into the clear sky. With Stephanos dead a vital link in the chain of communication had broken down. Although there were still a couple of radio officers held hostage on board, Palmer knew Lila would not allow her operation to hang on the integrity of a pressed man.

It was clear those two explosions were extremely puzzling to the terrorists. In an operation of such obviously meticulous planning such an obtrusion had a disconcerting effect. They were supposed to be remote, removed from all intervention while the fate of Palestine was resolved, their unknown whereabouts putting immense pressure on the forces of reaction that supported the usurping state of Israel.

So ran the theory.

From time to time Palmer heard Giorgio trying to make a point. The only word he recognized was the repetition of the Spanish noun 'libertad'. He assumed it had some connection with their allies, the Costa Mayans. They took little notice of Palmer. He waited and watched, of them all he was perhaps most interested in the source of those explosions, but in the silence of reaction the tatty edges of his dream came back to him and he turned away, crossed the bridge and looked upwards. The towering summit of the island reared against the rose sky of midnight.

He knew what he had to do. What worried him most was why he was doing it.

They had heard the exploding of the torpedoes in the cinema not as airborne concussions but as massive hammer blows transmitted through the sea and delivered with tremendous force against the largely hollow and silent hull of the *Adventurer*.

The entire population of the great room jerked with nervous horror and the rising wave of murmured terror was supressed by a shout from the guards and the waving of gun barrels.

An uneasy quiescence fell upon them all. The stale air was heavy with the stink of urine, sweat and the sweet and cloying scent of exuded secretions produced by fear.

Some minutes later the man known as Giorgio returned, muttered something to his men and the hostages sensed a relaxation of tension among the terrorists. Such was their own empathy with their captors that they too relaxed, aware that their worst fears were again postponed.

Jonathan Aymes felt the concussions in the hull and also through the air. Under guard, he had been allowed to occupy the hospital; like Palmer he was reprieved for his skill. He had left a distraught Melanie, dragged reluctantly from her just when a kind of contentment had begun to permeate him. He had held her asleep for so long that his desire for drink had ebbed a little. Now, taken into the hospital and confronted by the spectacle that lay on one of the half-dozen beds there, he wanted a drink badly.

He knew her, a girl with a surname that was inextricably connected with the aeronautical industry. The irony occurred to his lateral mind at once: warplanes bearing an acronym of her surname must have often bombed, if not the villages of Palestine, then those of Costa Maya.

She was a healthy, fit young creature whose body would recover from the brutal enthusiasm of the young Arab Stephanos. But she had remained rigid, staring up at him, her outraged eyes refusing to believe the horror she had been party to. The invasion of her own body, the pain, degradation and disgust to which she had been so swiftly reduced from a normality that was never less than pleasant, had shattered her; but to see then the terrible death of the hate-object as some fierce and spectacular retributive answer to her own screamed prayer for release, seemed beyond sane comprehension.

Aymes sat on the bed and stroked her hand. It was the only therapy he could devise and he himself derived some restoration of the equanimity he had felt in comforting Melanie.

The girl's face, pale and drawn, seemed disembodied. The slender shape of her defiled abdomen seemed shrunk, out of sight, disowned, under the clinical white bed linen.

The sudden shock of the explosions made him jump. Sudden concern made him look down at his patient and smile reassuringly. He squeezed her hand gently.

"It's all right, my dear."

The gunman, or was it a woman?, made for the hospital door,

anxious to determine the cause of the concussions. Aymes ignored the commotion, continuing to stroke the girl's hand, hoping he would feel it warm again under his caress.

Zelda Rebanowicz squealed at the noise, shrinking against the buttoned headboard of the bed. The loneliness of the cabin filled her with foreboding. When would Giorgio come again?

She looked old now. Her poise, her self-esteem, built on such flimsy foundations, lacked character to sustain it. She mewed for her lover, demanding his attentions, wondering what she had done wrong that he should ignore her at such a time.

"High explosive."

"You should know, Mr Blumenthal," said Galvin, patting Margaret Allen's hand.

"Those poor children. . . ." They could hear the cries of fright from the youngsters in the adjacent cabin. It was quickly silenced by a shout from one of the terrorists.

Margaret was shaking, the twin explosions seemed to have set up an uncontrollable nervous response. Galvin got up and drew another blanket off Captain Smythe's bed. There was the dark stain of dry blood on it, but he wrapped it around her. There was no time for niceties now. He recalled that rats had been eaten during the Seige of Paris. That no longer seemed disgusting to him. He looked at the old Israeli.

"I apologize, Mr Blumenthal."

"Eh?" The old man's eyes were rheumy. Galvin had not noticed before how blue they must once have been. "I do not regret what I did, Dr Galvin. It had to be done . . . after what we had suffered in my own lifetime at the hands of the Nazis, it had to be done."

"D'you regret nothing?" Margaret suddenly asked. "I mean I can see that as a general principle liberating the Holy Land and returning to the land of milk and honey was justifiable, but in detail, as a fighter dealing in death, in killing other human beings, was there no act you regretted?"

Galvin looked at Margaret. She appeared to have mastered her little nervous paroxysm. It seemed, however, that it was the question, not the extra blanket he had put over her, that had calmed her. She seemed eager for an answer. He turned to Blumenthal, willing the old guerrilla not to disappoint her.

Blumenthal remained sunk in thought for some time, then he half-turned towards them, his tongue running over his shrunken mouth.

"Yes. There are some regrets, not all of conscience. I lost friends at the hands of the British in Palestine, lost friends and someone close to me. All this was after we had survived the Holocaust, you see, somehow it seemed much worse at the hands of a nation we regarded as liberators governed by a new socialist ministry. Perhaps the irony was too great to appreciate . . . you must understand this perspective."

Blumenthal wiped his mouth.

"I forget why now, but many of our people had been arrested by the British and some guns were found. The Israelis who had the guns were hanged after a trial. The order came from the leaders for a reprisal; we were at war with the forces of opposition to the creation of Israel as expressed by the British presence in Palestine.

"I was ordered to carry out part of the reprisal. We ambushed a British sergeant outside his quarters and took him to a secret location. There we hanged him in cold blood. It was necessary. . . ."

Galvin felt Margaret's hand clutch his own. Somehow, Blumenthal had failed her.

"But you regretted it," he prompted.

"Yes. The sergeant was a tall man, very British . . . admirable I suppose, except that he was an enemy. It was an eye for an eye and I felt no sentiment about it. I had seen too much death, too many bodies in the camps in Germany."

He drew back his left sleeve. The withered skin with the brown blotches of age was crossed by the blue tattoo of his concentration camp number.

"I emptied his pockets. He had a wallet. In it was a photograph of his wife and a son. I expected to find such a photograph. It came as no surprise. The only surprise was that it looked like a photograph I had once carried, one that had been taken from me by a German under-officer. I remember looking up at the British sergeant and our eyes met.

"It was terrible. I regret that . . . yes, very much."

Margaret Allen was crying silently.

Galvin got up, feeling the need to move about. He crossed the captain's cabin and stared sadly from the window. The surrounding mountains across the bay reflected the low angle of the sun. The beauty of the scene seemed overwhelming, his feeling of despair equally so. He had left England in 1939, a conscientious objector to the war which had just broken out in Europe. Now it seemed the evil had pursued him to this remote spot.

As if in confirmation he saw suddenly something else, something that seemed the embodiment of this thought. A black submarine was crossing the bay towards them.

Chapter Twelve

DOWNING STREET, LONDON

"No, Mr President, I am *not* going to support you if you escalate the Sidon situation any further and I am refusing you permission to use the East Anglian bases. No, I am not interested in buttressing the Israelis either ... Special Relationships, Mr President? I thought it was you who had reneged on that when you excluded us from your intelligence reports ... then why should you consider I am any more trustworthy now. Even politicians don't change their spots in the first week in office. Why? Because it's what I believe in. I'm not interested in the policies of my predecessor. You ask what kind of a policy this is and I will tell you, it is a statesmanlike policy, designed to terminate a problem, not nurture it ... then that is because the electorate have got the patriotism out of their system. ... Of course I have seen the list of hostages and like you I am not going to be blackmailed, but I want to see this as the last hijack, not just one more.

"I have nothing more to say. Hostages? Why, nothing will happen to them if you concede the territorial claim gained by force of arms in Sidon, really they're making it very easy for us. No, you have to appear to be backing down, because you rushed the Sixth Fleet in there ... of course it's naive, Mr President ... it's also honest. Good night."

"Bad?"

"Mad as a flea-bitten coyote, Johnnie."

"I must say you're remarkably cool about it, considering the damage you've just done to the Atlantic Alliance."

"I shouldn't think the Kremlin would believe it if you told them."

NEW SCOTLAND YARD, LONDON

"Alex, I know it's very late, but I particularly wanted to see you about your transfer application. I'm sorry I haven't had time to talk earlier. Please sit down."

Chief Superintendent Martin swallowed a building anger with the acceptance of 22 years pensionable service. However he could not resist a look at his watch.

"I know you wife's going to give you hell, but perhaps," and Nicholas's voice lost its avuncular, slightly apologetic tone, gaining a knife edge of seriousness that alarmed Martin, "perhaps this will be the last time."

"Sir?"

"I've been looking at your file. . . ."

"Sir?" Martin felt prickles of sweat break out from beneath his armpits.

"I'm afraid there are some questions I want to ask you ... it's unofficial you understand, it's just the information I want." Nicholas's voice had dropped to a low and utterly menacing tone.

"Sir?" Martin had difficulty speaking. Apprehension constricted his throat.

"I think you'd better tell me all about the assignment you were given to recruit Kate Meldrum's boyfriend."

Martin stared back, feeling the tightness in his throat ease. So that was it. He had heard, of course, that something had developed between Kate and Nicholas. Kate was his protégé and he had the greatest professional respect for Nicholas, but was the Commander abusing his position to oust Kate's lover?

"I think you'd better tell me, Alex. This is way beyond any in-house scandals."

Perceptive bastard, Martin thought, wondering how much he should or could reveal.

270

"Come on Alex, all of it. I know all about you. I know *your* motivation, it's this man Palmer I need to know about. And I need to know about it *now*. Tomorrow may be too late."

ADVENTURER, DESTITUTION ISLAND

The representatives of April 86 watched the black and sinister shape of the *Libertad* slide through the dark waters of Destitution Bay towards the waiting liner. To Palmer's eyes, the rounded conning tower and the soft nose of the low pressure hull was unmistakably Russian in origin. He noted the protuberance of the bow-mounted, passive sonar array around which a cluster of seamen stood preparing to secure alongside the *Adventurer*.

The hydroplanes were being retracted as *Libertad* eased her speed. The white bow wave died away. On top of the tower an officer waved. Anna waved back.

Ten minutes later the Costa Mayan submarine was secured alongside the luxury cruise liner. They represented the opposite ends of the maritime spectrum and Palmer was not unaware of the implied irony of their respective flags. Both seemed to epitomize the purpose of their creeds: domination and pleasure.

"Now, Palmer, it is time to lock you up again." He turned to appeal to Lila to refute Anna's instruction, but her eyes were hard again. Palmer's detachment was over; he sensed the thing was building to its climax.

"Chilean? Not British?"

Korolenko looked sharply at the pale-faced woman who was, he knew from his Moscow briefing, the leader of the Palestinian April 86 Group. The photograph had not done her justice but, while he admired her looks, her contradiction irritated him.

"Chilean, Comrade, emphatically!"

The conference between Korolenko, Vega, Lila, Anna and the leader of the Costa Mayan wing of April 86 was being held on the *Adventurer*'s bridge. Ironically, they spoke in English and Lila's query was the first sign that their combined sense of

271

triumph might be premature. Lila nodded and added, "There were two helicopters."

"Helicopters? What helicopters?" Korolenko frowned.

"We shot one down . . . an Alouette. . . ." explained Lila.

"Alouette? Hell, those Chilean frigates carry an Alouette . . . but you said *two* . . . they only carry one."

"Yes. Another flew over us here, a few hours ago . . . it was not the same."

Korolenko swore in Russian.

"Then there is another ship," he concluded, exchanging glances with Vega. In these noisy eutrophic seas Korolenko could not blame the inexpert Costa Mayans. But now his men, no, Vega's men, were wandering about the great liner's bars and doubtless drinking more than the simple luxury of fresh air. They were certainly not at their patrol stations and *Libertad*'s passive sonar was stuck up uselessly into the air.

"Fuck!" Korolenko swore again and then turned to Vega and addressed him in a spate of Spanish.

"Manuel, we must get your men aboard again without delay. The last place we want to be caught is this infernal bay!"

"But we have to clear the port hydroplane. . . ."

"Yes, yes, but quickly, go and see to it!"

Korolenko looked over the side. A chunk of drifting ice had, by bad luck, lodged itself between the retractable adjustable fin of the port hydroplane and jammed the thing. It could not be freed readily from the casing and the duty watch of the *Libertad* had launched one of *Adventurer*'s lifeboats to go round the submarine's hull and get access to the lump of blue-white ice. Vega left to chivvy his men and Korolenko confronted Lila. She reminded him of a more ample version of a favourite Bolshoi dancer he had once made love to while attending a staff course in Moscow. The same scraped-back hair, the same remorseless dedication. Lila was certainly a beauty compared with her ill-visaged companion. Shit, how did a man go to bed with *that*?

"How long has your deadline left to run?"

"Five hours," Anna answered.

"Then it seems this other ship may well be here within the time-frame."

"Yes," Lila's face was drawn with anxiety, "will you sink her too?"

Korolenko crinkled his eyes. How much leeway had he? "Perhaps," he prevaricated, "it depends upon her nationality."

He knew he had not satisfied Lila. She *had* no nationality, the matter of flags was irrelevant to her. But she had other things on her mind. "Comrade Captain, I have lost my radio operator, I need to know what is happening."

"I received a coded information transmission from my support vessel." Korolenko referred to a trawler fishing some 200 miles to the north, acting as a relay station and fuel source for the *Libertad*. "The heroic Palestinian freedom fighters have resisted every attempt of the imperialist lackeys to capture Sidon. The Israelis have been thrown back from every assault on the city and the Soviet Navy is maintaining a presence in the eastern Mediterranean to prevent intervention by the forces of the United States of America. You have only to hold out for a few hours, Comrade, and victory is assured."

In her pleasure at hearing this news Lila failed to notice Korolenko's use of the second person.

"And your hostages, Comrade, are the best advantage you have."

HMS *NORWICH*, WEDDELL SEA

A creditable, though misplaced caution had prevented Crosby-Milne from hearing the reverberating echoes of Korolenko's twin torpedo impacts upon the hull of Soto's ship. HMS *Norwich* had retracted her sonar antennae into her hull to avoid damage from ice. In pursuit of a hijacked liner, Crosby-Milne had thought his greatest danger was the ice and that the malice of man would not have to be faced until he intercepted the liner at Destitution Island.

Modern warships are thinly-built, their steel shells fragile and susceptible to damage. Crosby-Milne had been a junior officer when the first of the Royal Navy's old Tribal Class frigates had been crossing the Atlantic to visit the United States. Her scantlings proved shamefully light for the ocean passage. She had returned with her tail between her legs and Crosby-Milne had nursed that experience of vulnerability ever since. Now, it seemed to him in the absence of contrary evidence, Soto had been caught out by a similar cause. Doubtless the *O'Higgins* had been holed by ice, though why he had been unable to get off more than a brief Mayday on a low-powered set, remained a mystery. Crosby-Milne had already formed the opinion that Soto's impetuous nature had run him into trouble. It was an easy prejudice to give way to.

The captain raised his glasses. To the south, ahead of the ship, sunlight caught the flashing blades of his reconnoitring Lynx, gone ahead to spot the stricken Chilean frigate and begin any assistance the British could render their friends. The grey-green sea was vivid with colour, set off by the bergs that dotted its surface, the strange blues and greens of their shadows in marvellous contrast to the glittering white plane surfaces that reflected the full glory of the sun.

Far to the south the sky was clouded, lowering over the permanent ice sheet of the Weddell Sea, its gloom relieved along the horizon by a band of 'ice-blink', the upward diffusion of reflected light from the ice shelf into the sky.

Against this backdrop, Destitution Island rose over the horizon, its summits gleaming above the black mass of volcanic rock, the restless sea breaking about its cliffs. A torn shred of orographic cloud streamed to leeward of its highest peak. It looked innocently beautiful, even to Crosby-Milne's unaesthetic eye.

"Message from the Lynx, sir."

"Mmm?" Crosby-Milne turned to the officer-of-the-watch.

"He's sighted extensive wreckage but no sign of a ship."

An hour later, under the beetling cliffs of the looming island, Crosby-Milne looked down on the oil-slicked waters that had closed over the grave of the *Bernardo O'Higgins*. Sonar confirmed the presence of the frigate, many metres below, broken in two pieces and lying upon the sloping shoulder of the volcano.

Norwich rolled uneasily in the swell and backwash that the buttress of the island threw back. The sea was smoothed by the oil leaking from the shattered hull far below and moved with a mournful undulation over the area. The air was thick with the stink of it, the pungent putrescence of a dead ship.

There was little Crosby-Milne could do beyond launch inflatable boats and recover the few bodies that were all that remained of the crew of the *Bernardo O'Higgins*. The captain recalled the Hispano-Indian faces that had peered curiously at him as he had made his way from the after flight-deck to the frigate's bridge to meet her commander. Now Soto's body was being shrouded in the plastic bags provided for the purpose by a solicitous Admiralty. It was unfortunate that modern practice made a dead man look like a lump of garbage.

"Sir?"

"Hullo Doc. Depressing business I'm afraid. No survivors?"

"No sir, but something else. . . ." Crosby-Milne looked at the boyish face of Surgeon Lieutenant Cornell. It bore an expression of the most profound concern.

"Well?"

"The bodies we've recovered, sir. Most of them died from gunshot wounds, not hypothermia. . . ."

"The devil they did! Are you certain?"

"Absolutely, sir."

Crosby-Milne frowned and his eyes were drawn to the island a mile away on their starboard bow. Soon he would have an unimpeded view into the bay. Whatever had caused those mysterious gunshot wounds, it was obvious the liner, hidden by the shoulder of the mountain, contained the secret.

He turned towards the wheelhouse, his mind made up. "Officer-of-the-watch!"

"Sir?"

"Recover the Zodiacs and recall the Lynx for refuelling, pass word for the first lieutenant and the PeeWo to report at once!"

"Aye, aye, sir!"

HIGHWAY DINER NEAR CLARKSVILLE, TENNESSEE

"Fellow Americans. . . ."

The man with the pale face and shadowed eyes of a junkie

looked up from the greasy plate of steak and eggs in the highway diner and stared at the image of his country's President on the huge television screen over his head.

"As a family man I share the concern of many of you this morning. As an American I share the anxiety and outrage of all my fellow countrymen at the recent terrorist aggression perpetrated against innocent American men, women and children. As your President I bear the heavy responsibility of expressing our united abhorrence of indiscriminate terror and also of taking steps against specific targets to persuade those evil men who plan such destruction and intimidation that their policies are counter-productive, their evil bankrupt.

"I recall to mind those words of the great Irish Parliamentarian and today take them as my inspiration that 'the only thing necessary for the triumph of evil is for good men to do nothing'. . . ."

The heroin addict bent again to his meal, shovelling in the food without taking his eyes from the face speaking against the background of the Oval Office.

"This morning, air and naval forces of the United States of America operated in direct support of and in full co-operation with units of the Israeli armed forces, in carrying out counter-insurgency operations to protect the national integrity of Israel, to suppress lawless elements in the Lebanon. This action was carried out with the full unequivocal sanction of the Governments of Israel and Lebanon."

"Nuke the bastards," said a truck driver at the next table.

"Sure!"

"To those of you with loved ones held hostage aboard the ship *Adventurer* I say we are doing all that can be done and that the whole of America and the Free World waits with you. . . ."

HENDON, NORTH WEST LONDON

"'All that can be done' . . . what sort of a response is that?" Kate raised an eyebrow over her coffee cup and stared at Nicholas.

"That old buzzard is cleverer than you think," Nicholas said, switching off the transistor radio on the table between them as the focus of the London news switched to another item. "He has lent massive and showy, if relatively ineffective help, to ensure that the Israeli assault on the defences of Sidon is successful. By doing this he has removed the effective bargaining weight of the hijacked ship, defused public opinion urging him to appease the terrorists and given the Israelis a much-needed boost to their morale. At the same time he has rehabilitated the Lebanese government and rallied the Lebanese people to their own national loyalty.

"Without Sidon the piracy of the *Adventurer* is just another hijack. By the time the Royal Navy arrive it will be a matter of negotiation and trading the hostages for the lives of the hijackers; routine stuff, albeit in an unusual venue. Is there some more coffee?"

"But what about that shadowing Russian force?" Kate asked, refilling Nicholas's cup.

"Quietly withdrawn as soon as Admiral Backhouse showed his hand."

"You mean they've abandoned the Palestinians to their fate?"

"You sound as though you cared, Kate ... but come on, I don't think the thing is played out yet. There's still that other factor." Nicholas stood.

"Where are we going?"

"Nottingham."

DOWNING STREET, LONDON

"Last night several ships from Admiral Backhouse's fleet effectively blocked the seaward approaches to the port of Sidon. This despatch has just come in from the BBC's reporter Brian Lord on the spot.

"Last night destroyers of the United States Sixth Fleet approached Sidon from Cape Saharé and completed the iron ring around the beleaguered Al Fatah forces in Sidon, sealing them from any outside aid which might have been flown in from the Soviet helicopter carrier *Borodino*. From the seashore where I spent much of the night, I could see the lights of these ships and also from the aircraft carrier *Brandywine*, which made no attempt to conceal themselves. Aircraft from the *Brandywine* made almost continuous sorties, many of them penetrating Lebanese airspace. Some anti-aircraft fire was put up from Sidon, including the launch of SAM missiles, but no hits were claimed or observed, though heat-producing decoys were released by the warplanes.

"Indications here are that Fatah resistance is weakening and that a further Israeli push can be expected this morning. What *is* clear is that the United States, if not actively participating in the action, is giving tacit support to Tel Aviv and discouraging interference from any other party." The Prime Minister's wife pressed the remote control and turned to her husband.

"What about those poor hostages, David, where do they figure in the calculations?"

"I don't know darling, but I think that, after all, I'm going to have to change my speech today."

"At the University of Newcastle?"

"Nottingham, darling."

ADVENTURER, DESTITUTION ISLAND

"They're deserting us . . . that Russian dog is deserting us!"

Anna's face was made more terrible by rage, the white scarred tissue blanched by fury. She choked on further speech for it was inadequate to the violence of her protest.

Lila gripped her arm and stared after the departing submarine as it crossed the dark waters of the bay and turned for the entrance and the grey-green, ice-dotted sea beyond.

Had Korolenko received a signal to withdraw and from whom had such an order come? Was Anna being pessimistic and over-suspicious? Perhaps she had known in her bones that their mission was doomed from the moment she learned from Portishead Radio the British authorities were alert to the possibility of a hijack on the high seas. At any rate, Korolenko had taken with him the Costa Mayan wing of April 86. She was left with her own people, her *fedayeen*.

"Come Anna, it is the will of God. . . ."

Already *Libertad* had disappeared.

COSTA MAYAN SUBMARINE *LIBERTAD*, WEDDELL SEA

Korolenko saw the *Norwich* from a distance of seven miles. Vega had submerged the *Libertad* as they broke the cover of Destitution Bay. The British destroyer lay stopped, her Lynx helicopter flying about overhead. It was clear that they were searching for survivors of the sunken Chilean frigate. They would find precious little, Korolenko mused and he had his orders, a single coded group from Severomorsk.

Withdraw.

He had no need to ask why and less need to press Vega to comply. Some of his men were drunk and the thought of confronting an alert and fully-trained warship filled him with apprehension. Vega had been jumping to get the hell out of that bay.

Clear of the island *Libertad* slipped deeper into the eutrophic waters of the ocean, below the drifting ice and into the great spaces of the sea, heading northwards. Terrified, a pod of killer whales dispersed as the long dark hull tore through them.

ADVENTURER, DESTITUTION ISLAND

The tension of desperation passed like an induced current through the *fedayeen* left aboard the *Adventurer*. It communicated itself to the shivering hostages, deprived now of any food by the reduction in guards. Galvin watched the submarine disappear and Blumenthal knew that when next the Fatah gunmen came to the captain's cabin, it would be for him.

Zelda Rebanowicz did not understand much of what was happening. For her it was enough that Giorgio came to her, wanting her to fulfill her promises. As for Anna, it took all Lila's powers of restraint to prevent the wholesale massacre of the crew and hostages.

Palmer, meanwhile, waited and watched the distant gap in the surrounding mountains. For what? he asked himself.

But he already knew the answer.

PART FOUR

STORM

'There is no home left for universal souls,
except perhaps in Antarctica or on the high seas.'

J. M. Coetzee
The Life and Times of Michael K.

Chapter Thirteen

A1, CAMBRIDGESHIRE

"Now the timing of the speech is going to be crucial, Johnnie, d'you have the Press organized?"

"Prime Minister, this is your first major speech since you took office, the Press would cover it without all the other hullabaloo."

"Yes, a hostage crisis and a major diplomatic row between Downing Street and the White House is enough to choke the entire Press Corps. D'you know I had Murchison of the *Commentator* on the telephone this morning, he got hold of my private number and actually begged me to intervene, apparently his granddaughter is one of the youngsters on this ship. It's inconceivable that a man who slams me with the most scurrilous and unfounded libel in his bloody tabloid has the nerve to do that!"

"Perhaps he's genuinely concerned about his grandchild, David?"

"It's not that, John, it was the way he demanded I did something. Hadn't even the decency to apologize for the filth he spread during the election campaign about Jill and me."

"I suppose moral principles aren't necessary qualifications for newspaper ownership."

"Too bloody right they're not ... now, how long have we got?"

"Three hours. At least the destroyer, er, *Norwich*, will be on the spot to handle that end of things. The only thing that bothers me is her captain does not fully understand his instructions."

"Didn't see the signal ... left that to Their Lordships."

"Not a wise thing, Prime Minister. They concocted a rather

283

ambiguous message. Frankly I don't think your intentions were made at all clear."

"Well, we mustn't have the works gummed up now. This captain doesn't have rules of engagement, he'll have to refer for instructions as soon as he confronts the hijackers."

"You can make a call on the Vodaphone from the car."

"No, no, not necessary."

"At least his presence takes the sting out of the press and opposition's accusations of your doing nothing."

"Yes, I wonder if the White House know about it yet?"

"And I wonder how our man is getting on. . . ." His voice was drowned by the roar of a Harrier lifting off from RAF Wittering, the shadow of which passed over the car.

ADVENTURER, DESTITUTION ISLAND

Palmer was exhausted by fatigue and the long, strained hours of navigation, always under the surveillance of a guard who might at any moment have misunderstood a movement of his. There had only been a brief interlude with Lila which had been shattered by the Lynx from, as only *he* knew, a British warship.

God! Would it never arrive?

He had not been told to expect one, but neither had he expected to fall in love with the leader of a terrorist gang.

What would the warship do when it arrived? It *must* have instructions from London and they would not conflict with his own. It was too much to think about; time to decide when things became clearer. In the meantime he lay back on the chart room settee and closed his eyes.

He could see Rosie in his mind's eye as if he had last seen her yesterday. The long, light brown hair, her grey eyes and the slim, shapely legs. And beside her, laughing, looking up as she held her mother's hand, the toddling Suki, bright as a button, relinquishing her mother's grasp to run towards her proud, indulgent and infatuated father.

Suki's death had not been sudden. The slow decline had begun just before he had left home for a four-month voyage; a passing childhood ailment, they had been patronizingly assured. Rosie's agonized phone calls and long, self-recriminatory letters caused him a distress permeating every waking hour. He felt a powerless frustration as Rosie's letters revealed the progress of the disabling disease. The ignorance of their family doctor and the poverty of the resources available to contest the advance of the auto-immune condition appalled him; even when a diagnosis was finally achieved, the three precise syllables with their Greek roots meant only that it was too late.

He had arrived home just in time to sit stupefied beside his daughter's deathbed. It was the longest week of his life. He and Rosie drifted apart afterwards. Death and his career, the one an enemy, the other a treacherous competitor, destroyed the bond between them. The process of parting came quite naturally, and in the end his return to sea was but a physical manifestation of what had already taken place between them mentally.

Palmer would never forget the guilty comfort of his next voyage: his life had meaning beyond the terminated life of his baby daughter. For Rosie the thing had been very different; it was impossible they could comprehend each other's viewpoint.

The memory stirred him. He turned over restlessly. First Rosie, then Rosie and Suki, and then Kate appeared before him. Kate had been a consolation to him. Rosie remained a reproach to which, despite their ineradicable estrangement, he had sought to make amends, for only Rosie knew the burden of protracted illness, and he had never been able to console her. After Suki's death Rosie had survived in the condition we call existence, after the dreams and expectancies of life have passed us by. Now perhaps, he might repay her for her devotion.

Palmer drifted into semi-consciousness. He walked with Rosie and Suki beneath a canopy of leaves; sunlight dappled down, lighting the blubells which covered the floor of the wood. An enchanted Suki ran laughing amid this wild proliferation.

The shout of alarm brought him to. Out on the port bridge wing Anna was pointing. Lila appeared and Palmer stared over the heads of the two young women at the Type 42 destroyer swinging as she came through the entrance to the bay. The clean lines of her sheer, the blocks of her superstructure topped by the domes of her weapons guidance systems, the huge, bedstead aerial and the other revolving antennae, twinkled as the sunshine caught them. At her gaff fluttered the British naval ensign. She was as sinister in her way as the dark and streamlined menace of the *Libertad*.

Palmer picked up the binoculars. Above the flurry of white water at the destroyer's stern marking the reversal of her screws, he read her name in neat, red letters: *Norwich*. As he watched, he saw the barrel of her automatic rapid-fire 4.5 inch gun turret foreshorten on the *Adventurer*.

Though Palmer was never to know it, it was Crosby-Milne's fatal mistake.

Even as the VHF radio beside him squarked into life, calling the *Adventurer*, the clipped precise naval voice was obliterated in the sudden whoosh of the Katyusha. Smoke and fumes rolled back over the bridge and Palmer had only the haziest picture of Anna beside the launcher which had been fitted by Giorgio on the bridge extremity.

There was an almost instantaneous crump. As the wind whipped the gases aside Palmer saw the black pall of smoke and the flicker of fire from beneath *Norwich*'s foremast. Dulled by sleep it took him a second to realize the enormity of what had happened. His heart was pumping frantically and he felt adrenalin pour into his bloodstream. When the *Adventurer*'s bridge was engulfed for a second time in the acrid stink of propellant, Palmer knew the time had come to throw off the mask.

Giorgio had arrived panting on the bridge, thrust Palmer aside and gone roaring out onto the bridge wing. It was obvious by the violence of his remonstration that he was furious at what had happened.

Palmer hesitated. Giorgio's arrival in such a state coincided with the new view of *Norwich*. Beyond the three April 86 leaders, the British warship lay. Anna's second rocket had destroyed the Lynx helicopter squatting aft on the flight deck. Palmer could see the men running about and the screening spray of AFFF foam shrouding the burst of flames as they fought to contain the blaze.

In the confusion he slipped away, aft along the fiddley behind the chart room, past the porcelain insulators of the radio aerials until he reached the base of that great, ugly swept-back funnel with the blue and orange logo showing faintly through the thin coat of white paint.

The door was as awkward for his height as it had been for Barclay's bulk, but once inside he grasped the vertical ladder that led upwards. Far below him rumbled the lone alternator supplying essential services to the anchored ship. He scrambled up the sooty rungs, flanked by the huge, lagged exhausts from the main Sulzers, the auxiliary generators, the compressors and pumps which culminated here before discharging their noxious fumes into the atmosphere. Oil feed pipes led downwards from a pair of upper settling tanks. He climbed above them, turning on their tops to take the last ladder upwards.

The inside of the funnel was vast, a great space formed by curved steel plates into a streamlined leading edge supported by vertical frames and horizontal stringers. The leading edge of its very top was curved back, an almost hemispherically dished plate stiffened by a web which was, in its turn, pierced by a lightening hole. Reaching upwards he found what he had long ago concealed. Grasping it firmly, he pulled hard and felt the light lashings of yarn break. Cautiously he eased the thing through the lightening hole. It was almost unsullied by the soot. Reaching aft and upwards he laid it on the platform over which the hemispherical cowling gave shelter, then he hoisted himself after it.

A second later he was standing amid the upright pipes of the exhausts, surrounded by a chest-high bulwark formed by the lip of the funnel. Bending down, he picked up the gun.

He had bought it the afternoon he had joined the ship. The man in London had said it would be easy in the States; no questions asked and ammunition to suit. He was quite familiar with the machine-carbine, the long hours of practice he had put in before the ship reached Rio were now to be tested. Clipping on the magazine he looked over the rim of the funnel. His insinct to act when he had, had been right.

Far below him on the port wing of the bridge Giorgio had stopped arguing. He was haranguing the two women, Lila and

Anna, pointing to the British warship that lay enshrouded by a dark pall of smoke three-quarters of a mile away. Palmer saw Lila shake her head and Anna start forward. Giorgio stepped backwards and suddenly brought up his gun. Lila and Anna stepped back. Even from here Palmer could sense their shock.

Palmer levelled his own gun and took aim. In the telescopic sight he could see the graticules intersect across Giorgio's square back. Palmer put the lever onto single shot, aware that exposed up here, his head, hands and shoulders were being cut by a wind as cold as the ice over which it blew. Gently he squeezed the trigger.

Giorgio crashed to his knees and slowly slumped forward, blood rushing from his mouth, his eyes wide with shock and then glazing over as he fell full length at the feet of the two women.

But Palmer saw none of this, already he was scrambling down the inside of the funnel, his mind working furiously. Giorgio had obviously decided to take matters into his own hands. Lila's emphatic refusal to Giorgio's pointing arm suggested to Palmer that the *fed'ai* wanted an accommodation, a compromise, with the British. Instinctively he knew that only a suggestion of that kind could produce such a reaction from Anna and Lila. And, thought Palmer as he worked through the door at the foot of the funnel, he had chosen his moment well. Neither Anna nor Lila had their guns, both having laid them down to aim and fire the Katyusha rocket launcher at the worship.

He was working round the side of the funnel now, running his greatest risk. Any one of the terrorists seeing him with a gun, would shoot him dead.

HMS *NORWICH*, DESTITUTION ISLAND

Captain Crosby-Milne was considering recalling the *Alert* which he had sent further north, towards South Georgia. He would have felt happier with her in company.

"Bloody clever camouflage. . . ." The first lieutenant said

beside him. They both stared across the comparatively smooth waters of the bay. Under the black and white cliffs, even at two miles, it was quite difficult to see the great ship.

"We could have missed her without the choppers spotting her."

"Just what I was thinking, sir, though gunnery radar found her quick enough."

Crosby-Milne grunted and ordered the helm steadied. His men were at action stations and he now ordered the first lieutenant to call the hijacked liner on the VHF radio-telephone. As he began to swing *Norwich* to port, keeping a discreet distance from her as he opened the delicate negotiations, he watched the bow swing and saw the automatic gun turret, programmed to lock on the targetted liner. He moved across the bridge and stepped out onto the exposed wing. The keen wind knifed him, causing an instant ache in his facial muscles.

A second later he was dead.

A1, HERTFORDSHIRE BORDER

The Rover swung with a squeal of tyres round the circus at Apex Corner and straightened out, accelerating into the outside lane of the A1.

"I suppose it was Alex who blew it," Nicholas said, slipping the car into overdrive. It was typical of him, Kate thought, to have retained a manual gearbox in his car. The low machine moved with ease past the other traffic and she guessed the speed to be over 90.

"I mean that your hypothesis was good, first-class in the event, but it was only a hypothesis. It needed the classical verification of experimental evidence. In the end the evidence didn't have to be experimental. It wasn't that much of a secret. In fact Alex gave up so easily I think he might have been worried about some other skeleton in his file."

A wry grin crossed Nicholas's face. He was obviously elated, keyed up for action. Kate recognized the symptoms, the reaction and antidote to desk-bound stress. She hoped he was not going to do anything rash. As was her custom, she sat quietly. They had a long way to go and Nicholas could take his own time. Her patience made his next move all the more shocking.

She was staring at the wooded hummock of Moat Mount as they rounded the bend and slowed for the roundabout at Stirling Corner. She heard the gear shift and expected his movements to be connected with the deceleration.

"Here, you know how to use one of these. . . ." His touch startled her and she looked down at her lap. The ugly shape of the police-issue revolver lay innocently on the dark cloth of her plain-clothes skirt. She had to brace herself as they took the roundabout and straightened out again, Nicholas racing through the gearbox as he pushed the accelerator down.

"What's this for?" she said.

"J.I.C." Just in case.

"In case of what?"

"Whatever might happen if all the threads of your damned thesis come together."

"And you think they will?"

"I think they already have!"

There was a pause. The traffic was thinning. They were passing the intersection with the M25 and it was creaming off half of the heavy lorries, leaving them a comparatively empty highway.

"Tell me about Palmer" he said.

"Is it relevant?"

"Yes."

"But it's personal . . ."

"About *him*. Not about you and him."

She shrugged, shifting mental gear to give a policemanlike description, not the subjective view of a lover. Impatiently, or was it kindly, Nicholas prompted her.

"I know he's tall, fair and handsome. But what about character, moods, that sort of thing?"

"Oh, he's an open sort of person, given to introspection more than moods; you know, long silences when you know he isn't in the room with you."

"Any reason?"

"None really. I rather put it down to his profession as much as

290

any innate characteristic: long night watches, silences, that sort of environment. Rather different from what we're used to."

"Sounds enviable. Did you know he used to have a commission in the naval reserve?"

"No, but there was no reason why he should tell me. He certainly wasn't the gung-ho type, not after finding himself beached through unemployment, anyway."

Nicholas fished in his breast pocket and handed Kate a snapshot. "Did you know he had a daughter?"

She caught her breath. "Where did you get this from?"

"Tucked inside that copy of Danton's 'Seamanship' I pulled out of your bookshelf. You didn't know?"

"No. I knew he had been married. . . ." She looked down at the little face, searching for Palmer in it. There was the hair and something about the mouth, but, to her consternation, she found she could no longer visualize clearly what Palmer looked like.

"Why all the questions?" She handed the snap back and Nicholas pocketed it.

"Because Palmer was recruited by Alex Martin for a special and most unusual mission."

"Good God," she paused, trying to make the jig-saw fit,

"And this ties in with my hypothesis?"

"It's pivotal."

Kate felt a cold shiver of apprehension pass through her. The picture of the child unnerved her. What could it all have to do with the crazy card-house of foreign policy she had outlined to Nicholas so many days ago?

"You see it *was* Martin who was the key to what is happening on that bloody ship. Your hypothesis gave me the Middle East connection, your affair with Palmer gave Martin a possible recruit, Martin's background suggested a crossover with your Middle East hypothesis. What I learned from Martin was that Palmer's suitability was reinforced by his reserve background as well as his unemployment. What I can't understand is, if he was as disaffected with politics and what I imagine he conceived to be the abandonment of his profession by the politicians, why he undertook the mission. I wondered if his past held a clue. I found out about the child, having taken the snap from the book in your flat. The child died, you see. . . ."

Kate understood, or thought she did, and knew now why they were racing north so fast.

"I think the child is what made Tim agree," she said, "I'm not sure how, but I'm sure the fact that he never spoke about her suggests it."

"The silences?"

"Yes. There were quite a lot of them."

"Obsessively so?"

"Perhaps."

ADVENTURER, DESTITUTION ISLAND

"Lila! Lila!"

He knew by the way they ran across the bridge with the guns at their hips that they were looking for him and they suspected treachery. Whoever killed Giorgio had struck at Al Fatah and was therefore an enemy. He heard her answer.

"Palmer? Where are you?"

"Lila! Hold your fire ... don't shoot! Cover me, but don't shoot!"

There was a pause. "Okay!"

He stood slowly, breaking cover from behind the lifejacket box on the starboard bridge wing. Lila, Anna and the *kaffiya*-shrouded bridge guard had their Kalashnikovs trained on him. They saw the gun he was holding at his side.

"I've got a gun. It's all right. I shot Giorgio, he was going to surrender wasn't he? Well?"

Doubt fluttered painfully in Palmer's gut, joining the hammering of his straining heart and the heave of his lungs as he reacted to the swift clamber down the funnel.

There was a sudden screaming howl, as of a great wind passing close overhead, so that they felt the shock wave of the passing shell. It was instantly followed by the explosion against the cliff beyond the liner. Spinning round they saw the rocks fly. Birds rose in clouds and the reverberations of gunshot and shell-burst played back and forth across the bay. Further shells screamed overhead, so close that the terrorists' *kaffiyas* fluttered in their wake. A cacophonous series of diminishing echoes burst about their ears. The warning salvo ceased abruptly, so abruptly that Palmer was shouting his next remark.

"I can help you!" He bawled, suddenly fearing the worst.

"How?" It was Anna who flashed back the question. There was deep suspicion in her dark chips of eyes.

He started to tell them as the hull of the destroyer began to foreshorten under her helm. The Kalashnikovs were no longer pointing at his belly.

HMS *NORWICH*, DESTITUTION ISLAND

"Check fire! Check fire!"

The first lieutenant cleared his head and passed a hand across his face. The navigating bridge of *Norwich* was filled with acrid smoke through which, behind him, he could see the orange flicker of fire. A brightness, of the sky he supposed, showed where there had been a cable-looped deckhead. A fire-fighting team under the direction of an indefatigable petty officer lumbered through the opening, tugging a hose behind them. In seconds a curtain of spray began to contain the flames.

Officers were making their reports now. The damage control state of the ship was emerging. The Lynx was destroyed by the second Katyusha's direct hit. There was local fire damage aft, but nothing more serious.

The first lieutenant's anxiety for the captain had already been answered. Now two stretcher bearers carried Crosby-Milne's body below.

"Hard a-starboard! Slow ahead! Pass word to the marine officer, I want an assault party ready in three minutes . . . small arms issue to officers and ratings on the upper decks! Upper deck gun crews resume stations! Close up!"

The first lieutenant's orders galvanized the ship as she turned towards the liner across the bay.

Chapter Fourteen

NOTTINGHAM UNIVERSITY

"For too long the world has been subjected to these outrages. Since the Second World War we have had every kind of extremist attacking innocent people in their daily lives to achieve political ends, and the United Kingdom has so often been caught in the crossfire.

"It is not my point to absolve successive British governments from measures of culpability, nor to claim guiltless association with the origins of such struggles, but the British *people*, as distinct from its leadership, has ever sought justice and freedom, whatever mistakes have been made along the way." The Prime Minister paused and regarded his audience of students.

"Today I say to you that old scores must not sustain *us*, we must look at problems with *new* eyes, *new* points of view. Today must be the beginning of all our tomorrows, for contemplating all our yesterdays has been too great a preoccupation of our country since it fell from greatness.

"Many years ago, long before you were born, a great and vicious evil was done to a helpless minority in Europe. A whole people was exterminated wholesale. In the reaction of post-war guilt the survivors were allowed to dispossess another people . . . we were forced to accept, in the then British Foreign Minister's words, the lesser of two evils! The dispossession of the Palestinians in favour of a homeland for the Jews. . . ."

The Rover swung onto the campus. The bare trees were waving against a grey sky as Nicholas slowed to cross a succession of 'sleeping-policemen' that straddled the road. He wound the steering wheel and drove up a side turning alongside the main hall. A convoy of official cars with smoking chauffers were gathered round the entrance. There were vans with BBC logos and the symbol of Central Television parked close by.

"Got your gun?"

"Yes."

"Come on then!"

". . . For too long we have cowered, waiting for the next strike by Al Fatah-inspired gunmen; for too long we have avoided grasping the nettle, writing these people off as evil. Of course they are evil! Of course they are despicable! Of course they will not stop these barbarous outrages!"

Nicholas could hear the Prime Minister's voice through the glass door. He could see above the crowded hall and the table on the stage where the Prime Minister stood, a surrounding gallery. It was festooned with cameras, cabling and the protruding gaffs of microphones behind which the tireless newshounds worked in obtrusive silence. He jerked his head in the direction of the stairs. Kate nodded.

". . . But they alone do not have the monopoly of evil. The Stern Gang was evil, the Irgun was evil, though we are accustomed to regard them as historically justified in the shadow of the Holocaust.

"What I have come here to say to you today is that the dictum of an eye for an eye and a tooth for a tooth has gone on for too long. Wrongs must be put right. The right of the Palestinian people, not their gunmen, shall be acknowledged. My government. . . ."

The shot rang out as Nicholas emerged onto the gallery. The Prime Minister crashed backwards and there was a moment of stunned silence, then everyone was looking round, shouting. Someone moved to the stage to bend over the assassin's victim.

But no one moved to run away. The media men looked at each other, astonishment registering in their faces. Then it dawned on them that they had scooped the greatest news story of the year and they waited to learn the Prime Minister's fate.

At the words "He's dead!" they made for the stairway door, while the students below rose in uproar.

Kate spotted their quarry, nudging Nicholas. A film camera-man and his gaffer in just too much of a hurry, just too-conveniently situated near to the door and too-unconcerned about their equipment.

They pushed past Kate and then Nicholas. He brought his right hand down on the camera in a karate chop that sent the thing crashing down the concrete steps and the man turned, his face a snarl, a hand reaching for another gun. His accomplice ducked and ran for the steps bending to pick up the camera.

Nicholas brought his knee up into the agent's groin and cut his right hand across the man's face. It slammed back against the wall with a sickening thud.

The second agent had reached the half-landing and turned, bringing up the camera so that Kate realized it was the murder weapon. Her hand squeezed the trigger of her revolver and she felt the kick of the thing. She fired again and the man crashed against the wall and slid downwards, blood bursting through his shirt.

An incredulous group of wide-eyed newsmen began to crowd out onto the landing, staring at the two bodies and Kate and Nicholas.

"Well gentlemen," said Nicholas, "I leave you to speculate whether they are Mossad or CIA." Then he came down the stairs and put his arm round Kate. She was shivering with reaction.

ADVENTURER, DESTITUTION ISLAND

Palmer reached for the Stornophone portable VHF radio and flung the strap over his shoulder. He struggled into his heavy greatcoat hanging in the chart room, then turned for the bridge wing. One look astern convinced him he was right. The bloody destroyer *was* making an approach to storm them and as they all knew, the *fedayeen* would be hopelessly outnumbered and out-fought.

He was as certain as Lila that it had gone wrong, but he could still salvage something, perhaps everything for Lila and at least prevent a massacre of the hostages which was what Anna wanted.

He took one last look at the bridge and ran for the boat deck.

The dark water of the bay was poppled now by a series of white horses where a more persistent wind blew down from the peaks behind him. As he hurried along the light went out of the air and the approaching warship became a grey shape. Palmer turned. The orographic cloud streamed from the summit of Mount Destitution, thickening by the minute. It was backed by a great darkness, a slab of lowering cumulus building behind the island. The wind was already stronger and not dying in gusts like the katabatic squalls they had become accustomed to. Moreover, its coldness could be felt as the first tiny spicules of ice were blown down from the rock ledges above.

The three prisoners in the captain's cabin froze at the commotion next door. Then it was their turn. The door was flung open and the ugly, maimed woman stood before them, her gun waving dangerously round the cabin. Margaret Allen vomited over the carpet.

"Out! Out! Quick!"

Blankets drawn about them they were shoved out onto the boat deck. Half a dozen children were with them. Galvin guessed they were selected hostages. He recognized one of the children as the son of a newspaper magnate, another as the daughter of a well-known and notorious film actress.

He saw Palmer, head and shoulders above the crowd of *fedayeen*, his unshaven face oddly relaxed and professional above the collar of a huge greatcoat. It was only when he turned and reached up to knock off the gripes from a lifeboat that Galvin felt a stab of disappointment. Over his shoulder Palmer had slung a machine-gun.

HMS *NORWICH*, DESTITUTION ISLAND

A gust of wind hit the wheelhouse windows and brought with it a flurry of ice. The stern of the *Adventurer* drew nearer, rising in tiers. *Norwich*'s first lieutenant saw a dark shape flit across the upper one, caught the flap of the *kaffiya* in the wind as the man disappeared.

The liner's stern seemed less substantial as the sudden blizzard drew a thick curtain of snow across the anchorage. It was amazing the speed with which weather systems moved in these high latitudes, thought the first lieutenant as he gauged the moment.

"Stop engines!"

"Stop her, sir!"

Adventurer's stern began to loom over the much-lower warship. Not a soul was visible which made the precaution of two marine sharpshooters kneeling on the bridge, their weapons trained, something of a nonsense. The lowermost deck, a platform for mooring the stern of the ship, was almost level with their own foredeck. He looked down; a huddle of marines waited behind the Sea Dart launcher. They were 100 yards from the *Adventurer*.

Eighty. "Port five."

The marine officer caught his eye and gave him the thumbs-up.

Sixty yards. "Half astern!"

"I think there's somebody up there, sir!" The first lieutenant dared not take his eyes off the liner's stern. She had begun to sheer in the wind. He would only have one chance and he was already losing control by stopping her forward speed. A chatter of machine-gun fire came suddenly from the destroyer's starboard bridge wing. He could not tell if there had been any from the liner first, so thick was the snow.

"Stop engines!"

The next instant *Norwich* rolled easily to port as her starboard bow collided with the port quarter of the liner.

"Go! Go!" he was out on the bridge wing, yelling madly as the marines scrambled aboard the liner. Behind them half a dozen seamen ran with a rope to secure the two ships in the time-honoured formula of a boarding. Above him the marines were already mounting the ladders leading up, storey by storey, storming the undefended hulk.

Aymes woke as the door slammed back. The sudden jar made him instinctively anxious for his patient. She was staring in fear at the figure in the doorway. The flak jacket was no different from that worn by the *fedayeen*. The beret above was green.

"You all right?" a voice asked curtly.

"As well as can be expected," Aymes replied, taking the girl's hand.

"What is it?" he asked as the man turned away with a nod.

"The navy's here, my dear. Everything's going to be quite all right now."

Zelda Rebanowicz waited patiently. She had drawn the curtains of her stateroom and lay in the dark. She had no idea how long she had been like this, but time had ceased to have any meaning. In her own way she tried to pray, but she remembered her silent blasphemy to the great Christ figure at Rio de Janeiro and felt waves of utter despair assault her. She heard the distant noises of rocket and gunfire beyond her double-glazed window, but did not look out. It seemed better not to. What happened outside could be ignored if she kept the curtains closed and did not make it her business to interfere. That was what Giorgio had told her. Soon they would be ashore in San Francisco, away from this awful ship and she would never, never go on a cruise again.

Her door was suddenly thrown open. She sat up, expecting her Greek.

The tall soldier in the combat jacket holding an ugly black gun was not familiar. She drew the sheet up round her throat.

"Anyone in there, Kev?" A voice came from the passageway.

The soldier turned. "Only an old bird," said the man and, pulling the door to, left Zelda Rebanowicz to her thoughts.

From somewhere far below came the sound of cheering.

Fifteen minutes later the marine lieutenant received the reports of his NCOs. It did not make sense. Frowning he pressed the TX button on his portable set and called *Norwich*.

"Not a bloody terrorist in sight, sir ... but one lifeboat is missing from the davits."

299

The lifeboat bucked across the choppy waters of the bay. Clear of the great arch of *Adventurer*'s bow the wind had caught them. Primitive though conditions on board the liner had been, they were now exposed to all the merciless indifference of nature. Spray and snow on the skin of their faces cooled rapidly in the wind, so that a painful ache gripped them all as the boat, with Palmer at the helm, slewed across the blizzard, its Lister engine roaring in competition with the gale.

Palmer did not look back. He knew the *Adventurer*'s white hull had merged with the snow by the expressions of the hostages. Galvin, Mrs Allen and Blumenthal and the ten teenagers ceased to look astern, but huddled in a group amidships, their eyes downcast, under blankets and the encircling guns of the Arabs.

It occurred to Palmer that they had no business here. The pricklingly angry thought stirred in him an old resentment; these were people of the *land*. Their presence at sea on a cruise was an indulgence. The world would be better off without indulgence, whether exclusive or demotic. He shrugged off the thought, an odd fulfilling happiness replaced it.

It was so quick a change of mood that he looked up at the sky to see if it was a response to a change in the weather. He was mistaken. The sky was obscured, hidden behind the low, snow-laden scud.

They grounded on the black shingle and laval sand of a small beach lying between two spurs of dark-ribbed rock. A great bull elephant seal looked up from the centre of his alarmed harem and snorted at them through his snout. The hostages were loaded with jerrycans of water from the lifeboat and a few ammunition boxes that bore the logos and appearance of packaged food. Palmer filled the pockets of his greatcoat with barley sugar sweets and the *fedayeen* followed his example. Picking up two jerrycans Palmer stumped up the beach, stopping only to swing round at the brief stutter of automatic fire.

Anna slung the gun and walked after them. Palmer could see the holes in the lifeboat. He resumed his trudging, the carbine tapping his shoulder uncomfortably.

Ahead of them, emerging into the centre of their vision as they leaned into the howling blizzard, were the corrugated iron buildings of the old whaling station.

He paused to catch his breath and look at the ugly angularity of the rotting sheds and trying-houses. Thus far, he thought, he could claim a limited success. Barclay was dead, it was true, but the hostages were still alive . . . just. The coming hours would be the most difficult, particularly as the *Norwich* had broken the rules by which he expected the game to be played. That puzzled him.

He felt Anna's gun jab his back. "No second thoughts, Palmer . . . it is too late for that."

"This is the April 86 Group of Al Fatah. We repeat our demand for immediate recognition of territorial rights for the dispossessed people of Palestine. We give you one hour to communicate to your government. At the expiration of that period we will execute our prisoners. They are Allen, Blumenthal, Galvin."

When Lila had read out the list Palmer heard the clipped English voice acknowledge it.

"One hour!"

"Acknowledged."

Lila lowered the portable Stornophone VHF radio.

Above their heads the rotten, rusty sheets of corrugated iron slatted and banged in the wind. They had holed up in what had once been the administrative office of the whaling station. It commanded a view of the slipway and the rusting winches once used to haul the dead whales up for flensing. An adjacent building housed the boilers and vats where chunks of blubber had been rendered down and tryed out for oil. Beyond the cracked concrete slipway snow drove across the bay so that they could see little beyond a dark patch of tossing water which faded to nothingness. Palmer shifted to the rear window of the building. The ground rose sharply, covered with broken scree lying at the foot of the mountains surrounding the submerged crater. He turned back, the darkness of the building stale and oppressive.

The hostages were huddled in the centre of the room as they

301

had been in the centre of the lifeboat. Palmer felt the eyes of Margaret Allen and Dr Galvin following him; to them he was a defector, a Quisling, collaborating with the enemy. The children sat quietly. Palmer wondered about their psychological state, how they perceived this outrage being done to them and whether they had been affected by Anna's propaganda. Had they succumbed to the Stockholm Syndrome? In a sense he hoped so, to a degree at any rate. They were destined for privileged lives; perhaps this experience would benefit them in their adult lives. If they survived.

So far Palmer had successfully extricated the terrorists, avoided the wholesale deaths of the hostages, yet preserved the soul of this act of terror. But the man in charge of *Norwich*, by attacking *Adventurer*, was not playing according to the rules. Lila's group could not have held the liner against the manpower of the destroyer without condemning many of the hostages to death.

He felt Anna's eyes upon him. She did not trust him, did not understand his motives. Between Palmer and Lila lay the intimate relationship of lovers that transcends bonds of normal loyalty.

To Anna he was a 'rogue', unpredictable, playing his own lone game, useful only in getting them off the ship. He could expect a bullet from Anna, or one of the *fed'ai*. He wondered how long the men would take orders from the two women. Ancient prejudices were apt to surface in moments of extremity. They had an hour. No more.

One of the girl hostages, a serious dark girl, Palmer remembered, for her detachment from the frivolous, rowdy and irresponsible behaviour of her friends, had produced a rosary. He could hear the whispered words of the Ave Maria ". . . Holy Mary, Mother of God, pray for us sinners, now and at the hour of our death. . . ."

Galvin held his arm about Margaret Allen's shoulder. She was much calmer now as they sat, almost meditatively, on the filthy concrete floor of the derelict building. He knew their plight was desperate and sought some communication with Blumenthal. The old Jew sat slightly apart, a *fed'ai* guarding him as though he presented a greater threat than all the others. All Galvin's lifelong abhorrence of violence seemed to culminate in that depressing scene. The old Jewish statesman, survivor of Hitler's death camps, founder of the state of Israel, had the deaths of British hostages lying upon his own conscience.

Galvin concentrated on the squares of daylight coming through the partly broken window. They began to swim before his eyes as he sought detachment, centring down as he had so often in the comfort of the Quaker Meeting House in Philadelphia.

Margaret Allen was quite calm now. She seemed to see a pattern of inevitability in her life which led to this moment and had brought her here to die in this squalid, abandoned building. She had to expiate guilt, the guilt of a life lived in luxurious comfort at a terrible expense to others. Her husband, provider of this wealth and, as she saw now only too well, perpetrator of great evil, had escaped such expiation, unless a quick and savage heart attack carried so great a pain as this prolonged agony in the scales of natural justice. But, it occurred to her, her death might remove the stain of guilt from her soul, though that did not justify the deaths of these young people. Might she not in dying claim back some credit for ensuring they lived?

And what of Palmer? Perhaps he was the worst. She had heard some loose talk on board the ship about him and the stewardess Lila. She had not then believed it, for Palmer was attractive enough to become the victim of such gossip. Now it seemed she was not the only sinner. She began to feel better. Beside her, Galvin was praying. His sincerity touched her, emphasized her own oppressive guilt. She looked at Blumenthal and something in the old man's expression sent a thrill of expectation through her. She caught it in his eyes, calculating, observing, like an ancient hawk upon its perch. Though the hawk's jesses of capture were about his legs he still looked about with the eye of a raptor.

Blumenthal had marked out the *fedayeen*. Fifteen of them. A lot, but he had faced worse odds and even an old man might be expected to call on his heart for one final effort for his country.

Very slowly he twisted his wrist. The watch showed 40 minutes until the deadline expired. He began to breathe deeply, calling on the holy name of Israel.

HMS *NORWICH*, DESTITUTION ISLAND

"It's a bloody mess, gentlemen." The first lieutenant came back onto the navigating bridge from the radio office and looked round. All *Norwich*'s officers were there, together with some from the liner *Adventurer*. Chief among these and the de facto commander of the liner was Staff Captain Meredith.

"What d'you mean?" Meredith demanded.

"London is delighted we have liberated the majority of the passengers and taken back the liner, but the situation is complex. The Americans are backing a massive assault on Sidon and the British Prime Minister's been assassinated."

There was a gasp of disbelief, and an outburst of speculation which gradually died away.

"I'm afraid we're pretty much on our own and with those hostages still in the hands of the terrorists, pretty much still at page one."

He looked up as *Norwich* ground against the side of *Adventurer*, the high-pitched squeal of fenders interrupting him as the two ships moved together in the wind which slammed down in increasingly violent gusts from the surrounding heights.

"I don't see that you've got much of a problem."

They looked at Meredith. Dishevelled, exhausted and irritable at the inglorious part he had played during the past days, inheriting command of the *Adventurer* in such a subordinate capacity as to be beholden for his very life to the Royal Navy, he sought to recapture some of his lost credibility.

"Captain Meredith?"

"You got a D/F on that VHF transmission. It's bloody obvious the bastards have gone to ground in the old whaling station. Get your men positioned under cover of this gale, before the bloody deadline expires, then tell 'em London have agreed."

"They won't believe it," said someone.

"Why shouldn't they believe it? It's what they've been expecting and they've no way of knowing otherwise now. Let 'em come out and you've got 'em."

"Take them out, sir . . . my men can do that from concealed positions," the marine officer volunteered, "the hostages will be quite all right."

A groundswell of enthusiasm greeted this idea.

"They might even forgive you for losing a Lynx and half your bridge, Colin," observed a tall, sardonic officer.

A sense of relief flooded the first lieutenant. He smiled back at the principal weapons officer. "That's all down to poor old C-M's account. . . okay, gentlemen, so we're agreed. Now we want a rough estimate as to the exact numbers of the opposition."

"Well one of them's a man called Palmer, our second officer. The bastard is collaborating with these scum. . . ."

Meredith's statement seemed to harden the resolution of the naval officers. Somehow treachery seemed to sully their own efforts and call for greater endeavours.

In the confusion then reigning in London, no one had mentioned Palmer's name to *Norwich*'s first lieutenant.

DESTITUTION ISLAND

Palmer must have been half-asleep leaning against the wall and staring at the bleak scene out of the window. The squawk of the Stornophone made him instantly alert. He felt his somnolent heart accelerate into sudden violent activity. The surge of adrenalin made him slightly light-headed. He knew the moment had come, though in what form he had yet to discover.

As he waited for Lila to acknowledge *Norwich*'s call he allowed himself a last moment of indulgence. This was for Suki, *in memoriam*, the only act possible to her father whose impotence at her death had destroyed her parents' marriage. He had the assurance of no less a person than the Prime Minister. It had been a personal guarantee.

"*Norwich* to April 86, I am instructed by my government to inform you that your terms have been met. The territorial rights

305

of the Palestine people are to be internationally recognized. Your resistance is no longer necessary and you can liberate your hostages."

Anna was translating into Arabic and even in the gloom of that abandoned room under the swirling overcast, Palmer could see the flash of fire kindled in those *kaffiya*-shrouded eyes. It was the gleam of victory.

Lila was still speaking and Palmer strained to hear what was being said as the *fedayeen* embraced, lowering their guns. Realisation dawned more slowly among the hostages, but Palmer turned and listened, sensing the most crucial hour of his own implication was just beginning.

" . . . What is the news from Sidon . . . what has happened at Sidon?" Lila asked.

There was a silence and Palmer saw her knuckles whiten as she sought some form of reassurance, some guarantee that this was not a bluff. After so long a trial she could scarcely believe in success.

"The Israelis have withdrawn and the Knesset has agreed. . . ."

Palmer saw the relief bloom on her face and all the hardness fell away. She turned towards him, her beauty restored.

"No!"

Only Margaret Allen had seen Blumenthal rise, seen him somehow rejuvenate as he filled his chest with air, the remnant of a one-time implacable member of the Irgun. Beside her ear the barrel of a machine-carbine wavered as Palmer put an impulsive arm about Lila. She recognized the gun. Margaret Allen's husband had peddled them like candy in every trouble spot Uncle Sam sought to foment. In a second she had twisted it from Palmer's grip and thrust it at Bluemthal. He caught the movement, turned and saw the gun and the smile on Margaret's face. He took it. "No!" he roared again swinging the gun to his hip and closing his fist on the trigger.

The *fedayeen* were bunched in jubilant groups. Blumenthal sprayed them with fire, swivelling round and filling the air with flying lead. The room exploded with noise, ricochets, ear-stunning echoes, screams and spatters of blood. Anna brought up her own gun, jumping clear of the arc of Blumenthal's fire, her back to the window.

Palmer saw her in silhouette, her disfigured face much as when he had first met her, obscured. She hit Blumenthal, puncturing his old-man's belly and sending him staggering backwards. His heels caught on the flattened and quivering body of one of the teenagers and he fell full length, his skull splitting on contact with the concrete.

But Anna's triumph was short-lived. The final outrage was committed upon her damaged body. Against the window her head had attracted notice from the British marines outside. The sudden unexpected burst of fire from within the building had brought up every gun in the shore party. Anna was destroyed by a concentrated hail of shot. The continuing noise of gunfire and the holes appearing in the corrugated iron of the walls turned the *fedayeen* who remained capable of returning fire to a last-ditch defence of their lives.

The whole incident had lasted perhaps ten or twelve seconds.

Palmer had crouched, half-concealed in the gloom by his heavy Melton greatcoat, dragging Lila down within its ample folds. He could feel her struggling to escape him, wanting to take part in this last bloody shambles that terminated the endeavour of her life.

Palmer had other ideas. He had no idea of the truth, for Blumenthal's reaction had clouded all hopes now of discovering it, unless they bought more time, but time was something they no longer had.

As the gunfire died away the derelict room filled with coughing, vomiting and groaning. The air was thick with smoke and the few *fedayeen* left on their feet were shouting at each other. Palmer dragged a shocked Lila behind him, leaving the charnel house and opening a rear door through which he quickly pushed her.

In the confusion no one saw them go. Fifteen minutes later Dr Galvin had arranged shouted terms. Three *fedayeen* surrendered as the hostages were liberated. All were dazed and shocked, bruised, cold and hungry. But with the exception of Mr Blumenthal they were all alive.

Palmer and Lila emerged into the trying shed, stumbling along behind the great vats, the rusty pipes and seized valves of the oil drains and boiler feeds. A parallelogram of sky appeared and vanished with a clatter, as a sheet of roofing lifted and then sank again, crashing against its neighbours as it worked itself loose from the roof. Looking right across the slipway where the ground rose in hummocks of grass and low rock outcrops, he could see the heads of the beseiging force.

By their numbers he knew he had been betrayed. He did not know what had gone wrong, but *Norwich* had never played her part correctly. All along it had been inconsistent. It did not matter now. All had been done that could be done and at the very least, Suki had not died in vain.

He turned towards Lila, shoving her sideways, up behind the trying shed where the ground rose steeply. He knew the storming party had not worked round there. There was no room to cover the whaling station without being pressed up against it and that would have attracted too much attention. Besides, there was no need to. The military mind knew that anyone breaking cover and attempting to escape faced a formidable clamber and once above the roof would be exposed to the guns across the slipway.

Palmer halted, briefly sheltered by a boiler. He turned to Lila and saw that she was wounded. Somehow a shot had hit her in the shoulder. He remembered she had been against the thin iron wall and the little stars of daylight that had suddenly blossomed in that insubstantial partition. Blood was welling through the tear in her jacket. He made a quick bandage from her neck scarf. She was panting, crouching gratefully, still stunned by what had happened back in the station office.

Bending, he kissed her on the lips and, looking upwards, gave a grim nod of satisfaction.

"Ten minutes hard run. Come on, now!"

They had worked to the end of the buildings. A hundred yards away the slope was less steep, giving way to a gully running back into the mountain, a gully formed by melt-water which, in the summer months, ran down from the summit, carving the valley and flattened its mouth. It was here that men had found a lodgement to establish their outstation for the slaughter of whales. Once in that gully they would be covered from direct fire and 70ft higher, be lost in a low shroud of orographic cloud.

Palmer led her by the arm; keeping low they moved as fast

308

as the tussocks of grass, patches of bare talus and rock outcrops allowed. In places they slipped in brown bog water, stumbling and gasping with the strain of effort. They had almost made the gully when a bullet smacked against a rock and whined off into the air. Another threw up hard chips of broken stones and then their feet slithered downwards, and they felt the security of rock behind them.

He paused and took a cautious look back, surprised how much they had already ascended. The slipway was covered by a crowd. He could see the military drab of combat clothing and the bright colours of the children. Dr Galvin stood out quite clearly, supporting a weeping Margaret Allen, whose reason had slipped beyond her grasp in the violent seconds of the terrible firefight she had precipitated. Before he turned and rejoined Lila he saw, too, the flutter of a few *kaffiyas*, set apart and guarded.

Waves of pain were passing across Lila's face as Palmer forced her upwards. On their right a twisting line of rich, green vegetation showed the bed of the stream. Higher up it broke surface, tumbling over smoothed boulders of dark, laval rock, streaking a silver path down from the heights that lay hidden in the cloud high above. Within minutes the cloud had swallowed them.

Palmer found a goat track that led to the left, traversing the shoulder of the mountain. Somewhere below he thought he could detect some evidence of pursuit and knew neither he nor Lila were any match for men who yomped such places for the hell of it. It was bitterly cold in the cloud, striking them through their clothes and the sweat of exertion, but Palmer would not stop. Only when they began to feel the wind blustering down the slope did he slacken his pace, aware that they could not go on indefinitely.

They reached the shoulder of the mountain and the wind caught them full face. They leant into it as the cloud thinned, swirling about them, a pale sun shining through the nacreous vapour. Palmer recalled the great buttress of rock that loomed above the whaling station. Something led him on, a fragment of recollection from his observations of the island.

He sensed it rather than saw it in the dense mist. The goat track gave way to short, sparse grass and the buttress of rock seemed to fall back. A flat area opened up, where an old rock fall had in-filled and erosion had generated a thin soil to support vegetation. Scrapes and broken eggshells revealed the nesting site of some species of seabird. Somewhere above them another rivulet of water cascaded down the mountain. He led Lila to the right and found what he was looking for; beneath two fallen rocks which leaned like drunken seamen for mutual support, they found a shallow hollow and crawled inside. Holding each other tight for warmth and comfort, they let the thudding of their hearts slow and their breathing become normal again.

They must have slept, for Palmer woke aware that the wind had shifted. There were no sounds of pursuit. Only the howl of the gale filled the air with its restless indifference. Palmer knew the 'liberators' had enough to do; when the mist cleared they could come after them if, indeed, they thought the two fugitives worthy of capture. He knew, too, that the actions of *Norwich*'s commander argued against any chance of explanation. Something had gone badly wrong.

He felt Lila stir beside him. She was flushed and feverish from her wound which pained her greatly. He found an Omnopon ampoule taken from the lifeboat and rolled her gently over. Beneath the hard drill of her combat trousers her dark, smooth skin stirred him. He inserted the needle and squeezed the morphine into her buttock and set about redressing her shoulder as best he could. When he had made her as comfortable as possible they sat in silence, leaning against the rock, sucking barley sugar tablets.

"Blumenthal," she breathed at last, "I should have killed him earlier, it would have been just ... he was the butcher of Deir Yasin."

Palmer knew nothing of the massacre of the 250 Arab men, women and children in the village of Deir Yasin by the Irgun. But he recognized a seed of violent reaction sown years earlier was now reaping its effect. History was littered with such seminal events whose results spurred acts long after their origins were past.

It had been Anna who had killed Blumenthal, revenging herself for her ruined life before being 'taken out' by a zealous marine in the line of what he conceived to be his duty.

310

"We were betrayed," he said, "I don't know how, or why, but we were betrayed."

She was staring at him now, the drugged, introspective glazing of her fine brown eyes giving way to the intensity of interest.

"*We? Betrayed?*" She paused, her mind clearing and seeking explanations. "You killed Giorgio because he wanted to negotiate with your navy . . . you helped us Palmer. Why?"

"Because . . . ." How could he explain it? Rosie, Suki's death, the broken marriage, the sense of guilt and failure, unemployment and disillusion, all these were causal factors. But so too were a sense of hope, a resistance to despair, a desire to do something other than sit supinely while others drove the wagon of materialism over him. But he could not explain them all to Lila. He was too tired and they were formed from the ugliness in his own society. To her they might seem utterly trivial.

"In Britain," he said slowly, "our new government is led by a man who wants to isolate international terrorism by destroying it at source. He is personally sympathetic to the claims of your people, though he cannot admit to support for Al Fatah. He thought that the shambles of the Lebanon could admit a new Arab state. I think he knew of the Sidon takeover and the planned hijack of the *Adventurer*. I was sent out to see it through, to shepherd it and ensure you were not overcome, so that the vast bargaining lever you gave to your cause could be used to best advantage."

"But you wanted to stop Barclay being killed."

"Yes. When it happened I didn't want him killed. I thought perhaps it could be accomplished without bloodshed. I was wrong."

"And what *do* you think happened? Was it a lie they told us back there?"

Palmer nodded. "Yes, I think so. You see *Norwich* should have referred to London before engaging."

"Even though we hit them with the Katyushas?"

"Yes, especially so. The whole matter was so delicate, but something went very wrong. I did not know *Norwich*, or any other ship, would be involved. Perhaps that just happened and events took their course; certainly it was not envisaged. I was

311

to stop reaction on board ... from the officers and crew ... by force, if need be."

"And so you had a gun?"

"Yes."

They fell silent for a while and then Lila asked, "What do you think will happen to us?"

He shrugged. "We are no threat now. Perhaps they will just sail away and leave us here marooned."

"Like Robinson Crusoe?"

"Yes ... you know about Robinson Crusoe?"

"I was educated at the American University in Beirut."

"I had no idea." But it explained so much that had not made sense before. Again silence fell between them. Beyond their shelter the wind moaned as the sun moved round the northern horizon. Palmer felt hungry but said nothing and Lila did not complain. He thought she had dozed off when she suddenly asked, "Why did *you* do this thing, Palmer? You have no connection with Palestine?"

He would have to tell her about Suki now.

"I had a daughter, she died of a debilitating disease and there was no money to pay for research. Plenty of money to buy Trident missiles and guns for those splendid men down below, but not enough to find out why little girls die. They promised money for research if I helped in their secret project."

"And you believed them?"

"Yes. The new Prime Minister is an honest man. I think he would have sacrificed *Norwich* to the success of your mission."

She was laughing at him. He had not expected that; it seemed the ultimate cruelty until he saw the tears in her eyes.

"I said you were a dreamer. . . ."

They slept as lovers and woke to brilliant sunshine. The gale had blown itself out and below them the sea was sapphire blue, ringed with the black, ice-capped cliffs and soaring summits of the surrounding peaks. Down in the bay *Adventurer* and *Norwich* had been joined by a third ship, the frigate *Alert*. There were boats moving between the ships and a shimmering disc on the stern of the frigate betrayed the presence of another helicopter warming up. Seconds later it lifted and flew below

312

them, straight for the hidden roofs of the old whaling station, its ugly protruding nose sniffing out the ground and moving up the gully and out of sight behind the shoulder of the mountain.

Palmer exchanged glances with Lila and they both stood, fearing the worst, yet powerless to stop it.

Suddenly the roar of the Lynx's turbines and the clatter of her rotors burst upon them as it rounded the rock buttress not 30 yards away. The Lynx levelled and moved towards them, slowing to the hover, the sun glancing off the Perspex windscreen like a gigantic, implacable eye.

Hovering almost overhead the pilot turned the machine to port, swinging the tail boom into sight and exposing the open door. A marine was squatting in the doorway, sunlight reflected from the barrel of his automatic. Palmer felt Lila squeeze his hand and he grabbed her in a last embrace.

"In'sh Allah," she said, "it is the will of God."

The light shining down from the helicopter exploded into an infinity of tiny fragments and he felt Lila sag against him. The pain was over very quickly and then he knew only the black void of a great wind.

An hour later HMS *Alert* led *Norwich* and the liner *Adventurer* to sea. A faint noise of jubilant music came over the liner's public address system. Gradually it faded and Destitution Island was left to the seals and the seabirds in the solitude of the Antarctic wind.